DOVER · THRIFT · EDITIONS

Les Liaisons Dangereuses

or

Letters Collected in a Private Society
and Published for the Instruction of Others

CHODERLOS DE LACLOS

Translated by Ernest Dowson

DOVER PUBLICATIONS, INC.
Mineola, New York

DOVER THRIFT EDITIONS

GENERAL EDITOR: MARY CAROLYN WALDREP
EDITOR OF THIS VOLUME: TOM CRAWFORD

Bibliographical Note

This Dover edition, first published in 2006, is an unabridged republication of the English translation by Ernest Dowson of *Les Liaisons Dangereuses ou Lettres Recuellies dans une Société, & publiées pour l'instruction de quelques autres,* originally published by Chez Durand Neveu, Libraire, a la Sagesse, Amsterdam, 1782. The present translation was published by Leonard Smithers, London, 1898. A new Note has been specially prepared for the Dover edition.

International Standard Book Number: 0-486-45245-X

Manufactured in the United States of America
Dover Publications, Inc., 31 East 2nd Street, Mineola, N.Y. 11501

Note

A *succès de scandale* when first published in 1782, this classic epistolary novel detailing the amorous schemes and calculated couplings of a gaggle of French aristocrats still has the power to shock. As Baudelaire put it, "*Les Liaisons Dangereuses* burns like ice." Much of the novel's negative force derives from the blatant cynicism and manipulative disregard for the feelings of others that drives the two central characters: the libertine Vicomte de Valmont, and the revenge-seeking Marquise de Merteuil.

As these two jaded sophisticates coldly plot the seduction of young, innocent Cécile de Volanges, recently out of a convent, and the virtuous married beauty, Madame de Tourvel, whose husband is away on court business, the malice and deceit at the bottom of their actions may discomfit us, but are not unfamiliar. Lust and revenge are all-too-familiar human motivators.

But of course, there are complications. Love, in particular, disrupts the smooth course of the seduction plots hatched by Valmont and Merteuil. Suffice it to say there are many twists and turns of the plot, before the tale winds down to its sad and tragic ending. And although the lascivious goings-on in the story are comparable to such classic erotic novels as *Fanny Hill* and *Lady Chatterley's Lover*, there is no vulgar language or graphic description. The events, and the thoughts of the characters, no matter how wanton or reprehensible, are recounted with exquisite refinement.

Pierre Choderlos de Laclos (1741–1803) was a highly regarded French military official, who eventually attained the rank of general. An expert on fortifications, he apparently survived the upheaval of the French Revolution because he was not important enough to guillotine. It could also be that *Les Liaisons Dangereuses*, which some critics have found to be a morality tale about the corrupt, squalid nobility of the *Ancien Régime*, helped spare him the wrath of the revolutionaries. And although the novel is, among other things, a portrayal of a consummate libertine, Choderlos de Laclos himself appears to have been a very happily married man.

Publisher's Note to the First Edition (1782)

We think it our duty to warn the public that, in spite of the title of this work and of what the Editor says of it in his Preface, we do not guarantee the authenticity of this narrative, and have even strong reasons for believing that it is but a romance. It seems to us, moreover, that the author, who yet seems to have sought after verisimilitude, has himself destroyed that, and maladroitly, owing to the period which he has chosen in which to place these adventures. Certainly, several of the personages whom he brings on his stage have morals so sorry that it were impossible to believe that they lived in our century, in this century of philosophy, where the light shed on all sides has rendered, as everyone knows, all men so honorable, all women so modest and reserved.

Our opinion is, therefore, that if the adventures related in this work possess a foundation of truth, they could not have occurred save in other places and in other times, and we must censure our author, who, seduced apparently by his hope of being more diverting by treating rather of his own age and country, has dared to clothe in our customs and our costumes a state of morals so remote from us.

To preserve the too credulous Reader, at least so far as it lies with us, from all surprise in this matter, we will support our opinion with an argument which we proffer to him in all confidence, because it seems to us victorious and unanswerable; it is that, undoubtedly, like causes should not fail to produce like effects, and that, nevertheless, we do not hear today of young ladies with incomes of sixty thousand livres turning nuns, nor of young and pretty dame presidents dying of grief.

Editor's Preface to the First Edition (1782)

This work, or rather this compilation, which the public will, perhaps, still find too voluminous, contains, however, but a very small portion of the letters which composed the correspondence whence it is extracted. Charged with the care of setting it in order by the persons into whose hands it had come, and whom I knew to have the intention of publishing it, I asked, for reward of my pains, no more than the permission to prune it of all that appeared to me useless, and I have, in fact, endeavored to preserve only the letters which seemed to me necessary, whether for the right understanding of events or the development of the characters. If there be added to this light labor that of arranging in order the letters I have let remain, an order in which I have almost invariably followed that of the dates, and finally some brief and rare notes, which, for the most part, have no other object than that of indicating the source of certain quotations, or of explaining certain abridgments which I have permitted myself, the share which I have had in this work will have been told. My mission was of no wider range.[1]

I had proposed alterations more considerable, and almost all in respect of diction or style, against which will be found many offenses. I should have wished to be authorized to cut down certain too lengthy letters, of which several treat separately, and almost without transition, of matters quite extraneous to one another. This task, which has not been permitted me, would doubtless not have sufficed to give merit to the work, but it would, at least, have freed it from a portion of its defects.

It has been objected to me that it was the letters themselves which it was desirable to make public, not merely a work made after those letters; that it would be as great an offense against verisimilitude as against truth, if all the eight or ten persons who participated in this correspondence

---

[1] I must also state that I have suppressed or altered all the names of persons which occur in these letters; and if, among those I have substituted for them, any is to be found which belongs to a real person, this arises solely from error on my part, and no conclusion is to be drawn therefrom.

had written with an equal purity. And to my representations that, far from that, there was not one of them, on the contrary, who had not committed grave faults, which would not fail to excite criticism, I was answered that any reasonable reader would be certainly prepared to meet with faults in a compilation of letters written by private individuals, since in all those hitherto published by sundry esteemed authors, and even by certain academicians, none has proved quite free of this reproach. These reasons have not persuaded me, and I found them, as I find them still, easier to give than to accept; but I was not my own master, and I gave way. Only, I reserved to myself the right of protest, and of declaring that I was not of that opinion: it is this protest I make here.

As for any degree of merit the work may have, perhaps it is not for me to discuss this, for my opinion neither ought to nor can influence that of anyone else. Yet those persons who, before they begin a book, like to know more or less what to expect, those persons, I say, can continue to read this preface; others had better pass straight to the work itself; they know enough about it already.

What I must say at the outset is that, if my advice has been, as I admit, to publish these letters, I am nevertheless far from hoping for their success: and let not this sincerity on my part be taken for the feigned modesty of an author; for I declare with equal frankness that, if this compilation had not seemed to me worthy of being offered to the public, I would not have meddled with it. Let us try to reconcile these apparent contradictions.

The deserts of a work are composed of its utility or of its charm, and even of both these, when it is susceptible of them: but success, which is not always a proof of merit, often depends more on the choice of a subject than on its execution, on the sum of the objects which it presents rather than on the manner in which they are treated. Now this compilation containing, as its title announces, the letters of a whole society, it is dominated by a diversity of interest which weakens that of the reader. Nay more, almost all the sentiments therein expressed being feigned or dissimulated, they but excite an interest of curiosity which is ever inferior to that of sentiment, which less inclines the mind for indulgence, and which permits a perception of the errors contained in the details that is all the more keen in that these are continually opposed to the only desire which one would have satisfied.

These blemishes are, perhaps, redeemed, in part, by a quality which is implied in the very nature of the work: it is the variety of the styles, a merit which an author attains with difficulty, but which here occurs of itself, and at least prevents the tedium of uniformity. Many persons will also be able to count for something a considerable number of observations, either new or little known, which are scattered through these letters. That is all, I fear, that one can hope for in the matter of charm, judging them even with the utmost favor.

The utility of the work, which, perhaps, will be even more contested, yet seems to me easier to establish. It seems to me, at any rate, that it is to render a service to morals, to unveil the methods employed by those whose own are bad in corrupting those whose conduct is good; and I believe that these letters will effectually attain this end. There will also be found the proof and example of two important verities which one might believe unknown, for that they are so rarely practiced: the one, that every woman who consents to admit a man of loose morals to her society ends by becoming his victim; the other, that a mother is, to say the least, imprudent who allows any other than herself to possess the confidence of her daughter. Young people of either sex might also learn from these pages that the friendship which persons of evil character appear to grant them so readily is never aught else but a dangerous snare, as fatal to their happiness as to their virtue. Abuse, however, always so near a neighbor to what is good, seems to me here too greatly to be feared; and far from commending this work for the perusal of youth, it seems to me most important to deter it from all such reading. The time when it may cease to be perilous and become useful seems to me to have been defined, for her sex, by a good mother, who has not only wit but good sense: "I should deem," she said to me, after having read the manuscript of this correspondence, "that I was doing a service to my daughter if I gave her this book on the day of her marriage." If all mothers of families think thus, I shall congratulate myself on having published it.

But if, again, we put this favorable supposition on one side, I continue to think that this collection can please very few. Men and women who are depraved will have an interest in decrying a work calculated to injure them; and, as they are not lacking in skill, perhaps they will have sufficient to bring to their side the austere, who will be alarmed at the picture of bad morals which we have not feared to exhibit.

The would-be freethinkers will not be interested in a God-fearing woman whom for that very reason they will regard as a ninny; while pious people will be angry at seeing virtue defeated and will complain that religion is not made to seem more powerful.

On the other hand, persons of delicate taste will be disgusted by the too simple and too faulty style of many of these letters; while the mass of readers, led away with the idea that everything they see in print is the fruit of labor, will think that they are beholding in certain others the elaborate method of an author concealing himself behind the person whom he causes to speak.

Lastly, it will perhaps be pretty generally said that everything is good in its own place; and that, although, as a rule, the too polished style of the authors detracts from the charm of the letters of society, the carelessness of the present ones becomes a real fault and makes them insufferable when sent to the printer's.

I sincerely admit that all these reproaches may be well founded: I think also that I should be able to reply to them without exceeding the length permissible to a preface. But it must be plain that, to make it necessary to reply to all, the book itself should be unable to reply to any; and that, had I been of this opinion, I would have suppressed at once the preface and the book.

PART I

1. Cécile Volanges to Sophie Carnay, at the Ursulines of . . .

You see, my dear friend, that I keep my word to you, and that bonnets and frills do not take up all my time; there will always be some left for you. However, I have seen more adornments in this one single day than in all the four years we passed together; and I think that the superb Tanville[1] will have more vexation at my first visit, when I shall certainly ask to see her, than she has ever fancied that she afforded us, when she used to come and see us *in fiocchi*. Mamma has consulted me in everything; she treats me much less as a schoolgirl than of old. I have a waiting maid of my own; I have a room and a closet at my disposition; and I write this to you at a very pretty desk, of which I have the key, and where I can lock up all that I wish. Mamma has told me that I am to see her every day when she rises, that I need not have my hair dressed before dinner, because we shall always be alone, and that then she will tell me every day when I am to see her in the afternoon. The rest of the time is at my disposal, and I have my harp, my drawing, and books as at the convent, only there is no Mother Perpétue here to scold me, and it is nothing to anybody but myself, if I choose to do nothing at all. But as I have not my Sophie here to chat and laugh with, I would just as soon occupy myself.

It is not yet five o'clock; I have not to go and join Mamma until seven: there's time enough, if I had anything to tell you! But as yet they have not spoken to me of anything, and were it not for the preparations I see being made, and the number of milliners who all come for me, I should believe that they had no thought of marrying me, and that that was the nonsense of the good Joséphine.[2] However, Mamma has told me so often that a young lady should stay in the convent until she marries that, since she has taken me out, I suppose Joséphine was right.

[1] A pupil at the same convent.
[2] The portress of the convent.

1

A carriage has just stopped at the door, and Mamma tells me to come to her at once. If it were to be the Gentleman! I am not dressed, my hand trembles and my heart is beating. I asked my waiting maid if she knew who was with my mother. "Certainly," she said, "it's Monsieur C★★★." And she laughed. Oh, I believe 'tis he! I will be sure to come back and relate to you what passes. There is his name, at any rate. I must not keep him waiting. For a moment, adieu. . . .

How you will laugh at your poor Cécile! Oh, I have really been disgraceful! But you would have been caught just as I. When I went in to Mamma, I saw a gentleman in black standing by her. I bowed to him as well as I could, and stood still without being able to budge an inch. You can imagine how I scrutinized him.

"Madame," he said to my mother, as he bowed to me, "what a charming young lady! I feel more than ever the value of your kindness." At this very definite remark, I was seized with a fit of trembling, so much so that I could hardly stand: I found an armchair and sat down in it, very red and disconcerted. Hardly was I there, when I saw the man at my feet. Your poor Cécile quite lost her head; as Mamma said, I was absolutely terrified. I jumped up, uttering a piercing cry, just as I did that day when it thundered. Mamma burst out laughing, saying to me, "Well! what is the matter with you? Sit down, and give your foot to Monsieur." Indeed, my dear friend, the gentleman was a shoemaker. I can't describe to you how ashamed I was; mercifully there was no one there but Mamma. I think that, when I am married, I shall give up employing that shoemaker.

So much for our wisdom—admit it! Adieu. It is nearly six o'clock, and my waiting maid tells me that I must dress. Adieu, my dear Sophie, I love you, just as well as if I were still at the convent.

P.S. I don't know by whom to send my letter, so that I shall wait until Joséphine comes.

Paris, 3rd August, 17★★.

2. The Marquise de Merteuil to the Vicomte de Valmont, at the Château de . . .

Come back, my dear Vicomte, come back; what are you doing, what *can* you be doing with an old aunt, whose whole property is settled on you? Set off at once; I have need of you. I have an excellent idea, and I should like to confide its execution to you. These few words should suffice; and only too honored at my choice, you ought to come, with enthusiasm, to receive my orders on your knees: but you abuse my kindness, even since you have ceased to take advantage of it, and between the alternatives of an eternal hatred and excessive indulgence, your happiness demands that my indulgence wins the day. I am willing then to inform you of my projects, but swear to me like a faithful cavalier that you will embark on no other adventure till this one be brought to an end. It is worthy of a hero: you will serve both love and vengeance; it will be, in short, one *rouerie*[1] the more to include in your Memoirs: yes, in your Memoirs, for I wish them to be printed, and I will charge myself with the task of writing them. But let us leave that, and come back to what is occupying me.

Madame de Volanges is marrying her daughter: it is still a secret, but she imparted it to me yesterday. And whom do you think she has chosen for her son-in-law? The Comte de Gercourt. Who would have thought that I should ever become Gercourt's cousin? I was furious. . . . Well! do you not divine me now? Oh, dull brains! Have you forgiven him then the adventure of the Intendante! And I, have I not still more cause to complain of him, monster that you are?[2] But I will calm myself, and the hope of vengeance soothes my soul.

You have been bored a hundred times, like myself, by the importance which Gercourt sets upon the wife who shall be his, and by his fatuous presumption, which leads him to believe he will escape the inevitable fate. You know his ridiculous preferences for convent education and his even more ridiculous prejudice in favor of the discretion of *blondes*. In fact, I would wager, that for all that the little Volanges has an income of sixty thousand livres, he would never have made this marriage if she had been dark or had not been bred at the convent. Let us prove to him then that he is but a fool: no doubt he will be made so one of these days; it isn't that of which I am afraid; but 'twould be pleasant indeed if he were to make his *début* as one! How we should amuse ourselves on the day after, when we heard him boasting, for he will boast; and then, if you once form this little girl, it would be a rare mishap if Gercourt did not become, like another man, the joke of all Paris.

For the rest, the heroine of this new romance merits all your attentions: she is really pretty; it is only fifteen, 'tis a rosebud, *gauche* in truth, incredibly so, and quite without affectation. But you men are not afraid of that; moreover, a certain languishing glance, which really promises great things. Add to this that I exhort you to it: you can only thank me and obey.

You will receive this letter tomorrow morning. I request that tomorrow, at seven o'clock in the evening, you may be with me: I shall receive

---

[1] The words *roué* and *rouerie*, which are now happily falling into disuse in good society, were much in vogue at the time when these Letters were written.

[2] To understand this passage, it must be mentioned that the Comte de Gercourt had deserted the Marquise de Merteuil for the Intendante de ***, who had sacrificed for him the Vicomte de Valmont, and it was then that the Marquise and the Vicomte formed an attachment. As this adventure is long anterior to the events which are in question in these Letters, it seemed right to suppress all that correspondence.

nobody until eight, not even the reigning Chevalier: he has not head enough for such a mighty piece of work. You see that love does not blind me. At eight o'clock I will grant you your liberty, and you shall come back at ten to sup with the fair object; for mother and daughter will sup with me. Adieu, it is past noon: soon I shall have put you out of my thoughts.

Paris, 4th August, 17**.

3. Cécile Volanges to Sophie Carnay

I know nothing as yet, my dear friend. Mamma had a great number of people to supper yesterday. In spite of the interest I took in regarding them, the men especially, I was far from being diverted. Men and women, everybody looked at me mightily, and then would whisper to one another, and I saw they were speaking of me. That made me blush; I could not prevent myself. I wish I could have, for I noticed that, when the other women were looked at, they did not blush: or perhaps 'tis the rouge they employ which prevents one seeing the red that is caused by embarrassment; for it must be very difficult not to blush when a man stares at you.

What made me most uneasy was that I did not know what they thought in my regard. I believe, however, that I heard two or three times the word *pretty*; but I heard very distinctly the word *gauche*; and I think that must be true, for the woman who said it is a kinswoman and friend of my mother; she seemed even to have suddenly taken a liking to me. She was the only person who spoke to me a little during the evening. We are to sup with her tomorrow.

I also heard, after supper, a man who, I am certain, was speaking of me, and who said to another, "We must let it ripen; this winter we shall see." It is, perhaps, he who is to marry me, but then it will not be for four months! I should so much like to know how it stands.

Here is Joséphine, and she tells me she is in a hurry. Yet I must tell you one more of my *gaucheries*. Oh, I am afraid that lady was right!

After supper they started to play. I placed myself at Mamma's side; I do not know how it happened, but I fell asleep almost at once. I was awakened by a great burst of laughter. I do not know if they were laughing at me, but I believe so. Mamma gave me permission to retire, and I was greatly pleased. Imagine, it was past eleven o'clock. Adieu, my dear Sophie; always love your Cécile. I assure you that the world is not so amusing as we imagined.

Paris, 4th August, 17**.

4. The Vicomte de Valmont to the Marquise de Merteuil, at Paris

Your commands are charming; your fashion of conveying them is more gracious still; you would make us in love with despotism. It is not the first time, as you know, that I have regretted that I am no longer your slave: and *monster* though I be, according to you, I never recall without pleasure the time when you honored me with sweeter titles. Indeed, I often desire to merit them again, and to end by setting, with you, an example of constancy to the world. But greater interests call us; to conquer is our destiny, we must follow it; perhaps at the end of the course we shall meet again; for, may I say it without vexing you, my fairest Marquise? you follow it at least as fast as I: and since the day when, separating for the good of the world, we began to preach the faith on our different sides, it seems to me that, in this mission of love, you have made more proselytes than I. I know your zeal, your ardent fervor; and if that god of ours judged us by our works, you would one day be the patroness of some great city, while your friend would be at most but a village saint. This language astounds you, does it not? But for the last week I hear and speak no other, and it is to perfect myself in it that I am forced to disobey you.

Listen to me and do not be vexed. Depositary of all the secrets of my heart, I will confide to you the most important project I have ever formed. What is it you suggest to me? To seduce a young girl, who has seen nothing, knows nothing, who would be, so to speak, delivered defenseless into my hands, whom a first compliment would not fail to intoxicate, and whom curiosity will perhaps more readily entice than love. Twenty others can succeed and these as well as I. That is not the case in the adventure which engrosses me; its success ensures me as much glory as pleasure. Love, who prepares my crown, hesitates, himself, betwixt the myrtle and the laurel; or rather he will unite them to honor my triumph. You yourself, my fair friend, will be seized with a holy veneration and will say with enthusiasm, "Behold a man after my own heart!"

You know the Présidente de Tourvel, her piety, her conjugal love, her austere principles. She it is whom I am attacking; there is the foe meet for me; there the goal at which I dare to aim:

> *And though to grasp the prize I be denied,*
> *Yet mine at least this glory—that I tried.*[1]

One may quote bad verses when a good poet has written them. You must know then that the President is in Burgundy, in consequence of some great lawsuit: I hope to make him lose one of greater import! His

---

[1] La Fontaine.

disconsolate better half has to pass here the whole term of this distressing widowhood. Mass every day; some visits to the poor of the district; morning and evening prayers, solitary walks, pious interviews with my old aunt, and sometimes a dismal game of whist, must be her sole distractions. I am preparing some for her which shall be more efficacious. My guardian angel has brought me here, for her happiness and my own. Madman that I was, I regretted twenty-four hours which I was sacrificing to my respect for the conventions. How I should be punished if I were made to return to Paris! Luckily, four are needed to play whist; and as there is no one here but the *curé* of the place, my eternal aunt has pressed me greatly to sacrifice a few days to her. You can guess that I have agreed. You cannot imagine how she has cajoled me since then, above all how edified she is at my regularity at prayers and mass. She has no suspicion what divinity I adore.

Here am I then for the last four days, in the throes of a doughty passion. You know how keen are my desires, how I brush aside obstacles to them: but what you do not know is how solitude adds ardor to desire. I have but one idea; I think of it all day and dream of it all night. It is very necessary that I should have this woman, if I would save myself from the ridicule of being in love with her: for whither may not thwarted desire lead one? O delicious pleasure! I implore thee for my happiness, and above all for my repose. How lucky it is for us that women defend themselves so badly! Else we should be to them no more than timid slaves. At present I have a feeling of gratitude for yielding women which brings me naturally to your feet. I prostrate myself to implore your pardon, and so conclude this too long epistle.

Adieu, my fairest friend, and bear me no malice.

                    At the Château de . . . , 5th August, 17**.

5. The Marquise de Merteuil to the Vicomte de Valmont

Do you know, Vicomte, that your letter is of an amazing insolence, and that I have every excuse to be angry with you? But it has proved clearly to me that you have lost your head, and that alone has saved you from my indignation. Like a generous and sympathetic friend, I forget my wrongs in order to concern myself with your peril; and tiresome though argument be, I give way before the need you have of it, at such a time.

You, to have the Présidente de Tourvel! The ridiculous caprice! I recognize there your froward imagination, which knows not how to desire aught but what it believes to be unattainable. What is the woman then? Regular features, if you like, but no expression; passably made, but lacking grace; and always dressed in a fashion to set you laughing, with her clusters of fichus on her bosom and her body running into her chin! I warn you as a friend, you need but to have two such women, and all your consideration will be lost. Remember the day when she collected at Saint-Roch, and when you thanked me so for having procured you such a spectacle. I think I see her still, giving her hand to that great gawk with the long hair, stumbling at every step, with her four yards of collecting bag always over somebody's head, and blushing at every reverence. Who would have said then that you would ever desire this woman? Come, Vicomte, blush too, and be yourself again! I promise to keep your secret.

And then, look at the disagreeables which await you! What rival have you to encounter? A husband! Are you not humiliated at the very word? What a disgrace if you fail! and how little glory even if you succeed! I say more; expect no pleasure from it. Is there ever any with your prudes? I mean those in good faith. Reserved in the very midst of pleasure, they give you but a half enjoyment. That utter self-abandonment, that delirium of joy, where pleasure is purified by its excess, those good things of love are not known to them. I warn you: in the happiest supposition, your Présidente will think she has done everything for you, if she treats you as her husband; and in the most tender of conjugal *tête-à-têtes* you are always two. Here it is even worse; your prude is a *dévote,* with that devotion of worthy women which condemns them to eternal infancy. Perhaps you will overcome that obstacle; but do not flatter yourself that you will destroy it: victorious over the love of God, you will not be so over the fear of the Devil; and when, holding your mistress in your arms, you feel her heart palpitate, it will be from fear and not from love. Perhaps, if you had known this woman earlier, you would have been able to make something of her; but it is two-and-twenty, and has been married nearly two years. Believe, me, Vicomte, when a woman is so *encrusted* with prejudice, it is best to abandon her to her fate; she will never be anything but a *puppet.*

Yet it is for this delightful creature that you refuse to obey me, bury yourself in the tomb of your aunt, and renounce the most enticing of adventures, and withal one so admirably suited to do you honor. By what fatality then must Gercourt always hold some advantage over you? Well, I am writing to you without temper: but, for the nonce, I am tempted to believe that you don't merit your reputation; I am tempted, above all, to withdraw my confidence from you. I shall never get used to telling my secrets to the lover of Madame de Tourvel.

I must let you know, however, that the little Volanges has already turned one head. Young Danceny is wild about her. He sings duets with her; and really, she sings better than a schoolgirl should. They must rehearse a good many duets, and I think that she takes nicely to the *unison;* but this Danceny is a child, who will waste his time in making love and will never finish. The little person, on her side, is shy enough; and in any event it will be much less amusing than you could have made it: wherefore I am in a bad humor and shall certainly quarrel with the Chevalier at his next appearance. I advise him to be gentle; for, at this moment, it would cost me nothing to break with him. I am sure that, if I had the sense to leave him at present, he would be in despair; and nothing amuses me so much as a lover's despair. He would call me perfidious, and that word "perfidious" has always pleased me; it is, after the word "cruel," the sweetest to a woman's ear, and less difficult to deserve.... Seriously, I shall have to set about this rupture. There's what you are the cause of; so I put it on your conscience! Adieu. Recommend me to the prayers of your lady President.

Paris, 7th August, 17★★.

6. The Vicomte de Valmont to the Marquise de Merteuil

There is never a woman then but abuses the empire she has known how to seize! And yourself, you whom I have so often dubbed my indulgent friend, you have discarded the title and are not afraid to attack me in the object of my affections! With what traits you venture to depict Madame de Tourvel! ... What man but would have paid with his life for such insolent boldness? What woman other than yourself would have escaped without receiving at least an ungracious retort? In mercy, put me not to such tests; I will not answer for my power to sustain them. In the name of friendship, wait until I have had this woman, if you wish to revile her. Do you not know that pleasure alone has the right to remove the bandage from Love's eyes? But what am I saying? Has Madame de Tourvel any need of illusion? No; for to be adorable, she has only need to be herself. You reproach her with dressing badly; I quite agree: all adornment is hurtful to her, nothing that conceals her adorns. It is in the freedom of her *negligé* that she is really ravishing. Thanks to the distressing heat which we are experiencing, a *déshabillé* of simple stuff permits me to see her round and supple figure. Only a piece of muslin covers her breast; and my furtive but penetrating gaze has already seized its enchanting form. Her face, say you, has no expression. And what should it express, in moments when nothing speaks to her heart? No, doubtless, she has not, like our coquettes, that false glance, which is sometimes seductive and always deceives. She knows not how to gloss over the emptiness of a phrase by a studied smile, and although she has the loveliest teeth in the world, she never laughs, except when she is amused. But you should see, in some frolicsome game, of what a frank and innocent gaiety she will present the image! Near some poor wretch whom she is eager to succor, what a pure joy and compassionate kindness her gaze denotes! You should see, above all, how, at the least word of praise or flattery, her heavenly face is tinged with the touching embarrassment of a modesty that is not feigned! . . . She is a prude and devout, and so you judge her to be cold and inanimate? I think very differently. What amazing sensibility she must have, that it can reach even her husband, and that she can always love a person who is always absent! What stronger proof would you desire? Yet I have been able to procure another.

I directed her walk in such a manner that a ditch had to be crossed; and, although she is very agile, she is even more timid. You can well believe how much a prude fears to *cross the ditch!*[1] She was obliged to trust herself to me. I held this modest woman in my arms. Our preparations and the passage of my old aunt had caused the playful *dévote* to peal with laughter; but when I had once taken hold of her, by a happy awkwardness our arms were interlaced. I pressed her breast against my own; and in this short interval, I felt her heart beat faster. An amiable flush suffused her face; and her modest embarrassment taught me well enough *that her heart had throbbed with love and not with fear.* My aunt, however, was deceived, as you are, and said, "The child was frightened," but the charming candor of *the child* did not permit her to lie, and she answered naively, "Oh no, but . . ." That alone was an illumination. From that moment the sweetness of hope has succeeded to my cruel uncertainty. I shall possess this woman; I shall steal her from the husband who profanes her: I will even dare ravish her from the God whom she adores. What delight, to be in turns the object and the victor of her remorse! Far be it from me to destroy the prejudices which sway her mind! They will add to my happiness and my triumph. Let her believe in virtue, and sacrifice it to me; let the idea of falling terrify her, without preventing her fall; and may she, shaken by a thousand terrors, forget them, vanquish them only in my arms. Then, I agree, let her say to me, "I adore thee"; she, alone among women, is worthy to pronounce these words. I shall be truly the God whom she has preferred.

Let us be candid: in our arrangements, as cold as they are facile, what we call happiness is hardly even a pleasure. Shall I tell you? I thought my heart was withered; and finding nothing left but my senses, I lamented my premature old age. Madame de Tourvel has restored to me the charming illusions of youth. With her I have no need of pleasure to be happy. The only thing which frightens me is the time which this adventure is going to take; for I dare leave nothing to chance. 'Tis in vain I recall my fortunate audacities; I cannot bring myself to put them in practice here. To become truly happy, I require her to give herself; and that is no slight affair.

---

[1]One sees here the deplorable taste for puns, which was becoming the fashion, and which has since made so much progress.

I am sure that you admire my prudence. I have not yet pronounced the word "love"; but we have already come to those of confidence and interest. To deceive her as little as possible, and above all to counteract the effect of stories which might come to her ears, I have myself told her, as though in self-accusation, of some of my most notorious traits. You would laugh to see the candor with which she lectures me. She wishes, she says, to convert me. She has no suspicion as yet of what it will cost her to try. She is far from thinking, that *in pleading,* to use her own words, *for the unfortunates I have ruined,* she speaks in anticipation in her own cause. This idea struck me yesterday in the midst of one of her dissertations, and I could not resist the pleasure of interrupting her to tell her that she spoke like a prophet. Adieu, my fairest of friends. You see that I am not lost beyond all hope of return.

P.S. By the way, that poor Chevalier—has he killed himself from despair? Truly, you are a hundredfold naughtier person than myself, and you would humiliate me, if I had any vanity.

At the Château de . . . , 9th August, 17★★.

7. Cécile Volanges to Sophie Carnay[1]

If I have told you nothing about my marriage, it is because I know no more about it than I did the first day. I am accustoming myself to think no more of it, and I am quite satisfied with my manner of life. I study much at my singing and my harp; it seems to me that I like them better since I have no longer a master, or perhaps it is because I have a better one. M. le Chevalier Danceny, the gentleman of whom I told you, and with whom I sang at Madame de Merteuil's, is kind enough to come here every day, and to sing with me for whole hours. He is extremely amiable. He sings like an angel, and composes very pretty airs, to which he also does the words. It is a great pity that he is a Knight of Malta! It seems to me that, if he were to marry, his wife would be very happy. . . . He has a charming gentleness. He never has the air of paying you a compliment, and yet everything he says flatters you. He takes me up constantly, now about my music, now about something else; but he mingles his criticisms with so much gaiety and interest, that it is impossible not to be grateful for them. If he only looks at you, it seems as though he were saying something gracious. Added to all that, he is very obliging. For instance, yesterday he was invited to a great concert; he preferred to

---

[1]Not to abuse the Reader's patience, many of the letters in this correspondence, from day to day, have been suppressed; only those have been given which have been found necessary for the elucidation of events. For the same reason all the replies of Sophie Carnay and many letters of the other actors in these adventures have been omitted.

spend the whole evening at Mamma's. That pleased me very much; for, when he is not here, nobody talks to me, and I bore myself: whereas, when he is here, we sing and talk together. He always has something to tell me. He and Madame de Merteuil are the only two persons I find amiable. But adieu, my dearest friend; I have promised to learn for today a little air with a very difficult accompaniment, and I would not break my word. I am going to practice it until he comes.

Paris, 7th August, 17**.

8. The Présidente de Tourvel to Madame de Volanges

No one, Madame, can be more sensible than I to the confidence you show in me, nor take a keener interest in the establishment of Mademoiselle de Volanges. It is, indeed, from my whole heart that I wish her a happiness of which I make no doubt she is worthy, and which your prudence will secure. I do not know M. le Comte de Gercourt; but being honored by your choice, I cannot but form a favorable opinion of him. I confine myself, Madame, to wishing for this marriage a success as assured as my own, which is equally your handiwork, and for which each fresh day adds to my gratitude. May the happiness of your daughter be the reward of that which you have procured for me; and may the best of friends be also the happiest of mothers!

I am really grieved that I cannot offer you by word of mouth the homage of this sincere wish, nor make the acquaintance of Mademoiselle de Volanges so soon as I should wish. After having known your truly maternal kindness, I have a right to hope from her the tender friendship of a sister. I beg you, Madame, to be so good as to ask this from her in my behalf, while I wait until I have the opportunity of deserving it.

I expect to remain in the country all the time of M. de Tourvel's absence. I have taken advantage of this leisure to enjoy and profit by the society of the venerable Madame de Rosemonde. This lady is always charming; her great age has deprived her of nothing; she retains all her memory and sprightliness. Her body alone is eighty-four years old; her mind is only twenty.

Our seclusion is enlivened by her nephew, the Vicomte de Valmont, who has cared to devote a few days to us. I knew him only by his reputation, which gave me small desire to make his further acquaintance; but he seems to me to be better than that. Here, where he is not spoilt by the hubbub of the world, he talks rationally with extraordinary ease, and excuses himself for his errors with rare candor. He speaks to me with much confidence, and I preach to him with great severity. You, who know him, will admit that it would be a fine conversion to make: but I suspect, in spite of his promises, that a week in Paris will make him forget all my sermons. His sojourn here will be at least so much saved from his ordinary course of conduct; and I think, from his fashion of life, that what he can best do is to do nothing at all. He knows that I am engaged in writing to you and has charged me to present you with his respectful homage. Pray accept my own also, with the goodness that I know in you; and never doubt the sincere sentiments with which I have the honor to be, etc.

At the Château de . . . , 9th August, 17★★.

9. Madame de Volanges to the Présidente de Tourvel

I have never doubted, my fair and youthful friend, either of the kindness which you have for me, or of the sincere interest which you take in all that concerns me. It is not to elucidate that point, which I hope is settled between us, that I reply to your *reply;* but I cannot refrain from having a talk with you on the subject of the Vicomte de Valmont.

I did not expect, I confess, ever to come across that name in your letters. Indeed, what can there be in common between you and him? You do not know this man; where should you have obtained any idea of the soul of a libertine? You speak to me of his *rare candor:* yes, indeed, the candor of Valmont must be most rare. Even more false and dangerous than he is amiable and seductive, never since his extreme youth has he taken a step or uttered a word without having some end in view which was either dishonorable or criminal. My dear, you know me; you know whether, of all the virtues which I try to acquire, charity be not the one which I cherish the most. So that, if Valmont were led away by the vehemence of his passions; if, like a thousand others, he were seduced by the errors of his age: while I should blame his conduct, I should pity him personally, and wait in silence for the time when a happy reformation should restore him the esteem of honest folk. But Valmont is not like that: his conduct is the consequence of his principles. He can calculate to a nicety how many atrocities a man may allow himself to commit, without compromising himself; and, in order to be cruel and mischievous with impunity, he has selected women to be his victims. I will not stop to count all those whom he has seduced: but how many has he not ruined utterly?

In the quiet and retired life which you lead, these scandalous stories do not reach your ears. I could tell you some which would make you shudder; but your eyes, which are as pure as your soul, would be defiled by such pictures: secure of being in no danger from Valmont, you have no need of such arms wherewith to defend yourself. The only thing which I may tell you is that out of all the women to whom he has paid attention, with or without success, there is not one who has not had cause to complain of him. The Marquise de Merteuil is the single exception to this general rule; she alone knew how to withstand and disarm his villainy. I must confess that this episode in her life is that which does her most honor in my eyes: it has also sufficed to justify her fully, in the eyes of all, for certain inconsistencies with which one had to reproach her at the commencement of her widowhood.[1]

However this may be, my fair friend, what age, experience, and above all, friendship, empower me to represent to you is that the absence of Valmont is beginning to be noticed, in the world; and that, if it becomes known that he has for some time made a third party to his aunt and you, your reputation will be in his hands: the greatest misfortune which can befall a woman. I advise you then to persuade his aunt not to keep him there longer; and, if he insists upon remaining, I think you should not hesitate to leave him in possession. But why should he stay? What is he doing in your part of the country? If you were to spy upon his proceedings, I am sure you would discover that he only came there to have a more convenient shelter for some black deed he is contemplating in the neighborhood. But, as it is impossible to remedy the evil, let us be content by ourselves avoiding it.

Farewell, my lovely friend; at present the marriage of my daughter is a little delayed. The Comte de Gercourt, whom we expected from day to day, tells me that his regiment is ordered to Corsica; and as military operations are still afoot, it will be impossible for him to absent himself before the winter. This vexes me; but it causes me to hope that we shall have the pleasure of seeing you at the wedding; and I was sorry that it was to have taken place without you. Adieu; I am, unreservedly and without compliment, entirely yours.

P.S. Recall me to the recollection of Madame de Rosemonde, whom I always love as dearly as she deserves.

Paris, 11th August, 17**.

10. The Marquise de Merteuil to the Vicomte de Valmont

Vicomte, are you angry with me? Or are you, indeed, dead? Or, what would not be unlike that, are you living only for your Présidente? This woman, who has restored you *the illusions of youth,* will soon restore you also its ridiculous prejudices. Here you are already timid and a slave; you might as well be amorous. You renounce *your fortunate audacities.* Behold you then conducting yourself without principles, and trusting all to hazard, or rather to caprice. Do you no longer remember that love, like med-

---

[1]The error, into which Madame de Volanges falls, shows us that, like other criminals, Valmont did not betray his accomplices.

icine, is *nothing but the art of assisting nature?* You see that I beat you with your own arms, but I will not plume myself on that: it is indeed beating a man when he is down. *She must give herself,* you tell me. Ah, no doubt, she must; she will give herself like the others, with this difference, that it will be with a bad grace.

But if the end is that she should give herself, the true way is to begin by taking her. This absurd distinction is indeed a true sign of love's madness! I say love; for you are in love. To speak to you otherwise would be to cheat you, it would be to hide from you your ill. Tell me then, languid lover, the women whom you have had, did you think you had violated them? Why, however desirous one may be of giving oneself, however eager one may be, one still needs a pretext; and is there any more convenient for us than that which gives us the air of yielding to force? For me, I confess, one of the things which flatter me the most is a well-timed and lively assault, where everything succeeds in order, although with rapidity; which never throws us into the painful embarrassment of having ourselves to repair a *gaucherie* from which, on the contrary, we should have profited; which is cunning to maintain the air of violence even in things which we grant, and to flatter adroitly our two favorite passions, the glory of resistance and the pleasure of defeat. I grant that this talent, rarer than one may think, has always given me pleasure, even when it has not seduced me, and that sometimes, solely for recompense, it has induced me to yield. So, in our ancient tourneys, beauty gave the prize of valor and skill.

But you, who are no longer you, are behaving as if you were afraid of success. Ah! since when do you travel by short stages and crossroads? My friend, when one wishes to arrive, post-horses and the highway! But let us drop this subject, which is all the more distasteful to me in that it deprives me of the pleasure of seeing you. At least write to me more often than you do, and keep me informed of your progress. Do you know that it is now more than a fortnight since you have been occupied by this ridiculous adventure, and have neglected all the world?

À propos of negligence, you are like those people who send regularly to enquire after their sick friends, but who never trouble to get a reply. You finish your last letter by asking me if the Chevalier be dead. I do not answer, and you are no longer in the least concerned. Are you no longer aware that my lover is your born friend? But reassure yourself, he is not dead; or if he were, it would be for excess of joy. This poor Chevalier, how tender he is! how excellently is he made for love! how well he knows how to feel intensely! It makes my head reel. Seriously, the perfect happiness which he derives from being loved by me gives me a real attachment for him.

The very same day upon which I wrote to you that I was going to promote a rupture, how happy I made him! Yet I was mightily occupied, when they announced him, about the means of putting him in despair. Was it reason or caprice: he never seemed to me so fine. I nevertheless received him with temper. He hoped to pass two hours with me, before the time when my door would be open to everybody. I told him that I was going out: he asked me whither I was going; I refused to tell him. He insisted: "Where I shall not have your company," I answered acidly. Luckily for himself, he stood as though petrified by this answer; for had he said a word, a scene would infallibly have ensued which would have led to the projected rupture. Astonished by his silence, I cast my eyes upon him, with no other intention, upon my oath, than to see what countenance he would show. I discovered on that charming face that sorrow, at once so tender and so profound, which, you yourself have admitted, it is so difficult to resist. Like causes produce like effects: I was vanquished a second time.

From that moment, I was only busy in finding a means of preventing him from having a grievance against me. "I am going out on business," said, I, with a somewhat gentler air; "nay, even on business which concerns you; but do not question me further. I shall sup at home; return, and you shall know all." At this he recovered the power of speech; but I did not permit him to use it. "I am in great haste," I continued; "leave me, until this evening." He kissed my hand and went away.

Immediately, to compensate him, perhaps to compensate myself, I decide to acquaint him with my *petite maison,* of which he had no suspicion. I called my faithful Victoire. I have my headache; I am gone to bed, for all my household; and left alone at last with my *Trusty,* while she disguises herself as a lackey, I don the costume of a waiting maid. She next calls a hackney coach to the gate of my garden, and behold us on our way! Arrived in this temple of love, I chose the most gallant of *déshabillés.* This one is delicious; it is my own invention: it lets nothing be seen and yet allows you to divine all. I promise you a pattern of it for your Présidente, when you have rendered her worthy to wear it.

After these preliminaries, while Victoire busies herself with other details, I read a chapter of *Le Sopha,*[1] a letter of Héloïse and two Tales of La Fontaine, in order to rehearse the different tones which I would assume. Meantime, my Chevalier arrives at my door with his accustomed zeal. My porter denies him, and informs him that I am ill: incident the first. At the same time he hands him a note from me, but not in my handwriting, after my prudent rule. He opens it and sees written therein in Victoire's hand: "At nine o'clock, punctually, on the Boulevard, in front of the *cafés*." Thither he betakes himself, and there a little lackey

---

[1] An ingenious but very gallant romance by Monsieur de Crébillon *fils.—Translator's Note.*

whom he does not know, whom he believes, at least, that he does not know, for of course it was Victoire, comes and informs him that he must dismiss his carriage and follow her. All this romantic promenade helped all the more to heat his mind, and a hot head is by no means undesirable. At last, he arrives, and love and amazement produced in him a veritable enchantment. To give him time to recover, we stroll out for a while in the little wood; then I take him back again to the house. He sees, at first, two covers laid; then a bed prepared. We pass into the boudoir, which was richly adorned. There, half pensively, half in sentiment, I threw my arms round him, and fell on my knees.

"O my friend," said I, "in my desire to reserve the surprise of this moment for you, I reproach myself with having grieved you with a pretence of ill humor; with having been able, for an instant, to veil my heart to your gaze. Pardon me my wrongs: the strength of my love shall expiate them."

You may judge of the effect of this sentimental oration. The happy Chevalier lifted me up, and my pardon was sealed on that very same ottoman where you and I once sealed so gallantly, and in like fashion, our eternal rupture.

As we had six hours to pass together, and I had resolved to make all this time equally delicious for him, I moderated his transports, and brought an amiable coquetry to replace tenderness. I do not think that I have ever been at so great pains to please, nor that I have ever been so pleased with myself. After supper, by turns childish and reasonable, sensible and gay, even libertine at times, it was my pleasure to look upon him as a sultan in the heart of his seraglio, of which I was by turn the different favorites. In fact, his repeated acts of homage, although always received by the same woman, were ever received by a different mistress.

Finally, at the approach of day, we were obliged to separate; and whatever he might say, or even do, to prove to me the contrary, he had as much need of separation as he had little desire of it. At the moment when we left the house, and for a last adieu, I took the key of this abode of bliss, and giving it into his hands: "I had it but for you," said I; "it is right that you should be its master. It is for him who sacrifices to have the disposition of the temple." By such a piece of adroitness, I anticipated him from the reflections which might have been suggested to him, by the possession, always suspicious, of a *petite maison*. I know him well enough to be sure that he will never make use of it except for me; and if the whim seized me to go there without him, I have a second key. He would at all costs fix a day for return; but I love him still too well, to care to exhaust him so soon. One must not permit oneself excesses, except with persons whom one wishes soon to leave. He does not know that himself; but happily for him, I have knowledge for two.

I perceive that it is three o'clock in the morning, and that I have written a volume, with the intention but to write a word. Such is the charm of confident friendship: 'tis on account of that, that you are always he whom I love the best; but, in truth, the Chevalier pleases me more.

Paris, 12th August, 17★★.

11. The Présidente de Tourvel to Madame de Volanges

Your severe letter would have alarmed me, Madame, if happily I had not found here more causes for security than you give me for being afraid. This redoubtable M. de Valmont, who must be the terror of every woman, seems to have laid down his murderous arms before coming to this *château*. Far from forming any projects there, he has not even advanced any pretensions: and the quality of an amiable man, which even his enemies accord him, almost disappears here, to be superseded by that of frank good nature.

It is apparently the country air which has brought about this miracle. What I can assure you is that, being constantly with me, even seeming to take pleasure in my company, he has not let fall one word which resembles love, not one of those phrases which all men permit themselves, without having, like him, what is required to justify them. He never compels one to that reserve which every woman who respects herself is forced to maintain nowadays, in order to repress the men who encircle her. He knows how not to abuse the gaiety which he inspires. He is perhaps somewhat of a flatterer; but it is with so much delicacy, that he would accustom modesty itself to praise. In short, if I had a brother, I should desire him to be such as M. de Valmont reveals himself here. Perhaps, many women would ask a more marked gallantry from him; and I admit that I owe him infinite thanks for knowing how to judge me so well as not to confound me with them.

Doubtless, this portrait differs mightily from that which you send me; and in spite of that, neither need contradict the other, if one compares the dates. He confesses himself that he has committed many faults; and some others will have been fathered on him. But I have met few men who spoke of virtuous women with greater respect, I might almost say enthusiasm. You teach me that at least in this matter he is no deceiver. His conduct toward Madame de Merteuil is a proof of this. He talks much to us of her, and it is always with so much praise, and with the air of so true an attachment, that I believed, until I received your letter, that what he called the friendship between the two was actually love. I reproach myself for this hasty judgment, wherein I was all the more wrong, in that he himself has often been at the pains to justify her. I confess that I took for cunning what was honest sincerity on his part. I do not know, but it seems to me a man who is capable of so persistent a friendship for a woman so estimable cannot be a libertine beyond salvation. I am, for the rest, ignorant as to whether we owe the quiet manner of life which he leads here to any projects he cherishes in the vicinity, as you assume. There are, indeed, certain amiable women near us, but he rarely goes abroad, except in the morning, and then he tells us that it is to shoot. It is true that he rarely brings back any game; but he assures us that he is not a skillful sportsman. Moreover, what he may do without causes me little anxiety; and if I desired to know, it would only be in order to be convinced of your opinion or to bring you back to mine.

As to your suggestion to me to endeavor to cut short the stay which M. de Valmont proposes to make here, it seems to me very difficult to dare to ask his aunt not to have her nephew in her house, the more so in that she is very fond of him. I promise you, however, but only out of deference and not for any need, to seize any opportunity of making this request, either to her or to himself. As for myself, M. de Tourvel is aware of my project of remaining here until his return, and he would be astonished, and rightly so, at my frivolity, were I to change my mind.

These, Madame, are my very lengthy explanations: but I thought I owed it to truth to bear my testimony in M. de Valmont's favor; it seems to me he stood in great need of it with you. I am nonetheless sensible of the friendship which dictated your counsels. To that also I am indebted for your obliging remarks to me on the occasion of the delay as to your daughter's marriage. I thank you for them most sincerely: but however great the pleasure which I promise myself in passing those moments with you, I would sacrifice them with a good will to my desire to know Mlle. de Volanges more speedily happy, if, indeed, she could ever be more so than with a mother so deserving of all her affection and respect. I share with her those two sentiments which attach me to you, and I pray you kindly to receive my assurance of them.

I have the honor to be, etc.

At the Château de . . . , 13th August, 17**.

12. Cécile Volanges to the Marquise de Merteuil

Mamma is indisposed, Madame; she cannot leave the house, and I must keep her company: I shall not, therefore, have the honor of accompanying you to the Opera. I assure you that I do not regret the performance nearly so much as not to be with you. I pray that you will be convinced of this. I love you so much! Would you kindly tell M. le Chevalier Danceny that I have not the selection of which he spoke to me, and that if he can bring it to me tomorrow, it will give me great pleasure? If he comes today, he will be told that we are not at home; but this is because

Mamma cannot receive anybody. I hope that she will be better tomorrow.

I have the honor to be, etc.

Paris, 13th August, 17★★.

13. The Marquise de Merteuil to Cécile Volanges

I am most grieved, my pretty one, both at being deprived of the pleasure of seeing you, and at the cause of this privation. I hope that the opportunity will recur. I will acquit myself of your commission with the Chevalier Danceny, who will certainly be distressed to hear of your Mamma's sickness. If she can receive me tomorrow, I will come and keep her company. She and I will assault the Chevalier de Belleroche[1] at piquet, and while we win his money, we shall have the additional pleasure of hearing you sing with your amiable master, to whom I will suggest it. If this is convenient to your Mamma and to you, I can answer for myself and my two cavaliers. Adieu, my pretty one; my compliments to dear Madame de Volanges. I kiss you most tenderly.

Paris, 13th August, 17★★.

14. Cécile Volanges to Sophie Carnay

I did not write to you yesterday, my dear Sophie, but it was not pleasure which was the cause; of that I can assure you. Mamma was ill, and I did not leave her all day. In the evening, when I retired, I had no heart for anything at all, and I went to bed very quickly, to make sure that the day was done; never have I passed a longer. It is not that I do not love Mamma dearly; but I do not know what it was. I was to have gone to the Opera with Madame de Merteuil; the Chevalier Danceny was to have been there. You know well that they are the two persons whom I like best. When the hour arrived when I should have been there, my heart was sore in spite of me. I did not care for anything, and I cried, cried, without being able to stop myself. Happily Mamma had gone to bed, and could not see me. I am quite sure that the Chevalier Danceny will have been sorry too, but he will have been amused by the spectacle, and by everybody; that's very different.

Luckily, Mamma is better today, and Madame de Merteuil is coming with somebody else and the Chevalier Danceny; but she always comes very late, Madame de Merteuil; and when one is so long all by oneself, it is very tiresome. It is not yet eleven o'clock. It is true that I must play on my harp; and then my toilette will take me some time, for I want my

---

[1] This is the same gentleman who is mentioned in the letters of Madame de Merteuil.

hair to be done nicely today. I think Mother Perpétue is right and that one becomes a coquette as soon as one enters the world. I have never had such a desire to look pretty as during the last few days, and I find I am not as much so as I thought; and then, by the side of women who use rouge, one loses much. Madame de Merteuil, for instance; I can see that all the men think her prettier than me: that does not vex me much, because she is so fond of me; and then she assures me that the Chevalier Danceny thinks I am prettier than she. It is very nice of her to have told me that! She even seemed to be pleased at it. Well, that's a thing I can't understand! It's because she likes me so much! and he! . . . Oh, that gives me so much pleasure! I think too that only to look at him is enough to make one prettier. I should look at him always, if I did not fear to meet his eyes: for every time that that happens to me, it puts me out of countenance, and seems as though it hurt me; but no matter!

Adieu, my dear friend: I am going to make my toilette. I love you as dearly as ever.

Paris, 14th August, 17★★.

15. The Vicomte de Valmont to the Marquise de Merteuil

It is very nice of you not to abandon me to my sad fate. The life I lead here is really fatiguing, from the excess of its repose and its insipid monotony. Reading your letter and the details of your charming day, I was tempted a score of times to invent some business, to fly to your feet, and beg of you an infidelity, in my favor, to your Chevalier, who, after all, does not merit his happiness. Do you know that you have made me jealous of him? Why talk to me of an eternal rupture? I abjure that vow, uttered in a moment of frenzy: we should not have been worthy to make it, had we meant to keep it. Ah, that I might one day avenge myself, in your arms, for the involuntary vexation which the happiness of your Chevalier has caused me! I am indignant, I confess, when I think that this man, without reasoning, without giving himself the least trouble, but quite stupidly following the instinct of his heart, should find a felicity to which I cannot attain. Oh, I will trouble it! . . . Promise me that I shall trouble it. You yourself, are you not humiliated? You take the trouble to deceive him, and he is happier than you. You believe he is in your chains! It is, indeed, you who are in his. He sleeps tranquilly, while you watch over his pleasures. What more would his slave do?

Listen, my lovely friend: so long as you divide yourself among many, I have not the least jealousy; I see then in your lovers only the successors of Alexander, incapable of preserving among them all that empire over which I reigned alone. But that you should give yourself entirely to one of them! That another man should exist as fortunate as myself! I will not suffer it; do not hope that I shall suffer it. Either take me back, or, at least, take someone else; and do not betray, by an exclusive caprice, the inviolate bond of friendship which we have sworn.

It is quite enough, no doubt, that I should have to complain of love. You see, I lend myself to your ideas, and confess my errors. In fact, if to be in love is to be unable to live without possessing the object of one's desire, to sacrifice to it one's time, one's pleasures, one's life, I am very really in love. I am no more advanced for that. I should not even have anything at all to tell you of in this matter, but for an incident which gives me much food for reflection, and as to which I know not yet whether I must hope or fear.

You know my *chasseur,* a treasure of intrigue, and a real valet of comedy: you can imagine that his instructions bade him to fall in love with the waiting maid, and make the household drunk. The knave is more fortunate than I: he has already succeeded. He has just discovered that Madame de Tourvel has charged one of her people to inform himself as to my behavior, and even to follow me in my morning expeditions, as far as he could without being observed. What is this woman's pretension? Thus then the most modest of them all yet dares do things which we should hardly venture to permit ourselves. I swear . . . ! But before I think of avenging myself for this feminine ruse, let us occupy ourselves over methods of turning it to our advantage. Hitherto, these excursions which are suspected have had no object; needs must I give them one. This deserves all my attention, and I take leave of you to ponder upon it. Farewell, my lovely friend.

Still at the Château de . . . , 15th August, 17★★.

16. Cécile Volanges to Sophie Carnay

Ah, my Sophie, I have a heap of news! I ought not, perhaps, to tell you: but I must talk to someone; it is stronger than I! This Chevalier Danceny . . . I am so perturbed that I can hardly write: I do not know where to begin. Ever since I related to you the sweet evening[1] which I passed at Mamma's, with him and Madame de Merteuil, I have said no more about him to you: it is because I did not want to speak of him to anybody; but I was thinking of him constantly. Since then he has grown so sad—oh, sad, sad!—that it gave me pain; and when I asked him why, he answered that it was not so; but I could well see that it *was.* Finally, yesterday he was even sadder than ordinarily. This did not prevent him from having the

---

[1]The letter in which this *soirée* is spoken of has not been found. There seems reason to believe it is that suggested in the note of Madame de Merteuil, and also mentioned in the preceding letter of Cécile Volanges.

kindness to sing with me as usual; but every time that he looked at me it gripped my heart. When we had finished singing, he went to shut up my harp in its case; and returning the key to me, begged me to play again that evening when I was alone. I had no suspicion of anything at all; I did not even want to play: but he begged me so earnestly that I told him yes. He, certainly, had his motive. In effect, when I had retired to my room and my waiting maid had gone, I went to get my harp. In the strings I found a letter, simply folded, with no seal, and it was from him. Ah, if you knew all he asks of me! Since I have read his letter, I feel so much delight that I can think of nothing else. I read it four times straight off, and then shut it up in my desk. I knew it by heart; and, when I was in bed, I repeated it so often that I had no thought to sleep. As soon as I shut my eyes, I saw him there; he told me himself all that I had just read. I did not get to sleep till quite late; and, as soon as I was awake (it was still quite early), I went to get his letter and read it again at my ease. I carried it to bed with me, and then I kissed it as if . . . Perhaps I did wrong to kiss a letter like that, but I could not check myself.

At present, my dear friend, if I am very happy, I am also much embarrassed; for, assuredly, I ought not to reply to this letter. I know that I should not, and yet he asks me to; and, if I do not reply, I am sure he will be sad again. All the same, it is very unfortunate for him! What do you advise me to do? But you can no more tell than I. I have a great desire to speak of it to Madame de Merteuil, who is so fond of me. I should indeed like to console him; but I should not like to do anything wrong. We are always recommended to cherish a kind heart! and then they forbid us to follow its inspiration, directly there is question of a man! That is not just either. Is not a man our neighbor as much as a woman, if not more so? For, after all, has not one one's father as well as one's mother, one's brother as well as one's sister? The husband is still something extra. Nevertheless, if I were to do something which was not right, perhaps M. Danceny himself would no longer have a good opinion of me! Oh, rather than that, I would sooner see him sad; and then, besides, I shall always have time enough. Because he wrote yesterday, I am not obliged to write today: I shall be sure to see Madame de Merteuil this evening, and, if I have the courage, I will tell her all. If I only do what she tells me, I shall have nothing to reproach myself with. And then, perhaps, she will tell me that I may answer him *a little,* so that he need not be so sad! Oh, I am in great trouble!

Farewell, my dear friend; tell me, all the same, what you think.

Paris, 19th August, 17★★.

17. The Chevalier Danceny to Cécile Volanges

Before succumbing, Mademoiselle, to the pleasure, or, shall I say, the necessity of writing to you, I commence by imploring you to hear me. I feel that, to be bold enough to declare my sentiments, I have need of indulgence; did I but wish to justify them, it would be useless to me. What am I about to do, after all, save to show you your handiwork? And what have I to tell you, that my eyes, my embarrassment, my conduct and even my silence have not told you already? And why should you take offense at a sentiment to which you have given birth? Emanating from you, it is doubtless worthy to be offered to you; if it is ardent as my soul, it is pure as your own. Shall it be a crime to have known how to appreciate your charming face, your seductive talents, your enchanting graces, and that touching candor which adds inestimable value to qualities already so precious? No, without a doubt: but without being guilty, one may be unhappy; and that is the fate which awaits me if you refuse to accept my homage. It is the first that my heart has offered. But for you, I should still be, not happy, but tranquil. I have seen you, repose has fled far away from me, and my happiness is insecure. Yet you are surprised at my sadness; you ask me its cause: sometimes, I have even thought to see that it affected you. Ah, speak but a word and my felicity will be your handiwork! But, before you pronounce it, remember that one word can also fill the cup of my misery. Be then the arbiter of my destiny. Through you I am to be eternally happy or wretched. In what dearer hands can I commit an interest of such importance?

I shall end as I have begun, by imploring your indulgence. I have begged you to hear me; I will dare more, I will pray you to reply to me. A refusal would lead me to think that you were offended, and my heart is a witness that my respect is equal to my love.

P.S. You can make use, to send a reply, of the same method which I employed to bring this letter into your hands; it seems to me as convenient as it is secure.

Paris, 18th August, 17**.

18. Cécile Volanges to Sophie Carnay

What, Sophie! You blame me in advance for what I am about to do! I had already enough anxiety, and here you are increasing it. Clearly, you say, I ought not to answer. You speak with great confidence; and besides, you do not know exactly how things are: you are not here to see. I am sure that, were you in my place, you would act like me. Assuredly, as a general rule, one ought not to reply; and you can see from my letter of yesterday that I did not want to either: but the thing is, I do not think anyone has *ever* found herself in quite my case.

And still to be obliged to take my decision all unaided! Madame de Merteuil, whom I counted on seeing yesterday evening, did not come. Everything conspires against me: it is through her that I know him! It is almost always with her that I have seen him, that I have spoken to him. It is not that I have any grudge against her; but she leaves me just in the embarrassing moment. Oh, I am greatly to be pitied!

Imagine! He came here yesterday just as usual. I was so confused that I dared not look at him. He could not speak to me, because Mamma was there. I quite expected that he would be grieved, when he should find that I had not written to him. I did not know what face to wear. A moment later he asked me if I should like him to bring me my harp. My heart beat so quick, that it was as much as I could do to answer yes. When he came back, it was even worse. I only looked at him for a second. He—he did not look at me, but he had such a look that one would have thought him ill. It made me very unhappy. He began to tune my harp, and afterward, on bringing it to me, he said, "Ah, Mademoiselle!" . . . He only said these two words; but it was with such an accent that I was quite overwhelmed. I struck the first chords on my harp without knowing what I was doing. Mamma asked me if we were not going to sing. He excused himself, saying that he was not feeling well, and I, who had no excuse—I had to sing. I could have wished that I had never had a voice. I chose purposely an air which I did not know; for I was quite sure that I could not sing anything, and was afraid that something would be noticed. Luckily, there came a visit, and as soon as I heard the carriage wheels, I stopped, and begged him to take away my harp. I was very much afraid lest he should leave at the same time; but he came back.

While Mamma and the lady who had arrived were talking together, I wanted to look at him again for one instant. I met his eyes, and it was impossible for me to turn away on my own. A moment later, I saw the tears rise, and he was obliged to turn away in order not to be observed. For an instant I could no longer hold myself in; I felt that I too should weep. I went out, and at once wrote in pencil, on a scrap of paper: "Do not be so sad, I implore you; I promise to give you a reply." Surely, you cannot see any harm in that, and then it was stronger than I. I put my paper in the strings of my harp, where his letter had been, and returned to the *salon*. I felt more calm.

It seemed to me very long until the lady went away. Luckily, she had more visits to pay; she went away shortly afterward. As soon as she was gone, I said that I wanted to have my harp again, and begged him to go and fetch it. I saw from his expression that he suspected nothing. But, on his return, oh, how pleased he was! As he set down my harp in front of me, he placed himself in such a position that Mamma could not see, and he took my hand, which he squeezed . . . but, in such a way! . . . it was only for a moment: but I could not tell you the pleasure which it gave me. However, I withdrew it; so I have nothing for which to reproach myself.

And now, my dear friend, you must see that I cannot abstain from writing to him, since I have given my promise; and then I am not going to give him any more pain; for I suffer more than he does. If it were a question of doing anything wrong, I should certainly not do it. But what harm can there be in writing, especially when it is to save somebody from being unhappy? What embarrasses me is that I do not know how to write my letter: but he will surely feel that it is not my fault; and then I am certain that as long as it only comes from me, it will give him pleasure.

Adieu, my dear friend. If you think that I am wrong, tell me; but I do not think so. The nearer the moment of writing to him comes, the more does my heart beat: more than you can conceive. I must do it, however, since I have promised. Adieu.

Paris, 20th August, 17★★.

19. Cécile Volanges to the Chevalier Danceny

You were so sad yesterday, Monsieur, and that made me so sorry, that I went so far as to promise to reply to the letter which you wrote me. I nonetheless feel today that I ought not to do this: however, as I have promised, I do not wish to break my word, and that must prove how much friendship I feel for you. Now that you know that, I hope you will not ask me to write to you again. I hope also that you will tell nobody that I have written to you, because I should be certainly blamed, and that might cause me a great deal of pain. I hope, above all, that you yourself will not form a bad opinion of me, which would grieve me more than anything. I can give you every assurance that I would not have done as much to anyone except yourself. I should be very glad if you would do me a favor in your turn, and be less sad than you were: it takes away all the pleasure that I feel in seeing you. You see, Monsieur, I speak to you very sincerely. I ask nothing better than that I may always keep your friendship; but I beg of you do not write to me again.

I have the honor to be,

Cécile Volanges.
Paris, 20th August, 17★★.

20. The Marquise de Merteuil to the Vicomte de Valmont

Ah, wretch, so you flatter me, for fear that I shall make a mock of you! Come, I pardon you: you write me such a heap of nonsense that I must even forgive you the virtue in which you are kept by your Présidente. I do not think my Chevalier would show as much indulgence as I do; he would not be the man to approve the renewal of our contract, or to find anything amusing in your mad idea. I have laughed mightily over it, however, and was really vexed that I had to laugh over it by myself. If you had been there, I know not whither this merriment might not have led me; but I have had time for reflection, and am armed with severity. I do not say that I refuse forever; but I postpone, and I am right to do so. I should bring my vanity with me, and once wounded at the game, one knows not where one stops. I should be the woman to enslave you again, to make you forget your Présidente; and if I—unworthy I—were to disgust you with virtue, consider the scandal! To avoid these dangers, here are my conditions:

As soon as you have had your lovely bigot, as soon as you can furnish me with the proof, come to me and I am yours. But you cannot be ignorant that, in affairs of importance, only written proofs are admitted. By this arrangement, on one part, I shall become a recompense instead of being a consolation, and that notion likes me better: on the other hand, your success will have added piquancy by being itself a means to an infidelity. Come then, come as soon as possible, and bring me the gauge of your triumph; like those valiant knights of ours, who came to lay at their ladies' feet the brilliant fruit of their victory. Seriously, I am curious to know what a prude can write after such a moment, and what veil she casts over her language, after having discarded any from her person. It is for you to say whether I price myself too high; but I forewarn you that there is no abatement. Till then, my dear Vicomte, you will find it good that I remain faithful to my Chevalier and amuse myself by making him happy, in spite of the slight annoyance this may cause you.

However, if my morals were less severe, I think he would have, at this moment, a dangerous rival: the little Volanges girl. I am bewitched by this child: it is a real passion. Unless I be deceived, she will become one of our most fashionable women. I see her little heart developing, and it is a ravishing spectacle. She already loves her Danceny with ardor; but she knows nothing about it yet. He himself, although greatly in love, has still the timidity of his age, and dares not as yet tell her too much about it. The two of them are united in adoring me. The little one especially has a mighty desire to confide her secret to me. A few days ago, particularly, I saw her really oppressed, and should have done her a great service by assisting her a little: but I do not forget that she is a child, and I should not like to compromise myself. Danceny has spoken to me somewhat more clearly; but with him my course is resolved; I refuse to hear him. As to the little one, I am often tempted to make her my pupil; it is a service that I would fain render Gercourt. He leaves me the time, since he is to stay in Corsica until the month of October. I have a notion to make use of that time, and that we will give him a fully informed woman, instead of his innocent schoolgirl. In effect, what must be the insolent sense of security of this man, that he dare sleep in comfort, while a woman who has to complain of him has not yet been avenged? Believe me, if the child were here at this moment, I do not know what I would not say to her.

Adieu, Vicomte; good night, and success to you: but do, for God's sake, make progress. Bethink you that, if you do not have this woman, the others will blush for having taken you.

Paris, 20th August, 17★★.

21. The Vicomte de Valmont to the Marquise de Merteuil

At last, my lovely friend, I have taken a step forward: a really great step, and one which, if it has not taken me to my goal, has at least let me know that I am on the right road, and dispelled the fear I was in, that I was lost. I have at last declared my love; and although the most obstinate silence has been maintained, I have obtained a reply that is, perhaps, the least equivocal and the most flattering: but let us not anticipate events, let us begin farther back.

You will remember that a watch was set upon my movements. Well, I resolved that this scandalous means should turn to public edification; and this is what I did. I charged my confidant with the task of finding me some poor wretch in the neighborhood who was in need of succor. This commission was not difficult to fulfill. Yesterday afternoon, he gave me the information that they were going to seize today, in the morning, the goods of a whole family who could not pay their taxes. I assured myself that there was no girl or woman among this household whose age or face might render my action suspicious; and, when I was well informed, I declared at supper my intention of going after game in the morning. Here I must render justice to my Présidente; doubtless she felt a certain remorse at the orders which she had given; and, not having the strength to vanquish her curiosity, she had at least enough to oppose my desire. It was going to be excessively hot; I ran the risk of making myself ill; I should kill nothing, and tire myself to no purpose; and during all this dialogue, her eyes, which spoke, perhaps, better than she wished, let me see quite sufficiently that she desired me to take these bad reasons for good. I was careful not to surrender, as you may believe, and I even resisted a little diatribe against sportsmen and sport and a little cloud of ill humor which obscured, during all the evening, that celestial brow. I feared for a moment that her orders had been revoked, and that her delicacy might hinder me. I did not calculate on the strength of a woman's curiosity; and so was deceived. My *chasseur* reassured me the same evening, and I went satisfied to bed.

At daybreak I rose and started off. Barely fifty yards from the *château,* I perceived the spy who was to follow me. I started after the game, and walked across country to the village whither I wished to make, with no other pleasure on the road than to give a run to the rogue who followed me, and who, not daring to quit the road, often had to cover, at full speed, a three times greater distance than mine. By dint of exercising him, I was excessively hot myself, and I sat down at the foot of a tree. He had the insolence to steal behind a bush, not twenty paces from me, and to sit down as well! I was tempted for a moment to fire my gun at him, which, although it only contained small shot, would have given him a sufficient lesson as to the dangers of curiosity: luckily for him, I remembered that he was useful and even necessary to my projects; this reflection saved him.

However, I reach the village; I see a commotion; I step forward; I question somebody; the facts are related. I have the collector called to me; and, yielding to my generous compassion, I pay nobly fifty-six livres, for lack of which five persons were to be left to straw and their despair. After this simple action, you cannot imagine what a crowd of benedictions echoed round me from the witnesses of the scene! What tears of gratitude poured from the eyes of the aged head of the family, and embellished his patriarchal face, which, a moment before, had been rendered really hideous by the savage marks of despair! I was watching this spectacle, when another peasant, younger, who led a woman and two children by the hands, advanced to me with hasty steps and said to them, "Let us all fall at the feet of this image of God"; and at the same instant I was surrounded by the family, prostrate at my knees. I will confess my weakness: my eyes were moistened by tears, and I felt an involuntary but delicious emotion. I am astonished at the pleasure one experiences in doing good; and I should be tempted to believe that what we call virtuous people have not so much merit as they lead us to suppose. However that may be, I found it just to pay these poor people for the pleasure which they had given me. I had brought ten louis with me, and I gave them these. The acknowledgments began again, but they were not pathetic to the same degree: necessity had produced the great, the true effect; the rest was but a simple expression of gratitude and astonishment at superfluous gifts.

However, in the midst of the loquacious benedictions of this family, I was by no means unlike the hero of a drama, in the scene of the *dénouement*. Above all, you will remark the faithful spy was also in this crowd.

My purpose was fulfilled: I disengaged myself from them all, and regained the *château*. On further consideration, I congratulated myself on my inventive genius. This woman is, doubtless, well worth all the pains I take; they will one day be my titles with her; and having, in some sort, as it were, paid in advance, I shall have the right to dispose of her, according to my fantasy, without having any cause to reproach myself.

I forgot to tell you that, to turn everything to profit, I asked these good people to pray for the success of my projects. You shall see whether their prayers have not been already in part hearkened to. . . . But they come to tell me that supper is ready, and it would be too late to dispatch this letter, if I waited to end it after rising from table. "To be continued," therefore, "in our next." I am sorry, for the sequel is the finest part. Adieu, my lovely friend. You steal from me a moment of the pleasure of seeing her.

At the Château de . . . , 20th August, 17★★.

22. The Présidente de Tourvel to Madame de Volanges

You will, doubtless, be well pleased, Madame, to hear of a trait in M. de Valmont which seems in great contrast to all those under which you have represented him to me. It is so painful to have to think unfavorably of anybody, so grievous to find only vices in people who should possess all the qualities necessary to make virtue lovable! Moreover, you love so well to be indulgent that, were it only to oblige you, I must give you a reason for reconsidering your too harsh judgment. M. de Valmont seems to me entitled to hope for this favor, I might almost say this justice; and this is on what I base my opinion.

This morning he made one of those excursions which might lead one to believe in some project on his part, in the vicinity, just as the idea came to you of one; an idea which I accuse myself of having entertained with too much precipitation. Luckily for him, and above all luckily for us, since we are thus saved from being unjust, one of my men happened to be going in the same direction,[1] and it is from this source that my reprehensible but fortunate curiosity was satisfied. He related to us that M. de Valmont, having found an unfortunate family in the village of —— whose goods were being sold because they were unable to pay their taxes, not only hastened to pay the debt of these poor people, but even added to this gift a considerable sum of money. My servant was a witness of this virtuous action; and he related to me in addition that the peasants, talking among themselves and with him, had said that a servant, whom they described, and who is believed by mine to be that of M. de Valmont, had sought information yesterday as to any of the inhabitants

---

[1]Madame de Tourvel then does not dare to say that it was by her order!

of the village who might be in need of help. If that be so, it was not merely a passing feeling of compassion, suggested by the opportunity: it was the deliberate project of doing good; it was a search for the chance of being benevolent; it was the fairest virtue of the most noble souls: but be it chance or design, it is nonetheless a laudable and generous action, the mere recital of which moved me to tears. I will add more, and still from a sense of justice, that when I spoke to him of this action, which he had never mentioned, he began by excusing himself, and when he admitted it had the air of attaching so little importance to it, that the merit of it was enhanced by his modesty.

After that, tell me, my esteemed friend, if M. de Valmont is indeed an irreclaimable libertine? If he can be no more than that and yet behave so, what is left for honest folk? What! are the wicked to share with the good the sacred joy of charity? Would God permit that a virtuous family should receive from the hands of a villain succor for which they render thanks to Divine Providence, and could it please Him to hear pure lips bestow their blessings upon a reprobate? No! I prefer to hold that errors, long as they may have lasted, do not endure forever; and I cannot think that he who does good can be the enemy of virtue. M. de Valmont is perhaps only one more instance of the danger of acquaintances. I remain of this opinion which pleases me. If, on one side, it may serve to justify him in your opinion, on the other, it renders more and more precious to me the tender friendship which unites me to you for life.

I have the honor to be, etc.

P.S. Madame de Rosemonde and I are going this moment to see for ourselves this worthy and unfortunate family, and to unite our tardy aid to that of M. de Valmont. We shall take him with us. We shall at least give these good people the pleasure of seeing their benefactor again: that is, I believe, all he has left for us to do.

At the Château de . . . , 20th August, 17★★.

23. The Vicomte de Valmont to the Marquise de Merteuil

I left off at my return to the *château:* I resume my tale.

I had only time to make a hurried toilette, ere I repaired to the drawing room, where my beauty was working at her tapestry, while the *curé* of the place was reading the gazette to my old aunt. I went and took my seat by the frame. Glances sweeter than were customary, and almost caressing, enabled me soon to divine that the servant had already given an account of his mission. Indeed, the dear, inquisitive lady could no longer keep the secret which she had acquired; and without fear of interrupting a venerable pastor, whose recital indeed resembled a sermon: "I too have a piece of news to recite," said she; and suddenly related my adventure, with an exactitude which did honor to the intelligence of her historian. You may conceive what play I made with my modesty: but who can stop a woman, when she praises the man whom, without knowing it, she loves? I decided therefore to let her have her head. One would have thought she was making the panegyric of a saint. All this time I was observing, not without hope, all the promises of love in her animated gaze; her gesture, which had become more lively; and, above all, her voice, which, by its already perceptible alteration, betrayed the emotion of her soul. She had hardly finished speaking when: "Come, my nephew," said Madame de Rosemonde to me, "come and let me embrace you." I felt at once that the pretty preacher could not prevent herself from being embraced in her turn. However, she wished to fly; but she was soon in my arms, and, so far from having the strength to resist, she had scarcely sufficient to maintain herself. The more I observe this woman, the more desirable she appears to me. She hastened to return to her frame, and to everybody had the appearance of resuming her tapestry. But I saw well her trembling hand prevented her from continuing her work.

After dinner, the ladies insisted on going to see the unfortunates whom I had so piously succored; I accompanied them. I spare you the tedium of this second scene of gratitude and praise. My heart, impelled by a delicious recollection, hurries on the moment for return to the *château*. On the way, my fair Présidente, more pensive than is her wont, said never a word. Occupied as I was in seeking the means of profiting by the effect which the episode of the day had produced, I maintained the same silence. Madame de Rosemonde was the only one to speak, and obtained from us but scant and few replies. We must have bored her; that was my intention, and it succeeded. Thus, on stepping from the carriage, she passed into her apartment and left my fair one and myself *tête-à-tête*, in a dimly lighted room—a sweet obscurity which emboldens timid love.

I had not to be at the pains to lead the conversation into the channel which I wished. The fervor of the amiable preacheress served me better than any skill of my own.

"When one is capable of doing good," said she, letting her sweet gaze rest on me, "how can one pass one's life in doing ill?"

"I do not deserve, either that praise or that censure," said I, "and I cannot imagine how you, who have so clear a wit, have not yet divined me. Though my confidence may damage me in your eyes, you are far too worthy of it that I should be able to refuse it. You will find the key to my conduct in my character, which is unhappily far too easygoing. Surrounded by persons of no morality, I have imitated their vices; I have perhaps made it a point of vanity to surpass them. In the same way, attracted here by the example of virtue, without ever hoping to come up to you, I have, at least, endeavored to imitate you. Ah, perhaps the action for which you praise me today would lose all value in your eyes if you knew its true motive!" (You see, my fair friend, how near the truth I touched.) "It is not to myself," I went on, "that these unfortunates owe their rescue. Where you think you see a praiseworthy action, I did but seek a means to please. I was nothing else, since I must say it, but the weak agent of the divinity whom I adore." (Here she would have interrupted me, but I did not give her time.) "At this very moment even," I added, "my secret only escapes from my weakness. I had vowed that I would be silent before you; I made it my happiness to render to your virtues as much as to your charms a pure homage of which you should always remain ignorant; but incapable of deception, when I have before my eyes the example of candor, I shall not have to reproach myself to you with guilty dissimulation. Do not believe that I insult you by entertaining any criminal hope. I shall be miserable, I know; but my sufferings will be dear to me: they will prove to me the immensity of my love; it is at your feet, it is on your bosom that I will cast down my woes. There shall I draw the strength to suffer anew; there shall I find compassionate bounty, and I shall deem myself consoled because you will have pitied me. Oh, you whom I adore! hearken to me, pity me, succor me!"

By this time I was at her feet, and I pressed her hands in mine; but she suddenly disengaged them and, folding them over her eyes, cried with an expression of despair, "Oh, wretched me!" then burst into tears. Luckily I was exalted to such a degree that I also wept; and, seizing her hands again, I bathed them with my tears. This precaution was most necessary; for she was so full of her grief that she would not have perceived my own, had I not taken this means of informing her. I moreover gained the privilege of considering at my leisure that charming face, yet more embellished by the potent charm of her tears. My head grew hot, and so little was I master of myself that I was tempted to profit by that moment.

What is this weakness of ours? of what avail is the force of circumstances if, forgetting my own projects, I risked losing, by a premature triumph, the charms of a long battle and the details of a painful defeat; if, seduced by the desires of youth, I thought of exposing the conqueror of Madame de Tourvel to the pain of plucking, for the fruit of victory, but the insipid consolation of having had one woman more? Ah, let her surrender, but let her first fight; let her, without having strength to conquer, have enough to resist; let her relish at her leisure the sentiment of her weakness and be constrained to confess her defeat! Let us leave it to the obscure poacher to kill at a bound the stag he has surprised; your true hunter will give it a run. Is not this project of mine sublime? Yet perhaps I should be now regretting that I had not followed it, had not chance come to the rescue of my prudence.

We heard a noise. Someone was coming to the drawing room. Madame de Tourvel, in alarm, rose precipitately, seized one of the candles, and left the room. I could not but let her go. It was only one of the servants. As soon as I was assured of this, I followed her. I had hardly gone a few paces, before, whether that she had recognized me, or for some vague sentiment of terror, I heard her quicken her steps, and flung herself into, rather than entered, her chamber, the door of which she closed behind her. I went after her; but the door was locked inside. I was careful not to knock; that would have been to give her the chance of a too easy resistance. I had the good and simple idea of peeping through the keyhole, and I saw this adorable woman on her knees, bathed with tears, and fervently praying. What God did she dare invoke? Is there one potent enough to resist love? In vain, henceforward, will she invoke extraneous aid! 'Tis I who will order her destiny.

Thinking I had done enough for one day, I too withdrew to my own room, and started to write to you. I hoped to see her again at supper; but she had given out that she was indisposed, and had gone to bed. Madame de Rosemonde wished to go up to her; but the cunning invalid alleged a headache which prevented her from seeing anybody. You may guess that after supper the interval was short, and that I too had my headache. Withdrawing to my room, I wrote a long letter to complain of this severity, and went to bed with the intention of delivering it to her this morning. I slept badly, as you can see by the date of this letter. I rose and reread my epistle. I discovered that I had not been sufficiently restrained, had exhibited less love than ardor, less regret than ill humor. It must be written again, but in a calmer mood.

I see the day break, and I hope the freshness which accompanies it will bring me sleep. I am going to return to my bed; and, whatever may be the power of this woman over me, I promise you never to be so occupied with her as to lack time to think much of you. Adieu, my lovely friend!

At the Chateau de . . . , 21st August, 17**.
at four o'clock in the morning.

24. The Vicomte de Valmont to the Présidente de Tourvel

Ah, Madame, deign in pity to calm the trouble of my soul, deign to tell me what I am to hope or fear. Cast between the extremes of happiness and misfortune, uncertainty is a cruel torment. Why did I speak to you? Why did I not know how to resist the imperious charm which betrayed my thoughts to you? Content to adore you in silence, I had at least the consolation of my love; and this pure sentiment, untroubled then by the image of your grief, sufficed for my felicity; but that source of happiness has become my despair, since I saw your tears flow, since I heard that cruel *Ah, wretched me!*

Madame, those words will echo long within my heart. By what fatality can the sweetest of the sentiments inspire nothing but terror? What then is this fear? Ah, it is not that of reciprocation: your heart, which I have misunderstood, is not made for love; mine, which you calumniate unceasingly, is the only one which is disturbed: yours is even pitiless. If it were not so, you would not have refused a word of consolation to the wretch who told you of his sufferings; you would not have withdrawn yourself from his sight, when he has no other pleasure than that of seeing you; you would not have played a cruel game with his anxiety by letting him be told that you were ill, without permitting him to go and inform himself of your health; you would have felt that the same night which did but mean for you twelve hours of repose would be for him a century of pain.

For what cause, tell me, have I deserved this intolerable severity? I do not fear to take you for my judge: what have I done, then, but yield to an involuntary sentiment, inspired by beauty and justified by virtue, always restrained by respect, the innocent avowal of which was the effect of trust and not of hope? Will you betray that trust, which you yourself seemed to permit me, and to which I yielded myself without reserve? No, I cannot believe that: it would be to imply a fault in you, and my heart revolts at the bare idea of detecting one. I withdraw my reproaches; write them I can, but think them never! Ah, let me believe you perfect; it is the one pleasure which is left me! Prove to me that you are so by granting me your generous aid. What poor wretch have you ever helped who was in so much need as I? Do not abandon me to the frenzy in which you have plunged me: lend me your reason since you have ravished mine; after having corrected me, give me light to complete your work.

I would not deceive you; you will never succeed in subduing my love; but you shall teach me to moderate it: by guiding my conduct, by dictating my speech, you will save me, at least, from the dire misfortune of displeasing you. Dispel above all that dreadful fear; tell me that you forgive me, that you pity me; assure me of your indulgence. You will never have as much as I should desire in you; but I invoke that of which I have need: will you refuse it me?

Adieu, Madame; be kind enough to receive the homage of my sentiments; it hinders not that of my respect.

At the Château de . . . , 20th August, 17**.

25. The Vicomte de Valmont to the Marquise de Merteuil

This is yesterday's bulletin. At eleven o'clock I visited Madame de Rosemonde, and, under her auspices, I was introduced into the presence of the pretended invalid, who was still in her bed. Her eyes looked very worn; I hope she slept as badly as I did. I seized a moment when Madame de Rosemonde had turned away to deliver my letter: it was refused; but I left it on the bed, and went decorously to the side of my old aunt's armchair. She wished to be near *her dear child*. It was necessary to conceal the letter to avoid scandal. The invalid was artless enough to say that she thought she had a little fever. Madame de Rosemonde persuaded me to feel her pulse, vaunting mightily my knowledge of medicine. My beauty then had the double vexation of being forced to give me her hand, and of feeling that her little falsehood was to be discovered. I took her hand, which I pressed in one of mine, while, with the other, I ran over her fresh and rounded arm. The naughty creature made no response, which impelled me to say, as I withdrew, "There is not even the slightest symptom." I suspected that her gaze would be severe, and to punish her, I refused to meet it: a moment later she said that she wished to rise, and we left her alone. She appeared at dinner, which was a somber one; she gave out that she would not take a walk, which was as much as to tell me that I should have no opportunity of conversing with her. I was well aware that, at this point, I must put in a sigh and a mournful look; no doubt she was waiting for that, for it was the one moment of the day when I succeeded in meeting her eyes. Virtuous as she is, she has her little ruses like another. I found a moment to ask of her if she had had the kindness to inform me of my fate, and I was somewhat astonished when she answered, "Yes, Monsieur, I have written to you." I was mighty anxious to have this letter, but whether it were a ruse again, or for awkwardness, or shyness, she did not give it to me till the evening, when she was retiring to her apartment. I send it you, as well as the first draft of mine; read and judge; see with what signal falsity she says that she feels no love, when I am sure of the contrary; and then she will complain if I deceive her afterward, when she does not fear to deceive me before! My lovely friend, the cleverest of men can do no more than keep on a level with the truest woman. I must needs, however, feign to believe all this nonsense, and weary myself with despair, because it pleases Madame to play at severity! It is hard not to be revenged on such baseness! Ah, patience! . . . But adieu. I have still much to write. By the way, return me the letter of the fair barbarian; it might happen later that she would expect one to attach a value to those wretched sheets, and one must be in order.

I say nothing to you of the little Volanges; we will talk of her at an early day.

At the Château de . . . , 22nd August, 17★★.

26. The Présidente de Tourvel to the Vicomte de Valmont

Assuredly, Monsieur, you would never have received any letter from me, did not my foolish conduct of yesterday evening compel me today to have an explanation with you. Yes, I wept, I confess it: perhaps, too, the words which you are so careful to quote to me did escape me; tears and words, you remarked everything; I must then explain to you everything.

Accustomed to inspire only honorable sentiments, to hear only conversation to which I can listen without a blush, and consequently to enjoy a feeling of security which I venture to say I deserve, I know not how either to dissimulate or to combat the impressions I receive. The astonishment and embarrassment into which your conduct threw me; a fear, I know not of what, inspired by a situation which should never have been thrust upon me; perhaps, even the revolting idea of seeing myself confounded with the women whom you despise, and treated as lightly as they are: all these causes in conjunction provoked my tears, and may have made me say, I think with reason, that I was wretched. This expression, which you think so strong, would certainly have been far too weak, if my tears and utterance had another motive; if, instead of disapproving sentiments which must need offend me, I could have feared lest I should share them.

No, Monsieur, I have not that fear; if I had, I would fly a hundred leagues away from you, I would go and weep in a desert at the misfortune of having known you. Perhaps even, in spite of the certainty in which I am of not loving you, of never loving you, perhaps I should have done better to follow the counsels of my friends, and forbid you to approach me.

I believed, and it is my sole error, I believed that you would respect a virtuous woman, who asked nothing better than to find you so and to do you justice; who already was defending you, while you were outraging her with your criminal avowals. You do not know me; no, Monsieur, you do not know me. Otherwise you would not have thought to make a right out of your error: because you had made proposals to me which I ought not to hear, you would not have thought yourself authorized to write me a letter which I ought not to read: and you ask me *to guide your conduct, to dictate to you your speech!* Very well, Monsieur, silence and forgetfulness, those are the counsels which it becomes me to give you, as it will you to follow them; then you will indeed have rights to my indulgence: it will only rest with you to obtain even my gratitude. . . . But no,

I will not address a request to a man who has not respected me; I will give no mark of confidence to a man who has abused my security. You force me to fear, perhaps to hate you: I did not want to; I wished to see in you naught else than the nephew of my most respected friend; I opposed the voice of friendship to the public voice which accused you. You have destroyed it all; and I foresee, you will not want to repair it.

I am anxious, Monsieur, to make it clear to you that your sentiments offend me; that their avowal is an outrage to me; and, above all, that, so far from my coming one day to share them, you would force me to refuse ever again to see you, if you do not impose on yourself, as to this subject, the silence which it seems to me I have the right to expect and even to demand from you. I enclose in this letter that which you have written to me, and I beg that you will similarly return me this: I should be sincerely grieved if any trace remained of an incident which ought never to have occurred.

I have the honor to be, etc.

At the Château de . . . , 21st August, 17★★.

27. Cécile Volanges to the Marquise de Merteuil

Lord! how good you are, Madame! how well you understood that it would be easier to me to write to you than to speak! What I have to tell you, too, is very difficult; but is it not true that you are my friend? Oh yes, my very dear friend! I am going to try not to be afraid; and then, I have so much need of you, of your counsels! I am so very grieved, it seems to me that everybody guesses my thoughts; and, especially when he is there, I blush as soon as anyone looks at me. Yesterday, when you saw me crying, it was because I wished to speak to you, and then, I do not know what prevented me; and, when you asked me what was the matter, my tears flowed in spite of myself. I could not have said a single word. But for you, Mamma would have noticed it; and what would have become of me then? That is how I pass my life, especially since four days ago!

It was on that day, Madame, yes, I am going to tell you, it was on that day that M. le Chevalier Danceny wrote to me: oh, I assure you that when I found his letter, I did not know at all what it was: but, not to tell a falsehood, I cannot tell you that I did not take a great deal of pleasure in reading it; you see, I would sooner have sorrow all my life than that he should not have written it. But I knew well that I ought not to tell him that, and I can even assure you that I told him I was vexed at it: but he said that it was stronger than himself, and I quite believe it; for I had resolved not to answer him, and yet I could not help myself. Oh, I have only written to him once, and even that was partly to tell him not to write to me again: but, in spite of that, he goes on writing to me; and, as I do not answer him, I see quite well that he is sad, and that pains me more still: so much that I no longer know what to do, nor what will happen, and I am much to be pitied.

Tell me, I beg you, Madame, would it be very wrong to reply to him from time to time? Only until he has been able to resolve not to write to me any more himself, and to stay as we were before: for, as for me, if this continues, I do not know what will happen to me. See, in reading his last letter, I cried as though I should never have done; and I am very sure that if I do not answer him again, it will cause us a great deal of pain.

I am going to send you his letter as well, or rather a copy, and you will decide; you will quite see there is no harm in what he asks. However, if you think that it must not be, I promise you to restrain myself; but I believe that you will think like me, and that there is no harm there.

While I am about it, Madame, permit me to ask you one more question. They have always told me that it was wrong to love anyone; but why is that? What makes me ask you is that M. le Chevalier Danceny maintains that it is not wrong at all, and that almost everybody loves; if that is so, I do not see why I should be the only one to refrain from it; or is it then that it is only wrong for young ladies? For I have heard Mamma herself say that Madame D★★★ was in love with Monsieur M★★★, and she did not speak of it as a thing which was so very wrong; and yet I am sure she would be angry with me, if she were only to suspect my liking for M. Danceny. She treats me always like a child, does Mamma; and she tells me nothing at all. I believed, when she took me from the convent, that it was to marry me; but at present it seems no: it is not that I care about it, I assure you; but you who are so friendly with her know, perhaps, how it stands; and, if you know, I hope you will tell me. This is a very long letter, Madame; but, since you have allowed me to write to you, I have profited by it to tell you all, and I count on your friendship.

I have the honor to be, etc.

Paris, 23rd August, 17★★.

28. The Chevalier Danceny to Cécile Volanges

What, Mademoiselle! you still refuse to answer me! Nothing can bend you, and each day bears away with it the hope which it had brought! What then is this friendship which you agree subsists between us, if it be not even powerful enough to render you sensible to my pain; if it leaves you cold and tranquil, while I experience the torments of a fire that I cannot extinguish; if, far from inspiring you with confidence, it does not even suffice to induce your pity? What! your friend suffers and you do nothing to help him! He does but ask you for a word, and you refuse him that! And you wish him to content himself with a sentiment so feeble, of which you even fear to reiterate the assurance!

You would not be ungrateful, you said yesterday: ah, believe me, Mademoiselle, to be ready to repay love with friendship is not to fear ingratitude, it is to dread only the having the appearance of it. However, I dare not discuss with you a sentiment which can only be a burden to you, if it does not interest you; I must at least confine it within myself until I learn how to conquer it. I feel how painful this task will be; I do not hide from myself that I shall have need of all my strength; I will attempt every means; there is one which will cost my heart most dearly, it is that of repeating to myself often that your own is insensible. I will even try to see you less often, and I am already busy in seeking a plausible excuse.

What! I should lose the sweet habit of seeing you every day! Ah, at least I shall never cease to regret it! An eternal sorrow will be the price of the most tender love; and you will have wished it, and it will be your work! Never, I feel it, shall I recover the happiness I lose today; you alone were made for my heart; with what delight I would take a vow to live only for you! But this vow you will not accept; your silence teaches me well enough that your heart says nothing to you in my behalf: it is at once the surest proof of your indifference and the most cruel fashion of announcing it to me. Adieu, Mademoiselle.

I dare not flatter myself with the hope of a reply: love would have written to me with impatience, friendship with pleasure, even pity with complacence; but pity, friendship and love are equally strangers to your heart.

Paris, 23rd August, 17**.

29. Cécile Volanges to Sophie Carnay

I told you, Sophie, that there were cases in which one might write, and I assure you that I reproach myself greatly with having followed your advice, which has brought so much grief to the Chevalier Danceny and to myself. The proof that I was right is that Madame de Merteuil, who is a woman who surely knows, thinks as I do. I confessed everything to her. She talked to me at first as you did: but when I had explained all to her, she agreed that it was very different; she only asks me to show her all my letters and all those of the Chevalier Danceny, in order to make sure that I say nothing but what I should; thus, at present, I am tranquil. Heavens, how I love Madame de Merteuil! She is so good! and she is a woman very much respected. Thus, there is nothing more to be said.

How I am going to write to M. Danceny, and how pleased he will be!

He will be even more so than he thinks, for hitherto I have only spoken of my friendship, and he always wanted me to tell him of my love. I think it was much the same thing; but anyhow, I did not dare, and he longed for that. I told this to Madame de Merteuil; she told me that I was right, and that one ought not to confess that one feels love, until one can no longer restrain oneself: now I am sure that I could not restrain myself any longer; after all, it is the same thing, and it will give him greater pleasure.

Madame de Merteuil told me also that she would lend me books which spoke of all that, and which would teach me to behave myself properly, and to write better than I know now: for, you see, she tells me of all my faults, which is a proof how much she likes me; she has only recommended me to say nothing to Mamma of these books, because that would seem to suggest that she has neglected my education, and that might vex her. Oh, I shall say nothing about it to her!

It is very extraordinary, however, that a woman who is scarcely related to me should take more care of me than my mother! It is very lucky for me to have known her!

She has also asked Mamma to bring me the day after tomorrow to the Opera, in her box; she has told me that we shall be quite alone there, and we are to talk all the time, without fear of being overheard: I like that much better than the opera. We shall speak also of my marriage: for she has told me that it was quite true that I was to be married; but we have not been able to say more about it. By the way, is it not astonishing that Mamma has said nothing about it at all?

Adieu, my Sophie, I am going to write to the Chevalier Danceny. Oh! I am very happy.

Paris, 24th August, 17★★.

30. Cécile Volanges to the Chevalier Danceny

At last, Monsieur, I consent to write to you, to assure you of my friendship, of my *love,* since without that you would be unhappy. You say that I have not a good heart; I assure you, indeed, that you are mistaken, and I hope, at present, you no longer doubt it. If you have been grieved that I have not written to you, do you suppose that that did not grieve me as well? But the fact is that, for nothing in the world, would I like to do anything that was wrong; and I would not even have told you of my love, if I could have prevented myself: but your sadness gave me too much pain. I hope that, at present, you will be sad no longer, and that we shall both be very happy.

I trust to have the pleasure of seeing you this evening, and that you will come early; it will never be so early as I could wish. Mamma is to sup at home, and I believe she will ask you to stay: I hope you will not be engaged as you were the day before yesterday. Was the supper you went to so very agreeable? For you went to it very early. But come, let us not talk of that: now that you know I love you, I hope you will remain with me as much as you can, for I am only happy when I am with you, and I should like you to feel the same.

I am very sorry that you are still sad at this moment, but it is not my fault. I will ask if I may play on the harp as soon as you arrive, in order that you may get my letter at once. I can do no more.

Adieu, Monsieur. I love you well, with my whole heart: the more I tell you so, the better pleased I am; I hope that you will be so too.

Paris, 24th August, 17★★.

31. The Chevalier Danceny to Cécile Volanges

Yes, without a doubt, we shall be happy. My happiness is well assured, since I am loved by you; yours will never end, if it is to last as long as the love which you have inspired in me. What! You love me, you no longer fear to assure me of your *love! The more you tell me so, the better pleased you are!* After reading that charming *I love you,* written by your hand, I heard your sweet mouth repeat the confession. I saw fixed upon me those charming eyes, which their expression of tenderness embellished still more. I received your vow to live ever for me. Ah, receive mine, to consecrate my whole life to your happiness; receive it and be sure that I will never betray it!

What a happy day we passed yesterday! Ah, why has not Madame de Merteuil secrets to tell your Mamma every day? Why must it be that the idea of constraint, which follows us, comes to mingle with the delicious recollection which possesses me? Why can I not hold unceasingly that pretty hand, which has written to me *I love you,* cover it with kisses, and avenge myself so for the refusal you have given me of a greater favor!

Tell me, my Cécile, when your Mamma had returned; when we were forced by her presence to have only indifferent looks for one another, when you could no longer console me, with the assurance of your love, for the refusal you made to give me any proofs of it: did you have no sentiment of regret? Did you not say to yourself: a kiss would have made him happier, and it is I who have kept this joy from him? Promise me, my charming friend, that on the first opportunity you will be less severe. With the aid of this promise, I shall find the courage to support the vexations which circumstances have in store for us; and the cruel privations will be at least softened by my certainty that you share my regret.

Adieu, my charming Cécile: the hour is at hand when I must go to your house. It would be impossible to quit you, were it not to go and see

you again. Adieu, you whom I love so dearly! you whom I shall love ever
more and more!

Paris, 25th August, 17**.

32. Madame de Volanges to the Présidente de Tourvel

You ask me then, Madame, to believe in the virtue of M. de Valmont? I
confess that I cannot bring myself to it, and that I should find it as hard
a task to believe in his honor, from the one fact that you relate to me, as
to believe in the viciousness of a man of known probity, for the sake of
one error. Humanity is not perfect in any fashion; no more in the case of
evil than in that of good. The criminal has his virtues, just as the honest
man has his weaknesses. This truth appears to me all the more necessary
to believe, in that from it is derived the necessity of indulgence toward
the wicked as well as to the good, and that it safeguards the latter from
pride as it does the former from discouragement. You will doubtless
think that I am practicing but sorrily, at this moment, the indulgence
which I preach; but I see in it only a dangerous weakness, when it leads
us to treat the vicious and the man of integrity alike.

I will not permit myself to criticize the motives of M. de Valmont's
action; I would fain believe them as laudable as the act itself: but has he
any the less spent his life in involving families in trouble, scandal and dishonor? Listen, if you will, to the voice of the wretched man he has succored; but let not that prevent you from hearing the cries of the hundred
victims whom he has sacrificed. Were he only, as you say, an instance of
the danger of acquaintances, would that make him any less a dangerous
acquaintance himself? You assume him to be capable of a happy reformation? Let us go farther: suppose this miracle accomplished; would not
public opinion remain against him, and does not that suffice to regulate
your conduct? God alone can absolve at the moment of repentance; he
reads in men's hearts: but men can only judge of thoughts by deeds; and
none among them, after having lost the esteem of others, has a right to
complain of the necessary distrust which renders this loss so difficult to
repair. Remember above all, my dear young friend, that to lose this respect, it sometimes suffices merely to have the air of attaching too little
value to it; and do not tax this severity with injustice: for, apart from our
being obliged to believe that no one renounces this precious possession
who has the right to pretend to it, he is, indeed, more liable to misdoing
who is not restrained by this powerful brake. Such, nevertheless, would
be the aspect under which an intimate acquaintance with M. de Valmont
would display you, however innocent it might be.

Alarmed at the warmth with which you defend him, I hasten to anticipate the objections which I foresee you will make. You will quote

Madame de Merteuil, to whom this acquaintance has been pardoned; you will ask me why I receive him at my house; you will tell me that, far from being repulsed by people of honor, he is admitted, sought after, even, in what is called good society. I believe I can answer everything.

To begin with, Madame de Merteuil, a most estimable person indeed, has perhaps no other fault save that of having too much confidence in her own strength; she is a skillful guide who delights in taking a carriage betwixt a mountain and a precipice, and who is only justified by success: it is right to praise her, it would be imprudent to imitate her; she herself admits it and reproaches herself for it. In proportion as she has seen more, have her principles become more severe; and I do not fear to assure you that she would think as I do.

As to what concerns myself, I will not justify myself more than others. No doubt I receive M. de Valmont, and he is received everywhere: it is one inconsistency the more to add to the thousand others which rule society. You know, as well as I do, how one passes one's life in remarking them, bemoaning them, and submitting to them. M. de Valmont, with a great name, a great fortune, many amiable qualities, early recognized that, to obtain an empire over society, it was sufficient to employ, with equal skill, praise and ridicule. None possesses as he does this double talent: he seduces with the one, and makes himself feared with the other. People do not esteem him; but they flatter him. Such is his existence in the midst of a world which, more prudent than courageous, would rather humor than combat him.

But neither Madame de Merteuil herself, nor any other woman, would for a moment think of shutting herself up in the country, almost in solitude, with such a man. It was reserved for the most virtuous, the most modest of them all to set the example of such an inconsistency: forgive the word, it escapes from my friendship. My lovely friend, your very virtue betrays you by the security with which it fills you. Reflect then that you will have for judges, on the one side, frivolous folk, who will not believe in a virtue the pattern of which they do not find in themselves, and on the other, the ill-natured, who will feign not to believe in it, in order to punish you for its possession. Consider that you are doing, at this moment, what certain men would not venture to risk. In fact, among our young men, of whom M. de Valmont has only too much rendered himself the oracle, I notice that the most prudent fear to seem too intimate with him; and you, are you not afraid? Ah, come back, come back, I conjure you! . . . If my reasons are not sufficient to convince you, yield to my friendship; it is that which makes me renew my entreaties, it is for that to justify them. You think it severe, and I trust that it may be needless; but I would rather you had to complain of its anxiety than of its neglect.

Paris, 24th August, 17**.

33. The Marquise de Merteuil to the Vicomte de Valmont

The moment that you are afraid of success, my dear Vicomte, the moment that your plan is to furnish arms against yourself and that you are less desirous to conquer than to fight, I have no more to say to you. Your conduct is a masterpiece of prudence. It would be one of folly in the contrary supposition; and, to tell the truth, I fear that you are under an illusion.

What I reproach you with is not that you did not take advantage of the moment. On the one side, I do not clearly see that it had arrived; on the other, I am quite aware, although they assert the contrary, that an occasion once missed returns, whereas one never recovers from a too precipitate action. But the real blunder is that you should have let yourself start a correspondence. I defy you at present to foretell whither that may lead you. Do you hope, by any chance, to prove to this woman that she must surrender? It appears to me that therein can only lie a truth of sentiment and not of demonstration; and that to make her admit it is a matter of acting on her feelings, and not of arguing; but in what will it serve you to move her by letter, since you will not be at hand to profit by it? If your fine phrases produce the intoxication of love, do you flatter yourself that it will last so long that there will be no time left for reflection to prevent the confession of it? Reflect only of the time it takes to write a letter, of that which passes before it can be delivered, and see whether a woman, especially one with the principles of your *dévote,* can wish so long that which it is her endeavor to wish never. This method may succeed with children, who, when they write, "I love you," do not know that they say "I yield myself." But the argumentative virtue of Madame de Tourvel seems to me to be fully aware of the value of terms. Thus, in spite of the advantage which you had over her in your conversation, she beats you in her letter. And then, do you know what happens? Merely for the sake of argument, one refuses to yield. By dint of searching for good reasons, one finds, one tells them; and afterward one clings to them, not because they are good, so much as in order not to give oneself the lie.

In addition, a point which I wonder you have not yet made: there is nothing so difficult in love as to write what you do not feel. I mean to write in a convincing manner: it is not that you do not employ the same words, but you do not arrange them in the same way; or rather, you arrange them, and that suffices. Read over your letter: there is an order presiding over it which betrays you at each turn. I would fain believe that your Présidente is too little formed to perceive it: but what matter? it has no less failed of its effect. It is the mistake of novels; the author whips himself to grow heated, and the reader remains cold. *Héloïse* is the only one which forms an exception, and, in spite of the talent of the author, this observation has ever made me believe that the substance of it was true. It is not the same in speaking. The habit of working the instrument gives sensibility to it; the facility of tears is added; the expression of desire in the eyes is confounded with that of tenderness; in short, the less coherent speech promotes more easily that air of trouble and confusion which is the true eloquence of love; and above all the presence of the beloved object forbids reflection, and makes us desire to be won.

Believe me, Vicomte: you are asked to write no more; take advantage of that to retrieve your mistake, and wait for an opportunity to speak. Do you know, this woman has more strength than I believed? Her defense is good; and, but for the length of her letter, and the pretext which she gives you to return to the question in her phrase about gratitude, she would not have betrayed herself at all.

What appears to me, again, to ensure your success is the fact that she uses too much strength at one time; I foresee that she will exhaust it in the defense of the word, and that no more will be left her for that of the thing.

I return you your two letters, and, if you are prudent, they will be the two last, until after the happy moment. If it were not so late, I would speak to you of the little Volanges who is coming on quickly enough, and with whom I am greatly pleased. I believe that I shall have finished before you, and you ought to be very glad thereat. Adieu, for today.

Paris, 24th August, 17**.

34. The Vicomte de Valmont to the Marquise de Merteuil

You speak with perfect truth, my fair friend: but why put yourself to so much fatigue to prove what nobody disputes? To move fast in love, 'tis better to speak than to write; that is, I believe, the whole of your letter. Why, those are the most simple elements in the art of seduction! I will only remark that you make but one exception to this principle, and that there are two. To children, who walk in this way from shyness and yield themselves from ignorance, must be added the *femmes beaux-esprits,* who let themselves be enticed therein by self-conceit and whom vanity leads into the snare. For instance, I am quite sure that the Comtesse de B★★★, who answered my first letter without any difficulty, had, at that time, no more love for me than I for her, and that she only saw an occasion for treating a subject which should be worthy of her pen.

However that may be, an advocate will tell you that principles are not applicable to the question. In fact, you suppose that I have a choice between writing and speaking, which is not the case. Since the affair of the 19th, my fair barbarian, who keeps on the defensive, has shown a skill in avoiding interviews which has disconcerted my own. So much so that, if this continues, I shall be forced to occupy myself seriously with the means of regaining this advantage; for assuredly I will not be routed by her in any way. My letters even are the subject of a little war; not content with leaving them unanswered, she refuses to receive them. For each one a fresh artifice is necessary, and it does not always succeed.

You will remember by what a simple means I gave her the first; the second presented no more difficulty. She had asked me to return her letter; I gave her my own instead, without her having the least suspicion. But whether from vexation at having been caught, or from caprice or, in short, virtue, for she will force me to believe in it, she obstinately refused the third. I hope, however, that the embarrassment into which the consequence of this refusal has happened to throw her will correct her for the future.

I was not much surprised that she would not receive this letter, which I offered her quite simply; that would already have been to grant a certain favor, and I am prepared for a longer defense. After this essay, which was but an attempt made in passing, I put my letter in an envelope; and seizing the moment of the toilette, when Madame de Rosemonde and the chambermaid were present, I sent it her by my *chasseur,* with an order to tell her that it was the paper for which she had asked me. I had rightly guessed that she would dread the scandalous explanation which a refusal would necessitate: she took the letter; and my ambassador, who had received orders to observe her face, and who has good eyes, did but perceive a slight blush, and more embarrassment than anger.

I congratulated myself then, for sure, either that she would keep this letter, or that, if she wished to return it to me, it would be necessary for her to find herself alone with me, which would give me a good occasion to speak. About an hour afterward, one of her people entered my room, and handed me, on behalf of his mistress, a packet of another shape than mine, on the envelope of which I recognized the writing so greatly longed for. I opened it in haste. . . . It was my letter itself, the seal unbroken, merely folded in two. I suspect that her fear that I might be less scrupulous than herself on the subject of scandal had made her employ this devil's ruse.

You know me: I need be at no pains to depict to you my fury. It was necessary, however, to regain one's *sang-froid,* and seek for fresh methods. This is the only one that I found:

They send from here every morning to fetch the letters from the post, which is about three quarters of a league away: they employ for this purpose a box with a lid almost like an almsbox, of which the postmaster has one key and Madame de Rosemonde the other. Everyone puts his letters in it during the day, when it seems good to him: in the evening they are carried to the post, and in the morning those which have arrived are sent for. All the servants, strange or otherwise, perform this service. It was not the turn of my servant; but he undertook to go, under the pretext that he had business in that direction.

Meantime I wrote my letter. I disguised my handwriting in the address, and I counterfeited with some skill upon the envelope the stamp of Dijon. I chose this town, because I found it merrier, since I was asking for the same rights as the husband, to write also from the same place, and also because my fair had spoken all day of the desire she had to receive letters from Dijon. It seemed to me only right to procure her this pleasure.

These precautions once taken, it was easy enough to add this letter to the others. I moreover succeeded by this expedient in being a witness of the reception; for the custom is to assemble for breakfast, and to wait for the arrival of the letters before separating. At last they came.

Madame de Rosemonde opened the box. "From Dijon," she said, giving the letter to Madame de Tourvel.

"It is not my husband's writing," she answered in a troubled voice, hastily breaking the seal.

The first glance instructed her; and her face underwent such an alteration that Madame de Rosemonde perceived it, and asked, "What is the matter with you?"

I also drew near, saying, "Is this letter then so very dreadful?"

The shy *dévote* dared not raise her eyes; she said not a word; and, to hide her embarrassment, pretended to run over the epistle, which she was scarcely in a state to read. I enjoyed her confusion, and not being sorry to gird her a little, I added, "Your more tranquil air bids me hope that this letter has caused you more astonishment than pain." Anger then inspired her better than prudence could have done.

"It contains," she answered, "things which offend me, and that I am astounded anyone has dared to write to me."

"Who has sent it?" interrupted Madame de Rosemonde.

"It is not signed," answered the angry fair one; "but the letter and its author inspire me with equal contempt. You will oblige me by speaking no more of it."

With that she tore up the audacious missive, put the pieces into her pocket, rose, and left the room.

In spite of this anger she has nonetheless had my letter; and I rely upon her curiosity to have taken care that she read it through.

The detailed relation of the day would take me too far. I add to this account the first draft of my two letters; you will thus be as fully informed as myself. If you want to be *au courant* with this correspondence, you must accustom yourself to deciphering my minutes; for nothing in

the world could I support the tedium of copying them. Adieu, my lovely
friend!

> At the Château de . . . , 25th August, 17**.

35. The Vicomte de Valmont to the Présidente de Tourvel

I must needs obey you, Madame; I must prove to you that, in the midst
of the faults which you are pleased to ascribe to me, there is left me at
least enough delicacy not to permit myself a reproach, and enough
courage to impose on myself the most grievous sacrifices. You order me
to be silent and to forget! Well! I will force my love to be silent; and I
will forget, if that be possible, the cruel manner in which you have met
it. Doubtless my desire to please you did not bear with it the right; and
more, I confess that the need I had of your indulgence was not a title to
obtain it: but you look upon my love as an outrage; you forget that if it
could be a wrong, you would be at once its cause and its excuse.

You forget also, that, accustomed to open my soul to you, even when
that confidence might hurt me, it was impossible for me to conceal from
you the sentiments by which I was penetrated; and that which was the
result of my good faith you consider as the fruit of my audacity. As a reward for the most tender, the most respectful, the truest love, you cast me
afar from you. You speak to me, lastly, of your hatred. . . . What other
than myself would not complain at being so treated? I alone submit; I
support it all, and murmur not; you strike, and I adore. The inconceivable power which you have over me renders you absolute mistress of my
feelings; and if only my love resists you, if you cannot destroy that, it is
because it is your work and not my own.

I do not ask for a love which I never flattered myself I should receive.
I do not even ask for that pity for which the interest you had sometimes
displayed in me might have allowed me to hope. But, I admit, I think I
can count on your sense of justice.

You inform me, Madame, that people have sought to damage me in
your opinion. If you had believed the counsels of your friends, you
would not even have let me approach you: those are your expressions.
Who then are these officious friends? No doubt those people of such
severity, and of so rigid a virtue, consent to be named; no doubt they
would not cover themselves in an obscurity which would confound
them with vile calumniators; and I shall not be left ignorant either of
their names or of their accusations. Reflect, Madame, that I have the
right to know both, since it is after them you judge me. One does not
condemn a culprit without telling him his crime, and naming his accusers. I ask no other favor, and I promise in advance to justify myself,
and to force them to retract.

If I have, perhaps, too much despised the vain clamors of a public of which I make so little case, it is not thus with your esteem; and when I devote my life to meriting that, I shall not let it be ravished from me with impunity. It becomes all the more precious to me, in that I shall owe to it doubtless that request which you fear to make me, and which would give me, you say, *rights to your gratitude*. Ah! far from exacting it, I shall believe myself your debtor, if you procure me the occasion of being agreeable to you. Begin then to do me greater justice by not leaving me in ignorance of what you desire of me. If I could guess it, I would spare you the trouble of saying it. To the pleasure of seeing you, add the happiness of serving you, and I will congratulate myself on your indulgence. What then can prevent you? It is not, I hope, the fear of a refusal: I feel that I could not pardon you that. It is no refusal that I do not return you your letter. More than you do I desire that it be no longer necessary to me: but accustomed as I am to believing in the gentleness of your soul, it is only in that letter that I can find you such as you would appear. When I frame the vow to render you less hard, I see there that, rather than consent, you would place yourself a hundred leagues away from me; when everything in you augments and justifies my love, it is that still which repeats to me that my love is an outrage to you; and when, seeing you, that love seems to me the supreme good, I needs must read you to feel that it is but a fearful torture. You can imagine now that my greatest happiness would be to be able to return you this fatal letter: to ask me for it now would be to authorize me to believe no longer what it contains; you do not doubt, I hope, of my eagerness to return it to you.

At the Château de . . . , 21st August, 17★★.

36. The Vicomte de Valmont to the Présidente de Tourvel
(BEARING THE POSTMARK OF DIJON)

Your severity augments daily, Madame; and, if I dare say it, you seem to be less afraid of being unjust than of being indulgent. After having condemned me without a hearing, you must have felt, in fact, that 'twere easier for you not to read my arguments than to reply to them. You refuse my letters obstinately; you send them back to me with contempt. You force me, at last, to have recourse to a ruse, at the very moment when my only aim is to convince you of my good faith. The necessity in which you have put me to defend myself will doubtless suffice to excuse my means. Convinced, moreover, by the sincerity of my sentiments that, to justify them in your eyes, it is sufficient merely that you should know them thoroughly, I thought that I might permit myself this slight artifice. I dare believe also that you will pardon me, and that you will be little surprised that love is more ingenious in presenting itself than indifference in repelling it.

Allow then, Madame, my heart to be entirely revealed to you. It belongs to you, and it is just that you should know it.

I was very far from foreseeing, when I arrived at Madame de Rosemonde's, the fate which awaited me. I did not know that you were there, and I will add, with the sincerity which characterizes me, that, if I had known, my sense of security would not have been troubled: not that I did not render to your beauty the justice which one could not refuse it; but, accustomed as I was to feel only desires, and to yield myself only to those which were encouraged by hope, I did not know the torments of love.

You were a witness of the efforts which Madame de Rosemonde made to keep me for some time. I had already passed one day with you, and yet I yielded, or at least believed that I yielded, only to the pleasure, so natural and so legitimate, of showing respect to a worthy relative. The kind of life which one led here doubtless differed greatly from that to which I was accustomed; it cost me nothing to conform to it; and, without seeking to penetrate into the cause of the change which was operating within me, I attributed it as yet solely to that easygoing character of which I believe I have already spoken to you.

Unfortunately (yet why need it be a misfortune?), coming to know you better, I soon discovered that that bewitching face, which alone had struck me, was but the least of your attractions; your heavenly soul astonished and seduced my own. I admired the beauty, I worshipped the virtue. Without pretending to win you, I bestirred myself to deserve you. In begging your indulgence for the past, I was ambitious of your support for the future. I sought for it in your utterance, I spied for it in your eyes, in that glance whence came a poison all the more dangerous in that it was distilled without design, and received without distrust.

Then I knew love. But how far was I from complaining! Determined to bury it in an eternal silence, I abandoned myself without fear, as without reserve, to this delicious sentiment. Each day augmented its sway. Soon the pleasure of seeing you was changed to a need. Were you absent for a moment? my heart was sore with sadness; at the sound which announced your return, it palpitated with joy. I only existed for you and through you. Nevertheless, it is yourself whom I call to witness: in the merriment of our heedless sports or in the interest of a serious conversation, did ever one word escape me which could betray the secret of my heart?

At last a day arrived when my evil fortune was to commence; by an inconceivable fatality, a good deed was to be the signal for it. Yes, Madame, it was in the midst of those unfortunates whom I had succored that, abandoning yourself to that precious sensibility which embellishes even beauty and adds value to virtue, you completed your work of destroying a heart which was already intoxicated with excess of love. You will remember, perhaps, what a moodiness came over me on our return! Alas! I was seeking to fight against an affection which I felt was becoming stronger than myself.

It was after I had exhausted my strength in this unequal contest, that an unforeseen hazard made me find myself alone with you. There, I confess, I succumbed. My heart was too full, and could withhold neither its utterance nor its tears. But is this then a crime? and if it be one, is it not amply punished by the dire torments to which I am abandoned?

Devoured by a love without hope, I implore your pity and I meet only with your hate: with no other happiness than that of seeing you, my eyes seek you in spite of myself, and I tremble to meet your gaze. In the cruel state to which you have reduced me, I pass my days in dissimulating my grief and my nights in abandoning myself to it; while you, peaceful and calm, know of these torments only to cause them and to applaud yourself for them. Nonetheless, it is you who complain and I who make excuse.

That, however, Madame, is the faithful relation of what you call my injuries, which it would, perhaps, be more just to call my misfortunes. A pure and sincere love, a respect which has never belied itself, a perfect submission; such are the sentiments with which you have inspired me. I would not fear to present my homage of them to the Divinity Himself. O you, who are His fairest handiwork, imitate Him in His indulgence! Think on my cruel pains; think, above all, that, placed by you between despair and supreme felicity, the first word which you shall utter will forever decide my lot.

At the Château de . . . , 23rd August, 17★★.

37. The Présidente de Tourvel to Madame de Volanges

I yield, Madame, to the counsels which your friendship gives me. Accustomed as I am to defer in all things to your opinions, I am ready to believe that they are always based on reason. I will even admit that M. de Valmont must be, indeed, infinitely dangerous, if he can, at the same time, feign to be what he appears here and remain such a man as you paint him. However that may be, since you request it, I will keep him away from me; at least I will do my utmost: for often things which ought to be at bottom the most simple become embarrassing in practice.

It still seems to me impracticable to make this request to his aunt; it would be equally ungracious both to her and to him. Neither would I adopt the course, without the greatest repugnance, of going away myself:

for apart from the reasons I have already given you relative to M. de Tourvel, if my departure were to annoy M. de Valmont, as is possible, would it not be easy for him to follow me to Paris? And his return, of which I should be—or at least should appear—the motive, would it not seem more strange than a meeting in the country, at the house of a lady who is known to be his relation and my friend?

There is left me then no other resource than to induce himself to consent to going away. I feel that this proposal is difficult to make; however, as he seems to me to have set his heart on proving to me that he has, effectually, more honesty than is attributed to him, I do not despair of success. I shall not be sorry even to attempt it, and to have an occasion of judging whether, as he has often said, truly virtuous women never have had, and never will have, to complain of his behavior. If he leaves, as I desire, it will indeed be out of consideration for me; for I cannot doubt but that he proposes to spend a great part of the autumn here. If he refuses my request and insists upon remaining, there will still be time for me to leave myself, and that I promise you.

That is, I believe, Madame, all that your friendship demanded of me; I am eager to satisfy it, and to prove to you that in spite of the *warmth* I may have used to defend M. de Valmont, I am nonetheless disposed, not only to heed, but also to follow, the counsels of my friends.

I have the honor to be, etc.

At the Château de . . . , 25th August, 17★★.

38. The Marquise de Merteuil to the Vicomte de Valmont

Your enormous budget, my dear Vicomte, has this moment arrived. If the date on it is exact, I ought to have received it twenty-four hours earlier; be that as it may, if I were to take the time to read it, I should have none left to reply to it. I prefer then simply to acknowledge it now, and we will talk of something else. It is not that I have anything to say to you on my own account; the autumn leaves hardly a single man with a human face in Paris, so that for the last month I have been perishing with virtue; and anyone else than my Chevalier would be fatigued with the proofs of my constancy. Being unable to occupy myself, I distract myself with the little Volanges, and it is of her that I wish to speak.

Do you know that you have lost more than you believe, in not undertaking this child? She is really delicious! She has neither character nor principles; judge how sweet and easy her society will be. I do not think she will ever shine by sentiment; but everything announces in her the liveliest sensations. Lacking wit and subtilty, she has, however, if one may so speak, a certain natural falseness which sometimes astonishes even me, and which will be all the more successful, in that her face presents the image of candor and ingenuousness. She is naturally very caressing, and I sometimes amuse myself thereby: her little head grows excited with incredible rapidity, and she is then all the more delightful, because she knows nothing, absolutely nothing, of all that she so greatly desires to know. She is seized with quite droll fits of impatience; she laughs, pouts, cries, and then begs me to teach her with a truly seductive good faith. Really, I am almost jealous of the man for whom that pleasure is reserved.

I do not know if I have told you that for the last four or five days I have had the honor of being in her confidence. You can very well guess that, at first, I acted severity: but as soon as I perceived that she thought she had convinced me with her bad reasons, I had the air of taking them for good ones; and she is intimately persuaded that she owes this success to her eloquence: this precaution was necessary in order not to compromise myself. I have permitted her to write, and to say *I love;* and the same day, without her suspecting it, I contrived for her a *tête-à-tête* with her Danceny. But imagine, he is still such a fool that he did not even obtain a kiss. The lad, however, writes mighty pretty verses! La, how silly these witty folks are! This one is, to such a degree that he embarrasses me; for, as for him, I cannot well drive him!

It is at this moment that you would be very useful to me. You are sufficiently intimate with Danceny to obtain his confidence, and, if he once gave it you, we should advance at full speed. Make haste, then, with your Présidente; for, indeed, I will not have Gercourt escape: for the rest, I spoke of him yesterday to the little person, and depicted him so well to her that, if she had been his wife for ten years, she could not hate him more. I preached much to her, however, upon the subject of conjugal fidelity; nothing could equal my severity on this point. By that, on the one side, I restore my reputation for virtue with her, which too much condescension might destroy; on the other, I augment in her that hatred with which I wish to gratify her husband. And, finally, I hope that, by making her believe that it is not permitted her to give way to love, except during the short time that she remains a girl, she will more quickly decide to lose none of that time.

Adieu, Vicomte; I am going to attend to my toilette, what time I will read your volume.

Paris, 27th August, 17★★.

39. Cécile Volanges to Sophie Carnay

I am sad and anxious, my dear Sophie. I wept almost all night. It is not that I am not, for the moment, very happy, but I foresee that it will not last.

I went yesterday to the Opera with Madame de Merteuil; we spoke much of my marriage, and I have learned no good of it. It is M. le Comte de Gercourt whom I am to wed, and it is to be in the month of October. He is rich, he is a man of quality, he is colonel of the Regiment of ——. So far, all very well. But, to begin with, he is old: imagine, he is at least thirty-six! and then, Madame de Merteuil says he is gloomy and stern, and she fears I shall not be happy with him. I could even see quite well that she was sure of it, only that she would not say so for fear of grieving me. She hardly talked to me of anything the whole evening, except of the duties of wives to their husbands: she admits that M. de Gercourt is not at all lovable, and yet she says I must love him. Did not she say also that, once married, I ought not to love the Chevalier Danceny any longer? as though that were possible! Oh, you can be very sure I shall love him always! Do you know, I would prefer not to be married. Let this M. de Gercourt look after himself, I never went in search of him. He is in Corsica at present, far away from here; I wish he would stay there ten years. If I were not afraid of being sent back to the convent, I would certainly tell Mamma that I don't want a husband like that; but that would be still worse. I am very much embarrassed. I feel that I have never loved M. Danceny so well as I do now; and when I think that I have only a month more left me, to be as I am now, the tears rush suddenly to my eyes; I have no consolation except the friendship of Madame de Merteuil; she has such a good heart! She shares in all my troubles as much as I do myself; and then she is so amiable that, when I am with her, I hardly think any more of them. Besides, she is very useful to me, for the little that I know she has taught me: and she is so good that I can tell her all I think, without being in the least ashamed. When she finds that it is not right, she scolds me sometimes; but only quite gently, and then I embrace her with all my heart, until she is no longer cross. Her, at any rate, I can love as much as I like, without there being any harm in it, and that pleases me very much. We have agreed, however, that I am not to have the appearance of being so fond of her before everybody, and especially not before Mamma, so that she may have no suspicions about the Chevalier Danceny. I assure you that, if I could always live as I do now, I believe I should be very happy. It's only that horrid M. de Gercourt . . . But I will say no more about him, else I should get sad again. Instead of that, I am going to write to the Chevalier Danceny; I shall only speak to him of my love and not of my troubles, for I do not want to distress him.

Adieu, my dear friend. You can see now that you would be wrong to complain, and that however *busy* I have been, as you say, there is time left me, all the same, to love you and to write to you.[1]

Paris, 27th August, 17**.

---

[1]We continue to omit the letters of Cécile Volanges and of the Chevalier Danceny, these being of little interest and containing no incidents.

40. The Vicomte de Valmont to the Marquise de Merteuil

Not content with leaving my letters without reply, with refusing to receive them, my inhuman wretch wishes to deprive me of the sight of her; she insists on my departure. What will astonish you more is that I am submitting to her severity. You will blame me. However, I thought I ought not to lose the opportunity of obeying a command, persuaded as I am, on the one side, that to command is to commit oneself; and on the other, that that illusive authority which we have the appearance of allowing women to seize is one of the snares which they find it most difficult to elude. Nay, more, the skill which this one has shown in avoiding a solitary encounter with me placed me in a dangerous situation, from which I thought I was bound to escape, whatever might be the cost: for, being constantly with her, without being able to occupy her with my love, there was reason to fear that she might grow accustomed to seeing me without trouble, a disposition from which you know how difficult it is to return.

For the rest, you may guess that I did not submit without conditions. I was even at the pains to impose one which it was impossible to grant, as much for the sake of remaining always free to keep my word or break it, as to promote a discussion, either by word of mouth or in writing, at a time when my beauty is more contented with me, or has need that I should be so with her: not to reckon that I should show a signal lack of skill if I did not find a means to obtain some compensation for my desisting from this pretension, untenable as it may be.

After having explained my motives in this long preamble, I come to the history of the last two days. I enclose as documentary evidence my beauty's letter and my reply. You will agree that few historians are as precise as I.

You will remember the effect produced by my letter from Dijon, on the morning of the day before yesterday; the rest of the day was most stormy. The pretty prude only appeared at dinnertime, and gave out that she had a violent headache: a pretext with which she masked one of the most furious fits of ill humor that a woman could have. It absolutely altered her face; the expression of gentleness, which you know, was changed into a rebellious air which gave it a fresh loveliness. I promise myself to make use of this discovery, and to replace sometimes the tender mistress with the sullen.

I foresaw that the time after dinner would be dull; and, to escape from ennui, I made a pretext of having letters to write, and retired to my own rooms. I returned to the salon about six o'clock; Madame de Rosemonde suggested a drive, which was agreed to. But just as we were getting into the carriage, the pretended invalid, with infernal malice, alleged in her turn—perhaps to avenge herself for my absence—an increase of the pain, and compelled me pitilessly to support a *tête-à-tête* with my old aunt. I know not whether the imprecations which I called down on this feminine demon were heeded; but we found her gone to bed on our return. On the following day, at breakfast, it was not the same woman. Her natural sweetness had returned, and I had reason to believe myself pardoned. Breakfast was hardly over, when the sweet person rose with an indolent air, and went into the park; as you may believe, I followed her. "Whence can spring this desire for walking?" said I, accosting her. "I wrote much, this morning," she answered, "and my head is a little tired." "I am not fortunate enough," I went on, "to have to reproach myself with this fatigue?" "Indeed, I have written to you," she answered again, "but I hesitate to give you my letter. It contains a request, and you have not accustomed me to hope for success." "Ah! I swear, if it be possible—" "Nothing could be easier," she broke in; "and although you ought, perhaps, to grant it out of justice, I consent to obtain it as a grace." As she said these words, she handed me her letter; seizing it, I also seized her hand, which she drew away, but without anger, and with more embarrassment than vivacity. "The heat is even greater than I thought," she said, "I must go indoors." And she retraced her steps to the *château*. I made vain efforts to persuade her to continue her walk, and I needed to remind myself that we might be observed, in order to employ no more than eloquence. She entered without a word, and I saw plainly that this pretended walk had no other object than to hand me my letter. She went up to her own room as soon as we came in, and I withdrew to mine, to read the epistle, which you will do well to read also, as well as my reply, before proceeding further. . . .

41. The Présidente de Tourvel to the Vicomte de Valmont

It seems to me, Monsieur, by your behavior, as though you did but seek to multiply daily the causes of complaint which I have against you. Your obstinacy in wishing unceasingly to approach me with a sentiment which I would not and may not heed, the abuse which you have not feared to take of my good faith, or of my timidity, in order to put your letters into my hands; above all the method, most indelicate I venture to call it, which you employed to make the last reach me, without the slightest fear of the effect of a surprise which might have compromised me; all ought to give occasion on my part to reproaches as keen as they are merited. However, instead of returning to these grievances, I confine myself to putting a request to you, as simple as it is just; and if I obtain it from you, I consent that all shall be forgotten.

You yourself have said to me, Monsieur, that I need not fear a refusal;

and, although, by an inconsistency which is peculiar to you, this very phrase was followed by the only refusal which you could make me,[1] I would fain believe that you will nonetheless keep today that word, given to me formally so few days ago.

I desire you then to have the complaisance to go away from me; to leave this *château*, where a further stay on your part could not but expose me more to the judgment of a public which is ever ready to think ill of others, and which you have but too well accustomed to fix its gaze upon the women who admit you to their society. Already warned, long ago, of this danger by my friends, I neglected, I even disputed their warning, so long as your behavior toward myself could make me believe that you would not confound me with the host of women who all have had reason to complain of you. Today, when you treat me like them, as I can no longer but know, I owe it to the public, to my friends, to myself, to adopt this necessary course. I might add here that you would gain nothing by denying my request, as I am determined to leave myself, if you insist on remaining; but I do not seek to diminish the obligation which you will confer on me by this complaisance, and I am quite willing that you should know that, by rendering my departure hence necessary, you would upset my arrangements. Prove to me then, Monsieur, that, as you have so often told me, virtuous women shall never have cause to complain of you; prove, at least, that, when you have done them wrong, you know how to repair it. If I thought I had need to justify my request to you, it would suffice to say that you have spent your life in rendering it necessary; and that, notwithstanding, it has not rested with me that I should ever make it. But let us not recall events which I would forget, and which would oblige me to judge you with rigor at a moment when I offer you an opportunity of earning all my gratitude. Adieu, Monsieur; your conduct will teach me with what sentiments I must be, for life, your most humble, etc.

At the Château de . . . , 25th August, 17★★.

42. The Vicomte de Valmont to the Présidente de Tourvel

However hard, Madame, the conditions that you impose on me, I do not refuse to fulfill them. I feel that it would be impossible for me to thwart any of your desires. Once agreed upon this point, I dare flatter myself in my turn that you will permit me to make certain requests to you, far easier to grant than your own, which, however, I do not wish to obtain, save by my complete submission to your will.

The one, which I hope will be solicited by your sense of justice, is to

---

[1]See Letter the Thirty-Fifth.

be so good as to name to me those who have accused me to you; they have done me, it seems, harm enough to give me the right of knowing them: the other, which I expect from your indulgence, is kindly to permit me to repeat to you sometimes the homage of a love which will now, more than ever, deserve your pity.

Reflect, Madame, that I am hastening to obey you, even when I can but do it at the expense of my happiness; I will say more, in spite of my conviction that you only desire my absence in order to spare yourself the spectacle, always painful, of the object of your injustice.

Admit, Madame, you are less afraid of a public which is too much used to respecting you to dare form a disrespectful judgment upon you than you are annoyed by the presence of a man whom you find it easier to punish than to blame. You drive me away from you as one turns away one's eyes from some poor wretch whom one does not wish to succor.

But, whereas absence is about to redouble my torments, to whom other than you can I address my complaints? From whom else can I expect the consolations which are about to become so necessary to me? Will you refuse me them, when you alone cause my pains?

Doubtless, you will not be astonished either that, before I leave, I have it on my heart to justify to you the sentiments which you have inspired in me; as also that I do not find the courage to go away until I receive the order from your mouth. This twofold reason compels me to ask you for a moment's interview. In vain would we seek to supply the place of that by letters: one may write volumes and explain poorly what a quarter of an hour's conversation were enough to leave amply understood. You will easily find the time to accord it me; for, however eager I may be to obey you, you know that Madame de Rosemonde is aware of my intention to spend a part of the autumn with her, and I must at least wait for a letter in order to have the pretext of some business to call me away.

Adieu, Madame; never has this word cost me so much to write as at this moment, when it brings me back to the idea of our separation. If you could imagine what it makes me suffer, I dare believe you would have some thanks for my docility. At least, receive with more indulgence the assurance and the homage of the most tender and the most respectful love.

At the Château de . . . , 26th August, 17★★.

40. The Vicomte de Valmont to the Marquise de Merteuil
CONTINUATION

And now let us sum up, my lovely friend. You can feel, like myself, how the scrupulous, the virtuous Madame de Tourvel cannot grant me the first of my requests, and betray the confidence of her friends, by naming to me my accusers; thus, by promising everything on this condition, I pledge myself to nothing. But you will feel also that the refusal which she will give me will become a title to obtain everything else; and that then I gain, by going away, the advantage of entering into a regular correspondence with her, and by her consent: for I take small account of the interview which I ask of her, and which has hardly any other object than that of accustoming her beforehand not to refuse me others when they become really needful.

The only thing which remains for me to do before my departure is to find out who are the people who busy themselves with damaging me in her eyes. I presume it is her pedant of a husband; I would fain have it so: apart from the fact that a conjugal prohibition is a spur to desire, I should feel sure that, from the moment my beauty has consented to write to me, I should have nothing to fear from her husband, since she would already be under the necessity of deceiving him.

But if she has a friend intimate enough to possess her confidence, and this friend be against me, it seems to me necessary to embroil them, and I count on succeeding in that: but before all I must be rightly informed.

I quite thought that I was going to be yesterday; but this woman does nothing like another. We were visiting her at the moment when it was announced that dinner was ready. Her toilette was only just completed; and while I bestirred myself and made my apologies, I perceived that she had left the key in her writing desk; and I knew her custom was not to remove that of her apartment. I was thinking of this during dinner, when I heard her waiting maid come down: I seized my chance at once; I pretended that my nose was bleeding, and left the room. I flew to the desk; but I found all the drawers open and not a sheet of writing. Yet one has no opportunity of burning papers at this season. What does she do with the letters she receives? And she receives them often. I neglected nothing; everything was open, and I sought everywhere; but I gained nothing except a conviction that this precious collection must be in her pocket.

How to obtain them? Ever since yesterday I have been busying myself vainly in seeking for a means: yet I cannot overcome the desire. I regret that I have not the talents of a thief. Should these not, in fact, enter into the education of a man who is mixed up in intrigues? Would it not be agreeable to filch the letter or the portrait of a rival, or to pick from the pockets of a prude the wherewithal to unmask her? But our parents have no thought for anything; and for me, 'tis all very well to think of everything, I do but perceive that I am clumsy, without being able to remedy it.

However that may be, I returned to table much dissatisfied. My beauty, however, soothed my ill humor somewhat, with the air of interest which my pretended indisposition gave her; and I did not fail to assure her that for some time past I had had violent agitations which had disturbed my health. Convinced as she is that it is she who causes them, ought she not, in all conscience, to endeavor to assuage them? But *dévote* though she be, she has small stock of charity; she refuses all amorous alms, and such a refusal, to my view, justifies a theft. But adieu; for all the time I talk to you, I am thinking of those cursed letters.

At the Château de . . . , 27th August, 17**.

43. The Présidente de Tourvel to the Vicomte de Valmont

Why seek, Monsieur, to diminish my gratitude? Why be willing to give me but a half obedience, and make, as it were, a bargain of an honorable action? Is it not sufficient for you then that I feel the cost of it? You not only ask much, but you ask things which are impossible. If, in truth, my friends have spoken to me of you, they have only done it in my interest: even if they have been deceived, their intention was nonetheless good; and you propose to me to reward this mark of attachment on their part by delivering you their secret! I have already done wrong in speaking to you of it, and you make me very conscious of that at this moment. What would have been no more than candor with another becomes a blunder with you, and would lead me to an ignominy did I yield to you. I appeal to yourself, to your honor; did you think me capable of such a proceeding? Ought you to have suggested it to me? No, without a doubt; and I am sure that, on further reflection, you will not repeat this request.

That which you make as to writing to me is scarcely easier to grant; and, if you care to be just, it is not me whom you will blame. I do not wish to offend you; but, with the reputation which you have acquired, and which, by your own confession, is at least in part deserved, what woman could own to be in correspondence with you? and what virtuous woman may determine to do something which she feels she will be obliged to conceal?

Again, if I were assured that your letters would be of a kind of which I need never have to complain, so that I could always justify myself in my own eyes for having received them! Perhaps then the desire of proving to you that it is reason and not hate which sways me would induce me to waive those powerful considerations, and to do much more than I ought, in allowing you sometimes to write to me. If indeed you desire to do so as much as you say, you will voluntarily submit to the one condition which could make me consent; and if you have any gratitude for what I am now doing for you, you will not defer your departure.

Permit me to remark to you on this subject that you received a letter this morning, and that you have not taken advantage of it to announce your going to Madame de Rosemonde, as you had promised me. I hope that at present nothing need prevent you keeping your word. I count, above all, on your not waiting for the interview which you ask of me, and to which I absolutely decline to lend myself; and I hope that, instead of the order which you pretend is necessary to you, you will content yourself with the prayer which I renew to you. Adieu, Monsieur.

At the Château de . . . , 27th August, 17★★.

44. The Vicomte de Valmont to the Marquise de Merteuil

Join in my joy, my lovely friend; I am beloved, I have triumphed over that rebellious heart. 'Tis in vain that it still dissimulates; my fortunate skill has surprised its secret. Thanks to my energetic pains, I know all that is of interest to me: since the night, the fortunate night of yesterday, I am once more in my element; I have resumed my existence; I have unveiled a double mystery of love and iniquity: I will delight in the one, I will avenge myself for the other; I will fly from pleasure to pleasure. The mere idea that I form of it transports me to such a degree that I have some difficulty in recalling my prudence; and shall have some, perhaps, in putting order into this narrative which I make for you. Let us try, however.

Yesterday, after I had written my letter to you, I received one from the celestial *dévote*. I send it you; you will see in it that she gives me, with as little clumsiness as is possible, permission to write to her: but she urges on my departure; and I quite felt that I could not defer it too long without injuring myself.

Tormented, however, by the desire to know who could have written against me, I was still uncertain as to what course I should take. I tried to win over the chambermaid, and would fain persuade her to give up to me her mistress's pockets, which she could have easily laid hold of in the evening, and which she could have replaced in the morning, without exciting the least suspicion. I offered ten louis for this slight service: but I only found a baggage, scrupulous or afraid, whom neither my eloquence nor my money could vanquish. I was still preaching to her when the supper bell rang. I was forced to leave her; only too glad that she was willing to promise me secrecy, on which you may judge I scarcely counted.

I had never been in a worse humor. I felt myself compromised, and I reproached myself all the evening for my foolish attempt.

When I had retired, not without anxiety, I sent for my *chasseur*, who, in his quality of happy lover, ought to have some credit. I wanted him either to persuade this girl to do what I had asked of her, or at least to make sure of her discretion; but he, who ordinarily is afraid of nothing, seemed doubtful of the success of the negotiation, and made a reflection on the subject the profundity of which amazed me.

"Monsieur surely knows better than I," said he, "that to lie with a girl is only to make her do what she likes to do: from that to making her do what we like is often a long way."

The fellow's good sense sometimes strikes me dumb.[1]

"I can the less answer for her," he added, "because I have reason to believe she has a lover, and that I only owe her to the idleness of country life. So that, were it not for my zeal in Monsieur's service, I should not have had her but once." (He is a real treasure this fellow!) "As for secrecy," he went on, "what will be the good of making her promise it, since she will run no risk in deceiving us? To speak again to her about it would only be to let her know that it was important, and thus make her all the more eager to use it for making up to her mistress."

The more just these reflections seemed to me, the more was my embarrassment heightened. Luckily the knave was started off to gossip; and as I had need of him, I let him run on. While he was relating to me his adventures with this wench, I learned that, as the chamber which she occupied was only separated from that of her mistress by a bare partition, through which any suspicious noise could be heard, it was in his own that they met every night. At once, I formed my plan; I communicated it to him, and we carried it out with success.

I waited until two o'clock in the morning; and then betook myself, as we had agreed, to the scene of the *rendezvous*, carrying a light with me, and pretending that I had rung several times to no purpose. My confidant, who plays his parts to a marvel, went through a little scene of surprise, despair, and excuses, which I terminated by sending him to heat me some water, of which I feigned to have a need; while the scrupulous chambermaid was all the more shamefaced, in that my rascal, wishing to improve on my projects, had induced her to make a toilette which the season suggested but did not excuse.

As I felt that the more this wench was humiliated, the more easily I should dispose of her, I allowed her to change neither her position nor her costume; and after ordering my valet to await me in my room, I sat down beside her on the bed, which was in great disorder, and commenced my conversation. I had need to maintain the control which the situation gave me over her; thus I preserved a coolness which would have done honor to the continence of Scipio; and without taking the slightest liberty with her—which, however, her freshness and the opportunity seemed to give her the right to expect—I spoke of business to her as calmly as I should have done with a lawyer.

My conditions were that I would faithfully keep her secret, provided that, on the morrow, at about the same hour, she would hand me the

---

[1] Piron, *Métromanie*.

pockets of her mistress. "Beside that," I added, "I offered you ten louis yesterday; I promise you them again today. I do not want to take advantage of your situation." Everything was granted, as you may well believe; I then withdrew, and allowed the happy couple to make up for lost time.

I spent mine in sleep; and, on my awakening, desiring to have a pretext for not replying to my fair one's letter before I had investigated her papers, which I could not do until the ensuing night, I resolved to go out shooting, which I did for the greater part of the day.

On my return, I was received coldly enough. I had a mind to believe that we were a little offended at the small zeal I had shown in not profiting by the time that was left, especially after the much kinder letter which she had written me. I judge so from the fact that, Madame de Rosemonde having addressed me some reproaches for this long absence, my beauty remarked with a tone of acrimony, "Ah! do not let us reproach M. de Valmont for giving himself up to the one pleasure which he can find here." I murmured at this injustice, and took advantage of it to vow that I took so much pleasure in the ladies' society that I was sacrificing for them a most interesting letter which I had to write. I added that, being unable to sleep for some nights past, I had wished to try if fatigue would restore it me; and my eyes were sufficiently explicit, both as to the subject of my letter and the cause of my insomnia. I was at the pains to wear all that evening a manner of melancholy sweetness, which seemed to sit on me well enough, and which masked the impatience I was in to see the hour arrive which was to deliver me the secret so obstinately withheld from me. At last we separated, and, some time afterwards, the faithful chambermaid came to bring me the price agreed upon for my discretion.

Once master of this treasure, I proceeded to the inventory with that prudence which you know I possess: for it was important to put back everything in its place. I fell at first upon two letters from the husband— an undigested mixture of details of lawsuits and effusions of conjugal love, which I had the patience to read in their entirety, and where I found no word that had any relation to myself. I replaced them with temper: but this was soothed when my hand lighted upon the pieces of my famous Dijon letter, carefully put together. Luckily the whim seized me to run through it. Judge of my joy when I perceived very distinct traces of my adorable *dévote*'s tears. I confess, I gave way to an impulse of youth, and kissed this letter with a transport of which I had not believed myself any longer capable. I continued my happy examination; I found all my letters in sequence and order of date; and what gave me a still more agreeable surprise was to find the first of all, the one which I thought the graceless creature had returned to me, faithfully copied by her hand, and in an altered and tremulous hand, ample witness to the soft perturbation of her heart during that employment.

Thus far I was entirely given over to love; soon it gave place to fury. Who do you think it is, that wishes to ruin me in the eyes of the woman whom I adore? What Fury do you suppose is vile enough to plot such a black scheme? You know her: it is your friend, your kinswoman; it is Madame de Volanges. You cannot imagine what a tissue of horrors this infernal Megæra has written concerning me. It is she, she alone, who has troubled the security of this angelic woman; it is through her counsels, through her pernicious advice, that I see myself forced to leave; it is she, in short, who has sacrificed me. Ah! without a doubt her daughter must be seduced: but that is not enough, she must be ruined; and, since this cursed woman's age puts her beyond the reach of my assaults, she must be hit in the object of her affections.

So she wishes me to come back to Paris! she forces me to it! be it so, I will go back; but she shall bewail my return. I am annoyed that Danceny is the hero of that adventure; he possesses a fundamental honesty which will embarrass us: however, he is in love, and I see him often; perhaps one may make use of him. I am losing sight of myself in my anger, and forgetting that I owe you an account of what has passed today. To resume.

This morning I saw my sensitive prude again. Never had I found her so lovely. It must ever be so: a woman's loveliest moment, the only one when she can produce that intoxication of the soul of which we speak so constantly and which we so rarely meet, is that one when, assured of her love, we are not yet of her favors; and that is precisely the case in which I found myself now. Perhaps too, the idea that I was going to be deprived of the pleasure of seeing her served to beautify her. Finally, with the arrival of the postman, I was handed your letter of the 27th; and while I read it, I was still hesitating as to whether I should keep my word: but I met my beauty's eyes, and it would have been impossible to me to refuse her aught.

I then announced my departure. A moment later, Madame de Rosemonde left us alone: but I was still four paces away from the coy creature when, rising with an affrighted air: "Leave me, leave me, Monsieur," she said; "in God's name, leave me."

This fervent prayer, which betrayed her emotion, could not but animate me the more. I was already at her side, and I held her hands which she had joined together with a quite touching expression; I was beginning some tender complaints, when some hostile demon brought back Madame de Rosemonde. The timid *dévote,* who had, in truth, some cause for fear, took advantage of this to withdraw.

I offered her my hand, however, which she accepted; and auguring well from this mildness, which she had not shown for a long time, I sought to press hers, while again commencing my complaints. At first she would fain withdraw it; but at my more lively insistence, she abandoned it with a good grace, although without replying either to the gesture or to my remarks. Arrived before the door of her apartment, I wished to kiss this hand, before I dropped it. The defense began by being hearty: but a "remember that I am going away," uttered most tenderly, rendered it awkward and inefficient. Hardly had the kiss been given, when the hand found strength enough to escape, and the fair one entered her apartment, where her chambermaid was in attendance. Here finishes my history.

As I presume that tomorrow you will be at the Maréchale's, where I certainly shall not go to look for you; as I think it very likely too that, at our first interview, we shall have more than one affair to discuss, and notably that of the little Volanges, whom I do not lose sight of, I have decided to have myself preceded by this letter, and, long as it is, I shall not close it, until the moment comes for sending it to the post: for, at the point which I have reached, everything may depend on an opportunity, and I leave you now to see if there be one.

P.S. *Eight o'clock in the evening.*

Nothing fresh; not the least little moment of liberty: care taken even to avoid it. However, at least as much sorrow shown as decency permits. Another incident which cannot be without consequences is that I am charged by Madame de Rosemonde with an invitation to Madame de Volanges to come and spend some time with her in the country.

Adieu, my lovely friend; until tomorrow, or the day after, at the latest.

At the Château de . . . , 28th August, 17**.

45. The Présidente de Tourvel to Madame de Volanges

M. de Valmont left this morning, Madame; you seemed to me so anxious for his departure, that I thought I ought to inform you of it. Madame de Rosemonde much regrets her nephew, whose society, one must admit, is agreeable: she passed the whole morning in talking of him, with that sensibility which you know her to possess; she did not stint his praises. I thought it was incumbent on me to listen to her without contradiction, more especially as I must confess that on many points she was right. In addition, I felt that I had to reproach myself with being the cause of this separation, and I cannot hope to be able to compensate her for the pleasure of which I have deprived her. You know that I have by nature small store of gaiety, and the kind of life we are going to lead here is not formed to increase it.

If I had not acted according to your advice, I should fear that I had behaved somewhat lightly; for I was really distressed at my venerable friend's grief; she touched me to such a degree that I could have willingly mingled my tears with her own.

We live at present in the hope that you will accept the invitation which M. de Valmont is to bring you, on the part of Madame de Rosemonde, to come and spend some time with her. I hope that you have no doubt of the pleasure it will give me to see you; and, in truth, you owe us this recompense. I shall be most delighted to have this opportunity of making an earlier acquaintance with Mademoiselle de Volanges, and to have the chance of convincing you more and more of the respectful sentiments, etc.

At the Château de . . . , 29th August, 17★★.

46. The Chevalier Danceny to Cécile Volanges

What has happened to you then, my adored Cécile? What can have caused in you so sudden and cruel an alteration? What has become of your vows of never changing? It was only yesterday that you repeated them with so much pleasure! Who can have made you forget them today? It is useless for me to examine myself; I cannot find the cause of it in me; and it is terrible that I should have to seek it in you. Ah! doubtless you are neither light nor deceitful; and even in this moment of despair, no insulting suspicion shall defile my soul. Yet, by what fatality comes it that you are no longer the same? No, cruel one, you are no longer the same! The tender Cécile, the Cécile whom I adore, and whose vows I have received, would not have avoided my gaze, would not have resisted the happy chance which placed me beside her; or, if any reason which I cannot understand had forced her to treat me with such severity, she would, at least, have condescended to inform me of it.

Ah, you do not know, you will never know, my Cécile, all that you have made me suffer today, all that I suffer still at this moment. Do you suppose then that I can live, if I am no longer loved by you? Nonetheless, when I asked you for a word, one single word to dispel my fears, instead of answering me you pretended to be afraid of being overheard; and that difficulty which did not then exist, you immediately brought about yourself by the place which you chose in the circle. When, compelled to leave you, I asked you at what hour I could see you again tomorrow, you pretended that you could not say, and Madame de Volanges had to be my informant. Thus the moment, ever desired so fondly, which is to bring me into your presence, tomorrow, will only excite in me anxiety; and the pleasure of seeing you, hitherto so dear to my heart, will give place to the fear of being intrusive.

I feel it already, this dread irks me, and I dare not speak to you of my love. That *I love you,* which I loved so well to repeat when I could hear it in my turn; that soft phrase which sufficed for my felicity, offers me, if you are changed, no more than the image of an eternal despair. I cannot believe, however, that that talisman of love has lost all its power, and I am fain to employ it once more.[1] Yes, my Cécile, *I love you*. Repeat after me then this expression of my happiness. Remember that you have accustomed me to the hearing of it, and that to deprive me of it is to condemn me to a torture which, like my love, can only end with my life.

Paris, 29th August, 17★★.

47. The Vicomte de Valmont to the Marquise de Merteuil

Today again I shall not see you, my lovely friend, and here are my reasons, which I beg you to receive with indulgence.

Yesterday, instead of returning here directly, I stopped with the Comtesse de ★★★, whose *château* lay almost upon my road, and of whom I asked a dinner. I did not reach Paris until about seven o'clock, and I alighted at the Opera, where I hoped to find you.

The Opera over, I went to see my fair friends of the green room; I found there my whilom Émilie, surrounded by a numerous court, women as well as men, to whom she was offering a supper that very evening at P——. I had no sooner entered this assemblage than I was invited to the supper by acclamation. I was likewise invited by a little fat and stumpy person, who stammered his invitation to me in the French of Holland, and whom I recognized as the true hero of the *fête*. I accepted.

I learned upon my way that the house whither we were going was the price agreed upon for Émilie's favors toward this grotesque figure, and that this supper was a veritable wedding breakfast. The little man could not contain himself for joy, in expectation of the pleasure which awaited him; he seemed to me so satisfied with the prospect that he gave me a longing to disturb it; which was, effectually, what I did.

The only difficulty I found was that of persuading Émilie, who was rendered somewhat scrupulous by the burgomaster's wealth. She agreed, however, after raising some objections, to the plan which I suggested of filling this little beer barrel with wine, and so putting him *hors de combat* for the rest of the night.

The sublime idea which we had formed of a Dutch toper caused us to employ all available means. We succeeded so well that, at dessert, he was already without the strength to lift his glass: but the helpful Émilie and myself vied with one another in filling him up. Finally, he fell be-

---

[1]Those who have not had occasion sometimes to feel the value of a word, an expression, consecrated by love will find no meaning in this sentence.

neath the table, in so drunken a state, that it ought to last for at least a week. We then decided to send him back to Paris; and, as he had not kept his carriage, I had him carried into mine, and remained in his stead. I thereupon received the congratulations of the company, which soon afterward retired, and left me in possession of the field. This gaiety, and perhaps my long rustication, made Émilie seem so desirable to me that I promised to stay with her until the Dutchman's resurrection.

This complaisance on my part is the price of that which she has just shown me, that of serving me for a desk upon which to write to my fair puritan, to whom I found it amusing to send a letter written in the bed, and almost in the arms, of a wench, a letter interrupted even to complete an infidelity, in which I send her an exact account of my position and my conduct. Émilie, who has read the epistle, laughed like a mad girl over it, and I hope that you will laugh as well.

As my letter must needs bear the Paris postmark, I send it to you; I leave it open. Will you please read it, seal it up, and commit it to the post. Above all, be careful not to employ your own seal, nor even any amorous device; a simple head. Adieu, my lovely friend.

P.S. I open my letter; I have persuaded Émilie to go to the *Italiens.* . . . I shall take advantage of that moment to come and see you. I shall be with you by six o'clock at the latest; and if it be agreeable to you, we will go together, about seven o'clock, to Madame de Volanges. Propriety commands that I do not postpone the invitation with which I am charged for her from Madame de Rosemonde; moreover, I shall be delighted to see the little Volanges.

Adieu, most fair lady. I shall be as pleased to embrace you, as the Chevalier will be jealous.

At P . . . , 30th August, 17★★.

48. The Vicomte de Valmont to the Présidente de Tourvel
(BEARING THE POSTMARK OF PARIS)

It is after a stormy night, during which I have not closed my eyes; it is after having been ceaselessly either in the agitation of a devouring ardor, or in an utter annihilation of all the faculties of my soul, that I come to seek with you, Madame, the calm of which I have need, and which, however, I have as yet no hope to enjoy. In truth, the situation in which I am, while writing to you, makes me realize more than ever the irresistible power of love; I can hardly preserve sufficient control over myself to put some order into my ideas; and I foresee already that I shall not finish this letter without being forced to interrupt it. What! Am I never to hope then that you will someday share with me the trouble which overcomes me at this moment? I dare believe, notwithstanding, that if you were well acquainted with it, you would not be entirely insensible. Believe me, Madame, a cold tranquillity, the soul's slumber, the imitation of death do not conduce to happiness; the active passions alone can lead us thither; and, in spite of the torments which you make me suffer, I think I can assure you without risk that at this moment I am happier than you. In vain do you overwhelm me with your terrible severities; they do not prevent me from abandoning myself utterly to love, and forgetting, in the delirium which it causes me, the despair into which you cast me. It is so that I would avenge myself for the exile to which you condemn me. Never had I so much pleasure in writing to you; never have I experienced, during such an occupation, an emotion so sweet and, at the same time, so lively. Everything seems to enhance my transports; the air I breathe is laden with pleasure; the very table upon which I write to you, consecrated for the first time to this office, becomes love's sacred altar to me; how much it will be beautified in my eyes! I shall have traced upon it the vow to love you forever! Pardon, I beseech you, the disorder of my senses. Perhaps, I ought to abandon myself less to transports which you do not share: I must leave you for a moment to dispel an intoxication which increases each moment, and which becomes stronger than myself.

I return to you, Madame, and doubtless, I return always with the same eagerness. However, the sentiment of happiness has fled far away from me; it has given place to that of cruel privation. What does it avail me to speak of my sentiments, if I seek in vain the means to convince you of them? After so many efforts, I am equally bereft of strength and confidence. If I still tell over to myself the pleasures of love, it is only to feel more keenly my sorrow at being deprived of them. I see no other resource, save in your indulgence; and I am too sensible at this moment of how greatly I need it, to hope to obtain it. Never, however, has my love been more respectful, never could it be less likely to offend you; it is of such a kind, I daresay, as the most severe virtue need not fear: but I am myself afraid of describing to you, at greater length, the sorrow which I experience. Assured as I am that the object which causes it does not participate in it, I must at any rate not abuse your kindness; and it would be to do that, were I to spend more time in retracing for you that dolorous picture. I take only enough to beg you to reply to me, and never to doubt of the sincerity of my sentiments.

Written at P . . . ; dated from Paris, 30th August, 17★★.

49. Cécile Volanges to the Chevalier Danceny

Without being either false or frivolous, Monsieur, it is enough for me to be enlightened as to my conduct, to feel the necessity of altering it; I have promised this sacrifice to God, until such a time when I can offer Him also that of my sentiments toward you, which are rendered even more criminal by the religious character of your estate. I feel certain that it will only bring me sorrow, and I will not even hide from you that, since the day before yesterday, I have wept every time I have thought of you. But I hope that God will do me the grace of giving me the needful strength to forget you, as I ask of Him morning and evening. I expect also of your friendship and of your honor that you will not seek to shake me in the good resolution which has been inspired in me, and in which I strive to maintain myself. In consequence, I beg you to have the kindness to write no more to me, the more so as I warn you that I should no longer reply to you, and that you would compel me to acquaint Mamma with all that has passed; and that would deprive me entirely of the pleasure of seeing you.

I shall, nonetheless, retain for you all the attachment which one may have without there being harm in it; and it is indeed with all my soul that I wish you every kind of happiness. I quite feel that you will no longer love me as much as you did, and that, perhaps, you will soon love another better than me. But that will be one penance the more for the fault which I have committed in giving you my heart, which I ought to give only to God and my husband when I have one. I hope that the Divine mercy will take pity on my weakness, and that it will give me no more sorrow than I am able to support.

Adieu, Monsieur; I can truly assure you that, if I were permitted to love anybody, I should never love anybody but you. But that is all I may say to you; and perhaps even that is more than I ought to say.

Paris, 31st August, 17**.

50. The Présidente de Tourvel to the Vicomte de Valmont

Is it thus then, Monsieur, that you carry out the conditions upon which I consented sometimes to receive your letters? And have I *no reason for complaint* when you speak to me only of a sentiment to which I should still fear to abandon myself, even if I could do so without violating all my duties? For the rest, if I had need of fresh reasons to preserve this salutary dread, it seems to me that I could find them in your last letter. In effect, at the very moment when you think to make an apology for love, what else are you doing but revealing to me its redoubtable storms? Who can wish for happiness bought at the expense of reason, whose short-lived pleasures are followed at any rate by regret, if not by remorse?

You yourself, in whom the habit of this dangerous delirium ought to diminish its effect, are you not, however, compelled to confess that it often becomes stronger than yourself; and are you not the first to lament the involuntary trouble which it causes you? What fearful ravages then would it not effect on a fresh and sensitive heart, which would still augment its empire, by the sacrifices it would be forced to make to it?

You believe, Monsieur, or you feign to believe that love leads to happiness; and I—I am so convinced that it would render me unhappy that I would not even hear its name pronounced. It seems to me that only to speak of it destroys tranquillity; and it is as much from inclination as from duty that I beg you to be good enough to keep silence on this subject.

After all, this request should be very easy for you to grant me at present. Returned to Paris, you will find there occasions enough to forget a sentiment which, perhaps, only owed its birth to the habit you are in of occupying yourself with such subjects, and its strength to the idleness of country life. Are you not then in that town where you had seen me with so much indifference? Can you take a step there without encountering an example of your readiness to change? And are you not surrounded there by women who, all more amiable than myself, have better right to your homage?

I am without the vanity with which my sex is reproached; I have still less of that false modesty which is nothing but a refinement of pride; and it is with the utmost good faith that I tell you here, I know how few pleasing qualities I possess: had I all there were, I should not believe them sufficient to retain you. To ask you then to occupy yourself no longer with me is only to beg you to do today what you had already done before, and what you would most assuredly do again in a short time, even if I were to ask the contrary.

This truth, which I do not lose sight of, would be, itself, a reason strong enough to disincline me to listen to you. I have still a thousand others, but without entering upon a long discussion, I confine myself to begging you, as I have done before, to correspond with me no further upon a sentiment to which I must not listen, and to which I ought even less to reply.

At the Château de . . . , 1st September, 17**.

Part II

51. The Marquise de Merteuil to the Vicomte de Valmont

Really, Vicomte, you are insupportable. You treat me as lightly as though I were your mistress. Do you know that I shall get angry, and that at the present moment I am in a fearful temper? Why! you have to see Danceny tomorrow morning; you know how important it is that I should speak to you before that interview; and without troubling yourself any more about it, you keep me waiting all day to run off I know not where. You are the cause of my arriving at Madame de Volanges' *indecently* late, and of my being found *surprising* by all the old women. I was obliged to flatter them during the whole of the evening in order to appease them: for one must never annoy the old women; it is they who make the young ones' reputations.

It is now one o'clock in the morning; and instead of going to bed, which I am dying to do, I must needs write you a long letter, which will make me twice as sleepy from the *ennui* it will cause me. You are most fortunate that I have not time to scold you further. Do not believe for that reason that I forgive you: it is only that I am pressed for time. Listen to me then, I hasten to come to the point.

However little skill you may exert, you are bound tomorrow to have Danceny's confidence. The moment is favorable for confidence: it is the moment of unhappiness. The little girl has been to confession: like a child, she has told everything; and ever since she has been tormented to such a degree by the fear of the devil that she insists on breaking it off. She related to me all her little scruples with a vivacity which told me how excited she was. She showed me her letter announcing the rupture, which was a real sermon. She babbled for an hour to me, without uttering one word of common sense. But she embarrassed me nonetheless; for you can imagine that I could not risk opening my mind to such a wrongheaded creature.

I saw, however, through all this verbiage, that she is as fond of her

73

Danceny as ever; I even remarked one of those resources which love never fails to find, and of which the little girl is an amusing dupe. Tormented by her desire to occupy herself with her lover, and by the fear of being damned if she does so, she has invented the plan of praying God that she may be able to forget him; and as she repeats this prayer at every moment of the day, she finds a means thereby of thinking of him unceasingly.

With anyone more *experienced* than Danceny, this little incident would perhaps be more favorable than the reverse; but the young man is so much of a Céladon that, if we do not help him, he will require so much time to overcome the slightest obstacles that there will be none left for us to carry out our project.

You are quite right; it is a pity, and I am as vexed as you, that he should be the hero of this adventure: but what would you have? What is done is done; and it is your fault. I asked to see his reply;[1] it was really pitiful. He produces arguments till he is out of breath, to prove to her that an involuntary sentiment cannot be a crime: as if it did not cease to be involuntary once one ceases to fight against it! That idea is so simple that it even suggested itself to the little girl. He complains of his unhappiness in a manner that is touching enough: but his grief is so gentle, and seems so strong and so sincere, that it seems to me impossible that a woman who finds occasion to reduce a man to such a degree of despair, and with so little danger, is not tempted to get rid of her fancy. Finally he explains that he is not a monk, as the little one believed; and that is, without contradiction, the best thing he has done: for, if it is a question of going so far as to abandon yourself to monastic loves, it is assuredly not the Knights of Malta who would deserve the preference.

Be that as it may, instead of wasting time in arguments which would have compromised me, perhaps without convincing, I approved her project of rupture: but I said that it was nicer, in such a case, to tell your reasons rather than to write them; that it was customary also to return letters and any other trifles one might have received; and appearing thus to enter into the views of the little person, I persuaded her to grant an interview to Danceny. We formed our plans on the spot, and I charged myself with the task of persuading the mother to go abroad without her daughter; it is tomorrow afternoon that this decisive moment will arrive. Danceny is already informed of it; but for God's sake, if you get an opportunity, please persuade this pretty swain to be less languorous, and teach him—since he must be told everything—that the true fashion to overcome scruples is to leave nothing to be lost by those who possess them.

---

[1] This letter has not been recovered.

For the rest, in order to save a repetition of this ridiculous scene, I did not fail to excite certain doubts in the little girl's mind, as to the discretion of confessors; and I assure you, she is paying now for the fright which she gave me, by her terror lest hers should go and tell everything to her mother. I hope that, after I have talked once or twice more with her, she will give up going thus to tell her follies to the first comer.[1]

Adieu, Vicomte; take charge of Danceny and guide his way. It would be shameful if we could not do what we will with two children. If we find it more difficult than we had thought at first, let us reflect, to animate our zeal—you, that it is the daughter of Madame de Volanges who is in question, I, that she is destined to become the wife of Gercourt. Adieu.

Paris, 2nd September, 17**.

52. The Vicomte de Valmont to the Présidente de Tourvel

You forbid me, Madame, to speak to you of my love; but where am I to find the necessary courage to obey you? Solely occupied by a sentiment which should be so sweet, and which you render so cruel; languishing in the exile to which you have condemned me; living only on privations and regrets; in prey to torments all the more dolorous in that they remind me unceasingly of your indifference; must I lose the only consolation which remains to me? And can I have any other, save that of sometimes laying bare to you a soul which you fill with trouble and bitterness? Will you avert your gaze, that you may not see the tears you cause to flow? Will you refuse even the homage of the sacrifices you demand? Would it not be worthier of you, of your good and gentle soul, to pity an unhappy one who is only rendered so by you, rather than to seek to aggravate his pain by a refusal which is at once unjust and rigorous?

You pretend to be afraid of love, and you will not see that you alone are the cause of the evils with which you reproach it. Ah, no doubt, the sentiment is painful, when the object which inspires it does not reciprocate; but where is happiness to be found, if mutual love does not procure it? Tender friendship, sweet confidence—the only kind which is without reserve—sorrow's alleviation, pleasure's augmentation, hope's enchantment, the delights of remembrance: where find them else than in love? You calumniate it, you who, in order to enjoy all the good which it offers you, have but to give up resisting it; and I—I forget the pain which I experience, to undertake its defense.

---

[1]The reader must have guessed already, by the conduct of Madame de Merteuil, how little respect she had for religion. This passage would have been suppressed, only it was thought that, while showing results, one ought not to neglect to make the causes known.

You force me also to defend myself; for, whereas I consecrate my life to your adoration, you pass yours in seeking reason to blame me: already you have assumed that I am frivolous and a deceiver; and, taking advantage of certain errors which I myself have confessed to you, you are pleased to confound the man I was then with what I am at present. Not content with abandoning me to the torment of living away from you, you add to that a cruel banter as to pleasures to which you know how you have rendered me insensible. You do not believe either in my promises or my oaths: well! there remains one guarantee for me to offer you, which you will not suspect. It is yourself. I only ask you to question yourself in all good faith: if you do not believe in my love, if you doubt for a moment that you reign supreme in my heart, if you are not sure that you have fixed this heart, which, indeed, has thus far been too fickle, I consent to bear the penalty of this error; I shall suffer, but I will not appeal: but if, on the contrary, doing justice to us both, you are forced to admit to yourself that you have not, will never have a rival, ask me no more, I beg you, to fight with chimeras, and leave me at least the consolation of seeking you no longer in doubt as to a sentiment which indeed will not finish, cannot finish, but with my life. Permit me, Madame, to beg you to reply positively to this part of my letter.

If, however, I give up that period of my life which seems to damage me so severely in your eyes, it is not because, in case of need, reasons had failed me to defend it.

What have I done, after all, but fail to resist the vortex into which I was thrown? Entering the world, young and without experience; passed, so to speak, from hand to hand by a crowd of women, who all hasten to forestall, by their good nature, a reflection which they feel cannot but be unfavorable to them; was it my part then to set the example of a resistance which was never opposed to me? Or was I to punish myself for a moment of error, which was often provoked by a constancy undoubtedly useless, and which would only have excited ridicule? Nay, what other cause, save a speedy rupture, can justify a shameful choice?

But, I can say it, this intoxication of the senses, perhaps even this delirium of vanity, did not attain to my heart. Born for love, intrigue might distract it, but did not suffice to occupy it; surrounded by seducing but despicable objects, none of them reached as far as my soul: I was offered pleasures, I sought for virtues; and in short, I even thought myself inconstant because I was delicate and sensitive.

It was when I saw you that I saw light: soon I understood that the charm of love sprang from the qualities of the soul; that they alone could cause its excess, and justify it. I felt, in short, that it was equally impossible for me not to love you, or to love any other than you.

There, Madame, is the heart to which you fear to trust yourself, and on whose fate you have to pronounce: but whatever may be the destiny you reserve for it, you will change nothing of the sentiments which attach it to you; they are as unalterable as the virtues which have given them birth.

Paris, 3rd September, 17★★.

53. The Vicomte de Valmont to the Marquise de Merteuil

I have seen Danceny, but only obtained his half confidence; he insists especially on suppressing the name of the little Volanges, of whom he only spoke to me as a woman of great virtue, even somewhat a *dévote:* apart from that, he gave me a fairly veracious account of his adventure, particularly the last incident. I excited him as best I could, I bantered him greatly upon his delicacy and scruples; but it seems that he clings to them, and I cannot answer for him: for the rest, I shall be able to tell you more after tomorrow. I am taking him tomorrow to Versailles, and I will occupy myself by studying him on the road. The interview which is to take place today also gives me some hope: everything may have happened to our satisfaction; and perhaps there is nothing left for us at present but to obtain a confession and collect the proofs. This task will be easier for you than for me: for the little person is more confiding or, what comes to the same thing, more talkative than her discreet lover. However, I will do my utmost.

Adieu, my lovely friend; I am in a mighty hurry; I shall not see you this evening, nor tomorrow: if you, on your side, know anything, write me a word on my return. I shall certainly come back to sleep in Paris.

At . . . , 3rd September, in the evening.

54. The Marquise de Merteuil to the Vicomte de Valmont

Oh yes, it is certainly with Danceny that there is something to discover! If he told you so, he was boasting. I know nobody so stupid in an affair of love, and I reproach myself more and more with the kindness we have shown him. Do you know that yesterday I thought I was compromised through him? And it would have been a pure loss! Oh, I will have my revenge, I promise you.

When I arrived yesterday to fetch Madame de Volanges, she no longer wanted to go out; she felt indisposed; I had need of all my eloquence to persuade her, and I foresaw that Danceny might arrive before our departure, which would have been all the more awkward, as Madame de Volanges had told him the day before that she would not be at home. Her daughter and I were on thorns. At last we went out; and the little one pressed my hand so affectionately as she bade me adieu that, in spite of her intended rupture, with which she believed herself, in all good faith, still to be occupied, I prophesied wonders in the course of the evening.

I was not at the end of my anxieties. We had hardly been half an hour at Madame de ★★★'s, when Madame de Volanges felt really unwell, and naturally she wanted to return home: as for me, I was the less inclined for it in that I was afraid, supposing we were to surprise the young people (as the chances were we should), that my efforts to make the mother go abroad might seem highly suspicious. I adopted the course of frightening her upon her health, which luckily is not difficult; and I kept her for an hour and a half, without consenting to drive her home, by feigning fear at the consequences of the dangerous motion of the carriage. We did not return until the hour that had been fixed. From the shamefaced air which I remarked on our arrival, I confess I hoped that at least my trouble had not been wasted.

The desire I had for further information made me stay with Madame de Volanges, who went to bed at once: and after having supped at her bedside, we left her at an early hour, under the pretext that she had need of repose, and passed into her daughter's apartment. The latter had done, on her side, all that I had expected of her; vanished scruples, fresh vows of eternal love, etc., etc.: in a word, she had performed properly. But the fool, Danceny, had not by one point passed the line where he had been before. Oh! one can safely quarrel with such a one: reconciliations are not dangerous.

The child assures me, however, that he wanted more, but that she knew how to defend herself. I would wager that she brags, or that she excuses him; indeed I made almost certain of it. The fantasy seized me to find out how much one might rely on the defense of which she was capable; and I, a mere woman, bit by bit, excited her to the point . . . In short, you may believe me, no one was ever more susceptible to a surprise of the senses. She is really lovable, this dear child! She deserves a different lover; she shall have at least a firm friend, for I am becoming really fond of her. I have promised her that I will form her, and I think I shall keep my word. I have often felt a need of having a woman in my confidence, and I should prefer her to another; but I can do nothing so long as she is not—what she needs to be; and that is one reason the more for bearing a grudge against Danceny.

Adieu, Vicomte; do not come to me tomorrow, unless it be in the forenoon. I have yielded to the entreaties of the Chevalier, for an evening at the *petite maison*.

Paris, 4th September, 17★★.

55. Cécile Volanges to Sophie Carnay

You were right, my dear Sophie; your prophecies succeeded better than your advice. Danceny, as you had predicted, has been stronger than my confessor, than you, than myself; and here we are returned precisely to our old position. Ah! I do not repent it; and if you scold me, it will be only because you do not know the pleasure of loving Danceny. It is very easy to say what one ought to do, nothing prevents you; but if you had any experience of how we suffer from the pain of somebody we love, of the way in which his pleasure becomes our own, of how difficult it is to say no, when what we wish to say is yes, you would be astonished at nothing: I myself, who have felt it, felt it most keenly, do not yet understand it. Do you suppose, for instance, that I could see Danceny weep, without weeping myself? I assure you that that would be utterly impossible to me; and, when he is happy, I am as happy as he. You may say what you like: what one says does not change things from what they are, and I am very certain that it is like that.

I should like to see you in my place. . . . No, it is not that I wish to say, for certainly I should not like to change places with anyone: but I wish that you too loved somebody; not only because then you would understand me better and scold me less; but also because you would be happier, or, I should rather say, you would only then begin to know happiness.

Our amusements, our merriment—all that, you see, is only child's play: nothing is left, when once it is over. But love, ah, love! . . . a word, a look, only to know he is there—that is happiness! When I see Danceny, I ask for nothing more; when I cannot see him, I ask only for him. I do not know how this is; but it would seem as though everything which I like resembles him. When he is not with me, I dream of him; and when I can dream of him utterly, without distraction, when I am quite alone, for instance, I am still happy; I close my eyes, and suddenly I think I see him; I remember his conversation, and think I hear him speak, it causes me to sigh; and then I feel a fire, an agitation . . . I cannot keep in one place. It is like a torment, and this torment gives me an unutterable pleasure.

I even think that when once one has been in love, the effect of it is shed even over friendship. That which I bear for you has not changed, however; it is always as it was at the convent: but what I tell you of I feel for Madame de Merteuil. It seems as though I love her more as I do Danceny than as yourself; and sometimes I wish that she were he. This is so, perhaps, because it is not a children's friendship like our own, or else because I see them so often together, which makes me deceive myself. Be that as it may, the truth is that, between the two of them, they make me very happy; and, after all, I do not think there is much harm in what

I do. I would only ask to stay as I am; and it is only the idea of marriage which distresses me: for if M. de Gercourt is such a man as I am told, and I have no doubt of it, I do not know what will become of me. Adieu, my Sophie; I love you always most tenderly.

                                        Paris, 4th September, 17★★.

56. The Présidente de Tourvel to the Vicomte de Valmont

How, Monsieur, would the answer which you ask of me serve you? To believe in your sentiments, would not that be one reason the more to fear them? And without attacking or defending their sincerity, does it not suffice, ought it not to suffice for yourself, to know that I will not and may not reply to them?

Supposing that you were to love me really (and it is only to prevent a return to this subject that I consent to the supposition), would the obstacles which separate us be less insurmountable? And should I have aught else to do, but to wish that you might soon conquer this love, and above all, to help you with all my power by hastening to deprive you of any hope? You admit yourself that *this sentiment is painful, when the object which inspires it does not reciprocate.* Now, you are thoroughly well aware that it is impossible for me to reciprocate; and even if this misfortune should befall me, I should be the more to be pitied, without making you any happier. I hope that you respect me enough, not to doubt of that for a moment. Cease then, I conjure you, cease from troubling a heart to which tranquillity is so necessary; do not force me to regret that I have known you.

Loved and esteemed by a husband whom I both love and respect, my duty and my pleasure are centred in the same object. I am happy, I must be so. If pleasures more keen exist, I do not desire them; I would not know them. Can there be any that are sweeter than that of being at peace with oneself, of knowing only days that are serene, of sleeping without trouble and awaking without remorse? What you call happiness is but a tumult of the senses, a tempest of passions of which the mere view from the shore is terrible. Ah! why confront these tempests? How dare embark upon a sea covered with the *débris* of so many thousand shipwrecks? And with whom? No, Monsieur, I stay on the shore; I cherish the bonds which unite me to it. I would not break them if I could; were I not held by them, I should hasten to procure them.

Why attach yourself to my life? Why this obstinate resolve to follow me? Your letters, which should be few, succeed each other with rapidity. They should be sensible, and you speak to me in them of nothing but your mad love. You besiege me with your idea, more than you did with your person. Removed in one form, you reproduce yourself under an-

other. The things which I asked you not to say, you repeat only in another way. It pleases you to embarrass me with captious arguments; you
shun my own. I do not wish to answer you, I will answer you no more.
. . . How you treat the women whom you have seduced! With what contempt you speak of them! I would fain believe that some of them deserve it: but are they all then so despicable? Ah, doubtless, since they have
violated their duties in order to give themselves up to a criminal love.
From that moment they have lost everything, even the esteem of him for
whom they have sacrificed everything. The punishment is just, but the
mere idea makes one tremble. What matters it, after all? Why should I
occupy myself with them or with you? By what right do you come to
trouble my tranquillity? Leave me, see me no more; do not write to me
again, I beg you; I demand it of you. This letter is the last which you will
receive from me.

At the Château de . . . , 5th September, 17★★.

57. The Vicomte de Valmont to the Marquise de Merteuil

I found your letter yesterday on my arrival. Your anger quite delighted
me. You could not have had a more lively sense of Danceny's delin-
quencies, if they had been exercised against yourself. It is no doubt out
of vengeance that you get his mistress into the habit of showing him
slight infidelities; you are a very wicked person! Yes, you are charming,
and I am not surprised that you are more irresistible than Danceny.

At last I know him by heart, this pretty hero of romance! He has no
more secrets for me. I have told him so often that virtuous love was the
supreme good, that one emotion was worth ten intrigues, that I was myself, at this moment, amorous and timid; he found in me, in short, a fashion of thinking so conformable with his own, that, in the enchantment
which he felt at my candor, he told me everything and vowed me a
friendship without reserve. We are no more advanced for that in our
project.

At first, it seemed to me that he went on the theory that a young girl
demands much more consideration than a woman, in that she has more
to lose. He thinks, above all, that nothing can justify a man for putting a
girl into the necessity of marrying him, or living dishonored, when the
girl is far richer than the man, which is the case in which he finds himself. The mother's sense of security, the girl's candor, all this intimidates
and arrests him. The difficulty would not be simply to dispute these arguments, however true they may be. With a little skill, and helped by passion, they would soon be destroyed; all the more, in that they tend to be
ridiculous, and one would have the sanction of custom on one's side. But
what hinders one from having any hold over him is that he is happy as

he is. Indeed, if a first love appears generally more virtuous, and, as one says, purer; if, at least, its course is slower, it is not, as people think, from delicacy or shyness; it is that the heart, astonished at an unknown emotion, halts, so to speak, at every step, to relish the charm which it experiences, and that this charm is so potent over a young heart that it occupies it to such an extent that it is unmindful of every other pleasure. That is so true, that a libertine in love—if such may befall a libertine—becomes from that instant in less haste for pleasure; in fact, between Danceny's behavior toward the little Volanges, and my own toward the more prudish Madame de Tourvel, there is but a shade of difference of degree.

It would have needed, to warm our young man, more obstacles than he has encountered; above all, that there should have been need for more mystery, for mystery begets boldness. I am coming to believe that you have hurt us by serving him so well; your conduct would have been excellent with a man of *experience,* who would have only felt desires: but you might have foreseen that, with a young man who is honorable and in love, the greatest value of favors is that they should be the proof of love; and, consequently, that, the surer he were of being beloved, the less enterprising he would become. What is to be done at present? I know nothing; but I have no hope that the child will be caught before marriage, and we shall have wasted our time: I am sorry for it, but I see no remedy.

While I am thus discoursing, you are doing better with your Chevalier. That reminds me that you have promised me an infidelity in my favor; I have your promise in writing, and I do not want it to be a dishonored draft. I admit that the date of payment has not yet come; but it would be generous of you not to wait for that; and on my side, I would take charge of the interest. What do you say, my lovely friend? Are you not tired of your constancy? Is this Chevalier then such a miracle? Oh, give me my way; I will indeed compel you to admit that if you have found some merit in him, it is because you have forgotten me.

Farewell, my lovely friend; I embrace you with all the ardor of my desire; I defy all the kisses of the Chevalier to contain as much.

At . . . , 5th September, 17★★.

58. The Vicomte de Valmont to the Présidente de Tourvel

Pray, Madame, how have I deserved the reproaches which you make me, and the anger which you display? The liveliest attachment and, withal, the most respectful, the most entire submission to your least wishes: there, in two words, is the history of my sentiments and my conduct. Oppressed by the pains of an unhappy love, I had no other consolation than that of seeing you; you bade me deprive myself of that; I obeyed you without permitting myself a murmur. As a reward for this sacrifice, you allowed me to write to you, and today you would rob me of that solitary pleasure. Shall I see it ravished from me without seeking to defend it? No, without a doubt: ah, how should it not be dear to my heart? It is the only one which remains to me, and I owe it to you.

My letters, you say, are too frequent! But reflect, I beseech you, that during the ten days of my exile, I have not passed one moment without thinking of you, and that yet you have only received two letters from me. *I only speak to you of my love!* Ah, what can I say, save that which I think? All that I could do was to weaken the expression of that; and you can believe me that I only let you see what it was impossible for me to hide. Finally, you threaten me that you will no longer reply to me! Thus, the man who prefers you to everybody, and who respects even more than he loves you: not content with treating him with severity, you would add to it your contempt! And why these threats and this anger? What need have you of them? Are you not sure of being obeyed, even when your orders are unjust? Is it possible for me then to dispute even one of your desires, have I not already proved it? But will you abuse this empire which you have over me? After having rendered me unhappy, after having become unjust, will you find it so easy then to enjoy that tranquillity which you assure me is so necessary to you? Will you never say to yourself: he has made me mistress of his fate, and I have made him unhappy? He implored my aid, and I looked at him without pity? Do you know to what point my despair may carry me? No. To be able to appreciate my sufferings, you would need to know the extent to which I love you, and you do not know my heart.

To what do you sacrifice me? To chimerical fears. And who inspires them in you? A man who adores you; a man over whom you will never cease to hold an absolute empire. What do you fear, what can you fear, from a sentiment over which you will ever be mistress, to direct as you will? But your imagination creates monsters for itself, and you attribute the fright which they cause you to love. A little confidence, and these phantoms will disappear.

A wise man said that, to dispel fears, it is almost always sufficient to penetrate into their causes.[1] It is in love especially that this truth finds its application. Love, and your fears will vanish. In the place of objects which affright you, you will find a delicious emotion, a lover tender and submissive, and all your days, marked by happiness, will leave you no other regret than that of having lost any by indifference. I myself, since I re-

---

[1]We believe it was Rousseau in *Émile:* but the quotation is not exact, and the application which Valmont makes of it entirely false; and then, had Madame de Tourvel read *Émile?*

pented of my errors and exist only for love, regret a time which I thought I had passed in pleasure; and I feel that it lies with you alone to make me happy. But, I beseech you, let not the pleasure which I take in writing to you be disturbed by the fear of displeasing you. I would not disobey you; but I am at your knees; it is there I claim the happiness of which you would rob me, the only one which you have left me; I cry to you, heed my prayers and behold my tears; ah, Madame, will you refuse me?

At . . . , 7th September, 17★★.

59. The Vicomte de Valmont to the Marquise de Merteuil

Tell me, if you know, what is the meaning of this effusion of Danceny? What has happened to him, and what has he lost? Has his fair one, perchance, grown vexed with his eternal respect? One must be just; we should be vexed for less. What am I to say to him this evening at the *rendezvous* which he asks of me, and which I have given him at all costs? Assuredly, I will not waste my time in listening to his complaints, if that is to lead us nowhither. Amorous complaints are not good to hear, save in a *recitato obbligato* or *arietta*. Let me know then what it is, and what I have to do, or really I shall desert, to avoid the tedium which I foresee. Shall I be able to have a talk with you this morning? If you are *engaged,* at least send me a word, and give me the cues to my part.

Where were you yesterday, pray? I never succeed in seeing you now. Truly, it was not worth the trouble of keeping me in Paris in the month of September. Make up your mind, however, as I have just received a very pressing invitation from the Comtesse de B★★★ to go and see her in the country; and, as she tells me, humorously enough, "her husband has the finest woods in the world, which he carefully preserves for the pleasure of his friends." Now you know I have certainly some rights over the woods in question; and I shall go and revisit them if I am of no use to you. Adieu; remember Danceny will be with me about four o'clock.

Paris, 8th September, 17★★.

60. The Chevalier Danceny to the Vicomte de Valmont
(ENCLOSED IN THE PRECEDING LETTER)

Ah, Monsieur, I am in despair, I have lost all! I dare not confide to writing the secret of my woes: but I feel a need to unburden them in the ear of a sure and trusty friend. At what hour could I see you, and ask you for advice and consolation? I was so happy on the day when I opened my soul to you! Now, what a difference! All is changed with me. What I suffer on my own account is but the least part of my torments; my anxiety on behalf of a far dearer object, that is what I cannot support.

Happier than I, you will be able to see her, and I count on your friendship not to refuse me this favor: but I must see you and instruct you. You will pity me, you will help me; I have no hope save in you. You are a man of sensibility, you know what love is, and you are the only one in whom I can confide; do not refuse me your aid.

Adieu, Monsieur; the only alleviation of my pain is the reflection that such a friend as yourself is left to me. Let me know, I beg you, at what hour I can find you. If it is not this morning, I should like it to be early in the afternoon.

Paris, 8th September, 17**.

61. Cécile Volanges to Sophie Carnay

My dear Sophie, pity your Cécile, your poor Cécile; she is very unhappy! Mamma knows all. I cannot conceive how she has come to suspect anything; and yet, she has discovered everything. Yesterday evening, Mamma seemed indeed to be in a bad humor, but I did not pay much attention to it. I even, while waiting till her rubber was finished, talked quite gaily to Madame de Merteuil, who had supped here, and we spoke much of Danceny. I do not believe, however, that we were overheard. She went away and I retired to my room.

I was undressing when Mamma entered, and sent away my maid; she asked me for the key of my desk. The tone in which she made this request caused me to tremble so that I could hardly stand. I made a pretense of being unable to find it; but at last I had to obey her. The first drawer which she opened was precisely that which contained the letters of the Chevalier Danceny. I was so confused that, when she asked me what it was, I did not know what to reply to her, except that it was nothing; but when I saw her begin to read the first which presented itself, I had barely time to sink into an armchair when I felt so ill that I swooned away. As soon as I came to myself again, my mother, who had called my maid, withdrew, telling me to go to bed. She carried off all Danceny's letters. I tremble every time I reflect that I must appear before her again. I did naught but weep all the night through.

I write to you at dawn, in the hope that Joséphine will come. If I can speak with her alone, I shall ask her to take a short note I am going to write to Madame de Merteuil; if not, I will put it in your letter, and will you kindly send it, as if from yourself. It is only from her that I shall get any consolation. At least, we can speak of him, for I have no hope to see him again. I am very wretched! Perhaps she will be kind enough to take charge of a letter for Danceny. I dare not trust Joséphine for such a purpose, and still less my maid; for it is perhaps she who told my mother that I had letters in my desk.

I will not write to you at any greater length, because I wish to have time to write to Madame de Merteuil and also to Danceny, to have my letter all ready, if she will take charge of it. After that I shall lie down again, so that they will find me in bed when they come into my room. I shall say that I am ill, so that I need not have to visit Mamma. It will not be a great falsehood: for indeed I suffer more than if I had the fever. My eyes burn from excessive weeping; and I have a weight on my chest which hinders me from breathing. When I think that I shall not see Danceny again, I wish that I were dead.

Adieu, my dear Sophie, I can say no more to you; my tears choke me.

Paris, 7th September, 17★★.

62. Madame de Volanges to the Chevalier Danceny[1]

After having abused, Monsieur, a mother's confidence and the innocence of a child, you will doubtless not be surprised if you are no longer received in a house where you have responded to the marks of a most sincere friendship, by a forgetfulness of all that is fitting. I prefer to beg you not to call upon me again, than to give orders at the door, which would compromise all alike, by the remarks which the lackeys would not fail to make. I have a right to hope that you will not force me to have recourse to such a means. I warn you also that if you make in future the least attempt to support my daughter in the folly into which you have beguiled her, an austere and eternal retreat shall shelter her from your pursuit. It is for you to decide, Monsieur, whether you will shrink as little from being the cause of her misery, as you have from attempting her dishonor. As for me, my choice is made, and I have acquainted her with it.

You will find enclosed the packet containing your letters. I reckon upon you to send me in return all those of my daughter, and to do your utmost to leave no trace of an incident the memory of which I could not retain without indignation, she without shame, and you without remorse.

I have the honor to be, etc.

Paris, 7th September, 17★★.

63. The Marquise de Merteuil to the Vicomte de Valmont

Indeed, yes, I will explain Danceny's letter to you. The incident which caused him to write it is my handiwork, and it is, I think, my *chef-d'oeu-*

---

[1]We have suppressed the letter of Cécile Volanges to the Marquise, as it contained merely the same facts as the preceding letter, but with less detail. That to the Chevalier Danceny has not been recovered: the reason of this will appear in letter the sixty-third, from Madame de Merteuil to the Vicomte.

vre. I wasted no time since your last letter, and I said with the Athenian architect, "What he has said, I will do."

It is obstacles then that this fine hero of romance needs, and he slumbers in felicity! Oh, let him look to me, I will give him some work: and if his slumber is going to be peaceful any longer, I am mistaken. Indeed, he had to be taught the value of time, and I flatter myself that by now he is regretting all he has lost. It were well also, said you, that he had need of more mystery: well, that need won't be lacking him now. I have this quality, I—that my mistakes have only to be pointed out to me; then I take no repose until I have retrieved them. Let me tell you now what I did.

When I returned home in the morning of the day before yesterday, I read your letter; I found it luminous. Convinced that you had put your finger on the cause of the evil, my sole concern now was to find a means of curing it. I commenced, however, by retiring to bed; for the indefatigable Chevalier had not let me sleep a moment, and I thought I was sleepy: but not at all; absorbed in Danceny, my desire to cure him of his indolence, or to punish him for it, did not let me close an eye, and it was only after I had thoroughly completed my plan, that I could take two hours' rest.

I went that same evening to Madame de Volanges, and, according to my project, I told her confidentially that I felt sure a dangerous acquaintance existed between her daughter and Danceny. This woman, who sees so clearly in your case, was so blind that she answered me at first that I was certainly mistaken, that her daughter was a child, etc., etc. I could not tell her all I knew; but I quoted certain looks and remarks *whereat my virtue and my friendship had taken alarm.* In short, I spoke almost as well as a *dévote* would have done; and to strike the decisive blow, I went so far as to say that I thought I had seen a letter given and received. "That reminds me," I added, "one day she opened before me a drawer in her desk in which I saw a number of papers, which she doubtless preserves. Do you know if she has any frequent correspondence?" Here Madame de Volanges' face changed, and I saw some tears rise to her eyes. "I thank you, my kind friend," she said, as she pressed my hand; "I will clear this up."

After this conversation, which was too short to excite suspicion, I went over to the young person. I left her soon afterward, to beg her mother not to compromise me in her daughter's eyes; she promised me this the more willingly, when I pointed out to her how fortunate it would be if the child were to take sufficient confidence in me to open her heart to me, and thus afford me the occasion of giving her *my wise counsels.* I feel certain that she will keep her promise, because she will doubtless seek to vaunt her penetration in her daughter's eyes. Thus I am authorized to maintain my friendly tone toward the child, without seeming false to Madame de Volanges, which I wished to avoid. I have also gained for the future the right to be as long and as privately as I like with the young person, without the mother being able to take umbrage.

I took advantage of this, that very evening; and when my game was over, I took the child aside in a corner, and set her on the subject of Danceny, upon which she is inexhaustible. I amused myself by exciting her with the pleasure she will have when she sees him tomorrow; there is no kind of folly that I did not make her say. I needs must restore to her in hope what I had deprived her of in reality; and besides, all that ought to render the blow more forcible, and I am persuaded that, the more she suffers, the greater will be her haste to compensate herself for it, on the next occasion. 'Tis wise, moreover, to accustom to great events anyone whom one destines for great adventures.

After all, may she not pay for the pleasure of having her Danceny with a few tears? She dotes on him! Well, I promise her that she shall have him, and even sooner than she would have done, but for this storm. It is like a bad dream, the awakening from which will be delicious; and, considering all, I think she owes me gratitude: after all, if I have put a spice of malice into it, one must amuse oneself:

The fool provides light pastime for the wise.[1]

I withdrew at last, thoroughly satisfied with myself. Either, said I to myself, Danceny's love, excited by obstacles, will redouble in intensity, and then I shall serve him with all my power; or, if he is nothing but a fool, as I am sometimes tempted to believe, he will be in despair, and will look upon himself as beaten: now, in that case, I shall at least have been as well avenged on him as he has been on me; on my way, I shall have increased the mother's esteem for me, the daughter's friendship, and the confidence of both. As for Gercourt, the first object of my care, I should be very unlucky, or very clumsy, if, mistress over his bride's mind, as I am, and as I intend to be even more, I did not find a thousand ways of making him what I mean him to be. I went to bed with these pleasant thoughts: I slept well, too, and awoke very late.

On my awakening I found two letters, one from the mother and one from the daughter; and I could not refrain from laughing when I encountered, in both, literally this same phrase: "*It is from you alone that I expect any consolation.*" Is it not amusing to console for and against, and to be the single agent of two directly contrary interests? Behold me, like the Divinity, receiving the diverse petitions of blind mortals, and altering nothing in my immutable decrees. I have deserted that august part, however, to assume that of the consoling angel; and have been, as the precept bids us, to visit my friends in their affliction.

I began with the mother; I found her wrapped in a sadness which al-

---

[1]Gresset: *Le Méchant.*

ready avenges you in part for the obstacles she has thrown in your way, on the side of your fair prude. Everything has succeeded marvelously, and my only anxiety was lest Madame de Volanges should take advantage of the moment to gain her daughter's confidence: which would have been quite easy, had she employed with her the language of kindness and affection, and given to reasonable counsels the air and tone of indulgent tenderness. Luckily she had armed herself with severity; in short, she had behaved so unwisely that I could only applaud. It is true that she thought of frustrating all our schemes, by the course which she had resolved on of sending her daughter back to the convent: but I warded off this blow, and induced her merely to make a threat of it, in the event of Danceny continuing his pursuit; this in order to compel both to a circumspection which I believe necessary to success.

I next went to the daughter. You would not believe how grief improves her! If she does but take to coquetry, I warrant that she will be often weeping; but this time she wept in all sincerity. . . . Struck by this new charm, which I had not known in her, and which I was very pleased to observe, I gave her at first but clumsy consolations, which rather increased her sorrow than assuaged it; and by this means I brought her well nigh to choking point. She wept no more, and for a moment I was afraid of convulsions. I advised her to go to bed, to which she agreed; I served her for waiting maid: she had made no toilette, and soon her disheveled hair was falling over her shoulders and bosom, which were entirely bare; I embraced her; she abandoned herself in my arms, and her tears began to flow again without an effort. Lord! how beautiful she was! Ah, if the Magdalen was like that, she must have been far more dangerous in her penitence than when she sinned.

When the disconsolate fair one was in bed, I started to console her in good faith. I first reassured her as to her fear about the content. I excited a hope in her of seeing Danceny in secret; and sitting upon the bed: "If *he* was here," said I; then, embroidering on this theme, I led her from distraction to distraction, until she had quite forgotten her affliction. We should have separated in a complete satisfaction with one another, if she had not wished to charge me with a letter to Danceny; which I consistently refused. Here are my reasons for this, which you will doubtless approve:

To begin with, it would have been to compromise myself openly with Danceny; and though this was the only reason I could employ with the little one, there are plenty of others which hold between you and me. Would it not have been to risk the fruit of my labors to give our young people so soon a means so easy of lightening their pains? And then, I should not be sorry to compel them to introduce some servants into this adventure; for, if it is to work out well, which is what I hope for, it must become known immediately after the marriage, and there are few surer methods of publishing it. Or if, by a miracle, the servants were not to speak, we would speak ourselves, and it will be more convenient to lay the indiscretion to their account.

You must give this idea, then, today to Danceny; and as I am not sure of the waiting maid of the little Volanges, and she seems to distrust her herself, suggest my own to him, my faithful Victoire. I will take care that the enterprise is successful. This idea pleases me all the more, as the confidence will only be useful to us and not to them: for I am not at the end of my story.

While I was excusing myself from carrying the child's letter, I was afraid every moment that she would suggest that I should send it by the post, which I could hardly have refused to do. Luckily, either in her confusion or in her ignorance, or again because she was less set on her letter than on a reply to it, which she could not have obtained by this means, she did not speak of it to me; but, to prevent this idea coming to her, or at least her being able to use it, I made up my mind on the spot; and on returning to her mother, persuaded her to send her daughter away for some time, to take her to the country. . . . And where? Does not your heart beat with joy? . . . To your aunt, to the old Rosemonde. She is to apprise her of it today; so, behold you authorized to return to your Puritan, who will no longer be able to reproach you with the scandal of a *tête-à-tête*; and thanks to my pains, Madame de Volanges will herself repair the wrong she had done you.

But listen to me, and do not be so constantly wrapped up in your own affairs as to lose sight of this one; remember that I am interested in it. I want you to become the go-between and counselor of the two young people. Inform Danceny of this journey and offer him your services. Find no difficulty, except as to getting your letter of credit into the fair one's hands; and demolish this obstacle on the spot by suggesting to him the services of my waiting maid. There is no doubt but that he will accept; and you will have, as reward for your trouble, the confidence of a young heart, which is always interesting. Poor child, how she will blush when she hands you her first letter! In truth, this *rôle* of confidant, against which a sort of prejudice has grown up, seems to me a very pretty relaxation, when you are occupied elsewhere; and that is the case in which you will be.

It is upon your attention that the *dénouement* of this intrigue will depend. Judge the moment when the actors must be reunited. The country offers a thousand ways; and Danceny cannot fail to be ready at your first signal. A night, a disguise, a window . . . what do I know? But mark me, if the little girl comes back as she went away, I shall quarrel with you. If you consider that she has need of any encouragement from me, send word to me. I think I have given her such a good lesson on the danger of keeping letters, that I may venture to write to her now; and I still cherish the design of making her my pupil.

I believe I forgot to tell you that her suspicions with regard to the surprised correspondence fell at first upon her waiting maid, but that I turned them toward the confessor. That was a way of killing two birds with one stone.

Adieu, Vicomte, I have been writing to you a long time now, and my dinner is the later for it: but self-love and friendship dictated my letter, and both are garrulous. For the rest, it will be with you by three o'clock, and that is all you need.

Pity me now, if you dare; and go and visit the woods of the Comte de B★★★, if they tempt you. You say that he keeps them for the pleasure of his friends! Is the man a friend of all the world then? But adieu, I am hungry.

Paris, 9th September, 17★★.

64. The Chevalier Danceny to Madame de Volanges
(A Draft Enclosed in Letter the Sixty-Sixth, from the Vicomte to the Marquise)

Without seeking, Madame, to justify my conduct, and without complaining of yours, I cannot but grieve at an event which brings unhappiness to three persons, all three worthier of a happier fate. More sensible to the grief of being the cause of it than even to that of being its victim, I have tried frequently, since yesterday, to have the honor to write to you, without being able to find the strength. I have, however, so many things to say to you that I must make a great effort over myself; and if this letter has little order and sequence, you must be sufficiently sensible of my painful situation to grant me some indulgence.

Permit me, first, to protest against the first sentence of your letter. I venture to say that I have abused neither your confidence nor the innocence of Mademoiselle de Volanges; in my actions I respected both. These alone depended on me; and when you would render me responsible for an involuntary sentiment, I am not afraid to add that that which Mademoiselle your daughter has inspired in me is of a kind which may be displeasing to you but cannot offend you. Upon this subject, which touches me more than I can say, I wish for no other judge than you, and my letters for my witnesses.

You forbid me to present myself at your house in future, and doubtless I shall submit to everything which it shall please you to order on this subject: but will not this sudden and total absence give as much cause for the remarks which you would avoid as the order which, for that very same reason, you did not wish to leave at your door? I insist all the more on this point, in that it is far more important for Mademoiselle de Volanges than for me. I beg you then to weigh everything attentively, and not to permit your severity to lessen your prudence. Persuaded that the simple interest of Mademoiselle your daughter will dictate your resolves, I shall await fresh orders from you.

Meanwhile, in case you should permit me to pay you my court sometimes, I undertake, Madame (and you can count on my promise), not to abuse the opportunity by attempting to speak privately with Mademoiselle de Volanges, or to send any letter to her. The fear of compromising her reputation decides me to this sacrifice; and the happiness of sometimes seeing her will be my reward.

This paragraph of my letter is also the only reply that I can make to what you tell me as to the fate you reserve for Mademoiselle de Volanges, and which you would make dependent on my conduct. I should deceive you were I to promise you more. A vile seducer can adapt his plans to circumstances, and calculate upon events; but the love which animates me permits me only two sentiments, courage and constancy. What, I! consent to be forgotten by Mademoiselle de Volanges, to forget her myself! No, no, never! I will be faithful to her, she has received my vow, and I renew it this day. Forgive me, Madame, I am losing myself, I must return.

There remains one other matter to discuss with you; that of the letters which you demand from me. I am truly pained to have to add a refusal to the wrongs which you already accuse me of: but I beg you, listen to my reasons, and deign to remember, in order to appreciate them, that the only consolation of my unhappiness at having lost your friendship is the hope of retaining your esteem.

The letters of Mademoiselle de Volanges, always so precious to me, have become doubly so at present. They are the solitary good thing which remains to me; they alone retrace for me a sentiment which is all the charm of life to me. However, you may believe me, I should not hesitate an instant in making the sacrifice, and my regret at being deprived of them would yield to my desire of proving to you my respectful deference; but considerations more powerful restrain me, and I assure you that you yourself cannot blame me for them.

You have, it is true, the secret of Mademoiselle de Volanges; but permit me to say that I am authorized to believe it is the result of surprise and not of confidence. I do not pretend to blame a proceeding which is, perhaps, authorized by maternal solicitude. I respect your rights, but they do not extend so far as to dispense me from my duties. The most sacred of all is never to betray the confidence which is entrusted to you. It would be to fail in this to expose to the eyes of another the secrets of a heart which did but wish to reveal them to mine. If Mademoiselle your daughter consents to confide them to you, let her speak; her letters are of no use to you. If she wishes, on the contrary, to lock her secret within herself, you doubtless cannot expect me to be the person to instruct you.

As for the mystery in which you desire this incident to be buried, rest assured, Madame, that, in all that concerns Mademoiselle de Volanges, I can rival even a mother's heart. To complete my work of removing all cause for anxiety from you, I have foreseen everything. This precious deposit, which bore hitherto the inscription: *Papers to be burned,* carries now the words: *Papers belonging to Madame de Volanges.* The course which I have taken should prove to you also that my refusal does not refer to any fear that you might find in these letters one single sentiment with which you could personally find fault.

This, Madame, is indeed a long letter. It will not have been long enough, if it leaves you the least doubt as to the honesty of my sentiments, my very sincere regret at having displeased you, and the profound respect with which I have the honor to be, etc.

Paris, 9th September, 17★★.

65. The Chevalier Danceny to Cécile Volanges
(Sent Open to the Marquise de Merteuil in Letter
the Sixty-Sixth from the Vicomte)

O my Cécile! what is to become of us? What God will save us from the misfortunes which threaten us? Let love, at least, give us the courage to support them! How can I paint for you my astonishment, my despair, at the sight of my letters, at the reading of Madame de Volanges' missive? Who can have betrayed us? On whom do your suspicions fall? Could you have committed any imprudence? What are you doing now? What have they said to you? I would know everything, and I am ignorant of all. Perhaps, you yourself are no better informed than I.

I send you your Mamma's note and a copy of my reply. I hope that you will approve of what I have said. I need also your approval of all the measures I have taken since this fatal event; they are all with the object of having news of you, of giving you mine; and, who knows? perhaps of seeing you again, and more freely than ever.

Imagine, my Cécile, the pleasure of finding ourselves together again, of being able to seal anew our vows of eternal love, and of seeing in our eyes, of feeling in our souls, that this vow will not be falsified! What pain will not so sweet a moment make us forget! Ah, well, I have hope of seeing it arrive, and I owe it to these same measures which I beg you to approve. What am I saying? I owe it to the consoling care of the most tender of friends; and my sole request is that you will permit this friend to become also your own.

Perhaps, I ought not to have given your confidence away without your consent; but I had misfortune and necessity for my excuse. It is love which has guided me; it is that which claims your indulgence, which begs you to pardon a confidence that was necessary, and without which we should, perhaps, have been separated forever.[1] You know the friend of whom I speak: he is the friend of the woman whom you love best. It is the Vicomte de Valmont.

My plan in addressing him was, at first, to beg him to induce Madame de Merteuil to take charge of a letter for you. He did not think this method could succeed, but, in default of the mistress, he answered for the maid, who was under obligations to him. It is she who will give you this letter; and you can give her your reply.

This assistance will hardly be of use to us, if, as M. de Valmont believes, you leave immediately for the country. But then it will be he himself who will serve us. The lady to whom you are going is his kinswoman. He will take advantage of this pretext to repair thither at the same time that you do; and it will be through him that our mutual correspondence will pass. He assures me, even, that if you let yourself be guided by him, he will procure us the means of meeting, without your running the risk of being in any way compromised.

Now, my Cécile, if you love me, if you pity my misery, if, as I hope, you share my regret, will you refuse your confidence to a man who will become our guardian angel? Without him, I should be reduced to the despair of being unable even to alleviate the grief I have caused you. It will finish, I hope: but promise me, my tender friend, not to abandon yourself overmuch to it, not to let it break you down. The idea of your grief is insupportable torture to me. I would give my life to make you happy! You know that well. May the certainty that you are adored carry some consolation to your soul! Mine has need of your assurance that you pardon love for the ills it has made you suffer.

Adieu, my Cécile, adieu, my tender love!

Paris, 9th September, 17**.

66. The Vicomte de Valmont to the Marquise de Merteuil

You will see, my lovely friend, by a perusal of the two enclosed letters, whether I have well fulfilled your project. Although both are dated today, they were written yesterday at my house, and beneath my eyes; that to

---

[1] M. Danceny does not confess the truth. He had already given his confidence to M. de Valmont before this event. See letter the fifty-seventh.

the little girl says all that we wanted. One can but humble oneself before the profundity of your views, when one judges of it by the success of your measures. Danceny is all on fire; and assuredly, at the first opportunity, you will have no moe reproaches to make him. If his fair *ingénue* chooses to be tractable, all will be finished a short time after her arrival in the country; I have a hundred methods all prepared. Thanks to your care, behold me decidedly *the friend of Danceny;* it only remains for him to become *Prince.*[1]

He is still very young, this Danceny! Would you believe it, I have never been able to prevail on him to promise the mother to renounce his love; as if there were much hindrance in a promise, when one is determined not to keep it! It would be deceit, he kept on repeating to me: is not this scruple edifying, especially in the would-be seducer of the daughter? That is so like men! all equally rascally in their designs, the weakness they display in the execution they christen probity.

It is your affair to prevent Madame de Volanges from taking alarm at the little sallies which our young man has permitted himself in his letter; preserve us from the convent; try also to make her abandon her request for the child's letters. To begin with, he will not give them up, he does not wish to, and I am of his opinion; here love and reason are in accord. I have read them, these letters; I have assimilated the tedium of them. They may become useful. I will explain.

In spite of the prudence which we shall employ, there may arise a scandal; this would break off the marriage, would it not? and spoil all our Gercourt projects. But, as on my side I have to be revenged on the mother, I reserve for myself in such a case the daughter's dishonor. By selecting carefully from this correspondence, and producing only a part of it, the little Volanges would appear to have made all the first overtures, and to have absolutely thrown herself at his head. Some of the letters would even compromise the mother, and would, at any rate, convict her of unpardonable negligence. I am quite aware that the scrupulous Danceny would revolt against this at first; but, as he would be personally attacked, I think he would be open to reason. It is a thousand chances to one that things will not turn out so; but one must foresee everything.

Adieu, my lovely friend: it would be very amiable of you to come and sup tomorrow at the Maréchale de ★★★'s; I could not refuse.

I presume I have no need to recommend you secrecy, as regards Madame de Volanges, upon my country project. She would at once decide to stay in Town: whereas, once arrived there, she will not start off again the next day; and, if she only gives us a week, I answer for everything.

                                        Paris, 9th September, 17★★.

---

[1]This expression refers to a passage in a poem by M. de Voltaire.

67. The Présidente de Tourvel to the Vicomte de Valmont

I did not mean to answer you again, Monsieur, and, perhaps, the embarrassment I feel at the present moment is itself an effectual proof that I ought not. However, I would not leave you any cause of complaint against me; I wish to convince you that I have done for you everything I could.

I permitted you to write to me, you say? I agree; but when you remind me of that permission, do you think I forget on what conditions it was given? If I had been as faithful to them as you have proved the reverse, would you have received a single reply from me? This is, however, the third; and when you do all that in you lies to compel me to break off this correspondence, it is I who am busy with the means of continuing it. There is one, but only one; and if you refuse to take it, it will prove to me, whatever you may say, how little value you set upon it.

Forsake, then, a language to which I may not and will not listen; renounce a sentiment which offends and alarms me, and to which you would perhaps be less attached, if you reflected that it is the obstacle which separates us. Is this sentiment the only one, then, that you can understand? And must love have this one fault the more in my eyes, that it excludes friendship? Would you yourself be so wrong as not to wish for your friend her in whom you have desired more tender sentiments? I would not believe it: that humiliating idea would revolt me, would divide me from you without hope of return.

In offering you my friendship, Monsieur, I give you all that is mine to give, all of which I can dispose. What can you desire more? To give way to this sentiment, so gentle, so suited to my heart, I only await your assent and the word which I ask of you, that this friendship will suffice for your happiness. I will forget all that I may have been told; I will trust in you to be at the pains of justifying my choice.

You see my frankness; it should prove to you my confidence; it will rest with you only, if it is to be further augmented: but I warn you that the first word of love destroys it forever, and restores to me all my fears; above all, that it will become the signal for my eternal silence with regard to you.

If, as you say, you have turned away from your errors, will you not rather be the object of a virtuous woman's friendship than of a guilty woman's remorse? Adieu, Monsieur; I feel that, after having spoken thus, I can say nothing more until you have replied to me.

At the Château de . . . , 9th September, 17★★.

68. The Vicomte de Valmont to the Présidente de Tourvel

How, Madame, am I to answer your last letter? How dare be true, when my sincerity may ruin my cause with you? No matter, I must; I will have the courage. I tell myself, I repeat to myself, that it is better to deserve you than to obtain you: and, must you deny me forever a happiness that I shall never cease to desire, I must at least prove to you that my heart is worthy of it.

What a pity, that, as you say, I have *turned away from my errors!* With what transports of joy I should have read that same letter, to which I tremble today to reply. You speak to me therein with *frankness,* you display me *confidence,* and you offer me your *friendship:* what good things, Madame, and how I regret that I can not profit by them! Why am I no longer what I was?

If I were, indeed, if I felt for you only an ordinary fancy, that light fancy which is the child of seduction and pleasure, which today, however, is christened love, I should hasten to extract advantage from all that I could obtain. With scant delicacy as to means, provided that they procured me success, I should encourage your frankness from my need of finding you out; I should desire your confidence with the design of betraying it; I should accept your friendship with the hope of beguiling it. . . . What, Madame! does this picture alarm you? . . . Ah, well, it would be a true picture of me, were I to tell you that I consented to be no more than your friend.

What, I! I consent to share with any one a sentiment which has emanated from your soul! If I ever tell you so, do not believe me. From that moment I should seek to deceive you; I might desire you still, but I should assuredly love you no longer.

It is not that amiable frankness, sweet confidence, sensible friendship are without value in my eyes. . . . But love! True love, and such as you inspire, by uniting all these sentiments, by giving them more energy, would not know how to lend itself, like them, to that tranquillity, to that coldness of soul, which permits comparisons, which even suffers preferences. No, Madame, I will not be your friend; I will love you with the most tender, even the most ardent love, although the most respectful. You can drive it to despair, but you cannot annihilate it.

By what right do you pretend to dispose of a heart whose homage you refuse? By what refinement of cruelty do you rob me of even the happiness of loving you? That happiness is mine; it is independent of you; I shall know how to defend it. If it is the source of my ills, it is also their remedy.

No, once more, no. Persist in your cruel refusals, but leave me my love. You take pleasure in making me unhappy! ah, well! be it so, endeavor to wear out my courage, I shall know how to force you at least to decide my fate; and perhaps some day you will render me more justice. It is not that I hope ever to make you susceptible: but, without being persuaded, you will be convinced; you will say to yourself: I judged him ill.

To put it rightly, it is to yourself that you are unjust. To know you without loving you, to love you without being constant, are two things which are equally impossible; and, in spite of the modesty which adorns you, it must be easier for you to feel pity than surprise at the sentiments which you arouse. For me, whose only merit is that I have known how to appreciate you, I will not lose that; and far from accepting your insidious offers, I renew at your feet my vow to love you always.

Paris, 10th September, 17★★.

69. Cécile Volanges to the Chevalier Danceny
(A NOTE WRITTEN IN PENCIL AND COPIED OUT BY DANCENY)

You ask me what I am doing; I love you and I weep. My mother no longer speaks to me; she has taken pens, ink, and paper away from me; I am making use of a pencil which has happily been left to me, and I am writing on a fragment of your letter. I needs must approve all you have done; I love you too well not to take every means of having news of you and of giving you my own. I did not like M. de Valmont, and I did not know he was so great a friend of yours; I will try to get used to him, and I will love him for your sake. I do not know who it is that has betrayed us; it can only be my waiting maid or my confessor. I am very miserable: we are going to the country tomorrow; I do not know for how long. My God! to see you no more! I have no more room: adieu, try to read me. These words traced in pencil will perhaps be effaced, but never the sentiments engraved on my heart.

Paris, 10th September, 17★★.

70. The Vicomte de Valmont to the Marquise de Merteuil

I have an important warning to give you, my dear friend. As you know, I supped yesterday with the Maréchale de ★★★: you were spoken of, and I said, not all the good which I think, but all that which I do not think. Everyone appeared to be of my opinion, and the conversation languished, as ever happens when one says only good of one's neighbor, when a voice was raised in contradiction: it was Prévan's.

"Heaven forbid," he said, rising, "that I should doubt the virtue of Madame de Merteuil! But I would dare believe that she owes it more to her lightness of character than to her principles. It is perhaps more difficult to follow her than to please her; and, as one rarely fails, when one

runs after a woman, to meet others on the way; as, after all, these others
may be as good as she is, or better; some are distracted by a fresh fancy,
others stop short from lassitude; and she is, perhaps, the woman in all
Paris who has had least cause to defend herself. As for me," he added, encouraged by the smile of some of the women, "I shall not believe in
Madame de Merteuil's virtue, until I have killed six horses in paying my
court to her."

This ill-natured joke succeeded, as do all those which savor of scandal;
and, during the laugh which it excited, Prévan resumed his place, and the
general conversation changed. But the two Comtesses de B★★★, by the
side of whom our skeptic sat, had a private conversation with him, which
luckily I was in a position to overhear.

The challenge to render you susceptible was accepted; word was
pledged that everything was to be told: and of all the pledges that might
be given in this adventure, this one would assuredly be the most religiously kept. But there you are, forewarned, and you know the proverb.

It remains for me to tell you that this Prévan, whom you do not know,
is infinitely amiable, and even more adroit. If you have sometimes heard
me declare the contrary, it is only that I do not like him, that it is my
pleasure to thwart his success, and that I am not ignorant of the weight
of my suffrage with thirty or so of our most fashionable women. In fact,
I prevented him for long, by this means, from appearing on what we call
the great scene; and he did prodigies, without for that winning any more
reputation. But the fame of his triple adventure, by turning people's eyes
on him, gave him that confidence which hitherto he had lacked, and
which has rendered him really formidable. He is, in short, today perhaps
the only man whom I should fear to meet in my path; and, apart from
your own interest, you will be rendering me a real service by making him
appear ridiculous by the way. I leave him in good hands, and I cherish the
hope that, on my return, he will be a ruined man.

. I promise, in revenge, to carry through the adventure of your pupil,
and to concern myself as much with her as with my fair prude.

The latter has just sent me a letter of capitulation. The whole letter
announces her desire to be deceived. It is impossible to suggest a method
more timeworn or more easy. She wishes me to become *her friend*. But I,
who love new and difficult methods, do not mean to cry quits with her
so cheaply; and I most certainly should not have been at such pains with
her, to conclude with an ordinary seduction.

What I propose, on the contrary, is that she should feel, and feel thoroughly, the value of each one of the sacrifices she shall make me; not to
lead her too swiftly for remorse not to follow her; to let her virtue expire in a slow agony; to concentrate her, unceasingly, upon the heart-
breaking spectacle; and only to grant her the happiness of having me in

her arms, after compelling her no longer to dissimulate her desire. In truth, I am of little worth indeed, if I am not worth the trouble of asking for. And can I take a less revenge for the haughtiness of a woman who seems to blush to confess that she adores?

I have, therefore, refused the precious friendship, and have held to my title of lover. As I do not deny that this title, which seems at first no more than a verbal quibble, is, however, of real importance to obtain, I have taken a great deal of pains with my letter, and endeavored to be lavish of that disorder which alone can depict sentiment. I have, in short, been as irrational as it was possible for me to be: for, without one be irrational, there is no tenderness; and it is for this reason, I believe, that women are so much our superiors in love letters.

I concluded mine with a piece of cajolery; and that is another result of my profound observation. After a woman's heart has been for some time exercised, it has need of repose; and I have remarked that cajolery was, to all, the softest pillow that could be offered.

Adieu, my lovely friend; I leave tomorrow. If you have any commands to give me for the Comtesse de ★★★, I will halt at her house, at any rate for dinner. I am vexed to leave without seeing you. Send me your sublime instructions, and aid me with your wise counsels, in this critical moment.

Above all, defend yourself against Prévan; and grant that I may make amends to you one day for the sacrifice! Adieu.

Paris, 11th September, 17★★.

71. The Vicomte de Valmont to the Marquise de Merteuil

My idiot of a *chasseur* has left my letter case in Paris! My fair one's letters, those of Danceny to the little Volanges: all have remained behind, and I have need of all. He is going off to repair his stupidity; and while he is saddling his horse, I will tell you my night's story: for I beg you to believe I do not waste my time.

The adventure in itself is but a small thing; a *réchauffé* with the Vicomtesse de M★★★. But it interested me in its details. I am delighted, moreover, to let you see that, if I have a talent for ruining women, I have nonetheless, when I wish it, that of saving them. The most difficult course or the merriest is the one I choose; and I never reproach myself for a good action, provided that it has kept me in practice or amused me.

I found the Vicomtesse here, and as she joined her entreaties to the persecutions with which they would make me pass the night at the *château:* "Well, I consent," I said to her, "on condition that I pass it with you." "That is impossible," she answered: "Vressac is here." So far, I had but meant to say the polite thing to her; but the word impossible revolted me as usual. I felt humiliated at being sacrificed to Vressac, and I resolved not to suffer it; I insisted therefore.

Circumstances were not favorable to me. This Vressac had been awkward enough to give offense to the Vicomte; so much so that the Vicomtesse can no longer receive him at home, and this visit to the good Comtesse had been arranged between them, in order to try and snatch a few nights. The Vicomte had at first even shown signs of ill humor at meeting Vressac there; but, as his love of sport is even stronger than his jealousy, he stayed nonetheless: and the Comtesse, always the same as you know her, after lodging the wife in the great corridor, put the husband on one side and the lover on the other, and left them to arrange things among themselves. The evil destiny of both willed that I should be housed opposite them.

That very day, that is to say, yesterday, Vressac, who, as you will well believe, cajoles the Vicomte, went out shooting with him in spite of his distaste for sport, and quite counted on consoling himself at night in the wife's arms for the *ennui* which the husband caused him all day: but I judged that he would have need of repose, and busied myself with the means of persuading his mistress to give him the time to take it.

I succeeded, and persuaded her to pick a quarrel with him concerning that very same shooting party to which, very obviously, he had only consented for her sake. She could not have chosen a more sorry pretext; but no woman is better endowed than the Vicomtesse with that talent, common to all women, of putting ill humor in the place of reason, and of being never so difficult to appease as when she is in the wrong. Neither was the moment convenient for explanations; and, as I only wished her for one night, I consented to their reconciliation on the morrow.

Vressac was greeted sullenly on his return. He sought to demand the cause; he was abused. He tried to justify himself; the husband, who was present, served for a pretext to break off the conversation; finally, he attempted to take advantage of a moment when the husband was absent, to ask that she would be kind enough to listen to him that night: it was then that the Vicomtesse became sublime. She declaimed against the audacity of men who, because they have experienced a woman's favors, suppose that they have the right to abuse her, even when she has cause of complaint against them; and, having thus skillfully changed the issue, she talked sentiment and delicacy so well that Vressac grew dumb and confused, and I myself was tempted to believe that she was right: for you must know that, as a friend of both of them, I made a third at this conversation.

In the end, she declared positively that she would not add the fatigues of love to those of the chase, and that she would reproach herself were she to disturb such sweet pleasures. The husband returned. The disconsolate Vressac, who was no longer at liberty to reply, addressed himself to me; and, having, at great length, expounded his reasons, which I knew as well as he, he begged me to speak to the Vicomtesse, and I promised him to do so. I spoke to her, in effect; but it was in order to thank her, and to arrange the hour and manner of our *rendezvous*.

She told me that, situated as she was between her husband and her lover, she had thought it more prudent to go to Vressac than to receive him in her apartment; and that, since I was placed opposite her, she thought it was safer also to come to me; that she would repair to my room as soon as her waiting maid had left her alone; that I had only to leave my door ajar and await her.

Everything was carried out as we had arranged; and she came to my room about one o'clock in the morning,

> "*In just such plain array,*
> *As beauty wears when fresh from slumber's sway.*"[1]

As I am quite without vanity, I will not go into the details of the night; but you know me, and I was satisfied with myself.

At daybreak, we had to separate. It is here that the interest begins. The imprudent woman had thought to have left her door ajar; we found it shut, and the key was left inside. You have no idea of the expression of despair, with which the Vicomtesse said to me at once: "Ah, I am lost!" You must admit it would have been amusing to have left her in this situation: but could I suffer a woman to be ruined for me who had not been ruined by me? And should I, like the commonalty of men, let myself be overcome by circumstances? A method had to be found therefore. What would you have done, my fair friend? Hear what was my conduct; it was successful.

I soon realized that the door in question could be burst in, on condition that one made a mighty amount of noise. I persuaded the Vicomtesse, therefore, not without difficulty, to utter some piercing cries of terror, such as *thieves, murder,* etc., etc. And we arranged that, at the first cry, I should break in the door, and she should rush to her bed. You would not believe how much time it needed to decide her, even after she had consented. However, it had to be done that way, and at my first kick the door yielded. The Vicomtesse did well not to lose time; for, at the same instant, the Vicomte and Vressac were in the corridor, and the waiting maid had also run up to her mistress's chamber. I alone kept my coolness, and I profited by it to go and extinguish a night-light which still burned, and throw it to the ground, for you can imagine how ridicu-

---

[1]Racine: *Britannicus*.

lous it would have been to feign this panic terror with a light in one's room. I then took husband and lover to task for their sluggish sleep, assuring them that the cries, at which I had run up, and my efforts to burst open the door, had lasted at least five minutes.

The Vicomtesse, who had regained her courage in bed, seconded me well enough, and swore by all her gods that there had been a thief in her chamber; she protested with all the more sincerity in that she had never had such a fright in her life. We searched everywhere and found nothing, when I pointed to the overturned night-light, and concluded that, without a doubt, a rat had caused the damage and the alarm; my opinion was accepted unanimously; and, after some well-worn pleasantries on the subject of rats, the Vicomte was the first to regain his chamber and his bed, praying his wife for the future to keep her rats quieter.

Vressac, who was left alone with us, approached the Vicomtesse to tell her tenderly that it was a vengeance of Love; to which she answered, glancing at me, "He was indeed angry then, for he has taken ample vengeance; but," she added, "I am exhausted with fatigue and I want to sleep."

I was in a good-humored moment; consequently, before we separated, I pleaded Vressac's cause and effected a reconciliation. The two lovers embraced, and I, in my turn, was embraced by both. I had no more relish for the kisses of the Vicomtesse; but I confess that Vressac's pleased me. We went out together; and after I had accepted his lengthy thanks, we both betook ourselves to bed.

If you find this history amusing, I do not ask you to keep it secret. Now that I have had my amusement out of it, it is but just that the public should have its turn. For the moment, I am only speaking of the story; perhaps, we shall soon say as much of the heroine.

Adieu! My *chasseur* has been waiting for an hour; I take only the time to embrace you, and to recommend you, above all, to beware of Prévan.

At the Château de . . . , 13th September, 17★★.

72. The Chevalier Danceny to Cécile Volanges
(NOT DELIVERED UNTIL THE 14TH)

O my Cécile! how I envy Valmont's lot! Tomorrow he will see you: it is he who will give you this letter, and I, languishing afar from you, must drag on my painful existence betwixt unhappiness and regret. My friend, my tender friend, pity my misfortunes; above all, pity me for your own: it is in the face of them that my courage deserts me.

How terrible it is to me that I should have caused your misfortune! But for me, you would be happy and tranquil. Can you forgive me? Ah, say, say that you forgive me; tell me also that you love me, that you will always love me. I need that you repeat it to me. It is not that I doubt it: but it seems to me that, the more sure I am of it, the sweeter it is to hear it said. You love me, do you not? Yes, you love me with all your soul. I do not forget that it is the last word I heard you utter. How I have treasured it in my heart! How deeply it is graven there! And with what transports has not mine replied to it!

Alas, in that moment of happiness, I was far from foreseeing the awful fate which awaited us! Let us occupy ourselves, my Cécile, with the means of alleviating it. If I am to believe my friend, it will suffice, to attain this, that you should treat him with the confidence which he deserves.

I was grieved, I confess, at the unfavorable opinion you appear to have had of him. I recognized there the prejudices of your Mamma; it was to submit to them that, for some time past, I had neglected that truly amiable man, who today does everything for me; who, in short, labors to reunite us, whom your Mamma has separated. I implore you, my dear friend, look upon him with a more favorable eye. Reflect that he is my friend, that he wishes to be yours, that he can afford me the happiness of seeing you. If these reasons do not convince you, my Cécile, you do not love me as well as I love you, you do not love me as much as you used to love me. Ah, if ever you were to come to love me less! But no, the heart of my Cécile is mine, it is mine for life; and if I have to dread the pain of a love which is unfortunate, her constancy will save me at least from the torments of a love betrayed.

Adieu, my charming friend; do not forget how I suffer, and that it only rests with you to make me happy, completely happy. Hear my heart's vow, and receive the most tender kisses of love.

Paris, 11th September, 17★★.

73. The Vicomte de Valmont to Cécile Volanges
(Delivered with the Preceding)

The friend who serves you knows that you have no writing materials, and he has already provided for this want. You will find in the anteroom of the apartment you occupy, beneath the great press, on the left-hand side, a supply of pens, ink, and paper, which he will renew when you require it, and which, so it seems to him, you can leave in the same place, if you do not find a surer one.

He asks you not to be offended with him, if he seems to pay no attention to you in public, and only to regard you as a child. This behavior seems to him necessary, in order to inspire the sense of security of which he has need, and to enable him to work more effectively for his friend's happiness and your own. He will try to find occasions for speaking with you, when he has anything to tell you or give to you; and he hopes to succeed, if you show any zeal to second him.

He also advises you to return to him, successively, the letters which you may have received, in order that there may be less risk of your compromising yourself.

He concludes by assuring you that, if you will give him your confidence, he will take every care to alleviate the persecution that a too harsh mother is using against two persons of whom one is already his best friend, while the other seems to him worthy of the most tender interest.

At the Château de . . . , 14th September, 17★★.

74. The Marquise de Merteuil to the Vicomte de Valmont

Ah, since when, my friend, do you take alarm so easily? Is this Prévan so very formidable then? But see how simple and modest am I! I have often met him, this haughty conqueror; I hardly looked at him! It required nothing less than your letter to cause me to pay him any attention. I repaired my injustice yesterday. He was at the Opera, almost exactly opposite me, and I took stock of him. He is handsome at any rate, yes, very handsome: fine and delicate features! He must gain by being seen close at hand. And you tell me he wants to have me! Assuredly it will be my honor and pleasure. Seriously, I have a fancy for it, and I now confide to you that I have taken the first steps. I do not know if they will succeed. Thus the matter stands.

He was not two paces off from me, as we came out from the Opera, and I, very loudly, made an appointment with the Marquise de ★★★ to sup on Friday with the Maréchale. It is, I think, the only house where I can meet him. I have no doubt that he heard me. . . . If the ungrateful fellow were not to come! But tell me, do you think he will come? Do you know that, if he were not to come, I should be in a bad humor all the evening? You see that he will not find so much difficulty in *following me;* what will more astonish you is that he will have still less in *pleasing me.* He would, he said, kill six horses in paying his court to me! Oh, I will save those horses' lives! I shall never have the patience to wait so long a time. You know it is not one of my principles to leave people languishing, when once I am decided; and I am for him.

Please now confess that there is some pleasure in talking reason to me! Has not your *important warning* been a great success? But what would you have? I have been vegetating for so long! It is more than six weeks since I permitted myself a diversion. This one presents itself; can I refuse myself it? Is not the object worth the trouble? Is there any more agreeable, in whatever sense you take the word?

You yourself are forced to do him justice; you do more than praise him, you are jealous of him. Ah, well! I will set up as judge between the two of you; but, to begin with, one should investigate, and that is what I want to do. I shall be an impartial judge, and you shall both be weighed in the same balance. As for you, I already have your papers, and your affair is thoroughly enquired into. Is it not only just that I should now occupy myself with your adversary? Come now, yield with a good grace; and as a commencement, let me hear, I beg you, what is this triple adventure of which he is the hero. You speak of it to me as though I knew of nothing else, and I do not know the first word of it. Apparently, it must have occurred during my expedition to Geneva, and your jealousy prevented you from writing to me about it. Repair this fault at the earliest possible; remember that *nothing which interests him is alien to me*. I certainly think that they were still talking of it when I returned; but I was otherwise occupied, and I rarely listen to anything of that sort which is not the affair of today or of yesterday.

Even if what I ask of you should go somewhat against the grain, is it not the least price you can pay for the pains I have taken for you? Have these not sent you back to your Présidente, when your blunders had separated you from her? Was it not I, again, who put into your hands the wherewithal to revenge yourself for the bitter zeal of Madame de Volanges? You have complained so often of the time you waste in searching after your adventures! Now, you have them under your thumb. Betwixt love and hate, you have but to choose; they both lie under the same roof; and you can double your existence, caress with one hand and strike with the other. It is even to me, again, that you owe the adventure of the Vicomtesse. I am quite satisfied with it; but, as you say, it must be talked about; for if the situation could induce you, as I conceive, to prefer for a moment mystery to *éclat,* it must be admitted, nonetheless, that the woman did not merit so honorable a procedure.

I have, besides, cause of complaint against her. The Chevalier de Belleroche finds her prettier than is to my liking; and, for many reasons, I shall be glad to have a pretext for breaking with her: now none is more convenient than to be obliged to say: One cannot possibly know that woman any longer.

Adieu, Vicomte; remember that, situated as you are, time is precious; I shall employ mine by occupying myself with Prévan's happiness.

Paris, 15th September, 17★★.

75. Cécile Volanges to Sophie Carnay

[*N.B. In this letter, Cécile Volanges relates with the utmost detail all that concerns her in the events which the Reader already knows from the conclusion of the fifty-ninth and following letters. It seemed as well to suppress this repetition. She finally speaks of the Vicomte de Valmont, and expresses herself thus:*]

... I assure you that he is a most remarkable man. Mamma speaks mighty ill of him, but the Chevalier Danceny says much in his favor, and I think that he is right. I have never seen a man so clever. When he gave me Danceny's letter, it was in the midst of all the company, and nobody saw anything of it: it is true I was terribly frightened, because I had not expected anything; but now I shall be prepared. I have already quite understood what he wants me to do when I give him my answer. It is very easy to understand him, because he has a look which says anything he wants. I don't know how he does it: he told me in his note that he would appear not to take any notice of me before Mamma; indeed, one would say, all the time, that he never thinks of me, and yet, every time I seek his eyes, I am sure to meet them at once.

There is a great friend of Mamma's here, whom I did not know, who also has the air of not loving M. de Valmont too well, although he is full of attentions for her. I am afraid that he will bore himself soon with the life one leads here, and go back to Paris; that would be very vexing. He must indeed have a good heart to have come on purpose to do a service to his friend and me. I should much like to show my gratitude to him, but I do not know how to get speech with him; and when I find the occasion, I should be so ashamed that, perhaps, I should not know what to say to him.

It is only to Madame de Merteuil that I talk freely, when I speak of my love. Perhaps, even with you, to whom I tell everything, I should feel embarrassed if we were talking. With Danceny himself, I have often felt, as though in spite of myself, a certain alarm which prevented me from telling him all that I thought. I reproach myself greatly for this now, and I would give everything in the world to find a moment to tell him once, only once, how much I love him. M. de Valmont promised him that, if I would be guided by him, he would contrive an opportunity for us to see one another again. I will certainly do everything he wants; but I cannot conceive how it is possible. Adieu, my dear friend; I have no more room left.[1]

At the Château de ... , 14th September, 17✶✶.

---

[1] Mademoiselle de Volanges having shortly afterward changed her confidant, as will appear in the subsequent letters, this collection will include no more of those which she continued to write to her friend at the convent: they would teach the Reader nothing that he did not know.

76. The Vicomte de Valmont to the Marquise de Merteuil

Either your letter is a piece of banter which I have not understood, or you were in a dangerous delirium when you wrote it. If I knew you less well, my lovely friend, I should truly be most alarmed; and, whatever you may say, I do not take alarm too easily.

It is in vain that I read and reread your letter, I am none the more advanced; for to take it in the natural sense which it presents is out of the question. What was it then you wished to say? Is it merely that it was useless to take so much trouble with an enemy who was so little to be feared? In that case, you might be wrong. Prévan is really attractive; he is more so than you believe; he has, above all, the most useful talent of interesting people greatly in his love, by the skill with which he will bring it up in society, and before the company, by making use of the first conversation which occurs. There are few women who do not fall into the trap and reply to him, because, all having pretensions to subtlety, none wishes to lose an opportunity of displaying it. Now you are well aware that the woman who consents to talk of love soon finishes by feeling it, or at least by behaving as if she did. He gains again at this method, which he has really brought to perfection, in that he can often call the women themselves in testimony of their defeat; and this I tell you, as one who has seen it.

I was never in the secret except at secondhand; for I have never been intimate with Prévan: but, in a word, there were six of us: and the Comtesse de P★★★, thinking herself very artful all the time, and having the air indeed, to any one who was not initiated, of conversing in the abstract, told us, with the utmost detail, both how she had succumbed to Prévan, and all that had passed between them. She told this narrative with such a sense of security that she was not even disturbed by a smile which came over all our six faces at the same time; and I shall always remember that one of us, having sought, by way of excuse, to feign a doubt as to what she said, or rather of what she had the air of saying, she answered gravely that we were certainly, none of us, so well informed as she was; and she was not afraid even to address herself to Prévan, and ask him if she had said a word which was not true.

I was right then in believing this man dangerous to everybody: but for you, Marquise, was it not enough that he was *handsome, very handsome,* as you tell me yourself? Or that he should make *one of those attacks on you which you sometimes amuse yourself by rewarding, for no other reason than that you find them well contrived?* Or that you should have found it amusing to succumb for any reason whatever? Or—what do I know? Can I divine the thousand and one caprices which govern a woman's head, and in which alone you continue to take after your sex? Now that you are forewarned of the danger, I have no doubt that you will easily avoid it: but it was nonetheless necessary to forewarn you. I return to my text therefore: what did you mean to say?

If it is only a piece of banter against Prévan, apart from its being very long, it was of no use, addressed to me; it is in society that he must suffer some excellent piece of ridicule, and I renew my prayer to you on this subject.

Ah! I think I hold the key to the enigma! Your letter is a prophecy, not of what you will do, but of what he will think you ready to do, at the moment of the fall which you have prepared for him. I quite approve of this plan: it requires, however, great precautions. You know as well as I do that, as far as the public is concerned, to have a man or to receive his attentions is absolutely the same thing, unless the man be a fool, which Prévan is very far from being. If he can gain the appearances, he will boast, and all will have been said. Fools will believe him, the malicious will have the air of believing; where will your resources be? Remember, I am afraid. It is not that I doubt your skill: but it is the good swimmers who get drowned.

I hold myself to be no duller than another: as for means of dishonoring a woman, I have found a hundred, I have found a thousand; but when I have busied myself to seek how the woman could escape, I have never seen the possibility. You yourself, my fair friend, whose conduct is a masterpiece, I have a hundred times found you to have had more good luck than you have shown skill.

But, after all, I am, perhaps, seeking for a reason where none exists. I am amazed, however, to think that, for the last hour, I should have been treating seriously what is surely a mere jest on your part. You intend to make fun of me! Ah well! so be it; but make haste, and let us speak of something else. Something else! I am mistaken, it is always the same; always women to have or to ruin, and often both.

I have here, as you remark, the wherewithal to exercise myself in both kinds, but not with equal ease. I foresee that vengeance will go quicker than love. The little Volanges has succumbed, I answer for that; she only awaits an opportunity, and I undertake to bring it about. But it is not the same with Madame de Tourvel: this woman is disheartening, I did not conceive it of her; I have a hundred proofs of her love, but I have a thousand of her resistance; and, in truth, I am afraid lest she escape me.

The first effect which my return produced gave me more hope. You will guess that I wished to judge for myself; and, to make sure of seeing the first emotions, I sent no one ahead to announce me, and I calculated my stages so as to arrive when they should be at table. In fact, I dropped from the clouds, like a divinity at the opera, who comes to effect a dé-nouement.

Having made enough noise at my entry to attract all eyes to me, I could see, in one glance, the joy of my old aunt, the annoyance of Madame de Volanges and the confused pleasure of her daughter. My fair one, owing to the seat she occupied, had her back turned to the door. Busy at the moment in carving something, she did not even turn her head: but I said a word to Madame de Rosemonde; and at the first sound, the sensitive Puritan, recognizing my voice, uttered a cry in which I thought I distinguished more love than terror or surprise. I was then in a position to see her face; the tumult of her soul, the struggle between her ideas and sentiments, were depicted on it in a score of different fashions. I sat down to table by her side; she did not know precisely anything of what she did or said. She endeavored to go on eating; it was out of the question: finally, not a quarter of an hour later, her pleasure and confusion becoming too strong for her, she could devise nothing better than to ask permission to leave the table, and she escaped into the park, on the pretext that she needed to take the air. Madame de Volanges wanted to accompany her; the tender prude would not permit it, too happy, no doubt, to have a pretext for being alone, and to give way without constraint to the soft emotion of her heart!

I made the dinner as short as it was possible to do. Dessert was hardly served, when the infernal Volanges woman, pressed apparently by her need to injure me, rose from her seat to go and find the charming invalid: but I had foreseen this project and I thwarted it. I feigned therefore to take this particular movement for the general signal; and, having risen at the same time, the little Volanges and the *curé* of the place followed the double example; so that Madame de Rosemonde was left alone at the table with the old Commandant de T★★★; and they also both decided to leave. We all went then to rejoin my fair one, whom we found in the grove near the *château:* as it was solitude she wanted and not a walk, she was just as pleased to return with us as to make us stay with her.

As soon as I was certain that Madame de Volanges would have no opportunity to speak apart with her, I thought of fulfilling your orders, and busied myself about the interests of your pupil. Immediately after coffee, I went up to my room, and went into the others also, to explore the territory; I took measures to ensure the little girl's correspondence; after this first piece of benevolence, I wrote a word of instruction to her and to beg for her confidence; and I added my note to the letter from Danceny. I returned to the *salon.* I found my beauty reclining on a long chair, in an attitude of delicious unconstraint.

This spectacle, while exciting my desires, illumined my gaze; I felt that this must be tender and beseeching, and I placed myself in such a position that I could bring it into play. Its first effect was to cause the big, modest eyes of the heavenly prude to be cast down. For some time I considered that angelic face; then, glancing over all her person, I amused myself by divining forms and contours through the light clothing, which I could have wished away. After having descended from head to feet, I returned from feet to head. . . . My fair friend, her soft gaze was fixed upon me; it was immediately lowered; but wishing to promote its return, I averted my eyes. Then was established between us that tacit convention, a first treaty of bashful love, which, in order to satisfy the reciprocal need of seeing, allows the looks to succeed one another, until the moment comes when they are mingled.

Convinced that this new pleasure occupied my fair one completely, I charged myself with the task of watching over our common safety; but, having assured myself that conversation was brisk enough to save us from the notice of the company, I sought to obtain from her eyes that they should frankly speak their language. For this, I began by surprising certain glances, but with so much reserve that modesty could not take alarm; and to put the bashful creature more at her ease, I appeared to be as embarrassed as herself.

Little by little our eyes, grown accustomed to encounter, were fixed for a longer interval; until at last they quitted each other no more, and I saw in hers that sweet languor which is the happy signal of love and desire: but it was only for a moment; soon recovering herself, she changed, not without a certain shame, her attitude and her look.

Being unwilling that she should suspect I had observed her different movements, I rose with vivacity, asking her, with an air of alarm, if she were unwell. At once, everybody rushed round her. I let them all pass in front of me; and as the little Volanges, who was working at her tapestry near a window, needed some time before she could leave her task, I seized the moment to deliver Danceny's letter.

I was at a little distance from her; I threw the letter into her lap. In truth she did not know what to do. You would have laughed over much at her air of surprise and embarrassment; however, I did not laugh, for I feared lest so much clumsiness might betray us. But a quick glance and gesture, strongly accentuated, gave her to understand at last that she was to put the packet in her pocket.

The rest of the day contained nothing of interest. What has passed since will, perhaps, bring about events with which you will be pleased, at any rate in so far as your pupil is concerned: but it is better to employ one's time in carrying out one's projects than in describing them. This is, moreover, the eighth sheet I have written, and I am wearied; and so, adieu.

You will rightly suppose, without my telling it you, that the child has replied to Danceny.[1] I have also had a reply from my fair, to whom I

---

[1]This letter has not been recovered.

wrote on the morrow of my arrival. I send you the two letters. You will or you will not read them: for this incessant, tedious repetition, which already is none too amusing to me, must be insipid indeed to any person not concerned.

Once more, adieu. I am ever mightily fond of you; but I beg you, if you write to me of Prévan, do so in such a manner that I may understand you.

At the Château de . . . , 17th September, 17**.

77. The Vicomte de Valmont to the Présidente de Tourvel

Whence, Madame, can arise the cruel pains which you are at to shun me? How can it be that the most tender zeal on my part meets on yours only with the treatment which one would barely permit oneself with the man against whom one had the greatest cause to complain? What! Love calls me back to your feet; and when a happy chance places me at your side, you prefer to feign indisposition, to alarm your friends, rather than consent to remain near me! How many times, yesterday, did you not turn away your eyes to deprive me of the favor of a glance! And if for one single moment I was able to see less severity there, that moment was so short that it seemed as though you wished less to have me enjoy it than to make me feel what I should lose by being deprived of it.

That is not, I venture to say, either the treatment which love deserves, or that which friendship may be allowed; and yet, of these two sentiments, you know whether the one does not animate me; and the other I was, it seems to me, authorized to believe that you did not withhold. This precious friendship, of which you doubtless thought me worthy, since you were kind enough to offer it me—what have I done that I should lose it since? Could I have damaged myself by my confidence, and will you punish me for my frankness? At least, have you no fear lest you abuse the one and the other? In effect, was it not to the bosom of my friend that I entrusted the secret of my heart? Was it not face to face with her alone that I thought myself obliged to refuse conditions which I had only to accept in order to obtain the facility for leaving them unfulfilled, and perhaps of abusing them to my advantage? Would you, in short, by a rigor so undeserved, force me to believe that I had needed but to deceive you in order to obtain greater indulgence?

I do not repent of a conduct which I owed you, as I owed it to myself; but by what fatality does each praiseworthy action of mine become the signal for a fresh misfortune?

It was after giving occasion for the only praise you have ever yet deigned to accord my conduct that I had to groan, for the first time, over the misfortune of having displeased you. It was after proving my perfect submission by depriving myself of the happiness of seeing you, simply to reassure your delicacy, that you wished to break off all correspondence with me, to rob me of that feeble compensation for a sacrifice which you had required, and to take from me even the very love which alone had given you the right to ask it. It is, in short, after having spoken to you with a sincerity which even the interest of that love could not abate that you shun me today, like some dangerous seducer whose perfidy you have found out.

Will you, then, never grow weary of being unjust? At least, tell me what new wrongs can have urged you to such severity, and do not refuse to dictate to me the orders which you wish me to obey; when I pledge myself to fulfill them, is it too great a pretension to ask that I may know them?

At the Château de . . . , 15th September, 17★★.

The Présidente de Tourvel to the Vicomte de Valmont

You seem surprised at my behavior, Monsieur, and within an ace of asking me to account to you for it, as though you had the right to blame it. I confess that I should have thought it was rather I who was authorized to be astonished and to complain; but, since the refusal contained in your last letter, I have adopted the course of wrapping myself in an indifference which affords no ground for remarks or reproaches. However, as you ask me for enlightenment, and I, thanks be to Heaven, am conscious of naught within me which should prevent my granting your request, I am quite willing to enter once more into an explanation with you.

Anyone reading your letters would believe me to be fantastic or unjust. I think it is not in my deserts that anyone should have this opinion of me; it seems to me, above all, that you, less than any other, have cause to form it. Doubtless, you felt that, in requiring my justification, you forced me to recall all that has passed between us. Apparently, you thought you had only to gain by this examination: as I, on my side, believe I have nothing to lose by it, at least in your eyes, I do not fear to undertake it. Perhaps, it is indeed the only means of discovering which of us has the right to complain of the other.

To start, Monsieur, from the day of your arrival in this *château,* you will admit, I suppose, that your reputation, at least, authorized me to employ a certain reserve with you; and that I might have confined myself to the bare expression of the coldest politeness, without fearing to be taxed with excessive prudery. You yourself would have treated me with indulgence, and would have thought it natural that a woman so little formed should not have the necessary merits to appreciate yours. That, surely, had been the part of prudence; and it would have cost me the less to follow in that, I will not conceal from you, when Madame de Rosemonde informed me of your arrival, I had need to remind myself of my friendship for her, and of her own for you, not to betray how greatly this news annoyed me.

I admit willingly that you showed yourself at first under a more favorable aspect than I had imagined; but you will agree, in your turn, that it lasted but a little while, and you were soon tired of a constraint for which, apparently, you did not find yourself sufficiently compensated by the advantageous notion it had given me of you. It was then that, abusing my good faith, my feeling of security, you were not afraid to pester me with a sentiment by which you could not doubt but that I should be offended; and I, while you were occupied in aggravating your errors by repeating them, sought a reason for forgetting them, by offering you the opportunity of, at least in part, retrieving them. My request was so just that you yourself thought you ought not to refuse it; but making a right out of my indulgence, you profited by it to ask for a permission which, without a doubt, I ought not to have granted you, but which, however, you obtained. Conditions were attached to it: you have kept no one of them; and your correspondence has been of such a kind that each one of your letters made it my duty not to reply to you. It was at the very moment when your obstinacy was forcing me to send you away from me that, by a perhaps culpable condescension, I attempted the only means which could permit me to be concerned with you: but what value has virtuous sentiment in your eyes? Friendship you despise; and, in your mad intoxication, counting shame and misery for naught, you seek only for pleasures and for victims.

As frivolous in your proceedings as inconsequent in your reproaches, you forget your promises, or rather you make a jest of violating them; and, after consenting to go away from me, you return here without being recalled; without thought for my prayers or my arguments; without even having the consideration to inform me, you were not afraid to expose me to a surprise whose effect, although assuredly very simple, might have been interpreted to my detriment by the persons who surrounded us. Far from seeking to distract from or to dissipate the moment of embarrassment you had occasioned, you seem to have given all your pains to increase it. At table you choose your seat precisely at the side of my own; a slight indisposition forces me to leave before the others, and, instead of respecting my solitude, you contrive that all the company should come to trouble it. On my return to the drawing room, I cannot make a step but I find you at my side; if I say a word, it is always you who reply to me. The most indifferent remark serves you for a pretext to bring up a conversation which I refuse to hear, which might even compromise me; for, in short, Monsieur, whatever the address you may bring to bear, I think that what I understand may also be understood by the others.

Forced thus to take refuge in immobility and silence, you nonetheless continue to persecute me; I cannot raise my eyes without encountering yours. I am incessantly compelled to avert my gaze; and by an incomprehensible inconsequence you draw upon me the eyes of the company at a moment when I would have even wished it possible to escape from my own.

And you complain of my behavior! and you are surprised at my eagerness to avoid you! Ah, blame rather my indulgence; be surprised that I did not leave at the moment of your arrival. I ought, perhaps, to have done so, and you will compel me to this violent, but necessary, course, if you do not finally cease your offensive pursuit. No, I do not forget, I never shall forget what I owe to myself, what I owe to the ties I have formed, which I respect and cherish; and I pray you to believe that, if ever I found myself reduced to the unhappy choice of sacrificing them, or of sacrificing myself, I should not hesitate an instant. Adieu, Monsieur.

At the Château de . . . , 16th September, 17★★.

79. The Vicomte de Valmont to the Marquise de Merteuil

I intended to go hunting this morning: but the weather was detestable. All that I have to read is a new romance which would bore even a schoolgirl. It will be two hours, at the earliest, before we breakfast: so that, in spite of my long letter of yesterday, I will have another talk with you. I am very certain not to weary you, for I shall tell you of *the handsome Prévan*. How was it you never heard of his famous adventure, the one which separated the *inseparables?* I wager that you will recall it at the first word. Here it is, however, since you desire it.

You will remember that all Paris marveled that three women, all three pretty, all three with like qualities and able to make the same pretensions, should remain intimately allied among themselves, ever since the moment of their entry into the world. At first, one seemed to find the reason in their extreme shyness: but soon, surrounded, as they were, by a numerous court whose homages they shared, and enlightened as to their value by the eagerness and zeal of which they were the objects, their union only became the firmer; and one would have said that the triumph of one was always that of the two others. One hoped at least that the moment of love would lead to a certain rivalry. Our rakes disputed the honor of being the apple of discord; and I myself should have entered their ranks, had the great consideration in which the Comtesse de ★★★ was held at the time permitted me to be unfaithful to her before I had obtained the favors I demanded.

However, our three beauties, during the same carnival, made their choice as though in concert; and, far from this exciting the storms which had been predicted, it only rendered their friendship more interesting, by the charm of the confidences entailed.

The crowd of unhappy suitors was added, then, to that of jealous women, and such scandalous constancy was held up to public censure. Some pretended that, in this society of *inseparables* (so it was dubbed at that time), the fundamental law was the community of goods, and that love itself was included therein; others asserted that, if the three lovers were exempt from rivals of their own sex, they were not from those of the other: people went so far as to say that they had but been admitted for decency's sake, and had obtained only a title without an office.

These rumors, true or false, had not the effect which one would have predicted. The three couples, on the contrary, felt that they were lost if they separated at such a moment; they decided to set their heads against the storm. The public, which tires of everything, soon tired of an ineffectual satire. Borne on the wings of its natural levity, it busied itself with other objects: then, casting back to that one with its habitual inconsequence, its criticism was converted into praise. As all things go by fashion here, the enthusiasm gained; it was become a real delirium, when Prévan undertook to verify these prodigies, and settle the public opinion about them, as well as his own.

He sought out therefore these models of perfection. He was easily admitted into their society, and drew a favorable omen from this. He was well aware that happy persons are not so easy of access. He soon saw, in fact, that this so vaunted happiness was, like that of kings, rather to be envied than desired. He remarked that, among these pretended inseparables, they were beginning to seek for pleasures abroad, and even to occupy themselves with distractions; and he concluded therefrom, that the bonds of love or friendship were already loosened or broken, and that those of self-conceit and custom alone retained some strength. The women, however, whose need brought them together, kept up among themselves an appearance of the same intimacy: but the men, who were freer in their proceedings, discovered duties to fulfill, or affairs to carry on; they still complained of these, but no longer neglected them, and the evenings were rarely complete.

This conduct on their part was profitable to the assiduous Prévan, who, being naturally placed beside the deserted one of the day, found a means of offering alternately, and according to circumstances, the same homage to each of the three friends. He could easily perceive that to make a choice between them was to lose everything; that false shame at proving the first to be unfaithful would make the preferred one afraid; that the wounded vanity of the two others would render them the enemies of the new lover, and that they would not fail to oppose him with the severity of their high principles; in short, that jealousy would surely revive the zeal of a rival who might be still to fear. Everything would be an obstacle; in his triple project all became easy: each woman was indulgent because she was interested in it; each man, because he thought that he was not.

Prévan, who had, at that time, but one woman to sacrifice, was lucky enough to see her become a celebrity. Her quality of foreigner, and the homage of a great Prince, adroitly refused, had fixed on her the eyes of the Court and the Town; her lover participated in the honor, and profited from it with his new mistresses. The only difficulty was to conduct his three intrigues at an equal pace; their progress had, of course, to be regulated by that of the one which lagged the most; in fact, I heard from one of his confidants, that his greatest difficulty was to hold in hand one which was ripe for gathering nearly a fortnight before the rest.

At last the great day arrived. Prévan, who had obtained the three avowals, was already master of the situation, and arranged it as you will see. Of the three husbands, one was absent, the other was leaving the next day at daybreak, the third was in town. The inseparable friends were to sup at the future widow's; but the new master had not permitted the former gallants to be invited there. On the morning of that very day, he divided the letters of his fair into three lots; he enclosed in one the portrait which he had received from her, in the second an amorous device which she had painted herself, in the third a tress of her hair; each of the friends received this third of a sacrifice as the whole, and consented, in return, to send to her disgraced lover a signal letter of rupture.

This was much; but it was not enough. She whose husband was in town could only dispose of the day; it was arranged that a pretended indisposition should dispense her from going to supper with her friend, and that the evening should be given entirely to Prévan; the night was granted by her whose husband was absent; and daybreak, the moment of the departure of the third spouse, was appointed by the last for the shepherd's hour.

Prévan, who neglected nothing, next hastened to the fair foreigner, brought there and aroused the humor which he required, and only left after having brought about a quarrel which assured him four-and-twenty hours of liberty. His dispositions thus made, he returned home, intending to take some hours' repose. Other business was awaiting him.

The letters of rupture had brought a flash of light to the disgraced lovers: none of them had any doubt but that he had been sacrificed to Prévan; and spite at being tricked uniting with the ill humor which is almost always engendered by the petty humiliation of being deserted, all three, without communicating with one another, but as though in concert, resolved to have satisfaction, and took the course of demanding it from their fortunate rival.

The latter found the three challenges awaiting him; he accepted them loyally, but not wishing to sacrifice either his pleasures or the glamour of this adventure, he fixed the *rendezvous* for the following morning, and gave all three assignations at the same place and the same hour. It was at one of the gates of the Bois de Boulogne.

When evening came, he ran his triple course with equal success; at least, he boasted subsequently that each one of his new mistresses had received three times the wage and declaration of his love. In this, as you may imagine, proofs are lacking to history; all that the impartial historian can do is to point out to the incredulous reader that vanity and exalted imagination can beget prodigies; nay more, that the morning which was to follow so brilliant a night seemed to promise a dispensation from all concern for the future. Be that as it may, the facts which follow are more authentic.

Prévan repaired punctually to the *rendezvous* which he had selected; he found there his three rivals, somewhat surprised at meeting, and each of them, perhaps, a trifle consoled at the sight of his companions in misfortune. He accosted them with a blunt but affable air, and used this language to them—it has been faithfully reported to me:

"Gentlemen," said he, "as I find you all here together, you have doubtless divined that you have all three the same cause of complaint against me. I am ready to give you satisfaction. Let chance decide between you which of the three shall first attempt a vengeance to which you have all an equal right. I have brought with me neither second nor witnesses. I did not include any in my offense; I seek none in my reparation." Then, agreeable to his character as a gamester, he added, "I know one rarely holds in three hands running; but, whatever fortune may befall me, one has always lived long enough when one has had time to win the love of women and the esteem of men."

While his astonished adversaries looked at one another in silence, and their delicacy, perhaps, reflected that this triple contest rendered the game hardly fair, Prévan resumed:

"I do not hide from you that the night which I have just passed has cruelly fatigued me. It would be generous of you to permit me to recruit my strength. I have given orders for a breakfast to be served on the ground; do me the honor to partake of it. Let us breakfast together, and, above all, let us breakfast gaily. One can fight for such trifles; but they ought not, I think, to spoil our good humor."

The breakfast was accepted. Never, it is said, was Prévan more amiable. He was skilled enough to avoid humiliating any one of his rivals, to persuade them that they would have easily had a like success, and, above all, to make them admit that, no more than he, would they have let the occasion slip. These facts once admitted, everything arranged itself. The breakfast was not finished before they had repeated a dozen times that such women did not deserve that men of honor should fight for them. This idea promoted cordiality; it was so well fortified by wine that, a few moments later, it was not enough merely to bear no more ill will: they swore an unreserved friendship.

Prévan, who doubtless liked this *dénouement* as well as the other, would not for that, however, lose any of his celebrity. In consequence, adroitly adapting his plans to circumstances: "In truth," he said to the three victims, "it is not on me but on your faithless mistresses that you should take revenge. I offer you the opportunity. I begin to feel already, like yourselves, an injury which would soon be my share: for if none of you could succeed in retaining a single one, how can I hope to retain all three? Your quarrel becomes my own. Accept a supper this evening at my *petite maison,* and I hope your vengeance may not be long postponed." They wished to make him explain: but, with that tone of superiority which the circumstances authorized him to adopt, he answered, "Gentlemen, I think I have proved to you that my conduct is founded on a certain wit; trust in me." All consented; and, after having embraced their new friend, they separated till the evening to await the issue of his promises.

Prévan returns to Paris without wasting time, and goes, according to the usage, to visit his new conquests. He obtained a promise from each to come the same evening and sup *tête-à-tête* at his pleasure house. Two of them raised a few objections; but what can one refuse on the day after? He fixed the *rendezvous* for a late hour, time being necessary for his plans. After these preparations he retired, sent word to the other three conspirators, and all four went gaily to await their victims.

The first is heard arriving. Prévan comes forward alone, receives her with an air of alacrity, conducts her into the sanctuary of which she believed herself to be the divinity; then, disappearing under some slight pretext, he allows himself to be forthwith replaced by the outraged lover.

You may guess how the confusion of a woman who had not yet the habit of adventures rendered triumph easy at such a moment: any reproach not made was counted for a grace; and the truant slave, once more handed over to her former master, was only too happy to be able to hope for pardon by resuming her former chain. The treaty of peace was ratified in a more solitary place, and the empty stage was successively filled by the other actors in almost the same fashion, and always with the same result. Each of the women, however, still thought herself alone to be in question. Their astonishment and embarrassment increased when, at suppertime, the three couples were united; but confusion reached its height when Prévan, reappearing in their midst, had the cruelty to make his excuses to the three faithless ones, which, by revealing their secret, told them completely to what a point they had been fooled.

However, they went to table, and soon afterward countenances cleared; the men gave themselves up, the women submitted. All had hatred in their hearts; but the conversation was nonetheless tender: gaiety aroused desire, which, in its turn, lent to gaiety fresh charm. This astounding orgy lasted until morning; and, when they separated, the women had thought to be pardoned: but the men, who had retained their resentment, made on the following morning a rupture which was never healed; and, not content with leaving their fickle mistresses, they sealed their vengeance by making their adventure public. Since that time one has gone into a convent, and the two other languish in exile on their estates.

That is the story of Prévan; it is for you to say whether you wish to add to his glory, and tie yourself to his car of triumph. Your letter has really given me some anxiety, and I await impatiently a more prudent and clearer reply to the last I wrote you.

Adieu, my fair friend; distrust those queer or amusing ideas which too easily seduce you. Remember that, in the career which you are leading, wit alone does not suffice; one single imprudence becomes an irremediable ill. In short, allow a prudent friendship to be sometimes the guide of your pleasures.

Adieu. I love you nevertheless, just as much as though you were reasonable.

At the Château de . . . , 18th September, 17★★.

80. The Chevalier Danceny to Cécile Volanges

Cécile, my dear Cécile, when will the time come for us to meet again? How shall I learn to live afar from you? Who will give me the courage and the strength? Never, never shall I be able to support this fatal absence. Each day adds to my unhappiness: and there is no term to look forward to!

Valmont, who had promised me help and consolation, Valmont neglects and, perhaps, forgets me! He is near the object of his love; he forgets what one feels when one is parted from it. When forwarding your last letter to me, he did not write to me. It is he, however, who should tell me when, and by what means, I shall be able to see you. Has he nothing then to tell me? You yourself do not speak of it to me; could it be that you do not participate in my desire? Ah, Cécile, Cécile, I am very unhappy! I love you more than ever: but this love which makes the charm of my life becomes its torture.

No, I can no longer live thus; I must see you, I must, were it only for a moment. When I rise, I say to myself: I shall not see her. I lie down saying: I have not seen her. . . . The long, long days contain no moment of happiness. All is privation, regret, despair; and all these ills come to me from the source whence I expected every pleasure! Add to these mortal pains my anxiety about yours, and you will have an idea of my situation. I think of you uninterruptedly, and never without dismay. If I see you afflicted, unhappy, I suffer for all your sorrows; if I see you calm and consoled, my own are redoubled. Everywhere I find unhappiness.

Ah, how different it was from this, when you dwelt in the same places as I did! All was pleasure then. The certainty of seeing you embellished even the moments of absence; the time which had to be passed away from you brought you nearer to me as it glided away. The use I made of it was never unknown to you. If I fulfilled my duties, they rendered me more worthy of you; if I cultivated any talent, I hoped the more to please you. Even when the distractions of the world carried me far away from you, I was not parted from you. At the playhouse I sought to divine what would have pleased you; a concert reminded me of your talents and our sweet occupations. In company, on my walks, I seized upon the slightest resemblance. I compared you with all; everywhere you had the advantage. Every moment of the day was marked by fresh homage, and every evening I brought the tribute of it to your feet.

Nowadays, what remains to me? Dolorous regrets, eternal privations, and a faint hope that Valmont's silence may be broken, that yours shall be changed to inquietude. Ten leagues alone divide us, and that distance, so easy to traverse, becomes to me alone an insurmountable obstacle! And when I implore my friend, my mistress, to help me to overcome it, both remain cold and unmoved! Far from aiding me, they do not even reply.

What has become then of the active friendship of Valmont? What, above all, has become of your tender sentiments, which made you so ingenious in discovering the means of our daily meetings? Sometimes, I remember, without ceasing to desire them, I found myself compelled to forego them for considerations, duties; what did you not say to me then? With how many pretexts did you not combat my reasons? And let me remind you, my Cécile, my reasons always gave way to your wishes. I do not make a merit of it; it has not even that of sacrifice. What you desired to obtain I was burning to bestow. But now I ask in my turn; and what is the request? To see you for a moment, to renew to you and to receive a vow of eternal love. Does that no longer make your happiness as it makes mine? I thrust aside that despairing idea, which would set the crown upon my ills. You love me, you will always love me, I believe it, I am sure of it, I will never doubt it: but my situation is frightful, and I cannot endure it much longer. Adieu, Cécile.

Paris, 18th September, 17★★.

81. The Marquise de Merteuil to the Vicomte de Valmont

How your fears excite my pity! How they prove to me my superiority over you! And you want to teach me, to be my guide? Ah, my poor Valmont, what a distance there is between you and me! No, all the pride of your sex would not suffice to bridge over the gulf which separates us. Because you could not execute my projects, you judge them impossible! Proud and weak being, it well becomes you to seek to weigh my means and judge of my resources! In truth, Vicomte, your counsels have put me in an ill humor, and I will not conceal it from you.

That, to mask your incredible stupidity with your Présidente, you should blazon out to me, as a triumph, the fact of your having for a moment put out of countenance this woman who is timid and who loves you: I agree to that; of having obtained a look, a single look: I smile, and grant it you. That, feeling, in spite of yourself, the poor value of your conduct, you should hope to distract my attention from it by gratifying me with the story of your sublime effort to bring together two children who are both burning to see one another, and who, I may mention by the way, owe to me alone the ardor of their desire: I grant you that also. That, finally, you should feel authorized by these brilliant achievements to write to me, in doctorial tones, *that it is better to employ one's time in carrying out one's projects than in describing them:* such vanity does me no harm, and I forgive it. But that you could believe that I had need of your prudence, that I should lose my way unless I deferred to your advice, that I ought to sacrifice to it a pleasure or a whim: in truth, Vicomte, that is indeed to plume yourself over much on the confidence which I am quite willing to place in you!

And, pray, what have you done that I have not surpassed a thousand times? You have seduced, ruined even, very many women: but what difficulties have you had to overcome? What obstacles to surmount? What merit lies therein that is really your own? A handsome face, the pure result of chance; graces, which habit almost always brings; wit, in truth: but jargon would supply its place at need; a praiseworthy impudence, perhaps due solely to the ease of your first successes; if I am not mistaken, these are your means, for, as for the celebrity you have succeeded in acquiring, you will not ask me, I suppose, to count for much the art of giving birth to a scandal or seizing the opportunity of one.

As for prudence, *finesse,* I do not speak of myself: but where is the woman who has not more than you? Why, your Présidente leads you like a child!

Believe me, Vicomte, it is rarely one acquires qualities which can be dispensed with. Fighting without risk, you are bound to act without precaution. For you men, a defeat is but one success the less. In so unequal a match, we are fortunate if we do not lose, as it is your misfortune if you do not win. Even were I to grant you as many talents as ourselves, by how many should we not still need to surpass you, from the necessity we are under to make a perpetual use of them!

Supposing, I admit, that you brought as much skill to the task of conquering us as we show in defending ourselves or in yielding, you will at least agree that it becomes useless to you after your success. Absorbed solely in your new fancy, you abandon yourself to it without fear, without reserve: it is not to you that its duration is important.

In fact, those bonds reciprocally given and received, to talk love's jargon, you alone can tighten or break at your will: we are even lucky if, in your wantonness, preferring mystery to noise, you are satisfied with a humiliating desertion, without making the idol of yesterday the victim of tomorrow.

But when an unfortunate woman has once felt the weight of her chain, what risks she has to run, if she endeavors to shake it off, or tries but to lighten it! It is only with trembling that she can attempt to dismiss from her the man whom her heart repulses with violence. Does he insist on remaining, she must yield to fear what she had granted to love:

Her arms are open still; her heart is shut.

Her prudence must skillfully unravel those same bonds which you would have broken. At the mercy of her enemy, if he be without generosity, she is without resources: and how can she hope generosity from him when, although he is sometimes praised for having it, he is never blamed for lacking it?

Doubtless, you will not deny these truths, which are so evident as to have become trivial. If, however, you have seen me, disposing of opinions and events, making these formidable men the toys of my fantasy and my caprice, depriving some of the power, some of the will to hurt me; if I have known, turn by turn, according to my fickle fancy, how to attach to my service or drive far away from me

These unthroned tyrants that are now my slaves,[1]

if in the midst of these frequent revolutions my reputation has still remained

---

[1] We are unaware whether this line, "*These unthroned tyrants that are now my slaves,*" as well as that which occurs above, "*Her arms are open still; her heart is shut,*" are quotations from little-known works, or part of the prose of Madame de Merteuil. What would lead us to believe the latter is the number of faults of this nature which are found in all the letters of this correspondence. Those of the Chevalier Danceny form the only exception: perhaps, as he sometimes occupied himself with poetry, his more practiced ear rendered it easier for him to avoid this fault.

pure; ought you not to have concluded that, being born to avenge my sex and to dominate yours, I had devised methods previously unknown?

Oh! keep your advice and your fears for those delirious women who call themselves *sentimental;* whose exalted imagination would make one believe that nature has placed their senses in their heads; who, having never reflected, persist in confounding love with the lover; who, in their mad illusion, believe that he with whom they have pursued pleasure is its sole depository; and, truly superstitious, show the priest the respect and faith which is only due to the divinity. Be still more afraid for those who, their vanity being larger than their prudence, do not know, at need, how to consent to being abandoned. Tremble, above all, for those women, active in their indolence, whom you call *women of sensibility,* and over whom love takes hold so easily and with such power; who feel the need of being occupied with it, even when they are not enjoying it; and, giving themselves up unreservedly to the fermentation of their ideas, bring forth from them those letters so sweet, but so dangerous to write, and are not afraid to confide these proofs of their weakness to the object which causes it: imprudent ones, who do not know how to discern in their present lover their enemy to be.

But what have I in common with these unreflecting women? When have you ever seen me depart from the rules I have laid down, or be false to my principles? I say my principles, and I say so. designedly; for they are not, like those of other women, the result of chance, received without scrutiny, and followed out of habit; they are the fruit of my profound reflections; I have created them, and I may say that I am my own handiwork.

Entering the world at a time when, still a girl, I was compelled by my condition to be silent and inert, I knew how to profit by that in order to observe and reflect. While I was thought heedless or inattentive, and, in truth, listened little to the remarks that they were careful to make to me, I carefully gathered up those which they sought to hide from me.

This useful curiosity, while serving to instruct me, also taught me dissimulation; often forced to conceal the objects of my attention from the eyes of those who surrounded me, I sought to direct my own whither I desired; I learned then how to assume at will that remote look which you have so often praised. Encouraged by this first success, I tried to govern equally the different movements of my face. Did I experience some vexation, I studied to assume an air of serenity, even of joy; I have carried my zeal so far as to inflict voluntary pain on myself, in order to seek, at that time, an expression of pleasure. I labored, with the same care and greater difficulty, to repress the symptoms of unexpected joy. It was thus that I gained that command over my physiognomy at which I have sometimes seen you so astonished.

I was very young still, and almost without interest: my thoughts were all that I had, and I was indignant that these should be stolen from me or surprised against my will. Armed with these first weapons, I tried to use them; not satisfied with not letting my real self be manifest, I amused myself by showing myself under different forms. Sure of my gestures, I kept a watch upon my speech; I regulated both according to circumstances, or even merely according to my whim; from that moment the color of my thought was my secret, and I never revealed more of it than it was useful for me to show.

This labor spent upon myself had fixed my attention on the expression of faces and the character of physiognomy; and I thus gained that penetrating glance to which experience, indeed, has taught me not to trust entirely, but which, on the whole, has rarely deceived me. I was not fifteen years old, I possessed already the talents to which the greater part of our politicians owe their reputation, and I was as yet only at the rudiments of the science which I wished to acquire. You may well imagine that, like all young girls, I sought to find out about love and its pleasures; but having never been to the convent, having no confidential friend, and being watched by a vigilant mother, I had only vague notions, which I could not fix; even nature, which later I had, assuredly, no reason to do aught but praise, as yet afforded me no hint. One might have said that it was working in silence at the perfection of its handiwork. My head alone was in a ferment; I did not desire enjoyment, I wanted to know: the desire for information suggested to me the means.

I felt that the only man with whom I could speak on this matter without compromising myself was my confessor. I took my course at once; I surmounted my slight feeling of shame; and vaunting myself for a sin which I had not committed, I accused myself of having done *all that women do*. That was my expression; but, in speaking so, I did not know, in truth, what idea I was expressing. My hope was not altogether deceived, nor entirely fulfilled; the fear of betraying myself prevented me from enlightening myself: but the good father represented the ill as so great that I concluded the pleasure to be extreme; and to the desire of knowing it the desire of tasting it succeeded.

I do not know whither this desire would have led me; and, devoid of experience as I was at that time, perhaps a single opportunity would have ruined me: luckily for me, my mother informed me, a few days later, that I was to be married; the certainty of knowing extinguished my curiosity at once, and I came a virgin to the arms of M. de Merteuil.

I waited with calmness for the moment which was to enlighten me, and I had need of reflection, in order to exhibit embarrassment and fear. The first night, of which ordinarily one entertains an idea so painful or so sweet, presented itself to me only as an occasion of experience: pain and pleasure, I observed all carefully, and saw in these different sensations only facts upon which to reflect and meditate. This form of study soon succeeded in pleasing me: but, faithful to my principles, and feeling by instinct perhaps that no one ought to be farther from my confidence than my husband, I resolved to appear the more impassive in his eyes, the more sensible I really was. This apparent coldness was subsequently the impregnable foundation of his blind confidence; on fruitful reflection, I joined to it the mischievous air which my age justified; and he never thought me more of a child than when I was tricking him most.

Meanwhile, I will admit, I, at first, let myself be dragged into the vortex of society, and gave myself up completely to its futile distractions. But, after some months, M. de Merteuil having taken me to his dismal country estate, the dread of *ennui* revived the taste for study in me: and as I found myself there surrounded by people whose distance from me put me out of the reach of all suspicion, I profited by it to give a vaster field to my experience. It was there especially that I assured myself that love, which they vaunt to us as the cause of our pleasures, is, at the most, only the pretext for them.

The illness of M. de Merteuil came to interrupt these sweet occupations; it was necessary to follow him to Town, where he went to seek for aid. He died, as you know, shortly afterward; and although, considering all things, I had no complaint to make against him, I had, nonetheless, a lively feeling of the value of the liberty which my widowhood would give me, and I promised myself to take advantage of it. My mother calculated on my entering a convent, or returning to live with her. I refused to take either course, and all I granted to decency, was to go back to the same country estate, where there were still some observations left for me to make.

I supplemented these with the help of reading: but do not imagine it was all of the kind you suppose. I studied our manners in novels, our opinions in the philosophers; I even went to the most severe moralists to see what they expected from us; and I thus made sure of what one could do, of what one ought to think, and of how one must appear. My mind once settled upon these three matters, the last alone presented any difficulties in its execution; I hoped to overcome them, and I meditated on the means.

I began to grow tired of my rustic pleasures, which were not varied enough for my active brain; I felt the need of coquetry, which should reunite me to love, not in order that I might really feel it, but to feign and inspire it. In vain had I been told, and had I read, that one could not feign this sentiment; I saw that, to succeed there, it sufficed to join the talent of a comedian to an author's wit. I exercised myself in both kinds, and, perhaps, with some success: but, instead of seeking the vain applause of the theatre, I resolved to employ for my happiness that which so many others sacrificed to vanity.

A year passed in these different occupations. My mourning then allowing me to reappear, I returned to Town with my great projects; I was not prepared for the first obstacle which I encountered.

My long solitude and austere retreat had covered me with a veneer of prudery which frightened our *beaux;* they kept their distance, and left me at the mercy of a crowd of tedious fellows, who all were aspirants for my hand. The embarrassment did not lie in refusing them; but many of these refusals displeased my family, and in these internal disputes I lost the time of which I had promised myself to make such charming use. I was obliged, then, in order to recall some and drive away the others, to display certain inconsistencies, and to take as much pains in damaging my reputation as I had thought to take in preserving it. I succeeded easily, as you may believe: but, being carried away by no passion, I only did what I thought necessary, and measured out my doses of indiscretion with caution.

As soon as I had touched the goal which I would attain, I retraced my steps, and gave the honor of my amendment to some of those women who, being impotent as far as any pretensions to charm are concerned, fall back on those of merit and virtue. This was a move which was of more value to me than I had hoped. These grateful duennas set themselves up as my apologists; and their blind zeal for what they called their work was carried to such an extent that, at the least reflection which might be made on me, the whole party of prudes cried scandal and outrage. The same method procured me also the suffrages of the women with pretensions, who, being persuaded that I had renounced the thought of following the same career as theirs, selected me as a subject for their praise, each time they wished to prove that they did not speak ill of all the world.

Meanwhile, my previous conduct had brought back the lovers; and to compromise between them and the unfaithful women who had become my patronesses, I passed as a woman of sensibility, but of rigor, whom the excess of her delicacy furnished with arms against love.

I then began to display upon the great stage the talents which had been given me. My first care was to acquire the reputation of being invincible. To attain it, the men who did not please me were always the only ones whose homage I had the air of accepting. I employed them usefully to obtain for me the honors of resistance, while to the preferred lover I abandoned myself without fear. But the latter, my pretended shyness never permitted to follow me in the world; and the gaze of society has thus been always fixed on the unhappy lover.

You know with what rapidity I choose: it is because I have observed that it is nearly always the previous attentions which disclose a woman's secret. Whatever one may do, the tone is never the same before and after success. This difference does not escape the attentive observer; and I have found it less dangerous to be deceived in my choice than to let that choice be penetrated. I gain here again by removing probabilities, by which alone we can be judged.

These precautions and that of never writing, of never giving any proof of my defeat, might appear excessive, and to me have ever appeared insufficient. I have looked into my own heart, I have studied in it the heart of others. I saw there that there is nobody who does not keep a secret there which it is of importance to him should not be divulged: a truth which antiquity seems to have known better than we, and of which the history of Samson might be no more than an ingenious symbol. Like a new Delilah, I have always employed my power in surprising this important secret. Ah, of how many of our modern Samsons have not the locks fallen beneath my shears? And these, I have ceased to fear them; they are the only ones whom I have sometimes permitted myself to humiliate. More supple with the others, the art of rendering them unfaithful lest I should appear to them fickle, a feint of friendship, an appearance of confidence, a few generous measures, the flattering notion, which each one retains, of having been my only lover, have secured me their discretion. Finally, when these methods failed me, foreseeing the rupture, I knew how to crush in advance, beneath ridicule or calumny, the credence which these dangerous men could have obtained.

All this which I tell you you have seen me practice unceasingly; and you doubt of my prudence! Ah, indeed! recall to mind the time when you paid me your first attentions: no homage was ever more flattering to me; I desired you before I had ever seen you. Seduced by your reputation, it seemed to me that you were wanting to my glory; I burned with a desire for a hand-to-hand combat with you. It is the only one of my fancies which ever had a moment's empire over me. However, if you had wished to destroy me, what means would you have found? Empty talk which leaves no trace behind it, which your very reputation would have helped to render suspect, and a tissue of improbable facts, the sincere relation of which would have had the air of a badly conceived novel. It is true, since that time, I have handed you over all my secrets: but you know what interests unite us, and that, if it be one of us, it is not I who can be taxed with imprudence.[1]

Since I have started off to render account to you, I will do it precisely. I hear you tell me now that I am at any rate at the mercy of my cham-

---

[1] It will appear, in letter the hundred and fifty-second, not what M. de Valmont's secret was, but more or less of what nature it was; and the Reader will see that we have not been able to enlighten him further on the subject.

bermaid; in fact, if she is not in the secret of my sentiments, she is of my actions. When you spoke of it to me once before, I answered that I was sure of her; and my proof that this reply was sufficient then for your tranquillity is that you have since confided to her mighty dangerous secrets of your own. But, now that you have taken umbrage at Prévan, and that your head is turned, I doubt whether you will believe me anymore on my word. I must therefore edify you.

In the first place, the girl is my foster sister, and this bond, which does not seem one to us, is not without force among people of her condition: in addition, I have her secret and better still, the victim of a love madness, she was ruined, if I had not saved her. Her parents, bristling with honor, would be satisfied by nothing less than her imprisonment. They applied to me. I saw at a glance how useful their anger might be made to me. I seconded them and solicited the order, which I obtained. Then, suddenly turning to the side of clemency, to which I persuaded her parents, and profiting by my influence with the old minister, I made them all consent to make me the depositary of this order, free to stay it or demand its execution, according to the judgment I should form of the girl's future conduct. She knows, then, that I have her lot within my hands; and if, to assume the impossible, these potent reasons should not prevent her, is it not evident that the revelation of her conduct and her authentic punishment would soon deprive her language of all credit?

To these precautions, which I call fundamental, are joined a thousand others, local or occasional, which habit and reflection allow me to find at need; of which the details would be tedious, although their practice is important; and which you must take the trouble to pick out from the general view of my conduct, if you would succeed in knowing them.

But to pretend that I have been at so much pains, and am not to cull the fruit of them; that, after having raised myself, by my arduous labors, so high above other women, I am to consent to grope along, like them, betwixt imprudence and timidity; that, above all, I should fear any man to such an extent as to see no other salvation than in flight? No, Vicomte, never! I must conquer or perish. As for Prévan, I wish to have him, and I shall have him; he wishes to tell of it, and he shall not tell of it: that, in two words, is our little romance. Adieu.

Paris, 20th September, 17★★.

82. Cécile Volanges to the Chevalier Danceny

Ah, God, what pain your letter gave me! I need well have felt such impatience to receive it! I hoped to find in it consolation, and here am I more afflicted than I was ere I received it. I shed many tears when I read it: it is not that with which I reproach you; I have already wept many

times because of you, without its being painful to me. But this time, it is
not the same thing.

What is it that you wish to say, pray? that your love is grown a torment
to you, that you cannot longer live thus, nor any more support your situation? Do you mean that you are going to cease to love me, because it
is not so agreeable as it used to be? It seems to me that I am no happier
than you are, quite the contrary; and yet I only love you the more for
that. If M. de Valmont has not written to you, it is not my fault; I could
not beg him to, because I have not been alone with him, and we have
agreed that we would never speak before people: and that again is for
your sake, so that he can the sooner do what you desire. I do not say that
I do not desire it also, and you ought to be assured of this: but what
would you have me do? If you believe it to be so easy, please find the
means, I ask nothing better.

Do you think it is so very agreeable for me to be scolded every day by
Mamma, who once never said anything to me? Quite the contrary. Now
it is worse than if I were at the convent. I consoled myself for it, however, by reflecting that it was for you; there were even moments when I
found I was quite content; but when I see that you are vexed too, without its being in the least my fault, I have more grief than I had for all that
has hitherto happened to me.

Even merely to receive your letters is embarrassing, so that, if M. de
Valmont were not so obliging and so clever as he is, I should not know
what to do; and, as to writing to you, that is more difficult still. All the
morning I dare not, because Mamma is close by me, and she may come,
at any moment, into my room. Sometimes, I am able to, in the afternoon,
under pretense of singing or playing on the harp; even then I have to interrupt myself after every line, to let them hear I am studying. Luckily
my waiting maid sometimes grows sleepy in the evening, and I tell her
that I can quite well get to bed by myself, so that she may go away and
leave me the light. And then, I am obliged to get behind my curtain, so
that no light can be seen; and then, to listen for the least sound, so that I
can hide everything in my bed, if anyone comes. I wish you were there
to see! You would soon see that one must indeed love anyone to do it.
In short, it is quite true that I do all that I can, and I would it lay within
my power to do more.

Certainly, I do not refuse to tell you that I love you, and that I shall
always love you; I never told it you with a fuller heart, and you are
vexed! Yet you had assured me, before I said it, that that was enough
to make you happy. You cannot deny it; it is in your letters. Although
I have them no longer, I remember them as well as when I used to
read them every day. And you, because you are absent now, no longer
think the same! But perhaps this absence will not always last? Ah,

God, how unhappy I am! And it is indeed you who are the cause of
it! . . .

   With regard to your letters, I hope that you have kept those which
Mamma took from me, and which she sent back to you; a time must
come, someday, when I shall not be so restrained as at present, and you
will give them all back to me. How happy I shall be when I am able to
keep them for good, and no one can object! Now I return them to M. de
Valmont, because there would be too much danger otherwise; in spite of
that, I never give them to him without feeling a deal of pain.

   Adieu, my dear friend. I love you with all my heart. I shall love you all
my life. I hope that now you are no longer vexed, and, were I sure of it,
I should not be so myself. Write to me, as soon as you are able, for I feel
that till then I shall continue sad.

At the Château de . . . , 21st September, 17★★.

83. The Vicomte de Valmont to the Présidente de Tourvel

For mercy's sake, Madame, let us repeat that interview which was so unhappily broken! Oh, that I could complete my work of proving to you
how much I differ from the odious portrait which has been made of me;
that, above all, I could again enjoy that amiable confidence which you
began to grant me! How many are the charms with which you know
how to endow virtue! How you beautify, and render dear, every virtuous
sentiment! Ah, therein lies your fascination; it is the strongest; it is the
only one which is at once powerful and worthy of respect.

   Doubtless, it is enough to see you to desire to please you; to hear you
in company for that desire to be redoubled. But he who has the happiness of knowing you better, who can sometimes read in your soul, soon
yields to a more noble enthusiasm, and, penetrated by veneration as by
love, worships in you the image of all the virtues. Better made than another, perhaps, to love and follow them, although seduced by certain errors which had separated me from them, it is you who have brought me
back, who have caused me to feel anew all their charm: will you make a
crime of this new love of mine? Will you blame your handiwork? Would
you reproach yourself even with the interest which you might take in it?
What harm is to be feared from so pure a sentiment, and what sweetness
might there not be to taste in it?

   My love alarms you, to find it violent, unrestrained! Temper it with a
gentler love; do not disdain the empire which I offer you, from which I
swear never to escape, and which, I dare believe, would not be entirely
lost to virtue. What sacrifice could seem hard to me, once sure that your
heart could keep its price for me? Where is the man, then, who is so unhappy as not to know how to delight in the privations which he imposes

on himself, as not to prefer a word, a glance, accorded, to all the pleasures which he could steal or surprise? And you believed that I was such a man, and you feared me! Ah, why does not your happiness depend on my own! What vengeance I would take on you, by rendering you happy! But this gentle empire is no result of barren friendship; it is only due to love.

That word frightens you! And why? A more tender attachment, a stronger union, a common thought, a like happiness and a like pain, what is there in that alien to your soul? Yet love is all that! Such, at least, is the love which you inspire and I experience. It is that, above all, which, calculating without interest, knows how to appreciate actions according to their merit and not their price; it is the inexhaustible treasure of sensitive souls, and all things become precious that are done for or by it.

What, then, have these truths, so easy to grasp, so sweet to practice, that can alarm? What fear, either, can a man of sensibility cause you, to whom love permits no other happiness than your own? This is the solitary vow I make today: I will sacrifice all to fulfill it, except the sentiment by which it is inspired; and this sentiment itself, if you do but consent to share it, you shall order as you will. But let us suffer it no longer to divide us, when it should unite us. If the friendship you have offered me is not an idle word; if, as you told me yesterday, it is the sweetest sentiment known to your soul, let that be the bond between us; I will not reject it: but, being arbiter of love, let it consent to listen to it; a refusal to hear it would become an injustice, and friendship is not unjust.

A second interview will present no greater difficulty than the first: chance can again furnish the occasion; you could yourself indicate the right moment. I am willing to believe that I am wrong; would you not be better pleased to convince me than to combat me, and do you doubt my docility? If that inopportune third party had not come to interrupt us, perhaps I had already been brought round entirely to your opinion: who knows the full extent of your power?

Shall I say it to you? This invincible power, to which I abandon myself without venturing on calculation, this irresistible charm, which renders you sovereign of my thoughts as of my actions: it comes to me sometimes to fear them. Alas, perhaps it is I who should be afraid of this interview for which I ask! After it, perhaps, bound by my promises, I shall see myself compelled to consume away with a love which, I am well aware, can never be extinguished, without daring to implore your aid! Ah, Madame, for mercy's sake, do not abuse your authority! But what then! if you are to be the happier for it, if I am thereby to appear worthier of you, what pains are not alleviated by these consoling ideas! Yes, I feel it; to speak again with you is to give you stronger arms against me; it is to submit myself more entirely to your will. It is easier to defend myself against your letters; they are indeed your very utterances, but you are not there to lend them fresh strength. However, the pleasure of hearing you leads me to brave the danger: at least I shall have the pleasure of having dared everything for you, even against myself; and my sacrifices will become an homage. I am too happy to prove to you in a thousand manners, as I feel in a thousand fashions, that you are and ever will be, without excepting myself, the object dearest to my heart.

At the Château de . . . , 23rd September, 17★★.

84. The Vicomte de Valmont to Cécile Volanges

You saw how greatly the chance was against us yesterday. All day long I was unable to hand you the letter which I had for you; I know not whether I shall find it any easier today. I am afraid of compromising you, by showing more zeal than discretion; and I should never forgive myself for an imprudence which might prove so fatal to you, and cause the despair of my friend, by rendering you eternally miserable. However, I am aware of the impatience of love; I feel how painful it must be to you, in your situation, to meet with any delay in the only consolation you can know at this moment. By dint of busying myself with the means of removing the obstacles, I have found one the execution of which, if you take some pains, will be easy.

I think I have remarked that the key of the door of your chamber, which opens into the corridor, is always on your Mamma's mantelshelf. Everything would be easy with this key, you must be well aware; but in default of it, I will procure you one like it, which will serve in its stead. To succeed in this, it will be sufficient to have the other at my disposition for an hour or two. You will easily find an opportunity for taking it; and, in order that its absence may not be noticed, I enclose, in this, one of my own which is so far like it that no difference will be seen, unless they try it; this they are not likely to do. You must only take care to tie it to a faded blue ribbon, like that which is on your own.

It would be well to try and have this key by tomorrow or the day after, at breakfast time; because it will be easier for you to give it me then, and it can be returned to its place in the evening, a time when your Mamma might pay more attention to it. I shall be able to return it to you at dinnertime, if we arrange well.

You know that, when we move from the *salon* to the dining room, it is always Madame de Rosemonde who walks last. I shall give her my hand. You will only have to take some time in putting away your tapestry, or even to let something drop, so that you may remain behind: you will see then how to take the key from me, which I shall be careful to hold behind me. You must not neglect, as soon as you have taken it, to rejoin my old aunt and pay her a few attentions. If by chance you should let the key fall, do not lose your countenance; I will feign that it was done by me, and I answer for everything.

The lack of confidence your Mamma shows in you, and her harsh behavior toward you, authorize this little deception. It is, moreover, the only way to continue to receive the letters of Danceny, and to forward him yours; all others are really too dangerous and might ruin you both irretrievably: thus my prudent friendship would reproach itself, were I to employ them further.

Once having the key, there remain some precautions for us to take against the noise of door and lock; but they are very easy. You will find, beneath the same press where I placed your paper, oil and a feather. You sometimes go to your room at times when you are alone there: you must profit by it to oil the lock and hinges. The only attention you need pay is to be careful of stains which might betray you. You had better wait also until night arrives, because, if it be done with the intelligence of which you are capable, there will be no trace of it on the following morning. If, however, it should be perceived, then you must say that it is the indoor polisher. You must in this case specify the time, and even the conversation which you had with him: as, for instance, that he takes this precaution against rust with all the locks which are not in use. For you see that it would be unlikely that you should have witnessed this proceeding without asking the reason. It is these little details which give probability; and probability renders a lie without consequence, by diminishing people's desire to verify it.

After you have read this letter, I beg you to read it again and even to study it: to begin with, one should be well acquainted with what one wishes to do well; next, to assure yourself that I have omitted nothing. Little accustomed to employ *finesse* on my own account, I have no great use for it; indeed it needed nothing less than my keen friendship for Danceny, and the interest which you inspire in me, to induce me to employ these means, however innocent they may be. I hate anything which has the air of deception; that is my character. But your misfortunes have touched me to such a degree that I will attempt everything to alleviate them.

You can imagine that, with this means of communication once established between us, it will be far easier for me to procure for you the interview with Danceny which he desires. However, do not yet speak to him of all this: you would only increase his impatience, and the moment for satisfying it is not yet quite arrived. You owe it to him, I think, to calm rather than to excite him. I depend in this matter on your delicacy. Adieu, my fair pupil, for you are my pupil. Love your tutor a little, and above all be docile to him: you will be rewarded. I am occupied with your happiness; rest assured that I shall find therein my own.

> At the Château de . . . , 24th September, 17**.

85. The Marquise de Merteuil to the Vicomte de Valmont

At last you may be tranquil, and, above all, you can render me justice. Listen, and do not confound me again with other women. I have brought my adventure with Prévan to a close. *To a close!* Do you fully understand what that implies? Now you shall judge whether it is I, or he, who can vaunt himself. The story will not be as amusing as the adventure: neither would it be just that you, who have done no more than reason ill or well about the affair, should reap as much pleasure from it as I, who have given my time and labor.

In the meantime, if you have some great scheme to try, if you would attempt some enterprise in which this dangerous rival should seem to you to be feared, this is your time. He leaves the field free to you, at least for some time; perhaps, even, he will never recover from the blow I have given him.

How fortunate you are to have me for a friend! I am a benevolent fairy to you. You languish afar from the beauty who engrosses you; I say one word, and you find yourself once more at her side. You wish to revenge yourself on a woman who injures you; I point out to you the place where you have to strike, and abandon her to your tender mercies. Finally, to drive a formidable competitor from the lists, it is once more I whom you invoke, and I give heed to you. Truly, if you do not spend your life in thanking me, it means that you are an ingrate. I return to my adventure and take it up from the beginning.

The *rendezvous* made so loudly, on leaving the Opera,[1] was understood as I had hoped. Prévan repaired to it; and when the Maréchale said to him politely that she congratulated herself on seeing him twice in succession at her days, he was careful to reply that, since Tuesday night, he had cancelled a thousand engagements, in order that he might thus dispose of that evening. *À bon entendeur, salut!* As I wished, however, to know with more certainty whether I was, or was not, the veritable object of this flattering zeal, I resolved to compel the new aspirant to choose between me and his dominant passion. I declared that I should not play; and he, on his side, found a thousand pretexts for not playing, and my first triumph was over lansquenet.

I secured the Bishop of *** for my gossip; I chose him because of his intimacy with the hero of the day, to whom I wished to give every fa-

---

[1] See letter the seventy-fourth.

cility to approach me. I was contented also to have a respectable witness, who could, at need, depose to my behavior and my language. This arrangement was successful.

After the vague and customary remarks, Prévan, having soon made himself the leader of the conversation, tried different tones in turn, in order to discover which was likely to please me. I refused that of sentiment, as though I had no faith in it; I stopped, by my seriousness, his gaiety, which seemed to me too frivolous for a *début;* he fell back upon delicate friendship; and it was beneath this well-worn flag that we began our reciprocal attack.

At suppertime, the Bishop did not descend; Prévan then gave me his hand, and was naturally placed by my side at table. One must be just; he maintained with much skill our private conversation, while seeming only to be occupied with the general conversation, to which he had the air of being the largest contributor. At dessert, they spoke of a new piece which was to be given on the following Monday at the *Français.* I expressed some regret that I had not my box; he offered me his own, which at first, as is the usage, I refused: to which he answered humorously enough, that I did not understand him; that certainly, he would not make the sacrifice of his box to anyone whom he did not know; but that he only let me know it was at Madame la Maréchale's disposal. She lent herself to this pleasantry, and I accepted.

On our return to the *salon,* he asked, as you may well believe, for a place in this box; and when the Maréchale, who treats him with great kindness, promised him it, *if he were good,* he made it the occasion of one of those double-edged conversations, at which you have extolled his talent to me. Indeed, having fallen on his knees, like a submissive child, he said, under pretext of begging for her counsel and asking her opinion, he uttered many a flattering and tender thing, the application of which I could easily take to myself. Several persons having not returned to play after supper, the conversation was more general and less interesting: but our eyes spoke much. I say our eyes: I should have said his; for mine spoke but one language—that of surprise. He must have thought I was astonished, and quite absorbed in the prodigious effect which he had on me. I think I left him highly satisfied; I was no less pleased myself.

On the following Monday I was at the *Français,* as we had agreed. In spite of your literary curiosity, I can tell you nothing of the performance, except that Prévan has a marvelous talent for cajolery, and that the piece failed: that is all that I learned. I was sorry to see the evening come to an end; it had really pleased me mightily; and, in order to prolong it, I invited the Maréchale to come and sup with me: this gave me a pretext for

---

[1]See letter the seventieth.

proposing it to the amiable flatterer, who only asked the time to hasten to the Comtesse de P★★★,[1] and free himself from an engagement. This name brought back all my anger; I saw plainly that he was going to begin his confidences; I remembered your wise counsels, and promised myself . . . to proceed with the adventure; I was certain that I should cure him of this dangerous indiscretion.

Being new to my company, which was not very numerous that evening, he owed me the customary usages; thus, when we went to supper, he offered me his hand. I was malicious enough, when accepting it, to allow mine to tremble slightly, and to walk with my eyes cast down, and a quick respiration. I had the air of having a presentiment of my defeat, and of being afraid of my victor. He noticed it readily; then the traitor promptly changed his tone and aspect. He had been gallant, he became tender. It was not that his language did not remain much the same: circumstances compelled that; but his gaze had become less keen and more caressing; the inflection of his voice softer, his smile was no longer the smile of *finesse,* but of satisfaction. Finally, in his conversation, suppressing more and more the fire of his sallies, wit gave place to delicacy. I ask you, could you have done better yourself?

On my side, I grew pensive to such a point that the company was forced to perceive it; and when I was reproached for it, I was clever enough to defend myself indifferently, and to cast on Prévan a rapid, yet shy and embarrassed glance, that was to make him believe that all my fear was lest he should divine the cause of my trouble.

After supper, I profited by the moment when the good Maréchale was telling one of those stories which she is always telling, to settle myself on my ottoman, in that languorous condition which is induced by a tender *rêverie.* I was not sorry for Prévan to see me thus; in truth, he honored me with most particular attention. You may well imagine that my timid glances did not dare to seek the eyes of my conqueror: but directed toward him in a more humble fashion, they soon informed me that I was obtaining the effect which I sought to produce. I still needed to persuade him that I shared it; so that, when the Maréchale announced she was going to retire, I cried out in a faint and tender voice, "*Ah Dieu!* I was so comfortable here!" I rose, however: but, before taking leave of her, I asked her her plans, in order to have a pretext for telling her mine, and of letting her know that I should stay at home the whole of the next day but one. Upon this, we all separated.

I then started reflecting. I had no doubt but that Prévan would profit by the sort of *rendezvous* I had given him; that he would come early enough to find me alone, and that the attack would be a fierce one: but I was quite sure also that, owing to my reputation, he would not treat me with that lightness which, however little practice one has had, is only employed with women of occasion or with those who have no experience; and I foresaw a certain success, if he pronounced the word love, above all, if he had the pretension of obtaining it from me.

How convenient it is to have dealings with you *people of principles!* Sometimes a clumsy lover disconcerts us by his bashfulness or embarrasses us with his fiery transports; it is a fever which, like the other, has its chills and ardors, and sometimes varies in its symptoms. But the even tenor of your way is so easily divined!

The arrival, the aspect, the tone, the language: I knew it all the day before.

I will not report our conversation to you, then; you will easily supply it for yourself. Only remark that, in my feigned defense, I aided him with all my power: embarrassment, to give him time to speak; sorry reasons, that he might combat them; distrust and fear, to revive his protestations; and that perpetual refrain on his side of *I ask you only for a word;* and the silence on mine, which seemed but to delay him in order to make him desire the more: during all that, a hand seized a hundred times, a hand always withdrawn yet never refused. One might pass a whole day thus; we passed a mortal hour: we should be there, perhaps, still, if we had not heard a carriage entering my courtyard. This fortunate occurrence naturally rendered his entreaties livelier; and I, seeing the moment arrive when I was out of danger of any surprise, prepared myself by a long sigh, and granted him the precious word. The visitor was announced, and soon afterward, I was surrounded by a numerous circle.

Prévan begged to be allowed to come on the following morning, and I consented: but, careful to defend myself, I ordered my waiting maid to remain all through the time of this visit in my bedchamber, whence, you know, one can see all that passes in my dressing room, and it was there that I received him. Free in our conversation and having both the same desire, we were soon in agreement: but it was necessary to get rid of this inopportune spectator; it was for that I was waiting.

Then, painting an imaginative picture of my home life, I persuaded him without difficulty that we should never find a moment's liberty, and that he must consider as a sort of miracle that which we had enjoyed yesterday, and even that contained too great a risk for me to expose myself to, since at any moment someone might enter my *salon.* I did not fail to add that all these usages were established, because, until that day, they had never interfered with me; and I insisted at the same time upon the impossibility of changing them without compromising myself in the eyes of my household. He attempted sadness, assumed ill humor, told me that I had little love; and you can guess how much all that touched me! But, wishing to strike the decisive blow, I summoned tears to my aid. It was precisely the *Zaïre, you are weeping.* The empire which he thought to have gained over me, and the hope he had conceived of compassing my ruin at his will, stood him in good stead for all the love of Orosmane.

This dramatic scene accomplished, we returned to our arrangements. The day being out of the question, we turned our attention to the night: but my Swiss became an insurmountable obstacle, and I would not permit any attempt to bribe him. He suggested the wicket gate of my garden; but this I had foreseen, and I invented a dog who, although calm and silent enough by day, became a real demon at night. The ease with which I entered into all these details was well fitted to embolden him. Thus he went on to propose the most ridiculous of expedients to me, and it was this which I accepted.

To begin with, his servant was as trusty as himself: in this he did not lie to me; the one was quite as little so as the other. I was to give a great supper at my house; he was to be there, and was to select a moment when he could leave alone. The cunning confidant would call his carriage, open the door, while he, Prévan, instead of entering it, would slip adroitly on one side. In no way could his coachman perceive this; so that, while everybody believed him to have left, he had really remained with me; the question remained whether he could reach my apartment. I confess that, at first, I had some difficulty in finding reasons against this project weak enough for him to be able to destroy; he answered me with instances. To hear him, nothing was more ordinary than this method; he himself had often employed it; it was even that one which he used the most, as being the least dangerous.

Subjugated by these irrefutable authorities, I admitted with candor that I had a private staircase which led to the near neighborhood of my *boudoir;* that I could leave the key of it, and it was possible for him to shut himself in there and wait, without undue risk, until my women had retired; and then, to give more probability to my consent, the moment after I was unwilling: I only relented on the condition of a perfect docility, of a propriety—oh, a propriety! In short I was quite willing to prove my love to him, but not so much to gratify his own.

The exit, of which I was forgetting to tell you, was to be made by the wicket gate of my garden; it was only a matter of waiting for daybreak, when the Cerberus would not utter a sound. Not a soul passes at that hour, and people are in the soundest slumber. If you are astonished at this heap of sorry reasons, it is because you forget our reciprocal situation. What need had we of better ones? He asked nothing better than for the thing to be known, and as for me, I was quite certain that it should not be known. The next day but one was the day fixed.

You will notice that there is the affair settled, and that no one has yet seen Prévan in my society. I meet him at supper at the house of one of my friends, he offers her his box for a new piece, and I accept a place in it. I invite this woman to supper, during the piece and before Prévan; I can hardly avoid inviting him to be of the party. He accepts, and pays me two days later the visit exacted by custom. 'Tis true, he comes to see me on the morning of the next day: but besides the fact that morning visits no longer count, it only rests with me to find this one too free; and in fact I put him in the category of persons less intimate with me, by a written invitation to a supper of ceremony. I can well cry, with Annette: "*Albeit that is all!*"

The fatal day having come, the day on which I was to lose my virtue and my reputation, I gave my instructions to the faithful Victoire, and she executed them as you will presently see. In the meantime, evening arrived. I had already a great company with me, when Prévan was announced. I received him with a marked politeness, which testified to the slightness of my acquaintance with him; and I put him by the side of the Maréchale, as being the person through whom I had made it. The evening produced nothing but a very short note, which the discreet lover found a means of giving me, and which, according to my custom, I burned. It informed me that I could trust him; and this essential word was surrounded by all the parasitical words, such as love, happiness, etc., which never fail to appear at such a festival.

By midnight, the rubbers being over, I proposed a short medley.[1] I had the double design of favoring Prévan's escape, and at the same time of causing it to be noticed; that could not fail to happen, considering his reputation as a gamester. I was not sorry, either, that it might be remembered, if need were, that I had not been in a hurry to be left alone. The game lasted longer than I had thought. The devil tempted me, and I was succumbing to my desire to console the impatient prisoner. I was thus rushing on to my ruin, when I reflected that, once having quite surrendered, I should not have sufficient control over him to keep him in the costume of decency which my plans required. I had the strength to resist. I retraced my steps, and returned, not without some ill humor, to resume my place at the eternal game. It finished, however, and everyone left. As for me, I rang for my women, undressed very rapidly, and sent them also away.

Can you see me, Vicomte, in my light toilette, walking with timid and circumspect steps and trembling hand to open the door to my conqueror? He saw me; lightning is not more prompt. What shall I say to you? I was vanquished, quite vanquished, before I could say one word to arrest him or defend myself. He then wanted to take a convenient posi-

---

[1]Some persons may not, perhaps, be aware that a medley (*macédoine*) is a succession of sundry different games of chance, among which each player has a right to choose when it is his turn to deal. It is one of the inventions of the century.

tion and one more suitable to the circumstances. He cursed his finery which, he said, kept him aloof from me; he would combat me with equal arms: but my extreme timidity was opposed to this project, and my soft caresses did not leave him time. He was occupied with other things.

His rights were redoubled, his pretensions were renewed; but then: "Listen to me," I said; "you will have thus far a merry story enough to tell the two Comtesses de P★★★, and a thousand others; but I am curious to know how you will relate the end of the adventure." Speaking thus, I rang the bell with all my strength. For the nonce it was my turn, and my action was quicker than his speech. He had only stammered out something, when I heard Victoire running up and calling the servants, whom she had kept near her, as I had ordered. Then, assuming my queenly tone, raising my voice: "Leave me, Monsieur," I went on, "and never come into my presence again." Whereupon a crowd of my people entered.

Poor Prévan lost his head, and, fancying an ambush in what was at bottom no more than a joke, he betook himself to his sword. It did him no good, for my *valet-de-chambre,* who is brave and active, caught him round the body and hurled him to the ground. I was in a mortal fright, I vow. I cried to them to cease, and bade them let his retreat go unmolested, so long as they made certain that he was gone. My men obeyed me: but there was great commotion among them; they were indignant that anyone should have dared to fail in respect toward *their virtuous mistress.* They all accompanied the unfortunate Chevalier, noisily and with the scandal which I desired. Victoire only stayed behind, and we occupied ourselves during this interval in repairing the disorder of my bed.

My household returned in the same state of commotion; and I, *still upset by my emotion,* asked them by what lucky chance they happened to be not yet gone to bed. Victoire then related to me how she had asked two women friends to supper, how they had sat up with her, and, in short, all that we had together agreed upon. I thanked them all, and let them retire, bidding one of them, however, to go immediately and summon my physician. It seemed to me that I was justified in fearing ill effects from *my mortal fright;* and it was a sure means of giving wind and celebrity to the news. He came in effect, condoled with me mightily, and prescribed repose. In addition, I bade Victoire go abroad early in the morning and gossip in the neighborhood.

Everything succeeded so well that, before noon, and as soon as I was awake, my pious neighbor was already at my bedside, to know the truth and the details of this terrible adventure. I was obliged to moan with her for an hour over the corruption of the age. A moment later, I received from the Maréchale the note which I enclose. Finally, about five o'clock,

---

[1]The commanding officer of the regiment to which Prévan belonged.

to my great astonishment, Monsieur ★★★ arrived.[1] He came, he told me, to bring his excuses that an officer of his regiment should have been so grossly wanting in respect. He had only heard of it at dinner, at the Maréchale's, and had immediately sent word to Prévan to consider himself under arrest. I asked for his pardon, and he refused it me. I then thought that, as an accomplice, I ought to dispatch myself on my side, and at least keep myself under strict guard. I caused my door to be shut, and word to be given that I was indisposed.

'Tis to my solitude that you owe this long letter! I shall write one to Madame de Volanges, which she will be sure to read aloud, and from which you will hear this story as it is to be told. I forgot to tell you that Belleroche is enraged, and absolutely wants to fight Prévan. The poor fellow! Luckily I shall have time to calm his head. In the meantime, I am going to repose my own, which is tired with writing. Adieu, Vicomte.

Paris, 25th September, 17★★.

86. The Maréchale de ★★★ to the Marquise de Merteuil
(A NOTE ENCLOSED IN THE PRECEDING ONE)

Ah, heaven! what do I hear, my dear Madame? Is it possible that that little Prévan should commit such abominations? And to you above all! What is one not exposed to! One is no longer safe in one's own house! Truly such events console one for being old. But that for which I shall never console myself is that I have been partly the cause of your receiving such a monster at your house. I promise you that, if what I am told is true, he shall never more set foot within my doors; that is the course which all nice persons will adopt toward him, if they do their duty.

I am told that you have been quite ill, and I am anxious about your health. Give me, I pray you, your precious news, or send by one of your women, if you cannot come yourself. I only ask a word to reassure me. I should have hastened to you this morning, had it not been for my baths, which my doctor will not allow me to interrupt; and I must go to Versailles this afternoon, always on my nephew's business.

Adieu, dear Madame; count upon my sincere friendship for life.

Paris, September 25th, 17★★.

87. The Marquise de Merteuil to Madame de Volanges

I write to you from my bed, my dear, kind friend. The most disagreeable event, and the most impossible to have foreseen, has made me ill with fright and annoyance. It is, assuredly, not because I have aught to reproach myself with; but it is always so painful for a virtuous woman, who retains the modesty which becomes her sex, to have public attention drawn upon her that I would give anything in the world to have been able to avoid this unhappy adventure; and I am still uncertain whether I may not decide to go to the country and wait until it be forgotten. This is the affair I allude to.

I met at the Maréchale de ★★★'s a certain M. de Prévan, whom you are sure to know by name, and whom I knew in no other way. But, meeting him at such a house, I was, it seems to me, quite justified in believing him to be of good society. He is well enough made personally, and seemed to me not lacking in wit. Chance and the tedium of play left me the only woman alone with him and the Bishop of ★★★, the rest of the company being occupied with lansquenet. The three of us conversed together till suppertime. At the table, a new piece, of which there was some talk, gave him the occasion to offer his box to the Maréchale, who accepted it; and it was arranged that I should have a place in it. It was for Monday last at the *Français*. As the Maréchale was coming to sup with me at the close of the performance, I proposed to this gentleman to accompany her, and he came. Two days later he paid me a visit, which passed with the customary compliments, and without the occurrence of anything marked. On the following day, he came to see me in the morning, and this appeared to me a trifle bold; but I thought that, instead of making him feel this by my fashion of receiving him, it were better to remind him, by a politeness, that we were not yet on so intimate a footing as he seemed to imply. To this end I sent him that same day a very dry and very ceremonious invitation for a supper that I was giving the day before yesterday. I did not speak four words to him all the evening; and he, on his side, retired as soon as his game was finished. You will admit that thus far nothing has less the air of leading up to an adventure: after the other games, we played a medley which lasted till nearly two o'clock, and finally I went to bed.

It must have been a mortal half hour at least after my women had retired, when I heard a noise in my room. I opened my curtains with much alarm, and saw a man enter by the door which leads into my *boudoir*. I uttered a piercing cry; and I recognized, by the light of my night-light, this M. de Prévan, who, with inconceivable effrontery, told me not to alarm myself; that he would enlighten me as to the mystery of his conduct; and that he begged me not to make any noise. Thus speaking, he lit a candle; I was so confounded that I could not speak. His tranquil and assured air petrified me, I think, even more. But he had not said two words, when I saw what this pretended mystery was; and my only reply, as you will believe, was to clutch my bell rope. By an incredible piece of good fortune, all my household had been sitting up with one of my women, and were not yet in bed. My chambermaid, who, on coming to me, heard me speaking with much heat, was alarmed, and summoned all this company. You can imagine what a scandal! My people were furious; there was a moment when I thought my *valet-de-chambre* would kill Prévan. I confess that, at the moment, I was quite relieved to find myself in force: on reflection today, I should have found it preferable if only my chambermaid had come; she would have sufficed, and I should, perhaps, have escaped all this noise which afflicts me.

In place of that, the tumult awoke the neighbors, the household talked, and it is the gossip of all Paris since yesterday. M. de Prévan is in prison by order of the commanding officer of his regiment, who had the courtesy to call upon me to offer me his excuses, he said. This arrest will still further augment the noise, but I could not obtain that it should be otherwise. The Town and the Court have been to inscribe their names at my door, which I have closed to everyone. The few persons I have seen tell me that justice is rendered me, and that public indignation against Prévan is at its height: assuredly, he well merits it, but that does not detract from the disagreeables of this adventure. Moreover, the man has certainly some friends; and his friends are bound to be mischievous; who knows, who can tell what they will invent to my injury? Ah, Lord! how unfortunate to be a young woman! She has done nothing yet, when she has put herself out of the reach of slander; she has need even to give the lie to calumny.

Write me, I beg of you, what you would have done, what you would do in my place; in short, all your thought. It is always from you that I receive the sweetest consolation and the most prudent counsel; it is from you also that I love best to receive it.

Adieu, my dear and kind friend; you know the sentiments which forever attach me to you. I embrace your amiable daughter.

Paris, 26th September, 17**.

Part III

88. Cécile Volanges to the Vicomte de Valmont

In spite of all the pleasure that I take, Monsieur, in the letters of M. le Chevalier Danceny, and although I am no less desirous than he is that we might be able to see one another again without hindrance, I have not, however, dared to do what you suggest to me.

In the first place, it is too dangerous; this key, which you want me to put in the other's place, is like enough to it, in truth; but not so much so, however, that the difference is not to be seen, and Mamma looks at and takes notice of everything. Again, although it has not yet been made use of since we have been here, there needs but a mischance; and, if it was to be perceived, I should be lost for ever. And then, it seems to me too that it would be very wrong; to make a duplicate key like that: it is going very far! It is true that it is you who would be kind enough to undertake it; but in spite of that, if it became known, I should, nonetheless, have to bear the blame and the odium, since it would be for me that you had done it. Lastly, I have twice tried to take it, and certainly it would be easy enough if it were anything else: but I do not know why, I always started trembling, and have never had the courage. I think then we had better stay as we are.

If you continue to have the kindness to be as complaisant as hitherto, you will easily find a means of giving me a letter. Even with the last, but for the ill chance which made you suddenly turn round at a certain moment, we should have been quite secure. I can quite feel that you cannot, like myself, be thinking only of that; but I would rather have more patience and not risk so much. I am sure that M. Danceny would speak as I do: for, every time that he wanted something which caused me too much pain, he always consented that it should not be.

I will give you back, Monsieur, at the same time as this letter, your own, that of M. Danceny, and your key. I am nonetheless grateful for all your kindnesses, and I beseech you to continue them. It is very true that

I am most unhappy, and without you I should be even more so; but, after all, she is my mother; I must needs have patience. And provided that M. Danceny goes on loving me, and you do not abandon me, perhaps a happier time will come.

I have the honor to be, Monsieur, with much gratitude, your most humble and obedient servant.

At the Château de . . . , 26th September, 17★★.

89. The Vicomte de Valmont to the Chevalier Danceny

If your affairs do not always advance as quickly as you could wish, my friend, it is not entirely me whom you must blame. I have more than one obstacle to overcome here. The vigilance and severity of Madame de Volanges are not the only ones; your young friend also throws some in my way. Whether from coldness or timidity, she does not always do as I advise her; and I think, nonetheless, that I know better than she what must be done.

I had found a sure, convenient and simple means of giving her your letters, and even of facilitating, subsequently, the interviews which you desire: but I could not persuade her to employ it. I am all the more distressed at this, as I cannot see any other means of bringing you together; and as, even with your correspondence, I am constantly afraid of compromising us all three. Now you may imagine that I am no more anxious to run that risk myself than to expose either of you to it.

I should be truly grieved, however, if your little friend's lack of confidence were to prevent me from being useful to you; perhaps, you would do well to write to her on the subject. Consider what you want to do, it is for you alone to decide; for it is not enough to serve one's friends, one must also serve them in their own manner. This might also be one means the more to assure yourself of her sentiments toward you; for the woman who keeps a will of her own does not love as much as she says.

'Tis not that I suspect your mistress of inconstancy: but she is very young; she has a great fear of her Mamma, who, as you know, only seeks to injure you; and perhaps it would be dangerous to stay too long without occupying her with you. Do not, however, render yourself unduly anxious by what I tell you. I have at bottom no reason for distrust; it is entirely the solicitude of friendship.

I do not write to you at greater length, because I too have certain affairs of my own. I am not as far advanced as you, but I am as fond; that is a consoling thought; and, even if I should not succeed for myself, if I succeed in being useful to you, I shall consider that my time has been well employed. Adieu, my friend.

At the Château de . . . , 26th September, 17★★.

90. The Présidente de Tourvel to the Vicomte de Valmont

I am greatly desirous, Monsieur, that this letter should not cause you any distress; or that, if it must do so, it may be at least softened by that which I experience in writing to you. You must know me well enough by this time to be well assured that it is not my wish to grieve you; but neither would you wish, doubtless, to plunge me into eternal despair. I conjure you then, in the name of the tender friendship which I have promised you, in the name, even, of the sentiments, perhaps more vivid, but assuredly not more sincere, which you have for me: let us cease to see one another; depart; and, in the meantime, let us shun all those private and too perilous interviews in which, forced by some inconceivable power, though I never succeed in saying what I wish to say to you, I pass my time in listening to what I never ought to hear.

Only yesterday, when you came to join me in the park, my sole intention was to tell you that which I am writing to you today; and yet, what did I do, but occupy myself with your love—your love—to which I am bound never to respond! Ah, for pity's sake remove yourself from me!

Do not think that absence will ever alter my sentiments for you: how shall I ever succeed in overcoming them, when I have no longer the courage to combat them? You see, I tell you all; I fear less to confess my weakness than to succumb to it: but that control which I have lost over my feelings I shall retain over my actions; yes, I shall retain it, I am resolved, be it at the cost of my life.

Alas! the time is not far distant when I believed myself very sure of never having such struggles to undergo. I congratulated myself, I vaunted myself for this, perhaps overmuch. Heaven has punished, cruelly punished this pride: but, full of mercy, at the very moment when it strikes us it forewarns me again before a fall; and I should be doubly guilty if I continued to fail in prudence, warned as I am already that I have no more strength.

You have told me a hundred times that you would have none of a happiness purchased by my tears. Ah! let us speak no more of happiness, but leave me to regain some calm.

In acceding to my request, what fresh rights do you not acquire over my heart? And from those rights, founded upon virtue, I shall have no need to defend myself. What pleasure I shall take in my gratitude! I shall owe you the sweetness of tasting without remorse a delicious sentiment. At present, on the contrary, terrified by my sentiments, by my thoughts, I am equally afraid of occupying myself with either you or myself; the very idea of you alarms me: when I cannot escape from it, I combat it; I do not drive it from me, but I repel it.

Is it not better for both of us to put a stop to this state of trouble and anxiety? Oh, you, whose ever sensitive soul, even in the midst of its errors, has continued the friend of virtue, you will respect my painful situation, you will not reject my prayer! A sweeter, but not less tender interest will succeed to these violent agitations: then, breathing again through your benevolence, I shall cherish existence, and shall say, in the joy of my heart: This calm, I owe it to my friend.

In causing you to undergo a few deprivations, which I do not impose upon you, but which I beg of you, will you think you are buying the end of my torments at too dear a price? Ah! if, to make you happy, I had but to consent to unhappiness, you may believe me, I would not hesitate for a moment. . . . But to become guilty! . . . No, my friend, no; rather would I die a thousand deaths. Already, assailed by shame, on the eve of remorse, I dread both others and myself; I blush in the midst of company, and tremble in solitude; I lead only a life of pain; I shall have no peace unless you consent. My most praiseworthy resolutions do not suffice to reassure me; I formed this one yesterday, and yet I have passed the night in tears.

Behold your friend, she whom you love, suppliant and confused, begging you for innocence and repose. Ah, God! But for you, would she ever have been reduced to so humiliating a request? I reproach you with nothing; I feel too strongly, myself, how difficult it is to resist an imperious sentiment. A complaint is not a reproach. Do, out of generosity, what I do from duty; and to all the sentiments which you have inspired in me, I will add that of eternal gratitude. Adieu, Monsieur, adieu.

At the Château de . . . , 27th September, 17**.

91. The Vicomte de Valmont to the Présidente de Tourvel

In consternation at your letter, Madame, I am still ignorant as to how I can reply to it. Doubtless, if I needs must choose between your unhappiness and my own, it is for me to sacrifice myself, and I do not hesitate: but such important interests deserve, so it seems to me, to be, before all, investigated and discussed, and how can that be contrived, if we are to speak and see each other no more?

What! while the sweetest of sentiments unite us, shall an empty fear suffice to separate us, perhaps beyond return! In vain shall tender friendship and ardent love reclaim their rights: their voice shall not be heard: and why? What then is this pressing danger which besets you? Ah, believe me, such fears so lightly conceived are already, it seems to me, potent enough reasons for security.

Permit me to tell you that I find here traces of the unfavorable impressions that have been given you about me. One does not tremble before the man one esteems; one does not, above all, drive away him whom one has judged worthy of a certain friendship: it is the dangerous man whom one dreads and shuns.

Who, however, was ever more respectful and submissive than myself? Already, you may observe, I am circumspect in my language; I no longer permit myself those names so sweet, so dear to my heart, which it never ceases to give you in secret. It is no longer the faithful and unhappy lover, receiving the counsels and the consolations of a tender and sensitive friend; it is the accused before his judge, the slave before his master. Doubtless these new titles impose new duties; I pledge myself to fulfill them all. Listen to me, and, if you condemn me, I obey the verdict and I go. I promise more: do you prefer the tyranny which judges without a hearing? Do you feel you possess the courage to be unjust? Command, and I will still obey.

But this judgment, or this command, let me hear it from your own lips. And why, you will ask me in your turn. Ah, if you put this question, how little you know of love and of my heart! Is it nothing then to see you once again? Nay, when you shall have brought despair into my soul, perhaps one consoling glance will prevent me from succumbing to it. In short, if I must needs renounce the love, and the friendship, for which alone I exist, at least you shall see your work, and your pity will abide with me; even if I do not merit this slight favor, I am prepared, methinks, to pay dearly for the hope of obtaining it.

What! you are going to drive me from you! You consent, then, to our becoming strangers to one another! What am I saying? You desire it; and although you assure me that absence will not alter your sentiments, you do but urge my departure, in order to work more easily at their destruction. You speak already of replacing them by gratitude. Thus, the sentiment which an unknown would obtain from you for the most trivial service, or even your enemy for ceasing to injure you—this is what you offer to me! And you wish my heart to be satisfied with this! Interrogate your own; if your lover, if your friend came one day to talk to you of their gratitude, would you not say to them with indignation: Depart from me, you are ingrates?

I come to a stop, and beseech your indulgence. Pardon the expression of a grief to which you have given birth; it will not detract from my complete submission. But I conjure you, in my turn, in the name of those sweet sentiments which you yourself invoke, do not refuse to hear me; and in pity, at least, for the mortal distress in which you have plunged me, do not defer the moment long. Adieu, Madame.

At the Château de . . . , 27th September, 17★★.

92. The Chevalier Danceny to the Vicomte de Valmont

O my friend! your letter has made my blood run cold for fright. Cécile
. . . O God! is it possible? Cécile no longer loves me. Yes, I see this dire-
ful truth, through the veil in which your friendship covers it. You wished
to prepare me for the receipt of this mortal blow; I thank you for your
pains; but can one impose on love? It is ever in advance of all that interests it: it does not hear of its fate, it divines it. I have no more doubt of
mine: speak to me without concealment, you may do so, and I beg this
of you. Inform me of everything; what gave rise to your suspicions, what
has confirmed them? The least details are precious. Endeavor above all
to recall her words. One word in place of another can change a whole
sentence; the same word often bears two meanings. . . . You may have
been deceived: alas, I seek to beguile myself still! What did she say to
you? Does she make me any reproach? At least, does she not defend herself for her faults? I might have foreseen this change, from the difficulties
which she raises lately about everything. Love is not acquainted with so
many obstacles.

What course ought I to adopt? What do you counsel me? If I attempted to see her! Is that utterly impossible? Absence is so cruel, so dismal . . . and she has rejected a means of seeing me! You do not tell me
what it was; if there was in truth too much danger, she knows well that
I am unwilling for her to run too much risk. But I also know your prudence; so to my misfortune I cannot but believe in it! What am I to do
now? How write to her! If I let her see my suspicions, they will, perhaps,
grieve her; and, if they are unjust, could I pardon myself for having distressed her? To hide them from her is to deceive her, and I know not
how to dissimulate with her.

Oh, if she could only know what I suffer, my pain would move her! I
know her sensibility; she has an excellent heart, and I have a thousand
proofs of her love. Too much timidity, some embarrassment: she is so
young! And her mother treats her with such severity! I will write to her;
I will restrain myself; I will only beg her to leave herself entirely in your
hands. Even if she should still refuse, she can at least not take offence at
my prayer; and perhaps she will consent.

To you, my friend, to you I make a thousand excuses, both for her
and for myself. I assure you that she feels the value of your efforts, that
she is grateful for them. It is timidity, not distrust. Be indulgent; it is the
finest quality in friendship. Yours is very precious to me, and I know
not how to acknowledge all that you do for me. Adieu, I will write at
once.

I feel all my fears return: who would have told me that it should ever
cost me an effort to write to her! Alas, only yesterday it was my sweet-

est pleasure! Adieu, my friend, continue your cares for me, and pity me mightily.

Paris, 27th September, 17★★.

93. The Chevalier Danceny to Cécile Volanges
(ENCLOSED IN THE PRECEDING)

I cannot conceal from you how grieved I have been to hear from Valmont of the scant confidence you continue to place in him. You are not ignorant that he is my friend, that he is the only person who can bring us together once more: I had thought that these titles would be sufficient with you; I see with pain that I have made a mistake. May I hope that at least you will inform me of your motives? Will you again find fresh difficulties which will prevent you? I cannot, however, without your help, penetrate the mystery of this conduct. I dare not suspect your love; doubtless you too would not venture to betray mine. Ah! Cécile! . . .

Is it true then that you have rejected a means of seeing me? A *simple, convenient* and *sure* means?[1] And is it thus that you love me? An absence so short had indeed changed your sentiments. But why deceive me? Why tell me that you love me always, that you love me more? Your Mamma, in destroying your love, has she also destroyed your sincerity? If she has at least left you some pity, you will not learn without sorrow the fearful tortures which you cause me. Ah! I should suffer less were I to die.

Tell me then, is your heart closed to me beyond recall? Have you utterly forgotten me? Thanks to your refusals, I know not either when you will hear my complaints, nor when you will reply to them. Valmont's friendship had assured our correspondence: but you, you have not wished it; you found it irksome; you preferred it to be infrequent. No, I shall believe no more in love, in good faith. Nay, whom can I believe, if my Cécile has deceived me?

Answer me then: is it true that you no longer love me? No, that is not possible; you are under an illusion; you belie your heart. A passing fear, a moment of discouragement, which love has soon caused to vanish: is it not true, my Cécile? Ah, doubtless; and I was wrong to accuse you. How happy I should be to be proved wrong! How I should love to make you tender excuses, to repair this moment of injustice with an eternity of love!

Cécile, Cécile, have pity on me! Consent to see me, employ for that every means! Look upon the effects of absence! Fears, suspicions, perhaps even coldness! A single look, a single word, and we shall be happy. But what! Can I still talk of happiness? Perhaps it is lost to me, lost for ever. Tortured by fear, cruelly buffeted between unjust suspicions and the most

---

[1]Danceny is ignorant of what this means was; he merely repeats Valmont's expression.

cruel truth, I cannot stay in any one thought; I only maintain existence to love you and to suffer. Ah, Cécile, you alone have the right to make it dear to me; and I expect, from the first word that you will utter, the return of happiness or the certainty of an eternal despair.

Paris, 27th September, 17★★.

94. Cécile Volanges to the Chevalier Danceny

I can gather nothing from your letter, except the pain it causes me. What has M. de Valmont written to you, then, and what can have led you to believe that I no longer loved you? That would be, perhaps, far happier for me, for I should certainly be less tormented; and it is very hard, when I love you as I do, to find that you always believe that I am wrong, and that, instead of consoling me, it is from you always that I receive the hurts which give me most pain. You believe I am deceiving you, and am telling you what is not the truth; it is a pretty notion you have of me! But, if I were to be as deceitful as you reproach me with being, what interest should I have? Assuredly, if I loved you no longer, I should only have to say so, and everybody would praise me; but unhappily it is stronger than I; and it must needs be for some one who feels no obligation to me for it at all!

What have I done, pray, to make you so vexed? I did not dare to take a key, because I was afraid that Mamma would perceive it, and that it would cause me more trouble, and you too on my account, and again because it seems to me a bad action. But it was only M. de Valmont who had spoken to me of it; I could not know whether you wished it or no, since you knew nothing about it. Now I know that you desire it, do I refuse to take this key? I will take it tomorrow; and then we shall see what more you will have to say.

It is very well for M. de Valmont to be your friend; I think I love you at least as well as he can: and yet it is always he who is right, and I am always wrong. I assure you I am very angry. That is quite the same to you, because you know that I am quickly appeased: but, now that I shall have the key, I shall be able to see you when I want to; and I assure you that I shall not want to, when you act like this. I would rather have the grief that comes from myself, than that it came from you: you see what you are ready to cause.

If you liked, how we would love each other! And, at least, we should only know the troubles that are caused us by others! I assure you that, if I were mistress, you would never have any complaint to make against me: but if you do not believe me, we shall always be very unhappy, and it will not be my fault. I hope we shall soon be able to meet, and that then we shall have no further occasion to fret as at present.

If I had been able to foresee this, I would have taken the key at once; but, truly, I thought I was doing right. Do not be angry with me then, I beg you. Do not be sad any more, and love me always as well as I love you; then I shall be quite happy. Adieu, my dear love.

At the Château de . . . , 28th September, 17★★.

95. Cécile Volanges to the Vicomte de Valmont

I beg you, Monsieur, to be so kind as to return me the key which you gave me to put in the place of the other; since everybody wishes it, I must needs consent also.

I do not know why you wrote to M. Danceny that I no longer loved him: I do not believe I have ever given you reason to think so; and it has caused him a great deal of pain, and me too. I am quite aware that you are his friend; but that is not a reason for vexing him, nor me either. You would give me great pleasure by telling him to the contrary the next time you write to him, and that you are sure of it; for it is in you that he has the most confidence; and for me, when I have said a thing, and am not believed, I do not know what to do.

As for the key, you can be quite easy; I well remember all that you recommended me in your letter. However, if you still have it, and would like to give it me at the same time, I promise I will pay great attention to it. If it could be tomorrow as we go to dinner, I would give you the other key the day after tomorrow, at breakfast, and you could give it back to me in the same manner as the first. I should be very pleased if it does not take long, because there will be less time for the danger of Mamma's seeing it.

Again, when once you have that key, you will be very kind to make use of it to take my letters also; and, in that way, M. Danceny will more often receive news of me. It is true that it will be much more convenient than it is at present; but at first it frightened me too much: I beg you to excuse me, and I hope you will nonetheless continue to be as obliging as in the past. I shall always be very grateful to you.

I have the honor to be, Monsieur, your most humble and obedient servant.

At the Château de . . . , 28th September, 17★★.

96. The Vicomte de Valmont to the Marquise de Merteuil

I will wager that since your adventure, you have been daily expecting my compliments and praises; I doubt not even that you feel a trifle out of humor at my long silence: but what do you expect? I have always thought that, when one has naught but praise to give a woman, one may be at one's ease about her, and occupy oneself with other matters. However, I thank you on my own account and congratulate you on yours. I am even ready to make you completely happy by admitting that this time you have surpassed my expectations. After that, let us see if, on my side, I have come up to yours, at least in part.

It is not of Madame de Tourvel that I want to talk to you; her too laggard progress, I know, displeases you. You only love accomplished facts. Spun-out scenes weary you; for my part I had never tasted such pleasure as I find in these feigned delays. Yes, I love to see, to watch this prudent woman, engaged, without her perceiving it, on a course which admits of no return, whose rapid and dangerous declivity carries her on in spite of herself and forces her to follow me. Then, terrified at the danger she runs, she would fain halt, but cannot hold herself in. Her skill and caution can indeed shorten her steps; yet they must inevitably succeed one another. Sometimes, not daring to behold the danger, she shuts her eyes and, letting herself go, abandons herself to my care. More often, a fresh alarm reanimates her efforts: in her mortal terror she would attempt once more to turn back; she wastes her strength in painfully overcoming a short distance; and soon a magic power replaces her nearer to that danger which she had vainly sought to fly. Then, having only me for guide and support, with no more thought to reproach me for an inevitable fall, she implores me to retard it. Fervent prayers, humble supplications, all that mortals in their terror offer to the divinity—it is I who receive them from her; and you would have me, deaf to her entreaties, and myself destroying the cult which she pays me, employ, to precipitate her, the power which she invokes for her support! Ah, leave me at least the time to observe those touching combats between love and virtue.

How then! Do you think that the same spectacle which makes you run eagerly to the theater, which you applaud there with fury, is less engrossing in real life? Those sentiments of a pure and tender soul which dreads the happiness which it desires, and never ceases to defend itself even when it ceases to resist, you listen to with enthusiasm; should they be valueless only to him who has called them forth? That, however, is the delicious enjoyment which this heavenly woman offers me daily; and you reproach me for relishing its sweetness! Ah, the time will come only too soon when, degraded by her fall, she will be to me no more than an ordinary woman.

But, in talking of her to you, I forget that I did not want to talk to you of her. I do not know what power constrains me, drags me back to her ceaselessly, even when I outrage her. Away with her dangerous idea; let me become myself again to treat a gayer subject. It concerns your pupil, who is now become my own, and I hope that here you will recognize me.

Some days ago, being better treated by my gentle Puritan, and in consequence less engrossed by her, I remarked that the little Volanges was, in fact, extremely pretty, and, that if there was folly in being in love with her, like Danceny, there was, perhaps, no less on my part in not seeking from her a distraction rendered necessary by my solitude. It seemed to me just, moreover, to repay myself for the care I was giving her: I reminded myself as well that you had offered her to me, before Danceny had any pretensions; and I considered myself justified in claiming certain rights on a property which he only possessed because I had refused and relinquished it. The little person's pretty face, her fresh mouth, her infantile air, her very *gaucherie,* fortified these sage resolutions; I consequently resolved on action, and my enterprise has been crowned by success.

You must be already wondering by what means I have so soon supplanted the favored lover; what form of seduction befits such youth and such inexperience. Spare yourself the trouble; I employed none at all. Whereas you, wielding skilfully the weapons of your sex, triumph by subtlety, I, rendering his imprescriptible rights to man, subjugated by authority. Sure of my prey if I could get within reach of it, I only required a ruse to approach her; and even that which I employed barely merits the name.

I profited by the first letter which I received from Danceny for his fair; and, after having let her know of it by the concerted signal, instead of employing my skill to get it into her hands, I used it to find a lack of means to do so: the impatience to which this gave rise I feigned to share; and, after having caused the ill, I pointed out the remedy.

The young person occupies a chamber one door of which opens into the corridor; but, naturally, the mother had taken away the key. It was merely a question of obtaining possession of this. Nothing more easy of execution; I only asked to have it at my disposal for two hours, and I answered for the procural of one similar to it. Then, correspondence, interviews, nocturnal *rendezvous*—everything became easy and safe: however, would you believe it? The timid child took alarm and refused. Another man would have been in despair; for my part, I only saw there the occasion for a more piquant pleasure. I wrote to Danceny to complain of this refusal, and I did it so well that our blockhead had no peace until he had obtained from his timorous mistress, and even urged her, that she should grant my request and so surrender herself utterly to my discretion.

I was mighty pleased, I confess, at having thus changed the *rôles,* and induced the young man to do for me what he calculated I should do for him. This notion doubled, in my eyes, the value of the adventure: thus, as soon as I had the precious key, I hastened to make use of it; this was last night.

After assuring myself that all was quiet in the *château,* armed with my dark lantern, and in the costume, befitting the hour, which the circumstance demanded, I paid my first visit to your pupil. I had caused all preparations to be made (and that by herself) to permit of a noiseless entrance. She was in her first sleep, the sleep of her age; so that I reached her bedside before she had awakened. At first I was tempted to go even farther, and try to pass for a dream; but, fearing the effects of surprise and the noise which it entails, I preferred to awake the lovely sleeper with precautions, and did in fact succeed in preventing the cry which I feared.

After calming her first fears, as I had not come there for conversation, I risked a few liberties. Doubtless she has not been well taught at her convent to how many varied perils timid innocence is exposed, and all that it has to guard if it would not be surprised; for, devoting all her attention, all her strength, to defending herself from a kiss, which was only a feigned attack, she left all the rest without defense; who could fail to draw profit from it! I changed my tactics accordingly, and promptly took the position. Here we both alike had thought ourselves to be lost: the little girl, in a mighty scare, tried to cry out in good earnest; luckily her voice was drowned by tears. She had thrown herself upon the bell rope; but my adroitness restrained her arm in time.

"What would you do," I asked her then; "ruin yourself utterly? Let anyone come: what does it matter to me? Whom will you persuade that I am not here with your consent? Who else but you can have furnished me with the means of entering? And this key, which I have obtained from you, which I could only obtain from you—will you undertake to explain its use?"

This short harangue calmed neither her grief nor her anger; but it brought about her submission. I know not if I had the accents of eloquence; it is true, at any rate, that I had not its gestures. With one hand employed in force, the other in love, what orator could pretend to grace in such a situation? If you rightly imagine it, you will admit that at least it was favorable to the attack: but, as for me, I have no head at all; and, as you say, the most simple woman, a schoolgirl, can lead me like a child.

This one, while still in high dudgeon, felt that she must adopt some course, and enter into a compromise. As prayers found me inexorable, she had to resort to bargaining. You think I sold the important post dearly: no, I promised everything for a kiss. It is true that, the kiss once obtained, I did not keep my promise: but I had good reasons. Had we agreed whether it was to be taken or given? By dint of bargaining, we fell into an agreement over the second; and this one, it was said, was to be received. Then, guiding her timid arms round my body, and pressing her more amorously with one of mine, the soft kiss was effectually received; nay excellently, nay perfectly received: so much so, indeed, that love itself could have done no better. Such good faith deserved a reward;

thus I at once granted her request. My hand was withdrawn; but I know not by what chance I found myself in its place. You will suppose me then mighty eager, energetic, will you not? By no means. I have acquired a taste for delay, I have told you. Once sure of arriving, why take the journey with such haste? Seriously, I was mighty pleased to observe once more the power of opportunity, and I found it here devoid of all extraneous aid. It had love to fight against, however, and love sustained by modesty and shame, and above all, fortified by the temper which I had excited, and which had much effect. It was opportunity alone; but it was there, always offered, always present, and love was absent.

To verify my observations, I was cunning enough to employ no more force than could be resisted. Only, if my charming enemy, abusing my good nature, seemed inclined to escape me, I constrained her by that same fear whose happy effects I had just experienced. Well, well! without any other further trouble, the languishing fair, forgetful of her vows, began by yielding and ended by consenting: not that, after this first moment, there was not a return of mingled reproaches and tears; I am uncertain whether they were real or feigned; but, as ever happens, they ceased as soon as I busied myself in giving cause for them anew. Finally, from frailty to reproach, and reproach to frailty, we separated, well satisfied with one another, and equally agreed on the *rendezvous* tonight.

I did not retire to my own room until the break of day, and I was exhausted with fatigue and sleepiness: however, I sacrificed both to my desire to be present at breakfast this morning; I have a passion for watching faces on the day after. You can have no idea of this one. There was an embarrassment in the attitude! a difficulty in the gait! eyes always lowered, and so big, and so heavy! The face so round was elongated! Nothing could have been more amusing. And, for the first time, her mother, alarmed at this extreme alteration, displayed a most tender interest in her! And the Présidente too, who was very busy about her! Ah, those attentions of hers are only lent; a day will come when she will need them herself, and that day is not far distant. Adieu, my lovely friend.

At the Château de . . . , 1st October, 17**.

97. Cécile Volanges to Madame de Merteuil

Oh, my God, Madame, I am in such distress! I am so unhappy! Who will console me in my trouble? Who will advise me in the embarrassment in which I am? That M. de Valmont . . . and Danceny! No, the idea of Danceny fills me with despair. . . . How can I tell you? How can I relate it? I do not know what to do. However, my heart is full. . . . I must speak to someone, and you are the only one whom I can, whom I dare confide in. You have shown me so much kindness! But do not have any for me now, I am not worthy of it: what shall I say? I do not wish it. Everybody here has shown an interest in me today . . . they have all increased my grief. I felt so much that I did not deserve it! Oh, scold me on the contrary; scold me well, for I am very guilty: but afterward save me; if you have not the goodness to advise me, I shall die of grief.

Listen then . . . my hand trembles, as you see, I can hardly write, I can feel my face is all on fire. . . . Oh, it is indeed the blush of shame. Ah well, I will endure it; it will be the first punishment for my fault. Yes, I will tell you all.

You must know then, that M. de Valmont, who has hitherto always handed me M. Danceny's letters, suddenly found it was too difficult; he wanted to have a key to my chamber. I can truly assure you that I did not want this: but he went so far as to write to Danceny, and Danceny also wished it; and as for me, it gives me so much pain to refuse him anything, especially since my absence, which makes him so unhappy, that I ended by consenting. I never foresaw the misfortune which it would lead to.

Yesterday, M. de Valmont made use of this key to come into my room when I was asleep; I was so little prepared for this, that he frightened me very much when he awoke me: but as he spoke to me at once, I recognized his voice, and did not cry out; and then the idea came to me at first that he had come, perhaps, to bring me a letter from Danceny. It was very far from that. A moment afterward, he tried to kiss me; and while I defended myself, as was natural, he contrived to do what I would not have suffered for the whole world . . . but he would have a kiss first. It had to be done, for what was there to do? All the more, as I had tried to call out; but, in addition to my not being able, he was careful to tell me that, if anyone came, he would know how to put all the blame on me; and, indeed, it was very easy, because of the key. Then he still refused to retire. He wanted a second one; and this one, I do not know how it was, but it quite confused me; and afterward, it was even worse than before. Oh! indeed this is dreadful. In short, after . . . you will surely excuse me from telling the rest: but I am as unhappy as anyone can be.

What I reproach myself with the most, and of which I must nevertheless speak to you, is that I am afraid I did not resist as much as I might have. I do not know how it happened. I certainly do not love M. de Valmont, quite the contrary; and there were moments when it was just as though I loved him. . . . You can imagine that did not prevent me from always saying no to him: but I felt sure that I did not act as I spoke, and that was in spite of myself; and then again, I was mightily confused! If it is always as difficult as that to resist, one ought to be well accustomed to it! It is true that M. de Valmont has a way of saying things to which one does not know how to answer. At last, would you believe it, when he went away, it was as though I was sorry; and I was weak enough to consent to his returning this evening: that distresses me more even than all the rest.

Oh! in spite of it, I promise you truly that I will prevent him from coming. He had hardly gone away, before I felt how very wrong I had been in promising him. I wept too all the rest of the time. It is about Danceny, especially, that I am so grieved! Every time I thought of him, my tears flowed so fast that I was suffocated, and I did nothing but think of him . . . and now again, you see the result; here is my paper all soaked. No, I shall never be consoled, were it only because of him. . . . At last I was worn out, and yet I was not able to sleep one minute. And this morning, on rising, when I looked at myself in the mirror, I was frightened, so much had I changed.

Mamma perceived it as soon as she saw me, and asked me what was the matter. As for me, I started crying at once. I thought she was about to scold me, and, perhaps, that would have hurt me less: but on the contrary she spoke gently to me! Little did I deserve it. She told me not to grieve like that! She did not know the cause of my grief. I should make myself ill! There are moments when I should like to be dead. I could not contain myself. I threw myself sobbing into her arms, and said to her, "Oh, Mamma, your daughter is very miserable!" Mamma could not keep herself from crying a little; and all this only increased my grief. Luckily she did not ask me why I was so unhappy, for I should not have known what to tell her.

I implore you, Madame, write to me as soon as you can, and tell me what I ought to do: for I have not the courage to think of anything, and I can only grieve. Will you be so kind as to send your letter through M. de Valmont; but, if you write to him at the same time, do not, I beg you, tell him that I have said anything.

I have the honor to be, Madame, always with great affection, your most humble and obedient servant . . .

I dare not sign this letter.

At the Château de . . . , 1st October, 17▲▲.

98. Madame de Volanges to the Marquise de Merteuil

It is but a few days ago, my charming friend, that you were asking me for consolation and advice: today, it is my turn; and I make you the same request which you made to me. I am indeed in real distress, and I fear that I have not taken the best means to remove the vexations from which I suffer.

It is my daughter who is the cause of my anxiety. Since my departure I had seen she was always sad and melancholy; but I was prepared for that, and had armed my heart with the severity I judged necessary. I hoped that absence, distraction, would soon destroy a love which I looked upon rather as a childish error than as a real passion. However, far from having recovered since our sojourn here, I notice that the child abandons herself more and more to a dangerous melancholy; and I am actually afraid that her health is suffering. Particularly during the last few days, it has visibly altered. Yesterday, above all, it struck me, and everybody here was genuinely alarmed.

What proves to me, besides, how keenly she is affected is that I see her prepared to overcome the shyness she has always shown with me. Yesterday morning, at the mere question I put to her, as to whether she were ill, she threw herself into my arms, telling me that she was very miserable; and she cried till she sobbed. I cannot describe to you the pain it caused me; tears came to my eyes at once; and I had only the time to turn away, to prevent her from seeing them. Luckily I had sufficient prudence to put no questions to her, and she did not dare to tell me any more; but it is none the less clear that it is this unfortunate passion which is tormenting her.

What course am I to take, however, if it lasts? Am I to be the cause of my daughter's unhappiness? Shall I blame her for the most precious qualities of the soul, sensibility and constancy? Am I her mother only for that? And if I should stifle that so natural sentiment, which makes us desire the happiness of our children; if I should regard as a weakness what I hold, on the contrary, to be the first and most sacred of all duties; if I force her choice, shall I not have to answer for the disastrous consequences which may ensue? What a use to make of maternal authority, to give my daughter a choice between unhappiness and sin!

My friend, I shall not imitate what I have so often blamed. Doubtless, I might try to make a choice for my daughter; I did, in that, but aid her with my experience; it was not a right which I exercised, but a duty which I fulfilled. I should betray one, on the contrary, were I to dispose of her to the neglect of an inclination, the birth of which I have not been able to prevent, and of which neither she nor I can judge the duration or the extent. No, I will never endure that she should marry one man that she may love another; and I would rather compromise my authority than her virtue.

I think, therefore, that I shall be taking the more prudent course in retracting the promise I have given to M. de Gercourt. You have just heard my reasons for this; it seems to me they ought to outweigh my promises. I say more: in the state in which things are, to fulfill my engagement would really be to violate it. For, after all, if I owe it to my daughter not to betray her secret to M. de Gercourt, I owe it to him at least not to abuse the ignorance in which I keep him, and to do for him all that I believe he would do for himself, if he were informed. Shall I, on the contrary, betray him ignobly, when he relies on my faith, and, while he honors me by choosing me for his second mother, deceive him in the choice he wishes to make of the mother of his children? These reflections, so true, and to me irrefutable, alarm me more than I can say.

With the misfortunes which they make me dread I compare my daughter happy with the bridegroom her heart has chosen, knowing her duties only from the sweetness which she finds in fulfilling them; my son-in-law equally contented and congratulating himself each day upon his choice; neither of them finding happiness save in the happiness of the other, and in that of cooperating to augment my own. Ought the hope of so sweet a future to be sacrificed to vain considerations? And what are those which restrain me? Only interested views. Pray, what advantage will my daughter gain from being born rich, if she is, nonetheless, to be the slave of fortune?

I agree that M. de Gercourt is a better match, perhaps, than I ought to hope for my daughter; I confess, indeed, that I was extremely flattered at the choice he made of her. But, after all, Danceny is of as good a family as his; he yields no whit to him in personal qualities; he has over M. de Gercourt the advantage of loving and of being beloved: in truth, he is not rich; but has not my daughter enough for two? Ah, why ravish from her the sweet satisfaction of enriching him whom she loves!

Those marriages which one calculates instead of assorting, which one calls marriages of convenience, and which are in fact convenient in all save taste and character—are they not the most fertile source of those scandalous outbreaks which become every day more frequent? I prefer to delay; at least I shall have time to study my daughter, whom I do not know. I have, indeed, the courage to cause her a passing sorrow, if she is to gain, thereby, a more substantial happiness: but I have not the heart to risk abandoning her to eternal despair.

Those, my dear friend, are the ideas which torment me, and as to which I ask your advice. These serious topics contrast mightily with your amiable gaiety, and seem hardly fitting to your youth: but your reason has so far outgrown that! Your friendship, moreover, will assist your prudence; and I have no fear that either will be refused to the maternal solicitude which invokes them.

Adieu, my charming friend; never doubt the sincerity of my sentiments.

At the Château de . . . , 2nd October, 17**.

99. The Vicomte de Valmont to the Marquise de Merteuil

A few more small incidents, my lovely friend; but scenes merely, no more actions. Arm yourself, therefore, with patience, assume a stock of it even:

for while my Présidente advances so imperceptibly, your pupil retreats, which is worse still! Well, well! I have wit enough to amuse myself with these vexations. Truly, I am acclimatizing myself mighty well to my sojourn here; and I may say that I have not experienced a single moment of *ennui* in my old aunt's dreary *château*. In fact, do I not find here enjoyment, privation, uncertainty, and hope? What more has one upon a greater stage? Spectators? Ah, let me be, they will not be lacking! If they do not see me at work, I will show them my labor accomplished; they will only have to admire and applaud. Yes, they will applaud; for at last I can predict with certainty the moment of my austere Puritan's fall. I assisted this evening at the death struggle of virtue. Sweet frailty will now rule in its stead. I fix the time at a date no later than our next interview: but already I hear you crying out against vainglory. To announce one's victory, to boast in advance! Prithee, calm yourself! To prove my modesty, I will begin with the story of my defeat.

In very truth, your pupil is a most ridiculous little person! She is, indeed, a child, whom one should treat as such, and whom one would favor by doing no more than putting her under penance! Would you believe that, after what passed between us, the day before yesterday, after the amicable manner in which we separated yesterday morning, when I sought to return in the evening, as she had agreed, I found her door bolted on the inside? What say you to that? Such childishness one sometimes meets with on the eve: but on the morrow! Is it not amusing?

I did not, however, laugh at it at first; I had never felt so strongly the imperiousness of my character. Assuredly, I was going to this *rendezvous* without pleasure, and solely out of politeness. My own bed, of which I had great need, seemed to me, for the moment, preferable to anyone else's, and I had dragged myself from it with regret. No sooner, however, had I met with an obstacle than I burned to overcome it; I was humiliated, above all, that a child should have tricked me. I withdrew, then, in considerable ill humor; and, with the intention of concerning myself no further with this silly child and her affairs, I had written her a note, on the spur of the moment, which I intended to give her today, and in which I accounted her at her just value. But night brings counsel, as they say; methought this morning that, having no choice of distractions here, I had better keep this one: I suppressed, therefore, the severe letter. Since reflecting upon it, I wonder that I can ever have entertained the idea of concluding an adventure before holding in my hands the wherewithal to ruin the heroine. Observe, however, whither a first impulse impels us! Happy, my fair friend, is he who has trained himself, as you have, never to give way to one! In fine, I have postponed my vengeance; I have made this sacrifice to your intentions toward Gercourt.

Now that I am no longer angry, I see your pupil's conduct only in a ridiculous light. In fact, I should be glad to know what she hopes to gain thereby! As for myself, I am at a loss: if it be only to defend herself, you must admit that she is somewhat late in starting. Someday she will have to tell me herself the key to this enigma. I have a great desire to know it. It may be, perhaps, only that she found herself fatigued? Frankly, that might well be possible: for, without a doubt, she is still ignorant that the darts of love, like the lance of Achilles, bear their own remedy for the ills they cause. But nay, by the little wry face she pulled all day, I would wager that there enters into it . . . repentance . . . there . . . something . . . like virtue. . . . Virtue! It becomes her indeed to show it! Ah, let her leave it to the woman veritably born to it, to the only one who knows how to embellish it, who could make it lovable! . . . Pardon, my fair friend: but it is this very evening that there occurred between Madame de Tourvel and myself the scene of which I am about to send you an account, and I still feel some emotion at it. I have need to do myself violence, in order to distract me from the impression which it made upon me; 'tis even to aid me in this that I have sat down to write to you. Something must be pardoned to this first moment.

It is some days, already, since we are agreed, Madame de Tourvel and I, upon our sentiments; we only dispute about words. It was always, in truth, her *friendship* which responded to my *love;* but this conventional language did not change things in substance; and, had we remained thus, I should have gone, perhaps, less quickly, but not less surely. Already even there was no more question of driving me away, as she had wished at first; and as for the interviews which we have daily, if I devote my cares to offering her the occasions, she devotes her to seizing them. As it is ordinarily when walking that our little *rendezvous* occur, the shocking weather, which set in today, left me no hope; I was even really vexed by it; I did not foresee how much I was to gain from this *contretemps.*

Being unable to go out, they started play after rising from table; as I play little, and am no longer indispensable, I chose this time to go to my own room, with no other intention than to wait there until the game was likely to be over. I was on my way to rejoin the company, when I met the charming woman; she was about to enter her apartment, and, whether from imprudence or weakness, she said to me in her gentle voice, "Where are you going? There is nobody in the *salon.*" I needed no more, as you may believe, to try and enter her room; I met with less resistance than I expected. It is true that I had taken the precaution to commence the conversation at the door, and to commence it indifferently; but hardly were we settled, than I brought back the real subject, and spoke of *my love for my friend.* Her first reply, though simple, seemed to me sufficiently expressive: "Oh, I pray you," said she, "do not let us speak of that here"; and she trembled. Poor woman! She sees she is lost.

However, she was wrong to be afraid. For some time past, assured of success some day or other, and seeing that she was spending so much strength in useless struggles, I had resolved to husband my own, and to wait, without further effort, until she should surrender from lassitude. You are quite aware that here I require a complete triumph, and that I wish to owe nothing to opportunity. It was, indeed, owing to this preconceived plan, and in order to be pressing without engaging myself too far, that I came back to this word love, so obstinately declined: sure that my ardor was sufficiently believed in, I tried a tone more tender. Her refusal no longer put me out, it pained me: did not my sensitive friend owe me some consolation?

As she consoled me, withal, one hand lingered in my own, the lovely form leaned upon my arm, and we were drawn extremely near. You have surely remarked, in such a situation, how, in proportion to the weakening of the defense, entreaties and refusals pass at closer quarters; how the head is averted and the gaze cast down; while remarks, always uttered in a weak voice, become rare and intermittent. These precious symptoms announce, in no equivocal manner, the soul's consent: but it has rarely yet extended to the senses; I even hold that it is always dangerous to attempt just then any too marked assault; because, this state of self-abandonment being never without a very sweet pleasure, one knows not how to dispel it, without giving rise to a humor which is invariably in the favor of the defense.

But, in the present case, prudence was all the more necessary to me in that I had, above all, to dread the alarm which this forgetfulness of herself could not fail to induce in my gentle dreamer. Thus, this avowal which I demanded, I did not even require that it should be pronounced; a glance would suffice; only one glance, and I was happy.

My lovely friend, her fine eyes were, in fact, raised to mine; her celestial mouth even uttered, "Well yes, I . . ." But on a sudden her gaze was withdrawn, her voice failed, and this adorable woman fell into my arms. Hardly had I had time to receive her, when, extricating herself with convulsive force, her eyes wild, her hands raised to Heaven . . . "God . . . O my God, save me!" she cried; and at once, swifter than lightning, she was on her knees, ten paces from me. I could hear her ready to suffocate. I advanced to her assistance; but, seizing one of my hands, which she bedewed with tears, sometimes even embracing my knees: "Yes, it shall be you," she said, "it shall be you who will save me! You do not wish my death, leave me; save me; leave me; in the name of God, leave me!" And these inconsequent utterances barely escaped through her redoubled sobs. Meanwhile, she held me with a strength which did not permit me to withdraw: then, collecting my own, I raised her in my arms. At the same instant, her tears ceased; she said no more: all her limbs stiffened, and violent convulsions succeeded to this storm.

I was, I confess, deeply moved, and I believe I should have consented to her request, had not circumstances compelled me to do so. The fact remains that, after rendering her some assistance, I left her as she prayed me, and I congratulate myself on this. I have already almost received the reward.

I expected that, as on the day of my first declaration, she would not appear that evening. But, toward eight o'clock, she came down to the *salon,* and only informed the company that she had been greatly indisposed. Her face was dejected, her voice feeble, her attitude constrained; but her gaze was soft, and was often fixed upon me. Her refusal to play having even compelled me to take her place, she took up hers at my side. During supper, she remained alone in the *salon;* when we returned methought I saw that she had wept: to make certain, I told her that I feared she still felt the effects of her indisposition, to which she answered me obligingly, "The complaint does not go as quickly as it comes!" Finally, when we retired, I gave her my hand; and, at the door of her apartment, she pressed mine with vigor. 'Tis true, this movement seemed to me to have something involuntary; but so much the better; it is a proof the more of my empire.

I would wager that at present she is enchanted to have reached this stage; the cost is paid; there is nothing left but to enjoy. Perhaps, while I am writing to you, she is already occupied with this soft thought! And even if she is employed, on the contrary, on a fresh project of defense, do we not know well what becomes of all such plans? I ask you then, can it go farther than our next interview? I quite expect, by the way, that there will be some ceremony about the surrender; very good! But, once the first step taken, do these austere prudes ever know where to stop? Their love is a veritable explosion; resistance lends it greater force. My shy Puritan would run after me, if I ceased to run after her.

In short, my lovely friend, I shall on an early day be with you, to claim fulfillment of your word. You have not forgotten, doubtless, what you promised me after success: that infidelity to your Chevalier? Are you ready? For myself, I desire it as much as if we had never known each other. For the rest, to know you is perhaps a reason for desiring it more:

Justice, not courtesy, disposes me.[1]

Moreover it shall be the first infidelity I will make to my serious conquest, and I promise you to profit by the first pretext to be absent for four-and-twenty hours from her. It shall be her punishment for keeping

---

[1]Voltaire: *Nanine.*

me so long away from you. Do you know that this adventure has occupied me for more than two months? Yes, two months and three days; 'tis true that I include tomorrow, since it will not be truly consummated till then. That reminds me that Madame de B★★★ held out for three whole months. I am most pleased to see that frank coquetry possesses more power of resistance than austere virtue.

Adieu, my lovely friend; I must leave you, for it is mighty late. This letter has led me on farther than I had intended; but, as I am sending to Paris tomorrow, I was fain to profit by it to let you participate one day sooner in the joy of your friend.

At the Château de . . . , 2nd October, 17★★, in the evening.

100. The Vicomte de Valmont to the Marquise de Merteuil

My friend, I am tricked, betrayed, lost, I am in despair; Madame de Tourvel has gone. She has gone, and I did not know it! And I was not there to oppose departure, to reproach her with her unworthy treachery! Ah, do not think I would have let her leave; she would have stayed; yes, she would have stayed, if I had had to employ violence! But think! in credulous security, I slept tranquilly; I slept, and the thunderbolt has fallen upon me. No, I do not understand this departure at all; I must abandon all hope of understanding women.

When I recall the events of yesterday! What do I say? Even of yesterday night! That glance so sweet, that voice so tender, and that pressure of the hand! And all the time, she was planning flight from me! O women, women! After this, complain that you are deceived! Yes, any perfidy that one employs is a theft from your store.

What pleasure I shall take in avenging myself! I shall find her again, this perfidious woman; I shall resume my empire over her. If love sufficed to procure me the means of that, what will it not do when assisted by vengeance? I shall see her again at my knees, trembling and bathed in tears, crying for mercy with her deceitful voice; and I—I shall be pitiless.

What does she at present? What does she think? Perhaps she applauds herself for having deceived me; and, faithful to the tastes of her sex, this pleasure seems to her the sweetest. What the so greatly vaunted virtue could not obtain, the spirit of ruse has brought about without an effort. Madman that I was, I dreaded her virtue; it was her ill faith that I had to fear.

And to be obliged to swallow my resentment! To dare show no more than a gentle sorrow, when I have a heart full of rage! To see myself reduced once more to be suppliant to a rebellious woman who has escaped from my sway! Ought I to be humiliated to such a degree? And by whom? By a timid woman, who was never practiced in fight. What does it serve me to have established myself in her heart, to have scorched her with all the fires of love, to have carried the trouble of her senses to the verge of delirium, if, calm in her retreat, she can today plume herself more on her escape than I upon my victories? And should I suffer it? My friend, you do not believe it; you have no such humiliating idea of me!

But what fatality attaches me to this woman? Are there not a hundred others who desire my attentions? Will they not be eager to respond to them? Even if none were worth this one, does not the attraction of variety, the charm of fresh conquests, the pride of numbers offer pleasure sweet enough? Why run after that which eludes us, and neglect what is in our path? Ah, why? . . . I know not, but I feel it extremely.

There is no happiness or peace for me, save in the possession of this woman whom I hate and love with equal fury. I will only support my lot from the moment when I shall dispose of hers. Then, tranquil and satisfied, I shall see her in her turn given over to the storms which I experience at this moment; I will excite a thousand others more! Hope and fear, security and distrust, all the ills devised by hate, all the good that love affords, I want them to fill her heart, to succeed one another at my will. That time shall come. . . . But how many labors yet! How near I was yesterday! And how far away I see myself today! How to approach her again? I dare not take any measure; I feel that, before I adopt any course, I need greater calmness, and my blood leaps within my veins.

What enhances my torment is the calm with which everyone here replies to my questions upon this event, upon its cause, and all the extraordinary features it presents. . . . No one knows anything, no one cares to know anything: they would hardly have spoken of it, had I allowed them to speak of anything else. Madame de Rosemonde, to whom I hastened this morning when I learned the news, answered me, with the indifference of her age, that it was the natural result of the indisposition which seized Madame de Tourvel yesterday; that she had been afraid of an illness, and had preferred to be at home: she thinks it quite simple; she would have done the same, she told me: as if there could be anything in common between the two! Between her, who has only death before her, and the other, who is the charm and torment of my life!

Madame de Volanges, whom I at first suspected of being an accomplice, seems only to be affected in that she was not consulted as to the step. I am delighted, I confess, that she has not had the pleasure of harming me. That proves again that she is not in this woman's confidence to the extent I feared: that is always one enemy the less. How pleased she would be with herself, if she knew that it was I who was the cause of the flight! How swollen with pride, if it had been through her counsels! How her importance would have been enhanced! Great God, how I hate her! Oh, I will begin again with her daughter, I will mold her to my fantasy:

I think, therefore, I shall remain here for some time; at least, the little reflection I have been able to make leads me to this course.

Do you not think, in fact, that, after so marked a step, my ingrate must dread my presence? If then the idea has come to her that I might follow her, she will not fail to close her door to me; and I wish as little to accustom her to that means as to endure the humiliation. I prefer, on the contrary, to announce to her that I shall remain here; I will even make entreaties for her return; and when she is persuaded of my absence, I will appear at her house: we shall see how she supports the interview. But I must postpone it, in order to enhance the effect, and I know not yet if I have the patience; twenty times today I have opened my mouth to call for my horses. However, I will command myself; I promise to await your reply here; I only beg you, my lovely friend, not to keep me waiting for it.

The thing which would thwart me the most would be not to know what is passing; but my *chasseur,* who is in Paris, has certain rights of access to the waiting maid; he will be able to serve me. I am sending him instructions and money. I beg you to find it good that I join both to this letter, and also to be at the pains to send them to him by one of your people, with orders to place them in his own hands. I take this precaution because the rascal is in the habit of failing to receive the letters I write to him, when they command him some task which irks him. And for the moment he does not seem to me so enamored of his conquest as I could wish him to be.

Adieu, my lovely friend; if any happy idea comes to you, any means of accelerating my progress, inform me of it. I have, more than once, had experience of how useful your friendship can be to me; I experience it once again at this moment: for I feel calmer since I have written to you; at least I am speaking to some one who understands me, and not to the automata with whom I vegetate since this morning. In truth, the farther I go the more am I tempted to believe that you and I are the only people in the world who are of any consequence.

At the Château de . . . , 3rd October, 17★★.

101. The Vicomte de Valmont to Azolan, His *Chasseur*
(ENCLOSED IN THE PRECEDING)

You must be addle-pated, indeed, to start hence this morning without knowing that Madame de Tourvel was leaving also; or, if you knew, not to come and warn me. Of what use is it, pray, that you should spend my money in getting drunk with the valets; that you should pass the time which you ought to employ in my service in making yourself agreeable to the maids, if I am no better informed of what is passing? This, however, is what comes of your negligence! But I warn you, if a single instance occurs in this matter, it is the last you shall commit in my service.

I require you to keep me informed of all that happens with Madame de Tourvel: of her health; if she sleeps; if she is dull or gay; if she often goes abroad, and whom she frequents; if she receives company, and of whom it consists; how she passes her time; if she shows ill humor with her women, particularly with the one she brought here with her; what she does when she is alone; if, when she reads, she reads uninterruptedly, or often puts her reading aside to dream; and alike, when she is writing. Remember also to become the friend of him who carries her letters to the post. Offer often to do this commission for him in his stead; and if he accepts, only dispatch those which seem to you indifferent, and send me the others, above all those, if you come across any, addressed to Madame de Volanges. Make arrangements to be, for some time longer, the happy lover of your Julie. If she has another, as you believed, make her consent to a participation, and do not plume yourself on any ridiculous delicacy; you will be in the same case with many others who are worth more than you. If, however, your substitute should become too importunate; should you perceive, for instance, that he occupied Julie too much during the day, and that she was less often with her mistress, get rid of him by some means, or seek a quarrel with him: have no fear of the results, I will support you. Above all, do not quit that house. It is by assiduity that one sees all, and sees clear.

If chance even should cause one of the men to be dismissed, present yourself to seek his place, as being no longer attached to me. Say in that case that you left me to seek a quieter and more regular house. Endeavor, in short, to get yourself accepted. I shall nonetheless keep you in my service during this time: it will be as it was with the Duchesse de ★★★; and in the end Madame de Tourvel will recompense you as well.

If you had skill and zeal enough, these instructions ought to suffice; but to make up for both, I send you money. The enclosed note authorizes you, as you will see, to receive twenty-five louis from my man of business; for I have no doubt that you are without a sou. You will employ what is necessary of this sum to induce Julie to establish a correspondence with me. The rest will serve to make the household drink. Have a care that this takes place as often as possible in the lodge of the porter of the house, so that he may be glad to see you come. But do not forget that it is your services, and not your pleasures, that I wish to pay for.

Accustom Julie to observe and report everything, even what might appear to her trivial. It were better that she should write ten useless sentences than that she should omit one which was of interest; and often what appears indifferent is not so. As it is necessary that I should be informed at once, if anything were to happen which should seem to you to deserve attention, immediately on receipt of this letter you will send Philippe on the message horse to establish himself at . . . ;[1] he will remain there until further orders; it will make a relay in case of need. For the current correspondence, the post will suffice.

Be careful not to lose this letter. Read it over every day, to assure yourself that you have forgotten nothing, as well as to make sure that you still have it. In short, do all that needs to be done, when one is honored with my confidence. You know that, if I am satisfied with you, you will be so with me.

At the Château de . . . , 3rd October, 17★★.

102. The Présidente de Tourvel to Madame de Rosemonde

You will be greatly astonished, Madame, to learn that I am leaving you so precipitately. This proceeding will appear to you very extraordinary: but your surprise will be redoubled, when you learn my reasons for it! Perhaps, you will find that, in confiding them to you, I do not sufficiently respect the tranquillity necessary to your age; that I even infringe the sentiments of veneration which are your due by so many titles? Ah! Madame, forgive me: but my heart is oppressed; it feels a need to pour out its griefs upon the bosom of a friend who is as kind as she is prudent: whom else, save you, could it choose? Look upon me as your child. Show me the kindness of a mother; I implore it. Perhaps my sentiments toward yourself give me some right to expect it.

Where has the time gone when, absorbed entirely in those laudable sentiments, I was ignorant of those which, afflicting my soul with the mortal sorrow I feel, deprive me of the strength to combat them at the same time that they impose upon me the duty? Ah, this fatal visit has been my ruin! . . . What shall I say to you, in fine? I love, yes, I love to distraction. Alas! that word which I write for the first time, that word so often entreated without being ever obtained, I would pay with my life the sweet privilege of letting him who has inspired it hear it but a single time; and yet I must unceasingly withhold it. He will continue to doubt my feelings toward him; he will think he has cause to complain of them. I am indeed unhappy! Why is it not as easy for him to read in my heart as to reign there? Yes, I should suffer less, if he knew all that I suffer; but you yourself, to whom I say it, will still have but a feeble idea of it.

In a few moments, I am about to fly from him and cause him grief. While he will still believe he is near me, I shall already be far away; at the

---

[1] A village halfway between Paris and the *château* of Madame de Rosemonde.

hour when I was accustomed to see him daily, I shall be where he has never been, where I must not permit him to come. Already, all my preparations are complete, all is there beneath my eyes; I can let them rest on nothing which does not speak of this cruel separation. Everything is ready except myself . . . !

And the more my heart resists, the more does it prove to me the necessity of submission to it. Doubtless, I shall submit to it; it is better to die than to lead a life of guilt. I feel it already, I know it but too well; I have only saved my prudence, my virtue is gone. Must I confess it to you—what yet remains to me I owe to his generosity. Intoxicated with the pleasure of seeing him, of hearing him; with the sweetness of feeling him near me; with the still greater happiness of being able to make his own, I was powerless and without strength; hardly enough was left me to struggle: I had no longer enough to resist; I trembled at my danger, but could not flee it. Well! he saw my trouble and had pity on me. Could I do aught else than cherish him? I owe him far more than life.

Ah, if, by remaining near him, I had but to tremble for that, do not suppose I had ever consented to go away! What is life to me without him? Should I not be too happy to lose it? Condemned to be the cause of his eternal misery and my own; to dare neither to pity myself nor console him; to defend myself daily against him, and against myself; to devote my cares to causing him pain, when I would consecrate them all to his happiness; to live thus, is it not to die a thousand times? Yet that is what my fate must be. I will endure it, however; I will have the courage. O you, whom I chose for my mother, receive this vow.

Receive also that which I make, to hide from you none of my actions: receive it, I beseech you; I beg it of you as a succor of which I have need: thus, pledged to tell you all, I shall acquire the habit of believing myself always in your presence. Your virtue shall replace my own. Never, doubtless, shall I consent to come before you with a blush; and, restrained by this powerful check, while I shall cherish in you the indulgent friend, the confidant of my weakness, I shall also honor in you the guardian angel who will save me from shame.

Shame enough must I feel, in having to make you this request. Fatal effect of presumptuous confidence! Why did I not dread sooner this inclination which I felt springing up? Why did I flatter myself that I could master it or overcome it at my will? Insensate! How little I knew what love was! Ah, if I had fought against it with more care, perhaps it would have acquired less dominion; perhaps then this separation would not have been necessary; or, even if I had submitted to that sorrowful step, I need not have broken off entirely a relation which it would have been sufficient to render less frequent! But to lose all at one stroke, and forever! O my friend! . . . But what is this? Even in writing to you, shall I be led

away to vent criminal wishes? Ah! away, away! and at least let these involuntary errors be expiated by my sacrifices.

Adieu, my venerable friend; love me as your daughter, adopt me for
such; and be sure that, in spite of my weakness, I would rather die than
render myself unworthy of your choice.

At the Château de . . . , 3rd October, 17★★,
at one o'clock in the morning.

103. Madame de Rosemonde to the Présidente de Tourvel

I was more grieved at your departure, my fairest dear, than surprised at
its cause; a long experience and the interest which you inspire in me had
sufficed to enlighten me as to the state of your heart; and, if all must be
told, there was nothing, or almost nothing, that your letter taught me. If
it had been my only source of information, I should be still in ignorance
of whom it was you loved; for, in speaking to me of *him* all the time, you
did not even once write his name. I had no need of that; I am well aware
who it is. But I remark it, because I remind myself that that is ever the
style of love. I see that it is still the same as in past times.

I had hardly expected ever to be in the case to hark back to memories
so far removed from me, and so alien to my age. Since yesterday, nevertheless, I have truly been much occupied with them, through the desire
which I felt to find in them something which might be useful to you.
But what can I do, except admire and pity you? I praise the wise course
you have taken: but it alarms me, because I conclude from it that you
judged it necessary; and, when one has gone so far, it is very difficult to
remain always at a distance from him to whom our heart is incessantly
attracting us. However, do not lose courage. Nothing should be impossible to your noble soul; and, even if you should someday have the misfortune to succumb (which God forbid!), believe me, my fairest dear,
reserve for yourself at least the consolation of having struggled with all
your power. And then, what human prudence cannot effect, divine grace
will, if it be so pleased. Perhaps you are on the eve of its succor; and your
virtue, proved by these grievous struggles, will issue from them purer and
more lustrous. Hope that you may receive tomorrow the strength which
you lack today. Do not count upon this in order to repose upon it, but
to encourage you to use all your own.

While leaving to Providence the care of succoring you in a danger
against which I can do nothing, I reserve to myself that of sustaining and
consoling you, as far as within me lies. I shall not assuage your pains, but
I will share them. It is by virtue of this that I will gladly receive your confidences. I feel that your heart must have need of unburdening itself. I
open mine to you; age has not yet so chilled it that it is insensible to

friendship. You will always find it ready to receive you. It will be a poor solace to your sorrow; but at least you will not weep alone: and when this unhappy love, obtaining too much power over you, compels you to speak of it, it is better that it should be with me than with *him*. Here am I talking like you; and I think that, between us, we shall succeed in avoiding his name: for the rest, we understand one another.

I know not whether I am doing right in telling you that he seemed keenly grieved at your departure; it would be wiser, perhaps, not to speak of it: but I have no love for the prudence which grieves its friends. Yet I am forced to speak about it at no greater length. My weak sight and tremulous hands do not admit of long letters, when I have to write them myself.

Adieu then, my fairest dear; adieu, my amiable child: yes, I gladly adopt you for my daughter, and you have, indeed, all that is needed to make the pride and pleasure of a mother.

At the Château de . . . , 3rd October, 17**.

104. The Marquise de Merteuil to Madame de Volanges

In truth, my good and dear friend, I could hardly refrain from a movement of pride when I read your letter. What! you honor me with your entire confidence! You even deign to ask for my advice! Ah, I am happy indeed, if I deserve this favorable opinion on your part: if I do not owe it only to the prepossession of friendship. For the rest, whatever the motive may be, it is nonetheless precious to my heart; and to have obtained it is only one reason the more in my eyes why I should labor harder to deserve it. I am going then (but without pretending to give you a counsel) to tell you freely my fashion of thinking. I distrust myself, because it is different from yours; but when I have exposed my reasons to you, you will judge them; and if you condemn them, I subscribe to your judgment in advance. I shall at least show thus much wisdom, that I do not think myself wiser than you.

If, however, and in this single instance, my opinion should seem preferable, you must seek for the cause of this in the illusions of maternal love. Since this sentiment is a laudable one, it needs must have a place in you. Indeed, how very recognizable it is in the course which you are tempted to take! It is thus that, if it sometimes happens to you to make a mistake, it never arises except through a choice of virtues.

Prudence, it seems to me, is the quality to be preferred, when one is disposing of another's fate; and, above all, where it is a question of fixing it by an indissoluble and sacred bond, such as that of marriage. 'Tis then that a mother, equally wise and tender, ought, as you say so well, *to aid her daughter with her experience.* Now, I ask you, what is she to do in order to succeed in this, if it be not to distinguish for her between what is pleasant and what is suitable?

Would it not, then, be to degrade the maternal authority, would it not be to annul it, if you were to subordinate it to a frivolous inclination, the illusory power of which is only felt by those who dread it, and disappears as soon as it is despised? For myself, I confess, I have never believed in these irresistible and engrossing passions, through which, it seems, we are agreed to pay general excuses for our disorders. I cannot conceive how a fancy which is born in a moment, and in a moment dies, can have more strength than the unalterable principles of honor, modesty and virtue; and I can no more understand why a woman who is false to them can be held justified by her pretended passion, than a thief would be by his passion for money, or an assassin by that for revenge.

Ah, who is there that can say that she has never had to struggle? But I have ever sought to persuade myself that, in order to resist, it sufficed to have the will; and thus far, at least, my experience has confirmed my opinion. What would virtue be without the duties which it imposes? Its worship lies in our sacrifices, its recompense in our hearts. These truths cannot be denied except by those who have an interest in disregarding them, and who, already depraved, hope to have a moment's illusion by endeavoring to justify their bad conduct by bad reasons. But could one fear it from a shy and simple child; a child whom you have borne, and whose pure and modest education can but have fortified her happy nature? Yet it is to this fear, which I venture to call humiliating to your daughter, that you are ready to sacrifice the advantageous marriage which your prudence had contrived for her! I like Danceny greatly; and for a long time past, as you know, I have seen little of M. de Gercourt; but my friendship with the one and my indifference toward the other do not prevent me from feeling the enormous difference which exists between the two matches.

Their birth is equal, I admit; but one is without fortune, while that of the other is so great that, even without birth, it would have sufficed to obtain him everything. I quite agree that money does not make happiness, but it must be admitted, also, that it greatly facilitates it. Mademoiselle de Volanges is rich enough for two, as you say: however, an income of sixty thousand livres, which she will enjoy, is not over much when one bears the name of Danceny; when one must furnish and maintain a house which corresponds with it. We no longer live in the days of Madame de Sévigné. Luxury swallows up everything; we blame it, but we needs must imitate it, and in the end the superfluous stints us of the necessary.

As to the personal qualities which you count for much, and with good reason, M. de Gercourt is, assuredly, irreproachable on that score; and, as for him, his proof is over. I like to think, and, in fact, I do think, that Danceny is no whit his inferior: but are we as sure of that? It is true that thus far he has seemed exempt from the faults of his age, and that, in spite of the tone of the day, he shows a taste for good company which makes one augur favorably for him: but who knows whether this apparent virtue be not due to the mediocrity of his fortune? Putting aside the fear of being a cheat or a drunkard, one needs money to be a gambler or a libertine, and one may yet love the faults the excesses of which one dreads. In short, he would not be the first in a thousand to frequent good company solely because he lacked the means of doing otherwise.

I do not say (God forbid!) that I believe all this of him; but it would be always a risk to run; and what reproaches would you not have to make yourself, if the event were not happy! How would you answer your daughter, if she were to say to you, "Mother, I was young and without experience; I was seduced even by an error pardonable at my age: but Heaven, which had foreseen my weakness, had granted me a wise mother, to remedy it and protect me from it. Why, then, forgetful of your prudence, did you consent to my unhappiness? Was it for me to choose a husband, when I knew nothing of the marriage state? If I had wished to do so, was it not your duty to oppose me? But I never had this mad desire. Determined to obey you, I awaited your choice with respectful resignation; I never failed in the submission which I owed to you, and yet I bear today the penalty which is only the rebellious children's due. Ah! your weakness has been my ruin! . . ."

Perhaps, her respect would stifle these complaints: but maternal love would divine them; and the tears of your daughter, though hidden, would nonetheless drip upon your heart. Where then will you look for consolation? Will it be to that mad love against which you should have armed her, and by which, on the contrary, you would have yourself to be seduced?

I know not, my dear friend, whether I have too strong a prejudice against this passion: but I deem it redoubtable even in marriage. It is not that I disapprove of the growth of a soft and virtuous sentiment to embellish the marriage bond, and to sweeten, in some sort, the duties which it imposes: but it is not to that passion that it belongs to form it; it is not for the illusion of a moment to settle the choice of our life. In fact, in order to choose, one must compare; and how can that be done, when one is occupied by a single object, when even that object one cannot know, plunged as one is in intoxication and blindness?

I have, as you may well believe, come across many women afflicted with this dangerous ill; of some of them I have received the confidences. To hear them, there is not one of them whose lover is not a perfect being: but these chimerical perfections exist only in their imaginations.

Their feverish heads dream only of virtues and accomplishments; they adorn with them, at their pleasure, the object whom they prefer: it is the drapery of a god, often worn by an abject model; but whatever it may be, hardly have they clothed it than, the dupes of their own handiwork, they prostrate themselves to adore it.

Either your daughter does not love Danceny, or else she is under this same illusion; if their love is reciprocal, it is common to both. Thus your reason for uniting them for ever resolves itself into the certainty that they do not, and cannot, know each other. But, you will ask, do M. de Gercourt and my daughter know each other any better? No, doubtless; but at least they are simply ignorant, they are under no delusion. What happens in such a case between two married persons whom I assume to be virtuous? Each of them studies the other, looks face to face at the other, seeks and soon discovers what tastes and wishes he must give up for the common tranquillity. These slight sacrifices are not irksome, because they are reciprocal, and have been foreseen: soon they give birth to mutual kindness; and habit, which fortifies all inclinations which it does not destroy, brings about, little by little, that sweet friendship, that tender confidence, which, joined to esteem, form, so it seems to me, the true and solid happiness of marriage.

The illusions of love may be sweeter; but who does not know that they are less durable? And what dangers are not brought about by the moment which destroys them? It is then that the least faults appear shocking and unendurable, by the contrast which they form with the idea of perfection which had seduced us. Each one of the couple believes, however, that only the other has changed, and that he has always the same value as that which, in a mistaken moment, had been attributed to him. The charm which he no longer experiences he is astonished at no longer producing; he is humiliated at this: wounded vanity embitters the mind, augments injuries, causes ill humor, begets hate; and frivolous pleasures are paid for finally by long misery.

Such, my dear friend, is my manner of thinking upon the subject which occupies us; I do not defend it, I simply expound it; 'tis for you to decide. But if you persist in your opinion, I beg you to make me acquainted with the reasons which have outweighed my own: I shall be glad indeed to gather light from you, and, above all, to be reassured as to the fate of your amiable child, whose happiness I ardently desire, both through my friendship for her and through that which unites me to you for life.

Paris, 4th October, 17**.

105. The Marquise de Merteuil to Cécile Volanges

Well, well, little one! So here you are quite vexed, quite ashamed. And that M. de Valmont is a wicked man, is he not? How now! He dares to treat you as the woman he would love the best! He teaches you what you are dying with desire to know! In truth, these proceedings are unpardonable. And you, on your side, you wished to keep your virtue for your lover (who does not abuse it): you cherish only the pains of love and not its pleasures! Nothing could be better, and you will figure marvelous well in a romance. Passion, misfortune, above all, virtue: what a heap of fine things! In the midst of this brilliant pageant, one feels *ennui* sometimes, it is true, but one pays it back.

See the poor child, then, how much she is to be pitied! Her eyes looked worn, the day after? What will you say, pray, when it is your lover's that look thus? Nay, my sweet angel, you will not always have them so; all men are not Valmonts. And then, not to dare to raise those eyes! Oh, in truth, you were right there; everybody would have read in them your adventure. Believe me, however, if it were so, our women and even our damsels would have a far more modest gaze.

In spite of the praise I am forced to give you, as you see, I must, however, admit that you failed in your *chef-d'oeuvre;* which was to have told everything to your Mamma. You had started so well! You had, already, thrown yourself into her arms, you sobbed, she also wept: what a pathetic scene! And what a pity not to have completed it! Your tender mother, quite ravished with delight, and to assist your virtue, would have shut you up in a convent for the rest of your life; and there you could have loved Danceny as much as you wished, without rivals and without sin: you could have broken your heart at your ease; and Valmont, assuredly, would not have come to trouble your grief with vexatious pleasures.

Seriously, at past fifteen can one be so utterly a child as you are? You are right, indeed, to say that you do not deserve my kindness. Yet I would be your friend: you have need of one, perhaps, with the mother you possess and the husband whom she would give you! But if you do not form yourself more, what would you have one do with you? What can one hope for, when that which generally excites intelligence in girls seems, on the contrary, to deprive you of it?

If you could bring yourself to reason for a moment, you would soon find that you ought to congratulate yourself, instead of complaining. But you are shamefaced, and that disturbs you! Well, calm yourself; the shame caused by love is like its pain; it is only experienced once. Indeed one can feign it afterward, but one no longer feels it. The pleasure, however, remains, and that is surely something. I think even that I gathered the fact, from your little chattering letter, that you were inclined to count it for much. Come now, a little honesty. That trouble which prevented you *from acting as you spoke,* which made you find it *so difficult to resist,* which made you feel *as though you were sorry* when Valmont went away, was it really shame which caused it, or was it pleasure? and *his way of saying things to which one does not know how to answer,* may that not have arisen from his *way of acting?* Ah, little girl, you are fibbing, and you are fibbing to your friend. That is not right. But let us leave that.

What would be a pleasure to anybody, and could be nothing else, becomes in your position a veritable happiness. In fact, placed as you are between a mother whose love is necessary to you, and a lover by whom you desire to be loved always, do you not see that the only means of obtaining these opposite ends is to occupy yourself with a third party? Distracted by this new adventure, while, in your Mamma's eyes, you will have the air of sacrificing to your submission an inclination which displeases her, in the eyes of your lover you will acquire the honor of a fine defense. While assuring him incessantly of your love, you will not grant him the last proofs of it. Such refusals, so little painful to you in the case in which you will be, he will not fail to attribute to your virtue; he will complain of them, perhaps, but he will love you more for them; and to obtain the double merit of having sacrificed love in the eyes of one, of resisting it in those of the other, will cost you nothing more than to taste its pleasures. Oh, how many women have lost their reputation, which they would have carefully preserved, had they been able to retain it by similar means!

Does not the course which I propose to you seem to you the most reasonable, as it is the most pleasant? Do you know what you have gained from that which you have adopted? Only that your Mamma has attributed your increased melancholy to an increase of love, that she is incensed at it, and that, to punish you, she only waits for additional proof. She has just written to me; she will make every attempt to extract the admission from you. She will go so far, she told me, as to propose Danceny to you, as a husband, and that, in order to induce you to speak. And if, letting yourself be beguiled by this deceitful tenderness, you answered as your heart bade you, soon, confined for a long time, perhaps forever, you would weep for your blind credulity at your leisure.

This ruse which she wishes to employ against you you must combat with another. Begin then, by seeming less melancholy, to lead her to believe that you think less of Danceny. She will allow herself to be the more easily persuaded in that this is the ordinary effect of absence; and she will be the better disposed to you for it, since she will find in it an opportunity for applauding her own prudence which suggested this means to her. But if, some doubt still remaining, she were, nevertheless, to persist in proving you, and were to speak to you of marriage, fall back, as a well-bred daughter, upon perfect submission. As a matter of fact, what do you risk? As far as husbands are concerned, one is worth no more than another; and the most uncompromising is always less troublesome than a mother.

Once more satisfied with you, your mother will at last marry you; and then, less hampered in your movements, you will be able, at your choice, to quit Valmont and take Danceny, or even to keep them both. For, mark this, your Danceny is charming; but he is one of those men whom one has when one wills and as long as one wills: one can be at one's ease, then, with him. It is not the same with Valmont: it is difficult to keep him, and dangerous to leave him. One must employ with him much tact, or, if one has not that, much docility. On the other hand, if you could succeed in attaching him to you as a friend, what a piece of fortune that would be! He would set you, at once, in the first rank of our women of fashion. It is in this way that one acquires consideration in the world, and not by dint of tears and blushes, as when your nuns made you take your dinner on your knees.

If you are wise then, you will endeavor to be reconciled with Valmont, who must be mighty wroth with you; and, as one should know how to repair one's follies, do not fear to make a few advances to him; besides, you will soon learn that, if men make us the first, we are almost always obliged to make the second. You have a pretext for them: for you must not keep this letter; and I require you to hand it to Valmont as soon as you have read it. Do not forget, however, to seal it beforehand. First, in order to secure for yourself the merit of the step you are taking with regard to him, and to prevent your having the air of being advised to it; and, secondly, because there is no one in the world, save yourself, of whom I am sufficiently the friend to speak to as I do to you.

Adieu, sweet angel; follow my advice, and you shall tell me if you feel the better for it.

P.S. By the way, I was forgetting . . . one word more. Look to it that you cultivate your style more. You write always like a child. I quite see whence it arises; it is because you say all that you think, and no whit of what you do not think. That may pass between you and me, who have nothing to hide from one another: but with everybody! With your lover above all! You would always have the air of a little fool. You must remember that, when you write to anyone, it is for him and not for yourself: you must, therefore, think less of telling him what you think than what will give him most pleasure.

Adieu, sweetheart: I kiss you instead of scolding you, in the hope that you will become more reasonable.

Paris, 4th October, 17★★.

106. The Marquise de Merteuil to the Vicomte de Valmont

Amazing, Vicomte, and this time I love you furiously! For the rest, after the first of your two letters, I could expect the second: thus it did not astonish me; and while, proud already of your success to come, you were soliciting its reward, and asking me if I were ready, I saw clearly that I had no such need for haste. Yes, upon my honor; reading the beautiful account of that tender scene, which had *moved you so deeply,* observing your restraint, worthy of the fairest days of our chivalry, I said to myself a score of times: The affair has failed!

But that is because it could not befall otherwise. What do you expect a poor woman to do who surrenders, and is not taken? My faith, in such a case one must at least save one's honor; and that is what your Présidente does. I know well that, for myself, who can perceive that the step she has taken is really not without some effect, I propose to make use of it myself on the first rather serious occasion which presents itself: but I promise you that, if he for whom I go to that trouble profits no better than you from it, he may assuredly renounce me for ever.

Here you are then, reduced, brought to impotence! And that between two women, one of whom had already crossed the Rubicon, and the other was asking nothing better than to do so. Well, well, you will think that I am boasting, and say that it is easy to prophesy after the event; but I can swear to you that I expected as much. It is because you have not really the genius of your estate; you know nothing except what you have learned, and you invent nothing. Thus, as soon as circumstances no longer lend themselves to your accustomed formulas, and you are compelled to leave the beaten road, you pull up short like a schoolboy. In short, a piece of childishness on the one side, a return of prudery on the other, are enough to disconcert you, because you do not meet with them every day; and you know not how either to prevent or remedy them. Ah, Vicomte, Vicomte, you teach me not to judge men by their successes; and soon we shall have to say of you: On such and such a day, he was brave! And when you have committed follies after follies, you come running to me! It seems that I have nothing else to do but to repair them. It is true, that there would be work enough there.

Whatever may be the state of these two adventures, one was undertaken against my will, and I will not meddle in it; for the other, as you have brought some complaisance for me to bear upon it, I make it my business. The letter which I enclose, which you will read first and then give to the little Volanges, is more than sufficient to bring her back to you: but, I beg you, give some attention to this child, and let us make her, in concert, the despair of her mother and of Gercourt. You need not fear to increase the doses. I see clearly that the little person will not take alarm;

and, our views upon her once fulfilled, she may become what she will.

I am entirely without interest on her account. I had had some desire to make of her, at least, a subaltern in intrigue, and to take her to play *understudies* to me: but I see that she has not the stuff in her; she has a foolish ingenuousness, which has not even yielded to the specific you have employed, though it be one which rarely fails; and it is, according to me, the most dangerous disease a woman can have. It denotes, above all, a weakness of character almost always incurable, and opposed to everything; in such wise that, while we busied ourselves in forming this little girl for intrigue, we should have made nothing of her but a facile woman. Now I know nothing so insipid as that idiotic facility, which surrenders without knowing how or why, solely because it is attacked and knows not how to resist. Women of this kind are absolutely nothing more than pleasure machines.

You will tell me that this is all there is to do, and that it is enough for our plans. Well and good! But do not let us forget that, with that kind of machine, everybody soon attains to a knowledge of the springs and motors; in order therefore to employ this one without danger, one must hasten, stop at the right moment and break it afterward. In truth, there will be no lack of means to disembarrass ourselves of it, and Gercourt, at any rate, will shut it up securely, when it is our pleasure. Indeed, when he can no longer doubt of his dishonor, when it is quite public and notorious, what will it matter to us if he avenges, provided that he do not console, himself? What I say of the husband, you doubtless think of the mother; thus the affair is settled.

The course I deem the better, and upon which I have decided, has induced me to conduct the little person somewhat rapidly, as you will see by my letter; it also renders it most important that nothing should be left in her hands which might compromise us, and I beg you to pay attention to this. This precaution once taken, I charge myself with the moral teaching; the rest concerns you. If, however, we see in the issue that ingenuousness is cured, we have always time to change our project. We should, in any case, have had, one day or other, to occupy ourselves with what we are about to do: in no case will our pains be wasted.

Do you know that mine risked being so, and that the Gercourt's star came near to carrying the day over my prudence? Did not Madame de Volanges show a moment of maternal weakness? Did she not want to marry her daughter to Danceny? It was that which was presaged by that more tender interest which you remarked "*the day after.*" It is you again who would have been the cause of this noble masterpiece! Luckily, the tender mother wrote to me, and I hope that my reply will disillusion her. I talk so much virtue in it, and above all I flatter her so, that she is bound to think I am right.

I am sorry that I have not found time to make a copy of my letter, to edify you with the austerity of my morals. You would see how I despise women who are so depraved as to take a lover! 'Tis so convenient to be a rigorist in conversation! It does no hurt, except to others, and in no way impedes ourselves. . . . And then, I am quite aware that the good lady had her little peccadillos like any other in her young days, and I was not sorry to humiliate her, at least before her conscience; it consoled me a little for the praises I gave her against my own. It was similarly that, in the same letter, the idea of harming Gercourt gave me the courage to speak well of him.

Adieu, Vicomte; I thoroughly approve the course you adopt in remaining some time where you are. I have no means of spurring on your progress: but I invite you to distract yourself with our common pupil. As for myself, in spite of your obliging summons, you see well that you have still to wait, and you will doubtless admit that it is not my fault.

Paris, 4th October, 17★★.

107. Azolan to the Vicomte de Valmont

Monsieur,

Conformably to your orders, I went, immediately on the receipt of your letter, to M. Bertrand, who gave me the twenty-five louis, as you had ordered him. I asked him for two more for Philippe, whom I had told to set off immediately, as Monsieur had commanded me, and who had no money; but your man of business would not do so, saying that he had no order from you for that. I was obliged therefore to give him these myself, and Monsieur will hold me acquitted of them, if it be his good pleasure.

Philippe set off yesterday evening. I strongly impressed upon him not to leave the inn, so that we might be certain of finding him if we had need of him.

I went immediately afterward to Madame la Présidente's to see Mademoiselle Julie; but she was gone out, and I could only speak with La Fleur, from whom I could learn nothing, as, since his arrival, he has only been to the house at mealtimes. It is the second lackey who does all the service, and Monsieur knows that I was not acquainted with him. But I began today.

I returned this morning to Mademoiselle Julie, and she seemed delighted to see me. I questioned her upon the cause of her mistress's return; but she told me that she knew naught of it; and I believe she told the truth. I reproached her with having failed to inform me of her departure, and she assured me that she had not known it till the night before, when putting Madame to bed; so that she spent all the night in packing, and the poor wench had not two hours' sleep. She did not leave her mistress's chamber that night until past one, and left her just as she was sitting down to write.

In the morning, Madame de Tourvel, before leaving, handed a letter to the porter of the *château*. Mademoiselle Julie does not know for whom: she says that it was, perhaps, for Monsieur; but Monsieur does not speak of it.

During the whole journey, Madame had a great hood over her face; by reason of this one could not see her: but Mademoiselle Julie feels assured that she often wept. She did not speak one word, and she would not halt at . . . ,[1] as she had done on her coming, which was none too pleasing to Mademoiselle Julie, who had not breakfasted. But, as I said to her, the masters are the masters.

On arriving, Madame went to bed: but she only remained there two hours. On rising, she summoned her Swiss, and gave him orders to admit nobody. She made no toilette at all. She sat down to table for dinner, but only took a little soup, and went away at once. Her coffee was brought to her room, and Mademoiselle Julie entered at the same time. She found her mistress arranging papers in her writing desk, and she saw that they were letters. I would wager that they were those from Monsieur; and of the three which came to her in the afternoon, there was one which she had still before her all the evening. I am quite certain that it is also one from Monsieur. But why then did she leave like this? That is what astounds me. For that matter, Monsieur is sure to know, and it is no business of mine.

Madame la Présidente went in the afternoon to the library, and took thence two books which she carried to her *boudoir:* but Mademoiselle Julie is certain that she did not read a quarter of an hour in them during the whole day, and that she did nothing but read this letter and dream, with her head resting on her hand. As I thought that Monsieur would be pleased to know what these books are, and as Mademoiselle Julie could not say, I obtained admission today to the library under the pretence of wishing to see it. There are only two books missing: one is the second volume of the *Pensées chrétiennes,* and the other, the first of a book entitled *Clarissa.* I write the name as it is written: Monsieur will, perhaps, know what it is.

Yesterday evening, Madame did not sup; she only took some tea.

She rang at an early hour this morning; asked at once for her horses, and went, before nine o'clock, to the Cistercians, where she heard mass. She wished to confess; but her confessor was away, and he will not return for a week or ten days. I thought it well to inform Monsieur of this.

She returned immediately, breakfasted, and then began to write, and

---

[1]The aforementioned village, halfway on the road.

she remained thus for nearly an hour. I soon found occasion to do what
Monsieur desired the most; for it was I who carried the letters to the
post. There was none for Madame de Volanges: but I send one to
Monsieur which was for M. le Présidente: it seemed to me that this
should be the most interesting. There was one also for Madame de
Rosemonde; but I imagined that Monsieur could always see that when
he wished, and I let it go. For the rest, Monsieur is sure to know everything, since Madame la Présidente has written to him also. I shall in the
future obtain all those which Monsieur desires; for it is Mademoiselle
Julie, almost every day, who gives them to the servants, and she has assured me that, out of friendship for me, and for Monsieur too, she will
gladly do what I want.

She did not even want the money which I offered her: but I feel sure
that Monsieur would like to make her some little present; and if this is
his wish, and he is willing to charge me with it, I shall easily find out
what will give her pleasure.

I hope that Monsieur will not think that I have shown any negligence
in his service, and I have set my heart on justifying myself against the reproaches he makes me. If I did not know of Madame la Présidente's departure, it was, on the contrary, my zeal in Monsieur's service which was
the cause, since it was that which made me start at three o'clock in the
morning; which was the reason that I did not see Mademoiselle Julie the
night before, as usual, having gone to Tournebride to sleep, so that I
might not have to arouse the *château*.

As for the reproach Monsieur makes me of being often without
money; first, it is because I like to keep myself decent, as Monsieur may
see; and then one must maintain the honor of the coat one wears: I
know, indeed, that I ought, perhaps, to save a little for the future; but I
trust entirely to the generosity of Monsieur, who is so good a master.

As for entering the service of Madame de Tourvel while remaining in
that of Monsieur, I beg that Monsieur will not require this of me. It was
very different with Madame la Duchesse; but certainly I would not wear
a livery, and a livery of the robe no less, after having had the honor of
being Monsieur's *chasseur*. In every other way, Monsieur may dispose of
him who has the honor to remain, with as much affection as respect, his
most humble servitor.

> Roux Azolan, *chasseur.*
> Paris, 5th October, 17**, at eleven o'clock at night.

108. The Présidente de Tourvel to Madame de Rosemonde

O my indulgent mother, how many thanks I have to render you, and
what need I had of your letter! I have read it again and again; I cannot

put it away from me. I owe to it the few less painful moments I have spent since my departure. How good you are! Prudence and virtue know then how to compassionate weakness! You take pity on my ills! Ah, if you knew them! . . . they are terrible. I thought I had experienced the pains of love; but the inexpressible torment, that which one must have felt to have any idea of it, is to be separated from the object of one's love, to be separated for ever! . . . Yes, the pain which crushes me today will return tomorrow, the day after, all my life! My God, how young I am still, and how long a time I have to suffer!

To be one's self the architect of one's own misery; to tear out one's heart with one's own hands; and, while suffering these insupportable sorrows, to feel at each instant that one can make them cease with a word, and that this word is a crime! Ah, my friend! . . .

When I adopted this painful course, and separated myself from him, I hoped that absence would augment my courage and my strength: how greatly I was deceived! It seems, on the contrary, as though it had completed the work of destruction. I had more to struggle against, 'tis true: but, even while resisting, all was not privation; at least I sometimes saw him; often even, without daring to direct my eyes toward him, I felt his own were fixed on me. Yes, my friend, I felt them; it seemed as though they warmed my soul; and without passing through my eyes, they nonetheless arrived at my heart. Now, in my grievous solitude, isolated from all that is dear to me, closeted with my misfortune, every moment of my sorrowful existence is marked by my tears, and nothing sweetens its bitterness; no consolation is mingled with my sacrifices; and those I have thus far made have only served to render more dolorous those which are left to make.

Yesterday again, I had a lively feeling of this. Among the letters they brought me, there was one from him; they were still two paces off from me when I recognized it among the rest. I rose involuntarily, I trembled, I could hardly hide my emotion; and this state was not altogether unpleasant. A moment later, finding myself alone, this deceitful sweetness soon vanished, and left me but one sacrifice the more to make. Could I actually open this letter, which, however, I burned to read? In the fatality which pursues me, the consolations which seem to present themselves do nothing, on the contrary, but impose fresh privations; and those become crueler still from the thought that M. de Valmont shares them.

There it is at last, that name which so constantly fills my mind, and which it costs me so much to write; the sort of reproach you make me really alarmed me. I beg you to believe that a false shame has not altered my confidence in you; and why should I fear to name him? Ah, I blush for my sentiments, but not for the object which causes them! Who other than he is worthy to inspire them? However, I know not why, this name does not come naturally to my pen; and, even this time, I had need of reflection to write it. I return to him.

You tell me that he seemed to you *keenly grieved at my departure.* What, then, did he do? What did he say? Did he speak of returning to Paris? I beg you to dissuade him as much as you can. If he has judged me aright, he cannot bear me any ill will for this step: but he must feel also that it is a course from which there is no return. One of my greatest torments is not to know what he thinks. I have still his letter there ... but you are surely of my opinion that I ought not to open it.

It is only through you, my indulgent friend, that I can feel myself not entirely separated from him. I would not abuse your kindness; I understand, perfectly, that your letters cannot be long ones: but you will not deny your child two words: one to sustain her courage, and the other to console her. Adieu, my venerable friend.

Paris, 5th October, 17★★.

109. Cécile Volanges to the Marquise de Merteuil

It is only today, Madame, that I have given M. de Valmont the letter which you have done me the honor to write me. I kept it for four days, in spite of the alarm which I often felt lest it should be found; but I concealed it very carefully; and, when my grief once more seized me, I shut myself up to reperuse it.

I quite see that what I believe to be so great a misfortune is hardly one at all; and I must confess that there is certainly pleasure in it: so much so that I hardly grieve about it any more. It is only the thought of Danceny which still sometimes torments me. But there are already moments when I do not think of him at all! Moreover it is true that M. de Valmont is mighty amiable!

I was reconciled with him two days ago: it was very easy for me; for I had but said two words to him, when he told me that, if I had anything to say to him, he would come to my chamber in the evening, and I only had to answer that I was very willing. And then, as soon as he had come there, he seemed no more vexed than if I had never done anything to him. He did not scold me till afterward, and then very gently; and it was in a manner ... just like you; which proved to me that he also had much friendship for me. I should not know how to tell you all the odd things he related to me, and which I never should have believed, particularly about Mamma. You would give me much pleasure by telling me if it is all true. What is very sure is that I could not restrain my laughter; so that once I burst out laughing, which gave us a mighty fright: for Mamma might have heard; and if she had come to see, what would have become of me? I am sure she would have sent me to the convent that very moment.

As we must be prudent, and as M. de Valmont has told me himself that he would not risk compromising me for anything in the world, we have agreed that henceforward he should only come to open the door, and that we should go to his room. In that, there is nothing to fear; I have already been there, yesterday, and even now, while I write to you, I am again expecting him to come. Now, Madame, I hope you will not scold me any more.

There is one thing, however, which has greatly surprised me in your letter; it is what you tell me against the time when I am married, with regard to Danceny and M. de Valmont. I fancy that one day, at the Opera, you told me, on the contrary, that, once married, I could only love my husband, and that I should even have to forget Danceny: for that matter, I may have misunderstood you, and I would far rather have it different, as now I shall not be so much afraid of the time for my marriage. I even desire it, since I shall have more liberty; and I hope then that I shall be able to arrange in such a fashion that I need only think of Danceny. I feel sure that I shall never be really happy except with him: for the idea of him always torments me now, and I have no happiness except when I succeed in not thinking of him, which is very difficult; and, as soon as I think of him, I at once become sad again.

What consoles me a little is that you assure me Danceny will love me the more for this: but are you quite certain? . . . Oh, yes, you would not deceive me! It is amusing, however, that it is Danceny I love, and that M. de Valmont . . . But, as you say, perhaps it is fortunate! Well, we shall see.

I understood none too well what you said about my fashion of writing. It seems to me that Danceny finds my letters good as they are. I quite feel, however, that I ought to tell him nothing of what passes with M. de Valmont: thus you have no reason to be afraid.

Mamma has not yet spoken to me of my marriage: but let her do so; when she speaks to me of it, since it is to entrap me, I promise you I shall know how to lie.

Adieu, my dear, kind friend; I thank you mightily, and I promise you I will never forget all your kindnesses to me. I must finish now; it is near one o'clock; so M. de Valmont cannot be long now.

> At the Château de . . . , 10th October, 17★★.

110. The Vicomte de Valmont to the Marquise de Merteuil

"*Powers of Heaven! I had a soul for sorrow, grant me one now for felicity.*"[1] It is the

---
[1] *La Nouvelle Héloïse.*

tender Saint-Preux, I think, who thus expresses himself. Better balanced than he, I possess these two existences at once. Yes, my friend, I am at the same time most happy and most miserable; and since you have my entire confidence, I owe you the double relation of my pleasures and my pains.

Know then that my ungrateful Puritan treats me ever with the same rigor. I am at the fourth letter which has been returned. Perhaps I am wrong to call it the fourth; for, having excellently well divined, on the return of the first, that it would be followed by many others, and being unwilling thus to waste my time, I adopted the course of turning my complaints into commonplaces, and putting no date: and, since the second post, it is always the same letter which comes and goes; I merely change the envelope. If my fair one ends as ordinarily end the fair, and softens, if only from lassitude, she will keep the missive at last; and it will be time enough then to pick up the threads. You see that, with this new manner of correspondence, I cannot be perfectly well informed.

I have discovered, however, that the fickle creature has changed her confidant: at least, I have made sure that, since her departure from the *château,* no letter has come from her for Madame de Volanges, while there have been two for the old Rosemonde; and, as the latter says nothing to us of them, as she no longer opens her mouth on the subject of *her dearest fair,* of whom previously she never ceased to speak, I concluded that it was she who had her confidence. I presume that, on one side, the need of speaking of me and, on the other, a little shame at returning with Madame de Volanges to the subject of a sentiment so long disavowed have caused this great revolution. I fear that I have lost by the change: for, the older women grow, the more crabbed and severe do they become. The first would have told her far more ill of me: but the latter will say more of love; and the sensitive prude has far more fear of the sentiment than of the person.

The only means of getting at the facts, is, as you see, to intercept the clandestine correspondence. I have already sent the order to my *chasseur;* and I am daily awaiting its execution. So far, I can do nothing except at random: thus, for the last week, I run my mind in vain over all recognized means, all those in the novels and in my private recollections; I can find none which befits either the circumstances of the adventure or the character of the heroine. The difficulty would not be to present myself before her, even in the night, nor again to induce her slumber, and make of her a new Clarissa: but, after more than two months of care and trouble, to have recourse to means which are foreign to me! To follow slavishly in the track of others, and triumph without glory! . . . No, she shall not have *the pleasures of vice and the honors of virtue.*[1] 'Tis not enough for

---

[1]*La Nouvelle Héloïse.*

me to possess her, I wish her to give herself. Now, for that, I need not only to penetrate to her presence, but to reach her by her own consent; to find her alone and with the intention of listening to me; above all, to close her eyes as to the danger; for if she sees it, she will know how to surmount it or to die. But the more clearly I see what I need to do, the more difficult do I find its execution; and though it should induce you to laugh at me once more, I will confess that my embarrassment is enhanced in proportion to the extent to which it occupies me.

My brain would reel, I think, were it not for the lucky distraction which our common pupil affords me; I owe it to her that I have still something else to do than compose elegies. Would you believe that this little girl had taken such fright that three whole days passed before your letter produced its effect? 'Tis thus that one false idea can spoil the most fortunate nature! In short, it was not until Saturday that she came and hovered round me, and stammered out a few words, and those pronounced in so low a voice, so stifled with shame, that it was impossible to hear them. But the blush which accompanied them made me guess their sense. Thus far, I had retained my pride: but, subdued by so pleasant a repentance, I consented to promise a visit to the fair penitent that same evening; and this grace on my part was received with all the gratitude that so great a condescension demanded.

As I never lose sight either of your projects or my own, I resolved to profit by this occasion to gain a just estimate of the child's value, and also to accelerate her education. But to pursue this work with greater freedom, I found it necessary to change the place of our *rendezvous;* for a simple closet, which separates your pupil's room from that of her mother, could not inspire sufficient security to allow her to reveal herself at her ease. I promised myself then *innocently* to make some noise, which would cause her enough alarm to induce her, for the future, to seek a safer asylum; this trouble she spared me again.

The little person loves laughter; and to promote her gaiety, I bethought myself, during our *entr'actes,* to relate to her all the scandalous anecdotes which occurred to my mind; and, so as to render them more piquant and better to fix her attention, I attributed them all to her mother, whom I was thus pleased to bedaub with vice and ridicule. It was not without motive that I made this choice; it encouraged my timid schoolgirl better than anything else, and I inspired her, at the same time, with the most profound contempt for her mother. I have long remarked that, if it be not always necessary to employ this means to seduce a young girl, it is indispensable, and often even the most efficacious, when one wishes to deprave her; for she who does not respect her mother will not respect herself: a moral truth which I hold to be so useful that I have been glad indeed to have furnished an example in support of the precept.

Meanwhile, your pupil, who had no thought of morals, was stifling her laughter every moment; finally, she had almost thought to have burst out with it. I had no difficulty in persuading her that she had made *a terrible noise*. I feigned a huge fright, which she easily shared. That she might the better remember it, I did not allow pleasure to reappear, and left her alone, three hours earlier than was customary; we agreed, therefore, on separating, that, from the morrow, it was in my room that we should meet.

I have already twice received her there; and in this short period the scholar has become almost as learned as the master. Yes, in truth, I have taught her everything, even to complaisances! I have only made an exception of precautions.

Occupied thus all night, I gain thereby in that I sleep a great portion of the day; and as the actual society of the *château* has nothing to attract me, I hardly appear in the *salon* for an hour during the day. Today, I even adopted the course of eating in my room, and I do not intend to leave it again, except for short walks. These eccentricities pass on the ground of my health. I have declared that I am *worn out with vapors;* I have also announced a little fever. It cost me no more than to speak in a slow and faint voice. As for the alteration in my face, trust your pupil for that. "*Love will provide.*"[1]

I employ my leisure in meditating means of recovering over my ingrate the advantages I have lost; and also in composing a sort of catechism of debauch for the use of my scholar. I amuse myself by mentioning nothing except by its technical name; and I laugh in advance at the interesting conversation which this ought to furnish between Gercourt and herself on the first night of their marriage. Nothing could be more amusing than the ingenuity with which she makes use already of the little she knows of this tongue! She has no conception that one can speak differently. This child is really seductive! The contrast of naive candor with the language of effrontery does not fail to have an effect; and, I know not why, but it is only *bizarre* things which gave me any longer pleasure.

Perhaps, I am abandoning myself overmuch to this, since I am compromising by it both my time and my health: but I hope that my feigned malady, besides that it will save me from the *ennui* of the drawing room, will, perhaps, be of some use to me with the rigid Puritan, whose ferocious virtue is nonetheless allied with soft sensibility. I doubt not but that she is already informed of this mighty event, and I have a great desire to

---

[1]"*L'amour y pourvoira.*" Regnard: *Les Folies amoureuses.*

know what she thinks of it; all the more so in that I will wager she does not fail to attribute the honor of it to herself. I shall regulate the state of my health according to the impression which it makes upon her.

Here you are, my fair friend, as fully acquainted with my affairs as I am myself. I hope to have, shortly, more interesting news to tell you; and I beg you to believe that, in the pleasure which I promise myself, I count for much the reward which I expect from you.

At the Château de . . . , 11th October, 17★★.

111. The Comte de Gercourt to Madame de Volanges

All seems to be quiet in this country, Madame; and we expect, from day to day, the permission to return to France. I hope you will not doubt that I have always the same eagerness to betake myself thither, and to tie there the knots which are to unite me to you and to Mademoiselle de Volanges. Meanwhile, M. le Duc de ★★★, my cousin, to whom, as you know, I am under so many obligations, has just informed me of his recall from Naples. He tells me that he intends to pass through Rome, and to see, on his road, that part of Italy with which he is not yet acquainted. He begs me to accompany him on this journey, which will take about six weeks or two months. I do not hide from you that it would be agreeable to me to profit by this opportunity; feeling sure that, once married, I shall with difficulty find the time for other absences than those which my service demands. Perhaps, also, it would be more proper to wait till winter for the wedding, since it will not be till then that all my kinsmen will be assembled in Paris; and notably M. le Marquis de ★★★, to whom I owe my hope of belonging to you. In spite of these considerations, my plans in this respect will be entirely subordinate to your own; and if you should have the slightest preference for your first arrangements, I am ready to abandon mine. I beg you only to let me know, as early as possible, your intentions on this subject. I will await your reply here, and it alone shall regulate my action.

I am with respect, Madame, and with all the sentiments that befit a son, your most humble, etc.

The Comte de Gercourt,
Bastia, 10th October, 17★★.

112. Madame de Rosemonde to the Présidente de Tourvel
(DICTATED)

I have only this instant received, my dearest fair, your letter of the 11th,[1]

---

[1]This letter has not been recovered.

and the gentle reproaches which it contains. Confess that you were quite disposed to make one more; and that, if you had not recollected that you were *my daughter,* you would have really scolded me. Yet you would have been very unjust! It was the desire and hope I had of being able to reply to you myself which made me postpone this from day to day; and you see that, even today, I am obliged to borrow the hand of my maid. My wretched rheumatism has come back again; it has taken up its abode this time in the right arm, and I am absolutely crippled. That is what it is, young and fresh as you are, to have so old a friend! One suffers for those incongruities.

As soon as my pains give me a little respite, I promise to have a long talk with you. In the meantime, I merely tell you that I have received your two letters; that they would have redoubled, had that been possible, my tender friendship for you; and that I shall never cease to take a very lively interest in all that concerns you.

My nephew too is somewhat indisposed, but in no danger, nor is there need for the least anxiety; it is a slight indisposition which, as it appears to me, affects his humor more than his health. We see hardly anything of him now.

His retreat and your departure do not add to the gaiety of our little circle. The little Volanges, especially, misses you furiously, and yawns consumedly all day long. Since the last few days, in particular, she has done us the honor of falling into a profound sleep every afternoon.

Adieu, my dearest fair; I am always your very good friend, your mamma, your sister even, did my great age permit that title. In short, I am attached to you by all the most affectionate sentiments.

Signed: Adelaide, for Madame de Rosemonde .

At the Château de . . . , 14th October, 17★★.

113. The Marquise de Merteuil to the Vicomte de Valmont

I think I ought to warn you, Vicomte, that they are beginning to busy themselves with you in Paris; your absence is remarked there, and they are already divining the cause. I was yesterday at a very numerous supper; it was said positively that you were retained in the country by an un-happy and romantic love: joy was immediately depicted on the faces of all those envious of your success, and of all the women whom you have neglected. If you are advised by me, you will not let these dangerous ru-mors acquire credit, but will come at once to destroy them by your pres-ence.

Remember that, if you once allow the idea that you are irresistible to be lost, you will soon find that it will, as a matter of fact, become easier to resist you; that your rivals, too, will lose their respect for you, and dare to combat you: for which of them does not believe himself stronger than virtue? Reflect above all that, in the multitude of women whom you have advertised, all those whom you have not had will endeavor to undeceive the public, while the others will exert themselves to hoodwink it. In short, you must expect to be appreciated, perhaps, as much below your value, as you have been, hitherto, beyond it.

Come back, then, Vicomte, and do not sacrifice your reputation to a puerile caprice. You have done all we wished with the little Volanges; and as for your Présidente, it is not, apparently, by remaining ten leagues away from her, that you will get over your fantasy. Do you think she will come to fetch you? Perhaps she has already ceased to dream of you, or is only so far occupied with you as to congratulate herself on having humiliated you. At any rate, here you will be able to find some opportunity of a brilliant reappearance: and you have need of one; and even if you insist on your ridiculous adventure, I do not see how your return can hurt it . . . on the contrary.

In effect, if your Présidente *adores you,* as you have so often told me and said so little to prove, her sole consolation, her sole pleasure now, must be to talk of you, and to know what you are doing, what you are saying, what you are thinking, even the slightest detail which concerns you. These trifles increase in value according to the extent of the privations one endures. They are the crumbs that fall from the rich man's table: he disdains them; but the poor man collects them greedily, and feeds on them. Now the poor Présidente gathers up all these crumbs at present; and the more she has, the less will be her haste to abandon herself to her appetite for the rest.

Moreover, since you know her confidant, you cannot doubt but that each of her letters contains at least one little sermon, and all that she thinks befitting "*to corroborate her prudence and fortify her virtue.*"[1] Why, then, leave to the one resources to defend herself, to the other the means of injuring you?

It is not that I am at all of your opinion as to the loss you believe you have sustained by the change of confidant. In the first place, Madame de Volanges hates you, and hatred is always clearer-sighted and more ingenious than friendship. All the virtue of your old aunt will not persuade her to speak ill of her dear nephew for a single moment, for virtue also has its weaknesses. Next, your fears depend upon a consideration which is absolutely false.

It is not true that *the older women grow, the more crabbed and severe they become.* It is betwixt the ages of forty and fifty that their despair at the sight of their fading faces, their rage at feeling obliged to abandon their

---

[1]From the comedy, "*On ne s'avise jamais de tout!*"

pretensions and the pleasures to which they still cling, render almost all women scolds and shrews. They need this long interval to make the great sacrifice in its entirety; but, as soon as it is consummated, all distribute themselves into two classes. The most numerous, that of the women who have had nothing in their favor save their faces and youth, falls into an imbecile apathy, and only issues from this for the sake of play or of a few practices of devotion; this kind is always tiresome, often fond of scolding, sometimes a little mischievous, but rarely malicious. One cannot tell, either, whether these women are, or are not, severe: without ideas, without an existence, they repeat indifferently, and without understanding, all that they hear said, and in themselves remain absolutely null. The other class, far rarer, but really precious, is that of the women who, having possessed character, and not having neglected to cultivate their reason, know how to create an existence for themselves when that of nature fails them, and adopt the plan of transferring to their minds the adornments which they had before employed for their faces. These last have, as a rule, a very sound judgment and an intelligence at once solid, gay, and gracious. They replace seductive charms by ingratiating kindness, and even by sprightliness, the charm of which increases in proportion to their age: it is thus that they succeed, after a fashion, in attracting youth by making themselves loved by it. But then, far from being, as you say, *crabbed and severe,* the habit of indulgence, their long reflections upon human frailty, and, above all, the memories of their youth, through which alone they have a hold on life, would rather place them, perhaps too much, on the side of complaisance.

What I may say to you, finally, is that, having always sought out old women, the utility of whose support I recognized at an early age, I have encountered several among them to whom I was led as much by inclination as interest. I stop there: for nowadays, when you take fire so quickly and so morally, I should be afraid lest you fell suddenly in love with your aged aunt, and buried yourself with her in the tomb in which you have already lived so long. I resume then.

In spite of the state of enchantment in which you seem to be with your little schoolgirl, I cannot believe that she counts at all in your projects. You found her to your hand, you took her: well and good! But it cannot be that your fancy enters into it. To tell the truth, it is not even a complete pleasure: you possess absolutely nothing beyond her person! I do not speak of her heart, in which I do not doubt you take not the slightest interest; but you do not even fill her head. I know not whether you have perceived it, but, for myself, I have the proof of it in the last letter she sent me;[1] I send it you, that you may judge of it. Observe that

[1]See letter the hundred and ninth.

when she speaks of you, it is always as *M. de Valmont;* that all her ideas, even those which you give rise to, always end in Danceny; and she does not call him Monsieur, it is plain *Danceny* always. Thereby, she singles him out from all the rest; and, even while abandoning herself to you, she is familiar only with him. If such a conquest seems to you *seductive,* if the pleasures she gives *attach you,* you are assuredly modest and not hard to please! That you should retain her, I consent to that; it even forms part of my projects. But it seems to me that it is not worth putting yourself to a quarter of an hour's inconvenience; also, that you had best acquire some dominion over her, and not allow her, for instance, to approach Danceny until after you have made her forget him a little more.

Before I cease to occupy myself with you, and come to myself, I wish to tell you again that this means of sickness, which you announce it is your resolve to employ, is well known and mighty stale. Truly, Vicomte, you have no invention! I myself repeat myself sometimes, as you are about to see; but I try to save myself by the details, and, above all, I am justified by success. I am going to try another still, and run after a new adventure. I admit that it will not have the merit of difficulty; but at least it will be a distraction, and I am perishing with *ennui.*

I know not why, but, since the adventure of Prévan, Belleroche has become insupportable. He has redoubled his attention, his tenderness, his *veneration* to such a degree that I can no longer submit to it. His anger seemed to me, at the outset, amusing; it was very necessary, however, to calm it, for to let him go on would have been to compromise myself; and there was no means of making him listen to reason. I adopted the course then of showing him more love, in order to make an end of it more easily: but he has taken this seriously, and ever since surfeits me with his eternal delight. I notice, especially, the insulting trust which he shows in me, and the security with which he considers me as his forever. I am really humiliated by it. He must rate me lightly indeed, if he believes he has worth enough to make me constant! Did he not tell me recently that I could never have loved anyone but himself? Oh, for the moment I had need of all my prudence not to undeceive him on the spot, by telling him how matters stood. A merry gentleman, forsooth, to think he has exclusive rights! I admit that he is well made and of a fair enough countenance; but, all considered, he is, in fact, but a journeyman lovemaker. In short, the moment has come when we must separate.

I have been attempting this for the last fortnight, and have employed, in turn, coldness, caprice, ill humor, and quarrels; but the tenacious personage is not made thus to lose his hold: a more violent method must be adopted therefore; consequently, I am taking him to my country place. We leave the day after tomorrow. With us there will only be a few uninterested persons, by no means clear-sighted, and we shall have almost as much liberty as if we were there alone. There I will surfeit him with love and caresses to such a degree, we will live there so entirely for one another, that I wager he will be more desirous than I am myself for the end of this expedition, which he considers so great a piece of good fortune; and, if he does not return more weary of me than I am of him, tell me that I know no more than you, and I will admit it.

My pretext for this sort of retreat is that I wish to busy myself exclusively with my great lawsuit, which, in fact, will be at last decided at the commencement of the winter. I am very glad of it; for it is really disagreeable to have one's whole fortune hanging thus in the air. 'Tis not that I am at all anxious as to the result; in the first place, I am in the right, all my lawyers assure me so; and, even if I were not, I should be maladroit indeed if I knew not how to gain a suit where my only adversaries are minors, still of immature years, and their aged guardian! As nothing, however, should be neglected in a matter of so great importance, I shall have two advocates on my side. Does not this expedition seem to you gay? However, if it serves me to win my suit and rid myself of Belleroche, I shall not think the time wasted.

Now, Vicomte, divine his successor: I give you a hundred guesses. But what is the use? Do I not know that you never guess anything? Well then, it is Danceny! You are astonished, are you not? For after all I am not yet reduced to the education of children! But this one deserves to form an exception; he has but the graces of youth, and not its frivolity. His great reserve in society is well calculated to remove all suspicion, and one finds him only the more amiable, when he lets himself go in a *tête-à-tête*. Not that I have yet had one with him on my own account, I am still no more than his confidant; but beneath this veil of friendship, I believe I discern a very lively taste for me, and I feel that I am conceiving a great one for him. It were a mighty pity that so much wit and delicacy should be debased and wasted upon that little fool of a Volanges! I hope he is deceived in believing that he loves her: she so little deserves it! 'Tis not that I am jealous of her; it is because it would be a crime, and I would save Danceny. I beg you then, Vicomte, to take precautions that he may not approach *his Cécile* (as he still has the bad habit of calling her). A first fancy has always more sway than one thinks; and I should feel sure of nothing, were he to see her again at present, especially during my absence. On my return, I charge myself with everything, and answer for the result.

I thought seriously of taking the young man with me: but, as usual, I have made a sacrifice to my prudence; moreover I should have been afraid lest he discovered anything between Belleroche and myself, and I should be in despair if he were to have the least idea of what was passing. I would at least offer myself to his imagination as pure and spotless, such indeed as one should be, to be really worthy of him.

Paris, 15th October, 17★★.

114. The Présidente de Tourvel to Madame de Rosemonde

My dear friend, I yield to the impulse of my grave anxiety; and without knowing whether you will be able to reply to me, I cannot refrain from questioning you. The condition of M. de Valmont, which you tell me is *not dangerous,* does not leave me as much confidence as you appear to have. It not rarely happens that melancholy and disgust with the world are the symptoms and precursors of some grave illness; the sufferings of the body, like those of the mind, make us desirous of solitude; and often we reproach with ill humor him who should merely be pitied for his pain.

It seems to me that he ought at least to consult someone. How is it that you, who are ill yourself, have not a doctor by your side? My own, whom I have seen this morning, and whom, I do not conceal from you, I have indirectly consulted, is of opinion that, in persons naturally active, this sort of sudden apathy should never be neglected; and, as he said besides, sicknesses that are not taken in time no longer yield to treatment. Why let one who is so dear to you incur this risk?

What enhances my anxiety is that I have received no news of him for four days. My God! Are you not deceiving me as to his condition? Why should he have suddenly ceased to write? If it were only the effect of my obstinacy in returning his letters to him, I think he would have adopted this course sooner. In short, although I do not believe in presentiments, I have been, for some days past, in a state of gloom which alarms me. Ah, perhaps I am on the eve of the greatest of misfortunes!

You would not believe, and I am ashamed to tell you, how pained I am not to receive those same letters which, however, I should still refuse to read. I was at least sure that he was thinking of me, and I saw something which came from him! I did not open those letters, but I wept when I looked at them: my tears were sweeter and more easy, and they alone partially dissipated the customary depression in which I live since my return. I conjure you, my indulgent friend, write to me yourself as soon as you are able, and, in the meanwhile, have your news and his sent to me daily.

I perceive that I have hardly said a word as to yourself, but you know my sentiments, my unlimited attachment, my tender gratitude for your sensitive friendship; you will pardon my trouble, my mortal sufferings, the terrible torture of having to dread calamities of which I am, perhaps, the cause. Great Heaven! this agonizing idea pursues me and rends my heart:

this misfortune was lacking me, and I feel that I was born to experience all.

Adieu, my dear friend: love me, pity me. Shall I have a letter from you today?

Paris, 16th October, 17**.

115. The Vicomte de Valmont to the Marquise de Merteuil

It is an incredible thing, my lovely friend, how easily, when two people are separated, they cease to understand one another. As long as I was near you, we had never but one same feeling, one like fashion of seeing things; and, because for nearly three months I have ceased to see you, we are no longer of the same opinion upon anything. Which of us two is wrong? You would certainly not hesitate about your reply: but I, wiser or more polite, do not decide. I am only going to answer your letter, and continue to expound my conduct.

To begin with, I thank you for the notice you give me of the rumors which are current about me; but I am not yet uneasy: I believe I am certain to have something soon wherewith to make them cease. Reassure yourself; I shall reappear in the world only more celebrated than ever, and always more worthy of you.

I hope that even the adventure of the little Volanges will be counted for something to me, although you appear to make so little of it: as though it were nothing to carry off, in one evening, a young girl from her cherished lover; to make use of her afterward as much as one wishes, and absolutely as one's own property, without any further pother; to obtain from her favors which one does not even dare demand from all the wenches whose trade it is; and this without in the least distracting her from her tender love; without rendering her inconstant or even unfaithful: for, as you say, I do not even fill her head! So that, when my fantasy has passed, I shall restore her to the arms of her lover, so to speak, without her having perceived anything. Pray, is this a very ordinary achievement? And then, believe me, once issued from my hands, the principles which I am imparting to her will not fail to develop; and I predict that the shy scholar will soon soar upon a flight fitting to do honor to her master.

If, nevertheless, you prefer the heroic manner, I will show you the Présidente, that exemplary model of all the virtues! respected even by our veriest libertines! of such a virtue that one had given up even the thought of attacking her! I will show her, I say, forgetting her duties and her virtue, sacrificing her reputation and two years of prudence, to run after the happiness of pleasing me, to intoxicate herself with that of loving me, finding herself sufficiently compensated for such sacrifices by a word, a glance, things which she will not even always obtain. I will do more, I will leave her; and either I do not know this woman, or she will not give me a successor. She will resist her need of consolation, the habit of pleasure, even the desire of vengeance. In short, she will have existed only for me; and, be her career short or long, I alone shall have opened and shut the barrier. Once having attained this triumph, I will say to my rivals: Behold my handiwork, and seek throughout the century for a second example!

You will ask me, whence comes today this excessive assurance? It is because for the last week I have been in my fair one's confidence; she does not tell me her secrets, but I surprise them. Two letters from her to Madame de Rosemonde have sufficiently instructed me, and I shall only read the others out of curiosity. I require absolutely nothing else to ensure success than to approach her, and I have found the means. I shall instantly employ them.

You are curious, I believe? . . . But no, to punish you for not believing in my inventions, you shall not know them. Once for all, if you had your deserts, I should withdraw my confidence from you, at least in this adventure; indeed, were it not for the sweet price you have set on my success, I should speak of it no further to you. You see that I am vexed. However, in the hope that you will correct yourself, I am willing to stop with this slight punishment; and, once more grown indulgent, will forget my rash projects for a moment, to discuss your own with you.

There you are then, in the country, which is as tedious as sentiment and as sad as constancy! And that poor Belleroche! You are not contented with making him drink the waters of oblivion, you must also put him to the torture! How does he like it? Does he bear up well beneath the nausea of love? I would give much to see him become only the more enamored; I am curious to see what more efficacious remedy you would succeed in finding. I pity you, truly, that you have been compelled to have recourse to that. Once only in my life have I made love from calculation. I had certainly an excellent reason, since it was to the Comtesse de ***; and twenty times I was tempted to say, while in her arms, "Madame, I renounce the place I am soliciting; permit me to retire from that which I occupy." Wherefore, of all the women I have had, she is the only one of whom it gives me real pleasure to speak ill.

As for your own motive, I find it, to tell the truth, of a rare absurdity; and you were right in believing I should never guess the successor. What! It is for Danceny you are taking all this trouble! Oh, my dear friend, leave him to adore *his virtuous Cécile,* and do not compromise yourself at these childish games. Leave boys to form themselves in their *nurses'* hands, or to play with schoolgirls *at little innocent games.* How can you burden yourself with a novice, who will know neither how to take you nor how to leave you, and with whom all will have to be done by you! I tell you, seriously, I disapprove of this choice; and however secret it may remain, it will humiliate you at least in my eyes and in your own conscience.

You have taken, you say, a great fancy to him: nay, nay, you surely make a mistake; and I even believe I have found the source of your error. This fine disgust with Belleroche came to you at a time of famine; and, as Paris offered you no choice, your ideas, which are always too volatile, turned toward the first object they encountered. But reflect: on your return you will be able to choose between a thousand; and if, in fine, you dread the inaction in which you risk falling if you delay, I offer myself to you to amuse your leisure.

By the time of your arrival, my great affairs will be terminated in some fashion or other; and assuredly neither the little Volanges nor the Présidente herself will occupy me so much then as to prevent me from being with you as much as you desire. Perhaps, even, between now and then, I shall have already restored the little girl into the hands of her discreet lover. Without admitting, whatever you may say, that it is not a pleasure which *attaches,* as it is my intention that she should retain all her life a superior notion of me to that of all other men, I have adopted a tone with her, which I could not keep up long without injuring my health; and, from henceforth, I am only drawn to her by the care which one owes to family affairs. . . .

You do not understand me? . . . The fact is that I am awaiting a second period to confirm my hope, and to assure me that I have thoroughly succeeded in my projects. Yes, my lovely friend, I have already a first indication that the husband of my pupil will not run the risk of dying without posterity; and that the head of the house of Gercourt will be in future only a cadet of that of Valmont. But let me finish, at my fantasy, this adventure which I only undertook at your entreaty. Remember that, if you render Danceny inconstant, you destroy all the raciness of the story. Consider, finally, that offering, as I do, to represent him for you, I have, it seems to me, some right to be preferred.

I count so much on this, that I am not afraid to cross your views, by endeavoring myself to augment the discreet lover's tender passion for the first and worthy object of his choice. Yesterday, having found your pupil employed in writing to him, after I had first disturbed her at this sweet occupation for the sake of another, sweeter still, I asked to see her letter; and as I found it cold and constrained, I made her feel that it was not thus that she should console her lover, and persuaded her to write another at my dictation; in which, imitating, as well as I could, her little prattle, I tried to foster the young man's love by a more certain hope. The little person was quite enchanted, she said, to find herself expressing herself so well; and, for the future, I am to be charged with the correspondence.

What have I not done for this Danceny? I shall have been at once his
friend, his confidant, his rival and his mistress! Again, at this moment, I
am rendering him the service of saving him from your dangerous chains.
Yes, dangerous without a doubt: for to possess you and lose you is to buy
a moment of happiness with an eternity of regret. Adieu, my lovely
friend; have the courage to dispatch Belleroche as soon as you can. Leave
Danceny alone, and prepare yourself to receive once more, and to renew
to me, the delicious pleasures of our first *liaison*.

P.S. I congratulate you upon the approaching decision of the great
lawsuit. I shall be delighted if this happy event occurs during my reign.

At the Château de . . . , 19th October, 17★★.

116. The Chevalier Danceny to Cécile Volanges

Madame de Merteuil left this morning for the country; thus, my charming Cécile, I am now deprived of the sole pleasure which remained to
me during your absence, that of talking of you to your friend and mine.
For some time past, she has allowed me to give her that title; and I have
profited by it with all the more eagerness because it seemed to bring me
nearer to you. Lord! how amiable this woman is! And with what a flattering charm she knows how to endow friendship! It seems as though
that sweet sentiment is embellished and fortified in her by all that she denies to love. If you knew how she loves you, how it pleases her to hear
me speak of you! . . . 'Tis that, no doubt, which draws me so much toward her. What happiness it were, to be able to live entirely for you both,
to pass uninterruptedly from the delights of love to the sweets of friendship, to consecrate all my existence to it, to be in some measure the point
of union of your mutual attachment, and to feel always that, in occupying myself with the happiness of the one, I was working equally for that
of the other. Love, love dearly, my charming friend, this adorable woman.
Give greater value still to the attachment I have for her by participating
in it. Since I have tasted the charm of friendship, I am desirous that you
should experience it in your turn. From pleasures which I do not share
with you I seem only to obtain a half enjoyment. Yes, my Cécile, I would
fain surround your heart with all the softest sentiments, so that its every
vibration might give you a sensation of happiness; and I should still feel
that I could never repay you more than a part of the felicity which I
should derive from you.

Why must it be that these charming projects are only a chimera of my
imagination, and that reality offers me, on the contrary, only indefinite
and dolorous privations? The hope which you had held out to me of
seeing you in the country I see well that I must renounce. I have no other
consolation than that of persuading myself that you do really find it im-

possible. And you refrain from telling me this, from grieving over it with me! Twice already have my complaints on this subject been left without a reply. Ah! Cécile, Cécile, I do believe that you love me with all the faculties of your soul; but your soul is not ardent like my own. Why does it not lie with me to overthrow the obstacles? Why is it not my interests that have to be considered instead of yours? I should know how to prove to you that nothing is impossible to love.

You tell me nothing, either, of the duration of this cruel absence: here, at least, I should perhaps see you. Your charming eyes would reanimate my drooping soul; their touching expression would reassure my heart, which has sometimes need of it. Forgive me, my Cécile; this fear is not a suspicion. I believe in your love, in your constancy. Ah, I should be too unhappy, if I were to doubt it. But so many obstacles! And always renewed! I am sad, my friend, very sad. It seems as though the departure of Madame de Merteuil had renewed in me the sentiment of all my woes.

Adieu, my Cécile; adieu, my beloved. Remember that your lover is grieving, and that you alone can restore him to happiness.

Paris, 17th October, 17★★.

117. Cécile Volanges to the Chevalier Danceny
(Dictated by Valmont)

Do you think then, my dear friend, that I had any need of scolding to make me sad, when I know that you grieve? And do you doubt that I suffer as much as you, at all your sorrows? I even share those which I cause you knowingly; and I have one more than you when I see that you do not do me justice. Oh! that is not right! Indeed, I see what vexes you; it is that, the last two times you asked to come here, I did not answer you: but was the answer such an easy one to give? Do you suppose I do not know that what you want is very wicked? And yet, if I have already so much difficulty in refusing you at a distance, pray, what would it be if you were here? And then, because I had wished to console you for a moment, I should be sorry all my life.

See, I have nothing to conceal from you; here are my reasons, judge for yourself. I should, perhaps, have done what you wish, had it not been for what I have told you, the news that this M. de Gercourt, who is the cause of all our grief, will not arrive yet awhile; and as Mamma, for some time past, has shown me much more kindness; as I, on my side, caress her as much as I can, who knows what I may not be able to obtain from her? And if we could be happy without my having anything to reproach myself with, would not that be much better? If I am to believe what I have been often told, men no longer love their wives so much, if they have loved them overmuch before they were wives. That fear restrains me even more than the rest. My friend, are you not sure of my heart, and will there not be always time?

Listen; I promise you that, though I cannot avoid the misfortune of marrying M. de Gercourt, whom I hate so much already before I know him, nothing shall any longer prevent me from being yours as much as I am able, and even before everything. As I do not care to be loved except by you, and you must see quite well that, if I do wrong, it is not my fault, the rest will be just the same to me; provided that you promise to love me always as much as you do now. But until then, my friend, let me continue as I am; and ask me no more for a thing which I have good reasons for declining to do, and which it yet vexes me to refuse you.

I should be very glad, too, if M. de Valmont were not so urgent for you; it only serves to make me grieve still more. Oh, you have a very good friend in him, I assure you! He does everything that you would do yourself. But adieu, my dear love; it was very late when I began to write to you, and I have spent part of the night over it. I am going to bed now, and to make up for the lost time. I embrace you, but do not scold me any more.

At the Château de . . . , 18th October, 17★★.

118. The Chevalier Danceny to the Marquise de Merteuil

If I am to believe my almanac, my adorable friend, it is but two days that you have been absent; but, if I am to believe my heart, it is two centuries. Now, I have it from yourself, it is always one's heart that one should believe; it is therefore quite time then that you should return, and all your affairs must be more than finished. How can you expect me to be interested in your lawsuit, when, be it lost or won, I must equally pay the costs by the tedium of your absence? Oh, how querulous I feel! And how sad it is to have so fair a subject for ill humor, but no right to show it!

Is it not, however, a real infidelity, a black betrayal, to leave your friend far away from you, after having accustomed him to be unable to dispense with your presence? In vain will you consult your advocates, they will find you no justification for this ill behavior; and then those gentry do but talk of reasons, and reasons are not sufficient answer to sentiments.

For myself, you have told me so often that it was reason which sent you on this journey, that I have entirely done with it. I will no longer listen to it, not even when it tells me to forget you. That is, however, a most reasonable reason: in fact, it would not be so difficult as you suppose. It would be sufficient merely to lose the habit of always thinking of you; and nothing here, I assure you, would recall you to me.

Our loveliest women, those who are said to be the most amiable, are yet so far below you that they could but give a very feeble idea of you.

I think even that, with practiced eyes, the more one thought at first they resembled you, the more difference one would remark afterward: in vain their efforts, in vain their display of all they know, they always fail in being you; and therein, positively, lies the charm. Unhappily, when the days are so long, and one is unoccupied, one dreams, one builds castles in the air, one creates one's chimera; little by little the imagination is exalted; one would fain beautify one's work, one gathers together all that may please, finally one arrives at perfection; and, as soon as one is there, the portrait recalls the model, and one is astonished to find that one has but dreamed of you.

At this very moment, I am again the dupe of an almost similar error. You will believe, perhaps, that it was in order to occupy myself with you that I started to write to you? Not at all: it was to distract myself from you. I had a hundred things to say of which you were not the object, things which, as you know, interest me very keenly; and it is from these, nevertheless, that I have been distracted. And since when, pray, does the charm of friendship divert us from that of love? Ah, if I were to look closely into the matter, perhaps I should have a slight reproach to make myself! But hush! Let us forget this little error, for fear of reverting to it, and let my friend herself ignore it.

Why, then, are you not here to reply to me, to lead me back if I go astray, to talk to me of my Cécile, to enhance, if that be possible, the happiness I derive from her love by the sweet thought that, in loving her, I love your friend? Yes, I confess it, the love which she inspires in me has become even more precious since you have been kind enough to receive my confidence. I love so much to open my heart to you, to pour my sentiments unreservedly into yours! It seems to me that I cherish them the more, when you deign to receive them; and again I look at you and say to myself: It is in her that all my happiness is bound up.

I have nothing new to tell you with regard to my situation. The last letter I received from *her* increases and assures my hope, but delays it still. However, her motives are so tender and so pure that I can neither blame her for them nor complain. Perhaps you do not understand too well what I am telling you; but why are you not here? Although one may say all to one's friend, one dare not write it. The secrets of love, especially, are so delicate that one may not let them go thus upon their *parole*. If one allows them out sometimes, one must at least never let them out of sight; one must, as it were, see them reach their new refuge. Ah, come back then, my adorable friend; you see how very necessary is your return. Forget, in short, the *thousand reasons* which detain you where you are, or teach me to live where you are not.

I have the honor to be, etc.

Paris, 19th October, 17**.

119. Madame de Rosemonde to the Présidente de Tourvel

Although I am still suffering greatly, my dearest fair, I am endeavoring to write to you myself, in order to be able to speak to you of what interests you. My nephew still keeps up his misanthropy. He sends every day most regularly to ask after my health; but he has not come once to enquire for himself, although I have begged him to do so. Thus I see no more of him than if he were in Paris. I met him today, however, in a place where I little expected him. It was in my chapel, whither I had gone for the first time since my painful indisposition. I learned today that for the last four days he has gone regularly to hear mass. God grant that this last!

When I entered, he came up to me, and congratulated me most affectionately on the improved state of my health. As mass was beginning, I cut short the conversation, which I expected to resume afterward; but he had disappeared before I could rejoin him. I will not hide from you that I found him somewhat changed. But, my dearest fair, do not make me repent of my confidence in your reason, by a too lively anxiety; and, above all, rest assured that I would rather choose to pain than deceive you.

If my nephew continues to keep aloof from me, I will adopt the course, as soon as I am better, of visiting him in his chamber; and I will try to penetrate the cause of this singular mania, which, I can well believe, has something to do with you. I will write and tell you anything I may find out. Now I take leave of you, as I can no more move my fingers: besides, if Adelaide knew that I had written, she would scold me all the evening. Adieu, my dearest fair.

At the Château de . . . , 20th October, 17★★.

120. The Vicomte de Valmont to the Père Anselme
(A CISTERCIAN OF THE MONASTERY OF THE RUE SAINT-HONORÉ)

I have not the honor of being known to you, Monsieur. but I know of the entire confidence which Madame la Présidente de Tourvel reposes in you, and I know, moreover, how much this confidence is deserved. I believe, then, that I may address myself to you without indiscretion, in order to obtain a very essential service, truly worthy of your holy office, and one in which the interests of Madame de Tourvel and myself are one.

I have in my hands important papers which concern her, which cannot be entrusted to anybody, and which I would not, and must not, give up except into her hands. I have no means of informing her of this, because reasons which, perhaps, you will have heard from her, but which I do not consider myself authorized to state, have led her to take the course of refusing all correspondence with me; a course that, today, I confess willingly, I cannot blame, since she could not foresee events which I myself was very far from expecting, and which were only rendered possible by that superhuman force which we are forced to recognize in them. I beg you, therefore, Monsieur, to be so good as to inform her of my new resolutions, and to ask her to grant me a private interview, in which I can, at least in part, repair my errors by my excuses; and, as a last sacrifice, destroy in her presence the sole existing traces of an error or fault which has rendered me guilty in her eyes.

It will not be until after this preliminary expiation that I shall dare to lay at your feet the humiliating confession of my long disorders, and to entreat your mediation for an even more important and, unhappily, more difficult reconciliation. May I hope, Monsieur, that you will not refuse me this precious and necessary aid, and that you will deign to sustain my weakness and guide my feet into the new way which I desire most ardently to follow, but which, I blush to confess, I do not yet know?

I await your reply with the impatience of the repentance which desires to make reparation, and I beg you to believe me, with equal gratitude and veneration,

Your most humble, etc.

P.S. I authorize you, Monsieur, should you deem it proper, to communicate this letter in its entirety to Madame de Tourvel, whom I shall make it my duty to respect all my life long, and in whom I shall never cease to honor one whom Heaven has used to bring back my soul to virtue, by the touching spectacle of her own.

At the Château de . . . , 22nd October, 17★★.

121. The Marquise de Merteuil to the Chevalier Danceny

I have received your letter, my too youthful friend; but, before I thank you, I must scold you, and I warn you that, if you do not correct yourself, you shall have no more answers from me. Quit then, if you will believe me, that tone of flattery, which is no more than jargon, when it is not the expression of love. Pray, is that the language of friendship? No, my friend, every sentiment has its befitting speech, and to make use of any other is to disguise the thought which one expresses. I am well aware that our frivolous women understand nothing that is said to them, if it be not translated, in some way, into this customary jargon; but I confess that I thought I deserved that you should distinguish between them and me. I am truly grieved, and perhaps more than I ought to be, that you have judged me so ill.

You will only find then in my letter the qualities which yours lacks:

frankness and simplicity. I will certainly tell you, for instance, that it would give me great pleasure to see you, and that I am vexed to have only tiresome people round me instead of people who please me; but this very phrase you translate thus: *Teach me to live where you are not;* so that, I suppose, when you are with your mistress, you will not be able to live unless I make a third. The pity of it! And these women *who always fail in being me:* perhaps you find that your Cécile also fails in that! That, however, is the result of a language which, owing to the abuse made of it nowadays, is even lower than the jargon of compliments, and has become no more than a mere formula, in which one no more believes than in a most humble servant.

My friend, when you write to me, let it be to tell me your fashion of thinking and feeling, and not to send me phrases which I can find, without your aid, more or less well turned in any novel of the day. I hope you will not be angry at what I am telling you, even if you should detect a little ill humor; for I do not deny I feel some: but, to avoid even the shadow of the fault for which I reproach you, I will not tell you that this ill humor is, perhaps, somewhat augmented by the distance at which I am from you. It seems to me that, all considered, you are worth more than a lawsuit and two advocates, perhaps even more than the *attentive* Belleroche.

You see that, instead of despairing at my absence, you ought to congratulate yourself upon it, for I have never paid you so pretty a compliment. I believe your example is catching, and I, too, am inclined to flatter you; but nay, I prefer to keep to my frankness; it is that alone, then, which assures you of my tender friendship, and of the interest which it inspires in me. It is very sweet to have a young friend whose heart is occupied elsewhere. That is not the system of all women, but it is mine. It seems to me that one abandons oneself with more pleasure to a sentiment from which one can have nothing to fear: thus I have passed with you, early enough, perhaps, into the *rôle* of confidant. But you choose your mistresses so young that you have made me perceive for the first time that I begin to grow old! You have acted well in preparing for yourself a long career of constancy, and I wish with all my heart that it may be reciprocated.

You are right in yielding to the *pure and tender motives* which, according to what you tell me, *delay your happiness.* A long defense is the only merit left to those who do not resist always; and what I should find unpardonable in any other than a child like the little Volanges would be the lack of knowledge how to escape a danger of which she has been amply forewarned by the confession she has made of her love. You men have no idea of what virtue is, nor of what it costs to sacrifice it! But, however incapable a woman may be of reasoning, she ought to know that,

independently of the sin which she commits, a frailty is the greatest of
misfortunes to her; and I cannot conceive how anyone can ever let herself be caught, if she has time for a moment's reflection on the subject.

Do not proceed to dispute this idea, for it is this which principally attaches me to you. You will save me from the perils of love; and, although
I have known well enough hitherto to defend myself without your aid,
I consent to be grateful to you for it, and I shall love you for it the more
and better.

Upon this, my dear Chevalier, I pray God to have you in His good and
holy keeping.

> At the Château de . . . , 22nd October, 17★★.

122. Madame de Rosemonde to the Présidente de Tourvel

I had hoped, my amiable daughter, to be able at least to calm your anxieties; and I see with grief, on the contrary, that I must still augment them.
Be calm, however; my nephew is not in danger: I cannot even say that he
is really ill. But something extraordinary is assuredly passing within him.
I understand naught of it; but I left his room with a sentiment of sadness,
perhaps even of alarm, which I reproach myself for causing you to share,
although I cannot refrain from discussing it with you. This is the narrative of what passed: you may rest assured that it is a faithful one; for, if I
were to live another eighty years, I should never forget the impression
which this sad scene made upon me.

I visited my nephew this morning; I found him writing, surrounded
by sundry heaps of papers which seemed to be the object of his labors.
He was so busied that I was already in the middle of his chamber before
he turned his head to discover who had entered. As soon as he recognized me, I noticed clearly that, on rising, he made an effort to compose
his features, and it was this fact, perhaps, which further attracted my attention. In truth, he had made no toilette and wore no powder; but I
found him pale and wan, and, above all, of a changed expression. His
glance, which we have known so gay and keen, was sad and downcast; in
short, between ourselves, I should not have cared for you to see him thus;
for he had a very pathetic air, and most fitting, I dare believe, to inspire
that tender pity which is one of the most dangerous snares of love.

Although impressed by what I had noticed, I nonetheless commenced
the conversation as though I had perceived nothing. I spoke to him first
of his health; and, though he did not tell me that it was good, he nevertheless did not say that it was bad. Thereupon, I complained of his re-
tirement, which had almost the air of a mania, and I tried to infuse a
little gaiety into my mild reproof; but he only answered, in heartfelt accents, "It is one wrong the more, I confess; but it shall be retrieved with

the rest." His expression, even more than his words, somewhat disturbed my playfulness, and I hastened to tell him that he attached too much importance to a mere friendly reproach.

We then commenced to talk quietly. He told me soon afterward that perhaps an affair, *the most important affair of his life,* would shortly recall him to Paris: but as I was afraid of guessing it, my dearest fair, and feared lest this prologue should lead up to a confidence which I did not desire, I put no question to him, and contented myself with replying that a little more dissipation would benefit his health. I added that, this once, I would not press him to remain, as I loved my friends for themselves; at this simple expression, he grasped my hands, and, speaking with a vehemence which I cannot describe to you: "Yes, aunt," he said to me, "love, love well a nephew who respects and cherishes you; and, as you say, love him for himself. Do not grieve about his happiness, and do not trouble, with any regret, the eternal peace which he hopes soon to enjoy. Repeat to me that you love me, that you forgive me. Yes, you will forgive me, I know your goodness; but how can I hope for the same indulgence from whose whom I have so greatly offended?" He then stooped over me to conceal, as I think, the signs of grief which, in spite of himself, the sound of his voice betrayed to me.

Moved more than I can say, I rose precipitately; and doubtless he noticed my alarm, for, at once growing more composed: "Pardon me," he resumed, "pardon me, Madame; I feel that I am wandering, in spite of my will. I beg you to forget my remarks, and only to remember my profound veneration. I shall not fail," he added, "to come and renew my respects to you before my departure." It seemed to me that this last sentence suggested that I should bring my visit to a conclusion, and I went away.

But the more I reflect upon it, the less can I guess what he wished to say. What is this affair, *the most important of his life?* On what ground does he ask my forgiveness? Whence that involuntary emotion when he spoke to me? I have already asked myself these questions a thousand times without being able to reply to them. I do not even see anything therein which relates to you: however, as the eyes of love are more clear-sighted than those of friendship, I was unwilling to leave you in ignorance of anything that passed between my nephew and myself.

I have made four attempts to finish this long letter, which would be longer still, were it not for the fatigue I feel. Adieu, my dearest fair.

At the Château de . . . , 25th October, 17★★.

123. The Père Anselme to the Vicomte de Valmont

I have had the honor of receiving your letter, M. le Vicomte; and yesterday I betook myself, in accordance with your wishes, to the person in question. I explained to her the object and the motives of the visit you had asked me to pay her. Determined as she was upon the prudent course which she had adopted at first, upon my pointing out to her that by a refusal she, perhaps, incurred a risk of putting an obstacle in the way of your happy return, and thus of opposing, in some manner, the merciful decrees of Providence, she consented to receive your visit, always on condition that it shall be the last, and has charged me to tell you that she will be at home on Thursday next, the 28th. If this day should not be convenient to you, will you be so good as to inform her, and appoint another. Your letter will be received.

Meanwhile, M. le Vicomte, permit me to invite you not to delay, without grave reasons, in order that you may be able to abandon yourself the sooner and more entirely to the laudable dispositions which you display to me. Remember that he who hesitates to improve the moment of grace runs the risk of its being withdrawn from him; that, if the mercy of God is infinite, yet the use of it is regulated by justice; and that a moment may come when the God of mercy shall turn into a God of vengeance.

If you continue to honor me with your confidence, I beg you to believe that all my attention shall be yours, as soon as you desire it: however greatly I may be busied, my most important business will ever be to fulfill the duties of my sacred office, to which I am peculiarly devoted, and the finest moment of my life will be that in which, by the blessing of the Almighty, I shall see my efforts prosper. Weak sinners that we are, we can do nothing by ourselves! But the God who recalls you can do all; and we shall owe alike to His bounty—you, the constant desire to be reconciled to Him, and I the means of being your guide. It is by His aid that I hope soon to convince you that Holy Religion alone can give, even in this world, that solid and durable happiness which in the blindness of human passions we seek in vain.

I have the honor to be, with respectful consideration, etc.

Paris, 25th October, 17★★.

124. The Présidente de Tourvel to Madame de Rosemonde

In the midst of the astonishment, in which the news I received yesterday has thrown me, Madame, I cannot forget the satisfaction which it must cause you, and I hasten to acquaint you with it. M. de Valmont is no longer occupied either with me or with his love; he would only retrieve by a more edifying life the faults, or rather the errors, of his youth. I have been informed of this great event by the Père Anselme, to whom he applied for future direction, and also in order to contrive an interview with me, the principal object of which I judge to be the return of my letters, which he had hitherto retained, in spite of the request I had made him to the contrary.

Doubtless, I cannot but applaud this happy termination, and felicitate myself, if, as he states, I am in any way responsible for it. But why needed it that I should be the instrument, and why should it have cost me my life's repose? Could not M. de Valmont's happiness have been secured by any other means than my misery? Oh, my indulgent friend, forgive me this complaint! I know that it is not mine to question the decrees of God; but while I pray to Him ceaselessly, and always in vain, for strength to conquer my unhappy love, He lavishes it on one who has not prayed for it, and leaves me without succor, utterly abandoned to my weakness.

But let me stifle this guilty plaint. Do I not know that the prodigal son on his return obtained more favor from his father than the son who had never been absent? What account have we to ask from Him who owes us nothing? And even were it possible that we had any rights before Him, what had been my own? Could I boast of a virtue that already I do but owe to Valmont? He has saved me, and how should I dare complain if I suffer for his sake! No, my sufferings will be dear to me, if his happiness is the price. Doubtless, it was needful for him to return to the common Father. The God who made him must have cherished His handiwork. He did not create this charming being only to be a reprobate. 'Tis for me to pay the penalty of my audacious imprudence; ought I not to have felt that, since it was forbidden me to love him, I ought never to have allowed myself to see him?

'Tis my fault or my misfortune that I held out too long against this truth. You are my witness, my dear and venerable friend, that I submitted to this sacrifice as soon as I recognized its necessity: but it just failed in being complete, in that M. de Valmont did not share it. Shall I confess to you that it is this idea which, at present, torments me most? Insufferable pride, which sweetens the ills we bear by the thought of those we inflict! Ah, I will conquer this rebellious heart, I will accustom myself to humiliations!

It is above all to obtain this result that I have at last consented to receive, on Thursday next, the painful visit of M. de Valmont. Then I shall hear him tell me himself that I am nothing to him; that the weak and fugitive impression I had made upon him is entirely effaced! I shall see his gaze directed toward me without emotion, while the fear of betraying my own will make me lower my eyes. Those same letters which he refused so long to my repeated requests I shall receive from his indifference; he will give them up to me as useless things, which have no further interest for him; and my trembling hands, receiving this deposit of shame, will feel that it is given to them by a hand which is firm and tranquil! And then I shall see him depart from me . . . depart forever; and my eyes, which will follow him, will not see his own look back to me!

And I have been reserved for so much humiliation! Ah, let me, at least, make use of it by allowing it to impregnate me with the sentiment of my weakness. . . . Yes, these letters, which he no longer cares to keep, I will religiously preserve. I will impose on myself the shame of reading them daily until the last traces of them are effaced by my tears; and his own I will burn as infected by the dangerous poison which has corrupted my soul. Oh, what is this love then, if it makes us regret even the risks to which it has exposed us; if one can be afraid of feeling it still, even when one no longer inspires it? Let us shun this dire passion, which leaves no choice save betwixt misery or shame, nay, often unites them both: let prudence at least replace virtue.

How far away is Thursday still! Why can I not this instant consummate the grievous sacrifice, and forget at once its object and its cause! This visit troubles me; I repent of my promise of it. Alas! What need has he to see me again? What are we to one another now? If he has offended me, I forgive him. I congratulate him even on his wish to repair his faults; I praise him for it. I will do more, I will imitate him; and I, who have been beguiled by like errors, shall be brought back by his example. But, since his intention is to flee from me, why does he begin by seeking me out? What is most urgent for either of us, is it not that each should forget the other? Doubtless that is so; and that, henceforth, shall be my sole care.

If you will permit me, my amiable friend, I will come to you in order to occupy myself with this arduous task. If I have need of succor, perhaps even of consolation, I will not receive it from any other than you. You alone know how to understand me and to speak to my heart. Your precious friendship shall fill my whole existence. Nothing shall seem too difficult for me to second the care that you must take of yourself. I shall owe you my tranquillity, my happiness, my virtue, and the fruit of your kindness to me will be that, at last, I shall become worthy of it.

I have written very wildly, I think, in this letter; I gather so, at least, from the trouble which has unceasingly harassed me while writing. If any sentiments occur in it at which I ought to blush, cover them with the indulgence of your friendship; I rely upon it entirely. It is not from you that I would hide any of the movements of my heart.

Adieu, my venerable friend. I hope, in a few days, to announce the day of my arrival.

Paris, 25th October, 17★★.

Part IV

125. The Vicomte de Valmont to the Marquise de Merteuil

Behold her vanquished then, this proud woman who dared to think she could resist me! Yes, my friend, she is mine, mine entirely; since yesterday there is nothing left for her to grant me.

I am still too full of my happiness to be able to appreciate it: but I am amazed at the unknown charm I have experienced. Can it be true, then, that virtue enhances the value of a woman even at the very moment of her fall? Nay, let us relegate this puerile notion with other old wives' tales. Does one not almost always encounter a more or less well-feigned resistance at a first triumph? And have I found elsewhere the charm of which I speak? Yet it is not that of love; for, after all, if I have sometimes had, with this astounding woman, moments of weakness which resembled that pusillanimous passion, I have always known how to overcome them and return to my principles. Even if the scene of yesterday had carried me, as I believe it did, somewhat farther than I counted on; even if, for a moment, I shared the trouble and intoxication which I caused, that passing illusion would be dissipated by now: and nevertheless the same charm subsists. I should even find, I confess, a sweet enough pleasure in abandoning myself to it, if it did not cause me some anxiety. Shall I be dominated at my age, like a schoolboy, by an unknown and involuntary sentiment? Nay: I must before all combat it and understand it.

Perhaps, as far as that goes, I have already caught a glimpse of the cause! I am pleased with this idea, at any rate, and I would fain have it true.

In the crowd of women with whom I have hitherto played the part and performed the functions of lover, I had never yet met one who had not at least as much desire to give herself as I had to persuade her to it; I was even in the habit of calling those women prudes who did no more than meet me halfway, in contrast to so many others whose provocative defense did but imperfectly conceal the first advances they had made.

Here, on the contrary, I met with a preconceived unfavorable prejudice, which was subsequently strengthened by the advice and stories of a spiteful but clear-sighted woman; a natural and extreme timidity, fortified by an enlightened modesty; an attachment to virtue directed by religion, with already two years of victory to its account; finally, a vigorous course of conduct inspired by these different motives, which all had for their aim escape from my pursuit.

It is not then, as in my other adventures, a mere capitulation, more or less advantageous, whereof it is easier to take advantage than to be proud; it is a complete victory, purchased at the cost of a hard campaign, and determined by cunning maneuvres. 'Tis not surprising, then, that this success, due to myself alone, should seem all the more precious to me; and the excess of pleasure which I experienced when I triumphed, and which I feel still, is no more than the sweet impression of the sentiment of glory. I cherish this point of view, which saves me from the humiliation of thinking that I can be in any manner dependent upon the slave whom I have subjected; that I do not possess in myself alone the plenitude of my happiness; and that the power of giving me the whole energy of pleasure should be reserved to such or such a woman, excluding all the others.

These deliberate reflections shall regulate my conduct on this important occasion; and you may rest assured that I will not let myself be enchained to such a degree that I cannot always play with these new bonds and break them at my will. But I am talking to you already of my rupture, while you do not yet know the means by which I have acquired my rights: read then, and learn to what virtue is exposed when it seeks to succor folly. I studied so attentively my conversation and the replies I obtained that I hope to be able to repeat them to you with a precision that will delight you.

You will see from the two copies of letters enclosed[1] what mediator I chose to reconcile me with my fair, and what zeal the holy personage employed to reunite us. One thing more I must tell you, which I learned from a letter intercepted in the usual way: the fear and the petty humiliation of being quitted had somewhat disturbed the austere Puritan's prudence, and had filled her heart and head with sentiments and ideas which were nonetheless interesting because they were not common-sense. It was after these preliminaries, necessary for you to know, that yesterday, Thursday the twenty-eighth, the day settled and appointed by the ingrate, I presented myself before her in the quality of a timid and repentant slave, to leave her crowned with victory.

It was six o'clock in the evening when I came to the fair recluse; for

---

[1]Letters the hundred and twentieth and hundred and twenty-second.

since her return her door has been shut to everyone. She attempted to rise when I was announced; but her trembling knees did not allow her to remain in this position: she immediately resumed her seat. She showed signs of impatience, because the servant who had introduced me had some task to perform in the apartment. We filled up the interval with the customary compliments. But, in order to waste no time, when moments were so precious, I carefully examined the locality; and at once my eye fixed upon the scene of my victory. I could have chosen one more suitable, for there was an ottoman in that very room. But I noticed that, facing it, was a portrait of the husband; and I confess that, with such a singular woman, I was afraid lest one haphazard glance in that direction should destroy the result of all my labors. At last, we were left alone and I broached the question.

After having explained, in a few words, that the Père Anselme must have informed her of the motives of my visit, I complained of the severe treatment I had been subject to, and dwelt particularly on the *scorn* which had been displayed me. She defended herself, as I expected; and, as you would expect yourself, I founded my proofs on the distrust and fear which I had inspired, on the scandalous flight which had ensued, her refusal to answer my letters, even to receive them, etc., etc. As she was commencing a justification which would have been very easy, I felt bound to interrupt her; and, to obtain pardon for this brusque proceeding, I covered it at once with a flattery. "If so many charms," I went on, "have made so profound an impression on my heart, the effect of so many virtues has been no less upon my soul. Led away, no doubt, by my desire to approach them, I dared to deem myself worthy. I do not reproach you for having judged otherwise; but I am punished for my mistake." As she maintained an embarrassed silence, I continued:

"It was my wish, Madame, either to justify myself in your eyes, or to obtain from you pardon for the wrongs you suppose me to have committed; so that I can at least end, with a certain tranquillity, days to which I attach no more value since you have refused to embellish them."

Here, however, she endeavored to reply:

"My duty did not permit me. . . ." And the difficulty of completing the lie which duty required, did not permit her to finish her phrase. I resumed, therefore, in a more tender tone: "Is it true that it is from me you have fled?" "My departure was necessary." "And that you drive me away from you?" "It must be so." "And forever?" "I must." I have no need to tell you that, during this short dialogue, the voice of the gentle prude was oppressed, and that her eyes were not raised to mine.

I judged it my duty to give this languid scene a touch of animation; thus, rising with an air of vexation: "Your firmness," I then said, "restores to me all my own. Well, yes, Madame, we shall be separated even more than you think. And you may congratulate yourself at your leisure over the success of your handiwork." Somewhat surprised at this tone of reproach, she sought to reply: "The resolution you have taken . . ." said she. "It is but the result of my despair." I resumed with passion. "You wished me to be unhappy; I will prove that you have succeeded even beyond your hopes." "I desire your happiness," she answered. And the sound of her voice began to announce a strong emotion. Casting myself, therefore, on my knees before her, and in that dramatic tone which you know is mine: "Ah, cruel one!" I cried. "Can any happiness exist for me in which you have no share? Where can I find it away from you? Ah, never, never!" I confess that, in abandoning myself to this extent, I had counted much on the support of tears; but, either from ill disposition, or perhaps owing to the constant and painful attention I was giving to everything, it was impossible for me to weep.

Luckily I remembered that, in order to subjugate a woman, all means are equally good, and that it would be sufficient to astound her by some great change of manner in order to produce an impression at once favorable and profound. Thus, for the sensibility which proved lacking, I substituted terror; and for that, merely changing the inflection of my voice, and keeping in the same posture, "Yes," I continued, "I make this vow at your feet, to possess you or die." As I uttered these last words, our eyes met. I know not what the timid creature saw, or thought she saw, in mine; but she rose with a terrified air, and escaped from the arm with which I had encircled her. It is true, I did nothing to retain her: for I had often remarked that scenes of despair rendered in too lively a key became ridiculous, if they were unduly prolonged, or left one only such really tragic resources as I was very far from wishing to take. However, while she withdrew from me, I added in a low and ominous whisper, but loud enough for her to hear me: "Well then, death!"

I then rose; and, after a moment's silence, cast upon her, as if at random, wild glances, which were nonetheless clear-sighted and observant for their distracted air. Her ill-assured attitude, her heavy breathing, the contraction of all her muscles, the half-raised position of her trembling arms, all gave sufficient proof to me that the effect was such as I had wished to produce: but, since, in love, nothing ever finishes except at close quarters, and we were still at some distance from one another, it became necessary before all things to draw together. It was in order to succeed in this, that I passed, as soon as possible, to an appearance of tranquillity, capable of calming the effects of so violent a condition, without weakening its impression.

This was my transition: "I am very miserable! It was my wish to live for your happiness, and I have troubled it. I devote myself for your peace, and I trouble it to. . . ." Then, with a composed, but constrained, air: "Forgive me, Madame; little accustomed as I am to the storms of passion, I know ill how to repress its movements. If I was wrong to abandon myself to them, at least remember 'tis for the last time. Ah, be calm, be calm, I conjure you!" And, during this long speech, I insensibly drew nearer. "If you would have me be calm," replied the frightened fair, "pray be more tranquil yourself." "Ah, well! yes, I promise you," said I. I added, in a fainter voice, "If the effort be great, at least it is not for long. But," I continued, with a distraught air, "I came, did I not, to return you your letters? For mercy's sake, deign to take them back. This sorrowful sacrifice remains for me to perform; leave me naught which may tend to diminish my courage." And, drawing the precious collection from my pocket: "Behold," said I, "the deceitful receptacle of your assurances of friendship! It bound me to life; take it back from me. Give me thus, yourself, the signal which must separate me from you forever...."

Here, my timorous mistress gave way entirely to her tender concern: "But, M. de Valmont, what is the matter with you, and what is it you would say? Is not the step which you are taking today a voluntary one? Is it not the fruit of your own reflections? And are they not the same which led you yourself to approve the inevitable course which duty has made me adopt?" "Well, then," I answered, "that course is responsible for my own." "And what is that?" "The only one which, while it separates me from you, can put an end to my pain." "But answer me, what is it?" Here I clasped her in my arms, nor did she defend herself in any way; and, judging from this forgetfulness of the proprieties how strong and potent was her emotion: "Adorable creature," said I, risking a little enthusiasm, "you have no conception of the love which you inspire in me; you will never know to what an extent you were adored, and how much dearer this sentiment was to me than existence! May all your days be calm and fortunate; may they be adorned with all the happiness which you have ravished from me! Reward this sincere prayer by a regret, a tear at least; believe that the last sacrifice which I shall make will not be the most grievous to my heart. Farewell!"

While I spoke thus, I felt her heart throbbing violently; I observed the changed expression of her face; I saw, above all, that her tears were choking her and yet were few and painful in their flow. It was not till then that I resolved to feign departure; when, retaining me forcibly: "Nay, listen to me," she said quickly. "Leave me," I answered. "You *shall* listen to me; it is my wish." "I must flee from you, I must!" "No," she cried....

At this last word she flung herself, or rather fell swooning into my arms. As I was still doubtful of so fortunate a success, I feigned the utmost alarm; but, alarmed as I was, I led her, or carried her, to the spot I had originally fixed upon as the field of my triumph; and in truth she did not return to herself until she was submissive and already abandoned to her happy conqueror.

Thus far, my lovely friend, you will find, I believe, a purity of method which will give you pleasure, and you will see that I departed in nothing from the true principles of that war which, as we have often remarked, so strongly resembles the real war. Judge me then as though I had been Frederic or Turenne. I had forced to combat an enemy who would do nothing but temporize; by scientific maneuvres I obtained the choice of positions and of the field; I was able to inspire the enemy with confidence, in order the more easily to catch up with him in his retreat; I was able to add terror to this feeling before the fight was engaged; I left nothing to chance, except in my consideration of a great advantage in case of success, and the certainty of resources in case of defeat; in short, I did not engage until I had an assured retreat, by which I could cover and preserve all that I had previously conquered. That is, I believe, all that one can do: but I am afraid, at present, lest, like Hannibal, I may be enervated by the delights of Capua. Now for what has passed since.

I fully expected that such a great event would not be accomplished without the customary tears and despair; and, if I noticed at first somewhat more confusion and a sort of shrinking, I attributed both to the character of the prude: thus, without concerning myself with these slight differences, which I thought purely local, I simply followed the high road of consolation, thoroughly persuaded that, as happens ordinarily, sensations would assist sentiment, and that a single action would do more than any speech, which last, however, I did not neglect. But I met with a really alarming resistance, less indeed from its excessive character than from the form under which it was displayed.

Imagine a woman seated, of an immovable rigor, and an unchanging face; having the air neither of thinking, hearing, nor understanding; whose fixed eyes give issue to a continuous stream of tears, which fall, however, without an effort. Such was Madame de Tourvel, while I was speaking; but, if I tried to recall her attention to me by a caress, by even the most innocent gesture, this apparent apathy was at once succeeded by terror, gasping for breath, convulsions, sobs and, at intervals, cries, but with not an articulate word.

These cries were resumed several times, and always more loudly; the last even was so violent that I was entirely discouraged by it, and feared for a moment that I had won a useless victory. I fell back upon the customary commonplaces; and, among their number, found this one: "And you are in despair because you have made my happiness?" At this word, the adorable woman turned toward me; and her face, although still rather wild, had, nevertheless, resumed already its celestial expression. "Your happiness!" she said. You can guess my answer. "You are happy then?" I redoubled my protestations. "And happy through me!" I joined praises and tender speeches. While I was speaking, all her limbs grew supple; she sank down languorously, leaning back in her armchair; and yielding to me a hand which I had ventured to take: "I feel," said she, "that that idea consoles and relieves me."

You may judge that, thus shown the way, I no longer left it; it was really the right and, perhaps, the only one. So that, when I would fain attempt a second success, I met, at first, with a certain resistance, and what had passed before rendered me circumspect: but, having summoned this same idea of my happiness to my aid, I soon perceived its favorable effects: "You are right;" the tender creature said to me, "I can no longer support my existence, except in so far as it may serve to render you happy. I devote myself entirely to that: from this moment, I give myself to you, and you shall meet, on my side, neither with refusals nor regrets." It was with this candor, naive or sublime, that she abandoned to me her person and her charms, and enhanced my happiness by participating in it. The intoxication was reciprocal and complete; and for the first time mine survived the pleasure. I only left her arms to fall at her knees and swear an eternal love to her; and, to tell the whole truth, I believed what I said. And, even after we had separated, the idea of her never left me, and I was obliged to make an effort in order to distract myself.

Ah, why are you not here at least to counterbalance the charm of the action by that of the reward? But I shall lose nothing by waiting, is not that so? And I hope I may consider as settled the happy arrangement which I proposed to you in my last letter. You see that I fulfill my word, and that, as I promised you, my affairs will be sufficiently advanced to enable me to give you a portion of my time. Hasten then to dismiss your heavy Belleroche, and leave the mawkish Danceny where he is, to occupy yourself only with me. But what are you doing so long in the country, that you do not even answer me? Do you know that I should like to scold you? But happiness tends to indulgence. And then I do not forget that, in entering once more the ranks of your adorers, I must submit anew to your little fantasies. Remember, however, that the new lover will lose no whit of the former rights of a friend.

Adieu, as of old. . . . Yes, *adieu my angel! I send thee all the kisses of love.*

P.S. Do you know that Prévan, after his month of prison, has been obliged to leave his regiment? It is the news of all Paris today. Truly, he is cruelly punished for a sin which he did not commit, and your success is complete!

Paris, 29th October, 17**.

126. Madame de Rosemonde to the Présidente de Tourvel

I should have replied to you before, my amiable child, if the fatigue consequent on my last letter had not brought back my pains, which have once more deprived me during these last days of the use of my arm. I was most anxious to thank you for the good news which you have given me of my nephew, and I was no less eager to offer you my sincere congratulations on your own account. One is forced to recognize in this a real effect of Providence, which, by touching the heart of one, has also saved the other. Yes, my dearest fair, God, who only wished to try you, has succored you at a moment when your strength was exhausted; and, in spite of your little murmur, you owe Him, methinks, your thanksgiving. It is not that I do not feel that it would have been more agreeable to you, if this resolution had come to you first, and that Valmont's had been only the consequence of it; it seems even, humanly speaking, that the rights of our sex would have been better preserved, and we would not lose any of them! But what are these slight considerations in view of the important objects which have been obtained? Does a man who has been saved from shipwreck complain that he has not had a choice of means?

You will soon find, my dear daughter, that the sorrow which you dread will alleviate itself; and, even if it were to subsist forever and in its entirety, you would nonetheless feel that it was still easier to endure than remorse for crime and contempt of yourself. It would have been useless for me to speak to you earlier with this apparent severity: love is an involuntary sentiment which prudence can avoid, but which it could not vanquish, and which, once born, dies only by its fine death, or from the absolute lack of hope. It is this last case, in which you are, which gives me the courage and the right to tell you frankly my opinion. It is cruel to alarm one hopelessly sick, who is no longer susceptible to aught save consolations and palliation; but it is right to enlighten a convalescent as to the dangers he has incurred, in order to inspire him with that prudence of which he has need, and with submission to counsels which may still be necessary to him.

Since you choose me for your physician, it is as such that I speak to you, and that I tell you that the little indisposition which you experience at present, and which perhaps demands some remedies, is nothing in comparison with the alarming malady from which your recovery is assured. Next, as your friend, as the friend of a reasonable and virtuous woman, I will permit myself to add that this passion, which has subjugated you, already so unfortunate in itself, became even more so through its object. If I am to believe what is told me, my nephew, whom I confess I love, perhaps to weakness, and who, indeed, unites many laudable qualities to many attractions, is not without danger for women; there are women whom he has wronged, and he sets almost an equal price upon their seduction and their ruin. Indeed, I believe that you may have converted him. Never, doubtless, was there a person more worthy to do this: but so many others have flattered themselves with the same thought, and their hopes have been deceived, that I love better far to think you should not be reduced to this resource.

Consider now, my dearest fair, that instead of the many risks you would have had to run, you will have, besides the repose of your conscience and your own peace of mind, the satisfaction of having been the principal cause of Valmont's happy reformation. For myself, I do not doubt but that this is, in large part, the result of your courageous resistance, and that a moment of weakness on your part might have left my nephew, perhaps, in eternal error. I love to think so, and desire to see you think the same; you will find in that your first consolations, and I, fresh reasons for loving you more.

I expect you here within a few days, my amiable daughter, as you have announced. Come and recover calm and happiness in the same spot where you had lost it; come, above all, to rejoice with your fond mother that you have so happily kept the word you gave her, to do nothing unworthy of her or of yourself!

At the Château de . . . , 30th October, 17**.

127. The Marquise de Merteuil to the Vicomte de Valmont

If I have not replied to your letter of the 19th, Vicomte, it is not that I have not had the time; it is quite simply that it put me in a bad humor, and that I found it lacking in common sense. I thought, therefore, that I could not do better than leave it in oblivion: but, since you come back to it, since you appear to cling to the ideas it contains, and take my silence for consent, I must tell you plainly what I think.

I may sometimes have had the pretension to replace in my single person a whole seraglio; but it has never suited me to make a part of one. I thought you knew this. Now, at least, when you can no longer be ignorant of it, you will easily imagine how absurd your proposal must have appeared to me. I indeed! I am to sacrifice a fancy, and a fresh fancy moreover, in order to occupy myself with you! And to occupy myself in what way? By awaiting my turn, like a submissive slave, for the sublime favors of *Your Highness!* When, forsooth, you want a moment's distraction from *that unknown charm* which *the adorable, the celestial* Madame de Tourvel has alone made you experience; or when you are afraid of compromising, in the eyes of *the seductive Cécile,* the superior idea which it is your good pleasure that she should preserve of you: then, condescending even to myself, you will come in search of pleasures, less keen in truth, but without consequence; and your precious bounties, although somewhat rare, will, nevertheless, suffice for my happiness!

You, certainly, are rich in your good opinion of yourself: but, apparently, I am not equally so in modesty; for however I may look at myself, I cannot find myself reduced to such a point. Perhaps this is a fault of mine; but I warn you I have many others also.

I have, in especial, that of believing that the *schoolboy, the mawkish* Danceny, who is solely occupied with me, and sacrifices to me, without making a merit of it, a first passion, even before it has been satisfied, who, in a word, loves me as one loves at his age, may work more effectively than you, for all his twenty years, to secure my happiness and my pleasure. I will even permit myself to add that, if it were my whim to give him an assistant, it would not be you, at any rate not at this moment.

And for what reasons, do you ask me? But, to begin with, there might very well be none: for the caprice which might make me prefer you could equally cause your exclusion. However, I am quite willing, out of politeness, to give you the reason of my opinion. It seems to me that you would have too many sacrifices to make me; and I, instead of being grateful for them, as you would not fail to expect, might be capable of believing that you were still my debtor! You quite see that, far as we are from each other in our fashion of thinking, we cannot come together again in any manner: and I am afraid that it might need time, a long time, before I should change my sentiments. When I am converted, I promise I will inform you. Until then, believe me, make other arrangements, and keep your kisses; you have so many better occasions to dispose of them! . . .

Adieu, as of old, say you? But of old, it seems to me, you took a little more account of me; you had not relegated me entirely to minor parts; and, above all, you were quite willing to wait until I had said yes, before being sure of my consent. Be satisfied then, if instead of bidding you also adieu as of old, I bid you adieu as at present.

Your servant, M. le Vicomte.

At the Château de . . . , 31st October, 17★★.

128. The Présidente de Tourvel to Madame de Rosemonde

I only received yesterday, Madame, your tardy reply. It would have killed me on the instant, if my existence had still been in my own hands; but another is its possessor, and that other is M. de Valmont. You see that I hide nothing from you. If you must consider me no longer worthy of your friendship, I fear even less to lose it than to retain it by guile. All that I can tell you is that, placed by M. de Valmont between his death or his happiness, I resolved in favor of the latter. I neither vaunt myself on this, nor accuse myself; I simply state the fact.

You will easily understand, after this, what impression your letter must have made upon me, with the severe truths which it contains. Do not believe, however, that it was able to give birth to a regret in me, nor that it can ever cause me to change in sentiment or in conduct. It is not that I do not have cruel moments: but when my heart is most torn, when I fear that I can no longer endure my torments, I say to myself: Valmont is happy; and all vanishes before this idea, or rather it converts all into pleasures.

It is to your nephew then that I have devoted myself; it is for him that I have ruined myself. He has become the one center of my thoughts, my sentiments, my actions. As long as my life is necessary to his happiness, it will be precious to me, and I shall deem it fortunate. If someday he thinks differently . . . he shall hear from me neither complaint nor reproach. I have already dared to cast my eyes upon that fatal moment; and I have resolved on my course.

You see, now, how little I need be affected by the fear you seem to have, lest one day M. de Valmont should ruin me: for, ere he can wish for that, he will have ceased to love me; and what will then be vain reproaches to me which I shall not hear? He alone shall be my judge. As I shall have lived but for him, it will be in him that my memory shall repose; and if he is forced to admit that I loved him, I shall be sufficiently justified.

You have now read, Madame, in my heart. I preferred the misfortune of losing your esteem by my frankness to that of rendering myself unworthy of it by the degradation of a lie. I thought I owed this complete confidence to the kindness you have shown me. To add one word more would be to lead you to suspect that I have the vanity to count upon it still, when, on the contrary, I do myself justice in ceasing to pretend to it.

I am with respect, Madame, your most humble and obedient servant.

Paris, 1st November, 17**.

129. The Vicomte de Valmont to the Marquise de Merteuil

Tell me then, my lovely friend, whence comes the tone of bitterness and banter which prevails in your last letter? Pray, what crime have I committed, apparently without suspecting it, which put you in such ill humor? You reproach me with having the air of counting on your consent before I had obtained it: but I believed that what might seem presumption in the case of everybody could never be taken, between you and me, for aught save confidence: and since when has that sentiment done detriment to friendship or to love? In uniting hope to desire, I did but yield to the natural impulse which makes us ever place the happiness we seek as near to us as possible; and you took for the effect of pride what was no more than the result of my eagerness. I know mighty well that custom has introduced in such a case a respectful doubt: but you also know that it is but a form, a mere protocol; and I was authorized, it seems to me, to believe that these minute precautions were no longer necessary between us.

Methinks, even, that this free and frank method, when it is founded on an old *liaison,* is far preferable to the insipid flattery which so often takes the relish out of love. Perhaps, moreover, the value which I find in this manner does but come from that which I attach to the happiness which it recalls to me: but, for that very cause, it would be more painful still for me to see you judge of it otherwise.

That, however, is the only error which I am conscious of; for I do not imagine that you could have thought seriously that there existed any woman in the world whom I could prefer to you, and, even less, that I could appreciate you so ill as you feign to believe. You have looked at yourself, you tell me, in this connection, and you have not found yourself reduced to such a point. I well believe it, and it proves only that you have a faithful mirror. But could you not have drawn the conclusion, with more ease and justice, that I was very certain not to have judged you so?

I seek in vain for a cause for this strange idea. It seems, however, that it is due, more or less, to the praises I have permitted myself to make of other women. At least I infer it, from your affectation of picking out the epithets *adorable, celestial, seductive,* which I made use of in speaking to you of Madame de Tourvel or of the little Volanges. But are you not aware that these words, more often used by chance than from reflection, are less expressive of the account one takes of the person than of the situation in which one finds oneself at the time of speaking? And if, at the very moment when I was keenly affected either by one or the other, I was nonetheless desirous of you; if I showed you a marked preference over both of them; since, in short, I could not renew our former *liaison,* except to the prejudice of the two others, I do not find in that so great a matter for reproach.

It will be no more difficult for me to justify myself as to *the unknown charm* with which you seem to be also somewhat shocked: for, to begin with, it does not result that it is stronger from the fact that it is unknown. Ah, who could give it the palm over the delicious pleasures which you alone know how to render always fresh, as they are always keen? I did but wish to tell you, therefore, that it was of a kind which I had not experienced before, but I did not pretend to assign a class to it; and I added what I repeat today, that, whatever it may be, I shall know how to combat and to conquer it. I shall bring even more zeal to this, if I can see in this trivial task a homage to be offered to you.

As for the little Cécile, I think it hardly necessary to speak of her to you. You have not forgotten that it was at your request that I charged myself with the child, and I only await your permission to be rid of her. I may have remarked upon her ingenuousness and freshness; I may even, for a moment, have thought her *seductive,* because, in a more or less degree, one always takes pleasure in one's own handiwork; but, assuredly, she is not in any way of sufficient consequence to fix one's attention upon her.

And now, my lovely friend, I appeal to your justice, to your first kindness for me, to the long and perfect friendship, the entire confidence which has since welded the bonds between us: have I deserved the severe tone which you adopt with me? But how easy it will be for you to compensate me for it when you like! Say but one word, and you will see whether all the charms and all the seductions will detain me here, not for a day, but for a minute. I will fly to your feet and into your arms, and I will prove to you a thousand times, and in a thousand manners, that you are, that you will ever be the true sovereign of my heart.

Adieu, my lovely friend; I await your reply with much eagerness.

Paris, 3rd November, 17★★.

130. Madame de Rosemonde to the Présidente de Tourvel

And why, my dearest fair, would you cease to be my child? Why do you seem to announce to me that all correspondence will cease between us? Is it to punish me for not having guessed what was against all probability; or do you suspect me of having pained you willfully? Nay, I know your heart too well to believe that it can think thus of mine. The pain, therefore, which your letter caused me is far less relative to me than to yourself!

O my youthful friend! I tell it you with sorrow: you are far too worthy of being loved that ever love should make you happy. Ah! what woman who was truly delicate and sensitive has not found misfortune in this very sentiment which promised her so much felicity! Do men know how to appreciate the woman they possess?

'Tis not that many are not honorable in their actions, and constant in their affections: but, even among these, how few know how to put themselves in unison with our hearts! Do not suppose, my dear child, that their love is like our own. Indeed, they experience the same intoxication, often even they bring more ardor to it; but they do not know that anxious eagerness, that delicate solicitude which causes in us those tender and constant cares of which the beloved object is ever the single aim. The man's pleasure lies in the happiness which he feels, the woman's in that which she bestows. This difference, so essential and so little noticed, has, however, a very sensible influence on the sum of their respective conduct. The pleasure of the one is ever to gratify his desires; that of the other is, especially, to arouse them. To please, with him, is but a means to success; whereas, with her, it is success itself. And coquetry, with which women are so often reproached, is nothing else than the abuse of this manner of feeling, and by that very fact proves its reality. In short, that exclusive taste, which particularly characterizes love, is in the man naught but a preference, serving at the most to enhance a pleasure which, perhaps, another object would diminish, but would not destroy; while in women it is a profound sentiment, which not only destroys every extraneous desire, but which, stronger than nature, and removed from its dominion, allows them to experience only repugnance and disgust at the very point where it seems that pleasure should be born.

And do not deem that more or less numerous exceptions, which one might quote, can successfully contradict these general truths. They are guaranteed by the public voice, which has distinguished infidelity from inconstancy for men alone; a distinction by which they prevail when they should be humiliated, and which, for our sex, has never been adopted save by those depraved women who are its shame, and to whom all means seem good which they hope can save them from the painful feeling of their baseness.

I had thought, my dearest fair, that it might be of use to you to have these reflections to oppose to the chimerical ideas of perfect happiness with which love never fails to abuse our imagination: the lying spirit, to which one still clings even when forced to abandon it, and the loss of which irritates and multiplies the sorrows, already too real, that are inseparable from a lively passion! This task of alleviating your pains, or of diminishing their number, is the only one I would or can fulfill at this moment. In disorders without remedy it is to the regimen alone that advice can be applied. The only thing I ask of you is to remember that to pity a sick person is not to blame him. Who are we, pray, that any of us should blame another? Let us leave the right to judge to Him alone who reads in our hearts, and I even dare believe that, in His paternal sight, a host of virtues may redeem a single weakness.

But I conjure you, my dear friend, guard yourself above all from those violent resolutions which are less a proof of strength than of entire discouragement: do not forget that, in rendering another possessor of your existence, to employ your own expression, it is not in your power to deprive your friends of the part of it which they previously possessed and will never cease to reclaim.

Adieu, my dear daughter; think sometimes of your affectionate mother, and believe that you will ever be, and above all else, the object of her dearest thoughts.

At the Château de . . . , 4th November, 17★★.

131. The Marquise de Merteuil to the Vicomte de Valmont

'Tis well done, Vicomte, and I am better pleased with you this time than the last; but now, let us talk in all friendship, and I hope to convince you that, for you as for myself, the arrangement which you appear to desire would be a veritable piece of madness.

Have you not yet remarked that pleasure, which is, in effect, the sole motive of the union of the two sexes, does not, nevertheless, suffice to form a *liaison* between them; and that, if it is preceded by the desire which attracts, it is no less followed by the disgust which repels? 'Tis a law of nature which love alone can change; and love: does one have it when one wills? Yet one needs it ever; and it would be really too embarrassing, if one had not discovered that it happily suffices if it exists only on one side. The difficulty has thus been rendered less by one half, even without much being lost thereby; in fact, the one derives pleasure from the happiness of loving, the other from that of pleasing, which is a little less keen indeed, but to which is added the pleasure of deceiving; that sets up an equilibrium, and everything is arranged.

But tell me, Vicomte, which of us two will undertake to deceive the other? You know the story of the two sharpers, who recognized each other while playing: "We shall make nothing," said they, "let us divide the cost of the cards;" and they gave up the game. We had best follow, believe me, their prudent example, and not lose time together which we can so well employ elsewhere.

To prove to you that in this I am influenced as much by your interests as my own, and that I am acting neither from ill humor nor caprice, I do not refuse you the price agreed upon between us: I feel perfectly that each of us will suffice to the other for one night; and I do not even doubt but that we should know too well how to adorn it, not to see it end with regret. But do not let us forget that this regret is necessary to happiness; and, however sweet be our illusion, let us not believe that it can be lasting.

You see that I am meeting you in my turn, and even before you have yet set yourself right with me: for, after all, I was to have the first letter of the celestial prude; however, whether because you still cling to it, or because you have forgotten the conditions of a bargain which interests you, perhaps, less than you would fain have me believe, I have received nothing, absolutely nothing. Yet, unless I make a mistake, the tender Puritan must write frequently; else what would she do when she is alone? Surely she has not wit enough to distract herself? I could have, then, did I wish, some slight reproaches to make you; but I pass them over in silence, in consideration of a little temper that I showed, perhaps, in my last letter.

Now, Vicomte, it only remains for me to make one request of you, and this is again as much for your sake as my own; it is to postpone a moment which I desire, perhaps, as much as you, but the date of which must, I think, be deferred until my return to town. On the one hand, we should not find the necessary freedom here; and, on the other, I should incur some risk: for it needs but a little jealousy to attach this tedious Belleroche more closely than ever to my side, although he now only holds by a thread. He is already driven to exert himself in order to love me; to such a degree at present that I put as much malice as prudence into the caresses which I lavish on him. But at the same time you can see that this would not be a sacrifice to make to you! A reciprocal infidelity will render the charm far more potent.

Do you know I regret sometimes that we are reduced to these resources! In the days when we loved—for I believe it was love—I was happy; and you, Vicomte! . . . But why be longer concerned with a happiness which cannot return? Nay, say what you will, such a return is impossible. First, I should require sacrifices which, assuredly, you could not or would not make, and which, like enough, I do not deserve; and then, how is it possible to fix you? Oh, no, no. I will not even occupy myself with the idea; and, in spite of the pleasure which I derive at the present moment from writing to you, I far prefer to leave you abruptly.

Adieu, Vicomte.

At the Château de . . . , 6th November, 17★★.

132. The Présidente de Tourvel to Madame de Rosemonde

Deeply touched, Madame, with your kindness to me, I would abandon myself entirely to it, were I not prevented in some sort from accepting it by the fear of profaning it. Why must it be that, while I see it to be so precious, I feel at the same time that I am no longer worthy of it! Ah! I will at least venture to express to you my gratitude; I will admire above all that indulgent virtue which only knows our frailties to compassionate them, and whose potent charm preserves so soft and strong an empire over hearts, even by the side of the charm of love.

But can I still deserve a friendship which no longer suffices for my happiness? I say the same of your counsels: I feel their worth, but I cannot follow them. And how should I not believe in a perfect happiness, when I experience it at this moment? Yes, if men are such as you say, we ought to shun them, they deserve to be hated; but then Valmont is so far from resembling them! If, like them, he has that violence of passion which you call ardor, how far it is surpassed by his excessive delicacy. O my friend! You talk of sharing my troubles; take a part, then, in my happiness; I owe it to love, and how greatly does the object enhance its value!

You love your nephew, you say, perhaps, foolishly. Ah, if you did but know him as I do! I love him with idolatry, and, even so, far less than he deserves. He may, doubtless, have been led astray by certain errors; he admits it himself; but who ever knew true love as he does? What more can I say to you? He feels it as he inspires it.

You will think that this is *one of those chimerical ideas with which love never fails to abuse our imagination:* but, in that case, why should he have become more tender, more ardent, when he has nothing further to obtain? I will confess, before, I found in him an air of reflection, of reserve, which rarely abandoned him, and which often reminded me, in spite of myself, of the cruel and false impressions which had been given me of him. But, since he has been able to abandon himself without constraint to the movements of his heart, he seems to guess all the desires of mine. Who knows if we were not born for each other! If this happiness was not reserved for me, of being necessary to his! Ah, if it is an illusion, let me die, then, before it comes to an end. But no; I am fain to live to cherish, to adore him. Why should he cease to love me? What other woman could he render happier than me? And I feel, from my own experience, that the happiness one arouses is the strongest tie, the only one which really attaches. Yes, it is this delicious sentiment which ennobles love, which purifies it in some sort, and makes it worthy of a tender and generous soul, such as Valmont's.

Adieu, my dear, my venerable, my indulgent friend. It is in vain that I would write to you at greater length: here is the hour at which he has promised to come, and every other thought forsakes me. Forgive me! But you wish me happiness, and, at this moment, it is so great that I can scarcely support it.

Paris, 7th November, 17★★.

133. The Vicomte de Valmont to the Marquise de Merteuil

What, then, my lovely friend, are those sacrifices which you deem I would not make for you, the reward of which, however, would be to please you? Let me only know them, and if I hesitate to offer them to you, I permit you to refuse the homage. Pray, what opinion have you conceived of me of late, if even in your indulgence you doubt my sentiments or my energy? Sacrifices which I would not or could not make! You think, then, that I am in love and subjugated? And you suspect me of having attached to the person the price which I set upon success? Ah, thank Heaven, I am not yet reduced to that, and I offer to prove it to you. Yes, I will prove it to you, even if it should be at Madame de Tourvel's expense. After that, assuredly, you can have no further doubt.

I have been able, I believe, without compromising myself, to devote some time to a woman who has, at least, the merit of being of a sort that is rarely met with. Perhaps, moreover, the dead season at which this adventure befell, caused me to abandon myself more to it; and, even now, when the great current has scarcely begun to flow, it is not surprising that it should almost entirely occupy me. But remember, please, that it is scarce eight days since I culled the fruits of three months' labor. I have often dallied longer with what was of much less value and had not cost me so much! . . . And never did you draw a conclusion from it to my prejudice.

Besides, would you like to know the true cause of the zeal I am bringing to bear upon it? I will tell you. This woman is naturally timid; at first she doubted incessantly of her happiness, and this doubt sufficed to trouble it: so much so that I am only just beginning to see the extent of my power in this direction. Yet it was a thing I was curious to know; and the occasion is not so readily offered as you may think.

To begin with, for many women pleasure is always pleasure, and never aught else; and in the sight of these, whatever the title with which they adorn us, we are never more than factors, mere commissioners, whose activity is all our merit, and among whom he who does the most is always he who does best.

In another class, perhaps nowadays the most numerous, the celebrity of the lover, the pleasure of having carried him off from a rival, the fear of being robbed of him in turn, absorb the women almost entirely: we count, indeed, more or less, for something in the kind of enjoyment they obtain; but it depends more on the circumstances than on the person: it comes to them through us and not from us.

I needed, then, for the purposes of my observation, to find a delicate and sensitive woman, who made love her sole affair, and who in love itself saw only her lover; whose emotions, far from following the common road, ever started from the heart to reach the senses; whom I have seen, for instance (and I do not speak of the first day), rise from the moment of enjoyment in despair, and a moment later recover pleasure in a word which was responsive to her soul. Last, she must unite to all this that natural candor, grown insurmountable by force of habit, which would not permit her to dissimulate the least sentiment of her heart. Now you will admit, such women are rare; and I dare believe that, failing this one, I should never, perhaps, have met another. It should not be surprising therefore, that she should hold me longer than another; and if the trouble that I take with her makes her happy, perfectly happy, why should I refuse it, especially as it pleases me instead of being disagreeable to me? But, because the mind is engaged, does it follow that the heart is caught? Certainly not. Nor will the value which I admit I set upon this adventure prevent me from embarking on others, or even from sacrificing it to some more agreeable one.

I am free to such an extent that I have not even neglected the little Volanges, whom, nevertheless, I hold so cheap. Her mother brings her back to town in three days; and yesterday I assured my communications; a little money to the porter, a few compliments to his wife, did the business. Can you conceive that Danceny never thought of this simple method? And then they tell us that love creates ingenuity! On the contrary, it stupefies those whom it enslaves. Shall not I, then, know how to defend myself from it? Ah, you may be easy. Already, in a few days, I am about to weaken the impression, too lively perhaps, which I have experienced, by dividing it; and, if a simple division will not do, I will multiply them.

I shall be nonetheless ready to restore the little schoolgirl to her discreet lover as soon as you think proper. It seems to me that you have no longer any motive for preventing it; and I consent to do poor Danceny this signal service. 'Tis in truth, the least I can do in return for those he has done me. He is, at present, in the greatest anxiety to discover whether he will be received at Madame de Volanges'; I calm him, to the utmost of my power, by assuring him that, in one way or another, I will contrive his happiness on an early occasion; and, in the meantime, I continue to charge myself with the correspondence which he means to resume on the arrival of *his Cécile.* I have already six letters from him, and I shall, certainly, have one or two more before the happy day. The lad must have mighty little to do!

But let us leave this childish couple and return to ourselves, so that I may occupy myself exclusively with the sweet hope your letter gave me. Yes, without a doubt you will hold me, and I would not pardon you for doubting it. Pray, have I ever ceased to be constant to you? Our bonds have been relaxed, but never broken; our pretended rupture was only an error of our imagination. Our sentiments, our interests remained nonetheless united. Like the traveler who returns in disillusion, I will confess that I deserted happiness to run after hope; and will say with d'Harcourt:

> "*The more strange lands I saw, I loved my country more.*"[1]

Please, then, oppose no longer the idea, or rather the sentiment, which restores you to me; and, after having tasted all the pleasures, in our different courses, let us enjoy the happiness of feeling that none of them is

---

[1]"*Plus je vis d'étrangers, plus j'aimai ma patrie.*" Du Belloi's tragedy of *Le Siège de Calais.*

comparable with that which we had of old, and which we shall find more delicious still.

Adieu, my charming friend. I consent to await your return; but hasten it, I pray you, and do not forget how greatly I desire it.

Paris, 8th November, 17★★.

134. The Marquise de Merteuil to the Vicomte de Valmont

Truly, Vicomte, you are like the children, before whom one cannot say a word, and to whom one can show nothing because they would at once lay hold of it! A bare idea which comes to me, upon which I warned you even that I was not settled—because I speak of it to you, you take advantage of it to recall my attention to it when I am seeking to forget it, and to make me, in a measure, participate, in spite of myself, in your headstrong desires! Is it generous, pray, to leave me to support the whole burden of prudence alone? I tell you again, and repeat it more often to myself, the arrangement which you suggest is really impossible. Even if you were to include all the generosity you display at this moment, do you suppose that I have not my delicacy also, or that I should be ready to accept sacrifices which would be harmful to your happiness?

Now is it not true, Vicomte, that you are under an illusion as to the sentiment which attaches you to Madame de Tourvel? It is love, or love has never existed: you deny it in a hundred fashions, but you prove it in a thousand. What, for instance, of that subterfuge you employ toward yourself (for I believe you to be sincere with me), which makes you ascribe to curiosity the desire which you can neither conceal nor overcome of retaining this woman? Would not one say that you had never made any other woman happy, perfectly happy? Ah, if you doubt that, you have but a poor memory! Nay, it is not that. Quite simply, your heart imposes on your intelligence, and is rewarded with bad arguments: but I, who have great interest in not being deceived by them, am not so easily satisfied.

Thus, while remarking your politeness, which has made you rigorously suppress all the words which you imagined had displeased me, I saw, nevertheless, that, perhaps without taking notice of it, you nonetheless retained the same ideas. 'Tis true, it is no longer the adorable, the celestial Madame de Tourvel; but it is *an astounding woman, a delicate and sensitive woman,* even to the exclusion of all others; in short *a rare woman* and such that *you would never have met another.* It is the same with that unknown charm, which is not *the strongest.* Well, so be it: but, since you had never found it before, it is easy to believe that you would be no more likely to find it in the future, and the loss you would incur would be nonetheless irreparable. Either these are certain symptoms of love, Vicomte, or we must renounce all hope of ever finding any.

Rest assured that this time I am speaking to you without temper. I have promised I will no more indulge in it; I recognized too clearly that it might become a dangerous snare. Believe me, let us be no more than friends, and let us be content with that. Only do justice to my courage in defending myself: yes, my courage; for one has sometimes need of it, if it be only to refrain from taking a course which one feels to be a bad one.

It is only, then, in order to bring you to my opinion by persuasion that I am going to answer the question you put as to the sacrifices which I should exact, and which you could not make. I employ the word *exact* expressly, for I am very sure that, in a moment, you will, indeed, find me over exacting: so much the better! Far from being annoyed at your refusal, I shall thank you for it. Come, it is not with you that I care to dissimulate, although, perhaps, I had need do so.

I would exact then—observe my cruelty!—that this rare, this astounding Madame de Tourvel should become no more to you than an ordinary woman, merely a woman such as she is: for you must not deceive yourself; the charm which you think to find in others exists in us, and it is love alone which so embellishes the beloved object. What I now require, impossible as it may be, you would, perhaps, make a grand effort to promise me, to swear it even; but I confess, I should put no faith in empty words. I could only be convinced by the whole tenor of your conduct.

Nor is that even all: I should be capricious. The sacrifice of the little Cécile, which you offer me with so good a grace, I should not care about at all. I should ask you, on the contrary, to continue this troublesome service until fresh orders on my part, whether because I should like thus to abuse my empire, or that, more indulgent or more just, it would suffice me to dispose of your feelings, without wishing to thwart your pleasures. Be that as it may, I would fain be obeyed; and my orders would be very rigorous!

'Tis true that then I should think myself obliged to thank you; and who knows? Perhaps even to reward you. For instance, I should assuredly shorten an absence which would become insupportable to me. In short, I should see you again, Vicomte, and I should see you . . . how? . . . But you must remember this is no more than a conversation, a plain narrative of an impossible project, and I would not be the only one to forget it. . . .

Do you know that my lawsuit makes me a little uneasy? I wanted, at last, to know exactly what my prospects were; my advocates, indeed, quote me sundry laws, and above all many *authorities,* as they call them:

but I cannot see so much reason and justice in them. I am almost inclined to regret that I declined the compromise. However, I am reassured when I reflect that the attorney is skillful, the advocate eloquent, and the plaintiff pretty. If these three arguments were to be of no more worth, it would be necessary to change the whole course of affairs; and what, then, would become of the respect for ancient customs?

This lawsuit is now the only thing which retains me here. That of Belleroche is finished: nonsuited, costs divided. He is regretting this evening's ball; it is indeed the regret of the unemployed! I will restore him his complete liberty on my return to town. I make this grievous sacrifice for him, but am consoled by the generosity he finds in it.

Adieu, Vicomte; write to me often. The particulars of your pleasures will recompense me, at least in part, for the tedium I undergo.

At the Château de . . . , 11th November, 17★★.

135. The Présidente de Tourvel to Madame de Rosemonde

I am endeavoring to write to you, without yet knowing if I shall be able. Ah God! When I think of my last letter, which my excessive happiness prevented me from continuing! It is the thought of my despair which overwhelms me now, which leaves me only strength enough to feel my sorrows, and deprives me of the power of expressing them.

Valmont—Valmont no longer loves me, he has never loved me. Love does not vanish thus. He deceives me, betrays me, outrages me. All misfortunes and humiliations that can be heaped together I experience, and it is from him that they come!

Do not suppose that this is a mere suspicion: I was so far from having any! I have not even the consolation of a doubt: I have seen him: what could he say to justify himself? . . . But what matters it to him! He will not even make the attempt. . . . Unhappy wretch! What will thy reproaches and tears avail with him? He is far from thinking of thee!

'Tis true, then, that he has sacrificed me, exposed me even . . . and to whom? . . . A low creature. . . . But what am I saying? Ah, I have even lost the right to despise her! She has been false to fewer duties, she is not so guilty as I. Oh, how bitter is the sorrow which is founded upon remorse! I feel my torments redouble.

Adieu, my dear friend; however unworthy I may have made myself of your pity, you will still feel it for me, if you can form any idea of what I suffer.

I have just read over my letter, and I perceive it can tell you nothing; I will try, then, to muster up courage to relate the cruel incident. It was yesterday; for the first time since my return I was going to sup abroad.

Valmont came to see me at five o'clock; never had he seemed so fond. He gave me to understand that my project of going out vexed him, and you may judge that I soon formed that of remaining with him. However, two hours later, and suddenly, his air and tone underwent a sensible change. I know not whether I had let fall something which may have displeased him; be that as it may, shortly afterward he pretended to recollect some business which compelled him to leave me, and went away: not without displaying a very lively regret, which seemed affectionate, and which I then believed to be sincere.

Being left alone, I judged it more proper not to excuse myself from my first engagement since I was at liberty to fulfill it. I completed my toilette and entered my carriage. Unfortunately, my coachman took me by way of the Opera, and I was involved in the crowd of people leaving; four yards in front of me, and in the rank next to my own, I perceived Valmont's carriage. My heart instantly palpitated, but it was not from fear; and my only idea was the desire that my carriage should go forward. Instead of that, it was his own which was forced to retreat, and came alongside of mine. I instantly advanced; what was my astonishment to find a courtesan at his side, one well known as such! I withdrew, as you may well believe, and I had already seen quite enough to wound my heart; but you would hardly believe that this same woman, apparently informed by an odious confidence, never quitted the window of the carriage, nor ceased to stare at me, with peals of scandalous laughter.

In the condition of prostration to which I was reduced, I let myself, nevertheless, be driven to the house where I was to sup; but it was impossible for me to remain; I felt each instant on the point of swooning away, and, above all, I could not restrain my tears.

On my return, I wrote to M. de Valmont, and sent him my letter immediately; he was not at home. Wishing, at any price, to issue from this state of death, or to confirm it forever, I sent again with orders to wait for him; but before midnight my servant returned, telling me that the coachman, who was back, had told him that his master would not be home that night. I thought this morning that I had nothing else to do than ask him for the return of my letters, and beg him to visit me no more. I have, indeed, given orders to this effect, but doubtless they were superfluous. It is nearly noon; he has not yet presented himself, and I have not received a word from him.

Now, my dear friend, I have nothing further to add: you are informed of everything, and you know my heart. My sole hope is that I may not long afflict your tender friendship.

Paris, 15th November, 17**.

136. The Présidente de Tourvel to the Vicomte de Valmont

Doubtless, Monsieur, after what passed yesterday, you will not expect me to receive you again; nor, doubtless, are you at all desirous that I should! This note, therefore, is written less with the intention of begging you to come no more, than to request you to return the letters, which should never have existed, and which, if they may have interested you for a moment, as proofs of the infatuation you had occasioned, can only be indifferent to you now that this is dissipated, and that they only express a sentiment which you have destroyed.

I admit and confess that I am to blame for having shown in you a confidence of which so many before me have been victims; in that I accuse myself alone: but I believed, at least, that I had not deserved to be handed over by you to insult and contempt. I believed that, in sacrificing all for you, and losing for you alone my rights to my own and others' esteem, I could, nevertheless, expect to be judged by you not more severely than by the public, whose opinion still discriminates, by an immense interval, between the frail woman and the woman who is depraved.

These wrongs, which would be wrongs in the case of anybody, are the only ones I shall mention. I shall be silent on those of love; your heart would not understand mine. Adieu, Monsieur.

Paris, 15th November, 17★★.

137. The Vicomte de Valmont to the Présidente de Tourvel

This instant only, Madame, has your letter been handed to me; I shuddered as I read it, and it has left me with barely the strength to reply to it. What terrible idea, then, do you form of me? Ah, doubtless, I have my faults, and such faults as I shall never forgive myself, all my life, even were you to cover them with your indulgence. But how far from my soul have those ever been with which you reproach me! What, I! Humiliate you! Degrade you! When I respect you as much as I cherish you; when I have never felt a moment of pride save when you judged me worthy of you! You are deceived by appearances, and I admit they may have seemed against me: but did not your heart contain the wherewithal to contend against them, and did it not rebel at the mere thought that it could have a cause of complaint against mine? However, you believed it. So you not only judged me capable of this atrocious madness, but you even feared you had exposed yourself to it through your bounty to me. Ah, if you consider yourself to such a degree degraded by your love, I am myself, then, all that is vile in your eyes!

Oppressed by the painful emotion which this idea causes me, I am losing, in repelling it, the time I should employ in destroying it. I will confess all: I am restrained also by quite another consideration. Must I retrace facts which I would fain obliterate, and fix your attention and my own upon a moment of error which I would fain redeem with the rest of my life, the cause of which I cannot even now conceive, and the memory of which must for ever be my humiliation and my despair? Ah, if my self-accusation is to excite your anger, you will not, at any rate, have to seek far for your revenge; it will be sufficient to hand me over to my remorse.

However, who would believe it? The first cause of this incident is the supreme charm which I experience when I am by you. It was this which caused me too long to forget important business which could not be postponed. I left you too late, and did not find the person of whom I was in search. I hoped to meet him at the Opera, and my visit there was equally unsuccessful. Émilie, whom I met there, whom I had known in days when I was far from knowing you or love; Émilie was without her carriage, and begged me to set her down at her house, not a dozen yards away, and to this I consented, seeing no harm in it. But it was just then that I met you, and I felt immediately that you would be driven to hold me guilty.

The fear of displeasing or of grieving you is so potent with me that it was bound to be, and indeed was, speedily noticed. I admit even that it induced me to try and persuade the girl not to show herself; this precaution of delicacy was fatal to love. Accustomed, like all those of her condition, never to be certain of an empire, ever usurped, save by means of the abuse which they allow themselves to make of it, Émilie was by no means willing to allow so splendid an occasion to slip. The more she saw my embarrassment increase, the more she affected to shew herself; and her mad merriment—and I blush to think that you could for a moment have thought yourself its object—was only caused by the cruel pain I experienced, which itself was but due to my respect and love.

So far, doubtless, I am more unfortunate than guilty, and those wrongs, *which would be wrongs in the case of anybody, and the only ones you mention;* those wrongs, being wiped away, cannot be a cause of reproach to me. But 'tis in vain you pass over in silence those of love: I shall not maintain a like silence concerning them; I have too great an interest in breaking it.

In the confusion in which I am thrown by this unaccountable deviation, it is not without extreme sorrow that I can bring myself to recall the memory of it. Penetrated with a sense of my failings, I would consent to pay the penalty for them, or I would wait for time, my eternal tenderness, and repentance to bring my pardon. But how can I be silent, when what is left for me to say concerns your delicacy?

Do not think I seek a pretense to excuse or palliate my fault: I confess my guilt. But I do not confess, I will never admit, that this humiliating error can be looked upon as a fault in love. Nay, what can there be in common between a surprise of the senses, a moment's self-oblivion, soon followed by shame and regret, and a pure sentiment which can only be born in a delicate soul and sustained by esteem, and of which, finally, happiness is the fruit? Ah, do not profane love thus! Above all, fear to profane yourself by uniting in the same point of view things which can never be confounded. Leave vile and degraded women to dread a rivalry which they feel may be established in their own despite, and to know the pangs of a jealousy as humiliating as it is cruel: but do you turn away your eyes from objects which might sully their glance; and, pure as the Divinity, like it punish the offense without feeling it.

But what penalty will you impose on me that is more grievous than that which I undergo? What can be compared to the regret at having displeased you, the despair at having grieved you, the overwhelming idea of having rendered myself less worthy of you? You are absorbed in punishing me, and I ask you for consolations: not that I deserve them, but because they are necessary to me, and they can only come to me from you!

If, on a sudden, forgetful of our love, and setting no further price on my happiness, you wish, on the contrary, to hand me over to eternal sorrow, you have the right; strike: but if, more indulgent or more sensitive, you remind yourself once more of those tender sentiments which united our hearts; of that voluptuousness of the soul, always being born again and always felt more keenly; of those sweet and fortunate days which each of us owed to the other; all those benefits of love which love alone procures; perhaps you will prefer the power of renewing to that of destroying them. What can I say more? I have lost all, and lost it by my fault; but I can retrieve all by your bounty. It is for you to decide now. I will add but one word. Only yesterday you swore to me that my happiness was quite secure so long as it depended on you! Ah, Madame, will you abandon me today to an eternal despair?

Paris, 15th November, 17**.

138. The Vicomte de Valmont to the Marquise de Merteuil

I insist, my charming friend: no, I am not in love, and it is not my fault if circumstances force me to play the part. Only consent, and return; you shall soon see for yourself how sincere I am. I made proof of it yesterday, and it cannot be destroyed by what occurs today.

Know then I was with the tender prude, and was quite without any other business: for the little Volanges, in spite of her condition, was to pass the whole night at Madame V***'s infants' ball. My lack of employment had, at first, inclined me to prolong the evening, and I had even demanded a slight sacrifice with this view; but hardly was it granted, when the pleasure I had promised myself was disturbed by the idea of this love which you persist in ascribing to me, or at least, in reproaching me with; so much so that I felt no other desire except that of being able to assure myself, and convince you, that it was pure calumny on your part.

I made a violent resolve therefore; and, under some trivial pretext, left my fair much surprised and, doubtless, even more grieved. For myself, I went tranquilly to meet Émilie at the Opera; and she could testify to you, that, until this morning, when we separated, no regret came to trouble our pleasures.

I had, however, fine cause enough for uneasiness, had not my utter indifference saved me from it; for you must know that I was hardly four doors away from the Opera, with Émilie in my carriage, when that of the austere Puritan drew up exactly beside mine, and a block which occurred left us for nearly half a quarter of an hour side by side. We could see each other as clearly as at noon, and there was no means of escape.

Nor is this all; I took it into my head to confide to Émilie that it was the woman of the letter. (You will remember, perhaps, that piece of folly, and that Émilie was the desk).[1] She had not forgotten it, and, as she is a laughter-loving creature, she could not be at peace until she had examined, at her ease, *this piece of virtue,* as she said, and this with peals of such scandalous laughter as would have angered anyone.

Still this is not all; the jealous woman sent to my house the very same night! I was not there; but, in her obstinacy, she sent a second time, with orders to wait for me. As soon as I had made up my mind to sleep with Émilie, I had sent back my carriage, with no other order to the coachman but to return and fetch me this morning; and as, on reaching home, he found the messenger of love, he told him very simply that I should not be back that night. You can well imagine the effect of this news, and that on my return I found my dismissal announced with all the dignity proper to the occasion.

Thus this adventure, which in your view was never to be determined, could have been finished, as you see, this morning; if it is not finished, that is not, as you will believe, because I set any price on its continuation: it is, first, because I did not think it decent that I should let myself be quitted; and again, because I wished to reserve for you the honor of the sacrifice.

I answered this severe note, therefore, in a long letter full of sentiment; I gave lengthy reasons and relied on love to make them acceptable. I have already succeeded. I have just received a second note, still very rigorous and confirming the eternal rupture, as it ought to be; the tone of it, however, is not the same. Above all, I am not to be seen again: this resolution

---

[1]"Letters the forty-sixth and forty-seventh.

is announced four times in the most irrevocable fashion. I concluded thereby, that I was not to lose a moment before I presented myself. I have already sent my *chasseur* to win over the porter; and, in an instant, I shall go myself, to have my pardon sealed: for in sins of this nature, there is only one formula which carries a general absolution; and that can only be performed at an audience.

Adieu, my charming friend; I fly to make trial of this great event.

Paris, 15th November, 17★★.

139. The Présidente de Tourvel to Madame de Rosemonde

How I reproach myself, my tender friend, for having spoken to you too much and too soon of my passing sorrows! I am the cause if you are grieved at present; those sorrows which you derive from me still endure; and I—I am happy. Yes, all is forgotten, pardoned; rather let me say, all is redeemed. Peace and delight have succeeded to this state of sorrow and anguish. O joy of my heart, how can I express you! Valmont is innocent; no one is guilty who loves so well. Those serious, offensive wrongs for which I reproached him with so much bitterness he had not committed; and if, on a certain point, my indulgence was necessary, had I not also my injustice to repair?

I will not enter into the details of the facts or reasons which justify him; perhaps, even, the mind would but ill appreciate them: it is the heart alone which is capable of feeling them. If, however, you were to suspect me of weakness, I would summon your judgment to the aid of my own. With men, you have said yourself, infidelity is not inconstancy.

'Tis not that I do not feel that this distinction, which opinion justifies in vain, nonetheless wounds our delicacy; but of what should mine complain, when that of Valmont suffers even more? For the very wrong which I forget do not believe that he forgives himself, or is consoled. And yet how greatly has he retrieved this trivial error by the excess of his love and my happiness!

Either my felicity is greater, or I know the value of it better, since I have been afraid that I had lost it: but what I may tell you is that, if I felt I had sufficient strength to support again sorrows as cruel as those I have just undergone, I should not deem I paid too high a price for the excess of happiness I have tasted since. O my tender mother, scold your inconsiderate daughter for having grieved you by too much hastiness; scold her for having judged rashly and calumniated him whom she should ever adore: but, while recognizing her imprudence, see her happy, and enhance her joy by sharing it.

Paris, 16th November, 17★★, in the evening.

140. The Vicomte de Valmont to the Marquise de Merteuil

How comes it, my lovely friend, that I receive no reply from you? Yet my last letter seemed to me to deserve one; these three days I could have received it, and I am awaiting it still! Indeed, I am vexed; I shall not speak to you at all, therefore, of my grand affairs.

That the reconciliation had its full effect; that, instead of reproaches and distrust, it but called forth fresh proofs of fondness; that it is I, at present, who receive the excuses and reparation due to my suspected candor, I shall tell you no word of this: and but for the unexpected occurrence of last night, I should not write to you at all. But, as that concerns your pupil, who probably will not be in a condition to tell you of it herself, at any rate for some time to come, I have charged myself with the task.

For reasons which you may or may not guess, Madame de Tourvel has not engaged my attention for some days past; and as these reasons could not exist in the case of the little Volanges, I became more attentive to her. Thanks to the obliging porter, I had no obstacles to overcome, and we led, your pupil and I, a comfortable and regular life. But habit leads to negligence: during the first days, we could never take precautions enough for our safety; we trembled even behind the bolts. Yesterday, an incredible piece of forgetfulness caused the accident of which I have to inform you; and if, for my part, I escaped with a fright, it has cost the little girl considerably more.

We were not asleep, but were in that state of repose and abandonment which succeeds to pleasure, when we heard, on a sudden, the door of the room open. I at once seized my sword, as much for my own defense as for that of our common pupil; I advanced, and saw no one: but, indeed, the door was open. As we had a light, I made a search, but found no living soul. I remembered, then, that we had forgotten our ordinary precautions, and no doubt the door, which had been only pushed to or badly shut, had opened of itself.

On rejoining my timid companion, with a view to calming her, I no longer found her in the bed; she had fallen, or hidden herself, betwixt the bed and wall: she was stretched there without consciousness, with no other movements than violent convulsions. You may imagine my embarrassment! I succeeded, however, in putting her back in the bed, and even in bringing her to, but she had hurt herself in her fall, and it was not long before she felt the effects.

Pains in the loins, violent colic pains, symptoms even less ambiguous, had soon enlightened me as to her condition: but, to acquaint her with it, I had first to tell her of that in which she was before; for she had no suspicion of it. Never perhaps, before her, did anyone preserve so much innocence, after doing so well all that is necessary to get rid of it! Oh, this one loses no time in reflection!

But she lost a great deal in bewailing herself, and I felt it was time to come to a resolution. I agreed with her, then, that I would go at once to the physician and to the surgeon of the family, and, informing them they would be sent for, would confide the whole truth to them, under a promise of secrecy; that she, on her side, should ring for her waiting maid; that she should, or should not, take her into her confidence, as she liked, but that she should send her to seek assistance, and forbid her, above all, to awake Madame de Volanges; a natural and delicate attention on the part of a daughter who fears to cause her mother anxiety.

I made my two visits and my two confessions with what speed I could, and thence returned home, nor have I gone abroad since; but the surgeon, whom I knew before, came at noon to give me an account of his patient's condition. I was not mistaken; but he hopes that, if no accident occurs, nothing will be noticed in the house. The maid is in the secret; the physician has given the complaint a name; and this business will be settled like a thousand others, unless it be useful for us to speak of it hereafter.

But have we still any interests in common, you and I? Your silence would lead me to doubt it; I should not even believe it at all, did not my desire lead me to seek every means of preserving the hope of it.

Adieu, my lovely friend; I embrace you, though I bear you a grudge.

Paris, 21st November, 17★★.

141. The Marquise de Merteuil to the Vicomte de Valmont

Good God, Vicomte, how you trouble me with your obstinacy! What does my silence matter to you? Do you suppose, if I maintain it, that it is for lack of reasons to justify it? Ah, would to God it were! But no; it is only that it is painful for me to tell you them.

Tell me truly: are you under an illusion yourself, or are you trying to deceive me? The disparity between what you say and what you do leaves me no choice but between these two sentiments: which is the true one? Pray, what would you have me say to you, when I myself do not know what to think?

You appear to make a great merit of your last scene with the Présidente; but, pray, what does it prove for your system, or against mine? I certainly never said that you loved this woman well enough not to deceive her, or not to seize every occasion which might seem to you easy or agreeable: I never even doubted but that it would be very much the same to you to satisfy with another, with the first comer, the same desires which she alone could have raised; and I am not surprised that, in the licentiousness of mind which one would be wrong to deny you, you have done once from deliberation what you have done a thousand times from opportunity. Who does not know that this is the simple way of the world, and the custom of you all, whoever you are, to whatever class you belong, from the rascal to the *espèces?* Whoever abstains from it, nowadays, passes for a romantic; and that is not, I think, the fault with which I reproach you.

But what I have said, what I have thought, and what I still think, is that you are nonetheless in love with your Présidente. Truly not with a love that is very pure or very tender, but with that of which you are capable; that kind, for instance, which enables you to find in a woman attractions or qualities which she does not possess; which places her in a class apart, and puts all other women in the second rank; which keeps you attached to her even when you outrage her; such, in short, as I conceive a sultan may feel for a favorite sultana, which does not prevent him from preferring to her often a simple odalisque. My comparison seems to me all the more just because, like him, you are never either the lover or friend of a woman, but always her tyrant or her slave. Thus, I am quite sure you humbled and abased yourself mightily, to regain this lovely creature's good graces! And only too happy at having succeeded, as soon as you think the moment has arrived to obtain your pardon, you leave me *for this grand event.*

In your last letter, again, if you do not speak exclusively of this woman, it is because you will not tell me anything *of your grand affairs;* they seem to you so important that the silence which you maintain on this subject seems to you sufficient punishment for me. And it is after these thousand proofs of your decided preference for another that you ask me calmly whether we still have *any interests in common!* Take care, Vicomte! If I once answer you, my answer will be irrevocable: and to be afraid to give it at this moment is perhaps already to have said too much. I am resolved, therefore, to speak no more of it.

All that I can do is to tell you a story. May be you will not have time to read it, or to give so much attention to it as to understand it right? That is your affair. At worst it will only be a story wasted.

A man of my acquaintance was entangled, like you, with a woman who did him little honor. He had indeed, at intervals, the wit to feel that, sooner or later, this adventure would do him harm: but although he blushed for it, he had not the courage to break it off. His embarrassment was all the greater in that he had boasted to his friends that he was entirely free; and that he was well aware that, when one meets with ridicule, it is always increased by self-defense. He passed his life thus, never ceasing to commit follies, never ceasing to say afterward: *It is not my fault.* This man had a friend, and she was tempted at one moment to give him up to the public in this state of frenzy, and thus render his ridicule indelible: however, being more generous than malicious, or, perhaps, for some other motive, she wished to make one last attempt, so that, whatever happened, she might be in a position to say, like her friend: *It is not my fault.* She sent him, therefore, without any other explanation, the following letter, as a remedy whose application might be useful to his disease:

"One tires of everything, my angel: it is a law of nature; it is not my fault.

"If, then, I am tired today of an adventure which has occupied me exclusively for four mortal months, it is not my fault.

"If, for instance, I had just as much love as you had virtue, and that is saying much, it is not surprising that one should finish at the same time as the other. It is not my fault.

"Hence it follows that for some time past I have deceived you: but then your pitiless fondness in some measure forced me to it! It is not my fault.

"Today, a woman whom I love to distraction demands that I sacrifice you. It is not my fault.

"I am very sensible that here is a fine opportunity for calling me perjured: but, if nature has only gifted men with constancy, while it has given women obstinacy, it is not my fault.

"Believe me, take another lover, as I have taken another mistress. This advice is good, very good; if you think it bad, it is not my fault.

"Adieu, my angel; I took you with pleasure, I leave you without regret: perhaps I shall return. This is the way of the world. It is not my fault."

It is not the moment, Vicomte, to tell you the effect of this last attempt, and what resulted from it: but I promise to let you know in my next letter. You will find there also my *ultimatum* as to the renewal of the treaty you propose. Until then, quite simply, adieu. . . .

By the way, I thank you for your details as to the little Volanges; it is an article that will keep for the gazette of scandal on the day after her marriage. In the meantime I send you my condolences on the loss of your progeny. Good night, Vicomte.

At the Château de . . . , 24th November, 17**.

142. The Vicomte de Valmont to the Marquise de Merteuil

Upon my word, my lovely friend, I know not whether I have misread or misunderstood your letter, and the story you told me, and the model little epistle which it contained. All I can tell you is that this last seemed to me original and calculated to produce an effect: so that I simply copied it, and, quite simply again, sent it to the celestial Présidente. I did not lose a moment, for the tender missive was dispatched yesterday evening. I preferred it thus, because, first, I had promised to write to her yesterday; and again, because I thought a whole night would not be too long for her to reflect and meditate *upon this grand event,* even though you should reproach me a second time with the expression.

I hoped to be able to send you my beloved's reply this morning; but it is nearly noon, and I have as yet received nothing. I shall wait until five o'clock; and, if then I have no news of her, I shall go and enquire myself; for in matters of form, above all, 'tis only the first step that is difficult.

At present, as you may well believe, I am most anxious to hear the end of the story of this man of your acquaintance, so vehemently suspected of not knowing at need how to sacrifice a woman. Did he not amend? And did not his generous friend give him her pardon?

I am no less anxious to receive your *ultimatum,* as you so politically say! I am curious, above all, to know if you will find love again in this last proceeding. Ah, no doubt, there is, and much of it! But for whom? Still, I make no pretensions, and I expect everything from your charity.

Adieu, my charming friend; I shall not seal this letter until two o'clock, in the hope of being able to enclose the expected reply.

At two o'clock in the afternoon.

Still nothing; I am in a mighty hurry; I have not time to add a word: but this time, will you still refuse the tenderest kisses of love?

Paris, 25th November, 17★★.

143. The Présidente de Tourvel to Madame de Rosemonde

The veil is rent, Madame, upon which was painted the illusion of my happiness. Grim truth enlightens me, and shows me naught but a sure and speedy death, the road to which is traced between shame and remorse. I will follow it, . . . I will cherish my torments, if they cut short my existence. I send you the letter which I received yesterday; I will add no reflections on it, it contains them all. The time has passed for complaint; nothing is left but to suffer. It is not pity I need, but strength.

Receive, Madame, the one farewell that I shall utter, and grant my last prayer; it is to leave me to my fate, to forget me utterly, to consider me no longer upon the earth. There is a stage of misery in which even friendship augments our sufferings and cannot heal them. When wounds are mortal, all succor becomes inhuman. All emotion is foreign to me save that of despair. Nothing can befit me now save the profound darkness in which I will bury my shame. There I will weep over my faults, if I can still weep; for since yesterday I have not shed a tear. My withered heart no longer furnishes any.

Adieu, Madame. Do not answer me. I have made a vow upon that cruel letter never to receive another.

                              Paris, 27th November, 17★★.

144. The Vicomte de Valmont to the Marquise de Merteuil

Yesterday, at three o'clock in the evening, my lovely friend, being out of patience at having received no news, I presented myself at the house of the deserted fair; I was told that she was out. I saw nothing more in this phrase than a refusal to receive me, at which I was neither vexed nor surprised; and I retired, in the hope that this step would induce so polite a woman to honor me with at least a word of reply. The desire I had to receive it brought me home on purpose about nine o'clock, but I found nothing there. Astonished at this silence, for which I was not prepared, I sent my *chasseur* for information, and to discover if the sensitive person was dying or dead. At last, when I had returned, he informed me that Madame de Tourvel had, indeed, gone out at eleven in the forenoon with her waiting maid; that she was driven to the Convent of . . . ; and that, at seven o'clock in the evening, she sent back her carriage and servants, saying that they were not to expect her home. This is certainly acting according to rule. The convent is the widow's right asylum; and, if she persists in so laudable a resolution, I shall add to all the other obligations which I owe her that of the celebrity which this adventure will assume.

I told you some time ago that, in spite of your uneasiness, I should only reappear upon the stage of the world brilliant with new *éclat*. Let them show themselves, then, these severe critics, who accused me of a romantic and unhappy passion; let them make quicker or more brilliant ruptures: nay, let them do better, let them present themselves as consolers, the way is clear for them. Well, let them only dare to attempt the course which I have run from end to end; and, if one of them obtains the least success, I yield him the place of honor. But they will all discover that, when I am at any pains, the impression I leave is ineffaceable. This one I am sure will be so; and I should look upon all my other triumphs as nothing, if in this case I was ever to have a favored rival.

The course she has taken flatters my self-love, I admit; but I am annoyed that she should have found sufficient strength to separate herself so much from me. There will be no obstacles between us, then, save those of my own formation! What! If I wished to renew with her, she might be unwilling? What am I saying? She would not desire it, deem it no more her supreme happiness? Is it thus that one loves? And do you think, my lovely friend, that I ought to suffer it? Could I not, for instance, and would it not be better, endeavor to bring this woman to the point of seeing the possibility of a reconciliation, which one always desires, as long as one has hope? I could try this course without attaching any importance to it, and consequently without your taking umbrage. On the contrary, it would be a simple experiment which we would perform in concert; and, even if I should succeed, it would but be one means the more of repeating, when you wished it, a sacrifice which seems to have been agreeable to you. Now, my fair one, I am waiting to receive the reward, and all my prayers are for your return. Come quickly then to recover your lover, your pleasures, your friends and the current of adventure.

That of the little Volanges has turned out amazing well. Yesterday, my uneasiness not allowing me to remain in one place, I called, among my various excursions, upon Madame de Volanges. I found your pupil already in the *salon,* still in the costume of an invalid, but in full convalescence, looking only fresher and more interesting. You women, in a like situation, would have lain a month on your long chair: my faith, long live our *demoiselles!* This one, in truth, gave me a desire to see if the recovery was a complete one!

I have still to tell you that the little girl's accident had like to have turned your *sentimental* Danceny's head. At first it was grief; today it is joy. *His Cécile* was ill! You can imagine how the brain reels at such a calamity. Three times a day he sent to enquire after her, and on no occasion omitted to present himself; finally, in a noble epistle, he asked Mamma's permission to go and congratulate her on the convalescence of so dear an object, and Madame de Volanges consented: so much so that I found the young man established as in the old days, save for a certain familiarity which as yet he dares not permit himself.

It is from himself that I have learned these details, for I left at the same time with him, and made him chatter. You can have no notion of the effect this visit has had on him. Joy, desires, transports impossible to describe. I, with my fondness for grand emotions, completed the work of turning his head, by assuring him that, in a very few days, I would put him in the way of seeing his fair one at closer quarters.

Indeed, I am determined to hand her over to him as soon as I have made my experiment. I wish to consecrate myself to you wholly; and then, would it be worthwhile that your pupil should also be my scholar, if she were to deceive nobody but her husband? The masterpiece is to deceive her lover, and above all her first lover! As for myself, I have not to reproach myself with having uttered the word love.

Adieu, my lovely friend; return soon, then, to enjoy your empire over me, to receive its homage, and to pay me its reward.

Paris, 28th November, 17★★.

145. The Marquise de Merteuil to the Vicomte de Valmont

Seriously, Vicomte, have you left the Présidente? Have you sent her the letter which I wrote you for her? Really, you are charming; and you have surpassed my expectations! In all good faith, I confess that this triumph gratifies me more than all those I have hitherto obtained. You will think, perhaps, that I set a very high value on this woman, whom recently I so disparaged; not at all: but it is not over her that I have gained the advantage; it is over you: that is the amusing and really delicious part of it.

Yes, Vicomte, you loved Madame de Tourvel much, and you love her still; you are madly in love with her: but, because I amused myself by making you ashamed of it, you bravely sacrificed her. You would have sacrificed a thousand of her, rather than submit to raillery. To what lengths will not vanity carry us! The wise man was right, indeed, when he said that it was the enemy of happiness.

Where would you be now, if I had only wished to play you a trick? But I am incapable of deceit, as you well know; and, should you even reduce me in my turn to the convent and despair, I will run the risk, and surrender to my victor.

If I capitulate, however, it is really mere frailty: for, if I liked, what quibbles I might set up! And perhaps you would deserve them! I admire, for instance, the skill, or the awkwardness, with which you sweetly propose to me that you should be allowed to renew with the Présidente. It would suit you mightily, would it not? To take all the merit of this rupture, without losing thereby the pleasures of enjoyment? And then, as this apparent sacrifice would be no longer one for you, you offer to repeat it when I wish it! By this arrangement, the celestial prude would always believe herself to be the single choice of your heart, while I should plume myself on being the preferred rival; we should both of us be deceived, but you would be happy; and what does the rest matter?

'Tis a pity that, with such a genius for conceiving projects, you should have so little for their execution; and that, by a single ill-considered step, you should have yourself put an invincible obstacle to what you most desire.

What! You had an idea of renewing, and you could write my letter! You must have thought me clumsy indeed! Ah, believe me, Vicomte, when one woman strikes at another's heart, she rarely fails to find the vital spot, and the wound is incurable. When I was striking this one, or rather guiding your blows, I had not forgotten that the woman was my rival, that you had, for one moment, preferred her to me, and, in short, that you had rated me below her. If my vengeance has been deceived, I consent to bear the blame. Thus I am satisfied that you should try every means: I even invite you to do so, and promise you not to be vexed at your success, if you should attain it. I am so easy on the subject that I will trouble no further about it. Let us speak of something else.

For instance, of the health of the little Volanges. You will give me definite news of it on my return, will you not? I shall be very glad to have some. After that, it will be for you to judge whether it will suit you best to restore her to her lover or to endeavor to become once more the founder of a new branch of the Valmonts, under the name of Gercourt. This idea strikes me as rather diverting; and, in leaving you your choice, I ask you not to take any definite step until we have talked of it together. This does not delay you very long, for I shall be in Paris immediately. I cannot tell you the precise day; but you may be sure that you will be the first informed of my arrival.

Adieu, Vicomte; in spite of my peevishness, my malice, and my reproaches, I have still much love for you, and I am preparing to prove it to you. *Au revoir,* my friend.

At the Château de . . . , 29th November, 17★★.

146. The Marquise de Merteuil to the Chevalier Danceny

At last I am leaving, my young friend; and tomorrow evening I shall be back again in Paris. In the midst of all the confusion which a change of residence involves, I shall receive no one. However, if you have some very pressing confidence to make me, I am quite willing to except you from the general rule: but you will be the sole exception; I beg you, therefore, to keep the secret of my arrival. Valmont even will not be informed of it.

Had anyone told me, a short time ago, that soon you would have my exclusive confidence, I should not have believed it. But yours has attracted mine. I am tempted to believe that you have brought some skill to this end, perhaps even some seduction. That would be very wrong, to say the least! For the rest, it would not be dangerous now; you have really other and better occupations! When the heroine is on the scene, there is little notice taken of the confidant.

Indeed, you have not even found time to acquaint me of your new successes. When your Cécile was absent, the days were not long enough to hear your tender complaints. You would have made them to the echoes, if I had not been there to hear them. Since then, when she was ill, you honored me again with the recital of your anxieties; you wanted someone to whom to tell them. But now that she whom you love is in Paris, that she is recovered, and, above all, that you sometimes see her, she is all-sufficing, and your friends see no more of you.

I do not blame you; it is the fault of your twenty years. From Alcibiades down to yourself, do we not know that young people are unacquainted with friendship, save in their sorrows? Happiness sometimes makes them indiscreet, but never confiding. I am ready to say with Socrates: *I love my friends to come to me when they are unhappy*.[1] But, in his quality of a philosopher, he could dispense with them when they did not come. In that I show less wisdom than he, and I felt your silence with all a woman's weakness.

Do not, however, think me exacting: I am far from being that! The same sentiment which makes me notice these privations enables me to support them with courage, when they are the proof, or the cause, of my friends' happiness. I do not count on you, therefore, for tomorrow evening, save insofar as love may leave you free and disengaged, and I forbid you to make the least sacrifice for me.

Adieu, Chevalier; it will be a real festival to see you again: will you come?

At the Château de . . . , 29th November, 17**.

147. Madame de Volanges to Madame de Rosemonde

I am sure you will be as grieved as I am, my worthy friend, to learn of the condition in which Madame de Tourvel lies; she has been ill since yesterday: her disorder appeared so suddenly, and exhibits such grave symptoms, that I am really alarmed.

A burning fever, a violent and almost constant delirium, an unquenchable thirst: that is all that can be remarked. The doctors say they can make no diagnosis as yet; and the treatment will be all the more difficult, because the patient refuses every kind of remedy with such obstinacy that it was necessary to hold her down by force to bleed her; and the same course had to be followed on two other occasions to tie her bandage, which in her delirium she persists in tearing off.

You, who have seen her, as I have, so fragile, timid and quiet, cannot conceive that four persons are barely enough to hold her; and at the slightest expostulation she flies into indescribable fury! For my part, I am afraid it is something worse than delirium, and that she is really gone out of her mind.

What increases my fear on this subject is a thing which occurred the day before yesterday. Upon that day, she arrived about eleven o'clock in the forenoon, with her waiting maid, at the Convent of. . . . As she was educated in that house, and had continued the habit of sometimes visiting it, she was received as usual, and seemed to everyone calm and in good health. About two hours later, she enquired if the room she had occupied as a schoolgirl was vacant, and, on being answered in the affir-

---

[1]Marmontel: *Conte moral d'Alcibiade.*

mative, she asked to go and see it: the Prioress accompanied her with some other nuns. It was then that she declared that she had come back to take her abode in that room, which, said she, she ought never to have left, and which, she added, she would never leave *until her death:* those were her words.

At first they knew not what to say: but when their first astonishment was over, it was represented to her that her position as a married woman prevented them from receiving her without a special permission. Neither this, nor a thousand other reasons, made any impression; and from that moment she obstinately refused, not only to leave the convent, but even her room. At last, weary of the discussion, they consented, at seven o'clock in the evening, that she should pass the night there. Her carriage and servants were dismissed; and they awaited the next day to come to some decision.

I am assured that, all through the evening, her air and bearing, far from being wild, were composed and deliberate; only that she fell four or five times into a reverie so deep that they could not rouse her from it by speaking to her; and, that, each time before she issued from it, she carried her two hands to her brow, which she seemed to clasp vigorously: upon which, one of the nuns who were with her having asked her if her head pained her, she gazed at her a long time before replying, and said at last, "The hurt is not there!" A moment later, she asked to be left alone, and begged that no further question should be put to her.

Everyone retired except her waiting maid: who was fortunately obliged to sleep in the same chamber, for lack of other room. According to this girl's account, her mistress was pretty quiet until eleven o'clock. She then expressed a wish to go to bed: but, before she was quite undressed, she began to walk up and down her chamber, with much action and frequent gestures. Julie, who had been a witness of what had passed during the day, dared say naught to her, and waited in silence for nearly an hour. At length, Madame de Tourvel called to her twice in quick succession; she had but the time to run up, when her mistress fell into her arms, saying, "I am exhausted." She let herself be led to bed, and would not take anything, nor allow any help to be sent for. She merely had some water placed near her and ordered Julie to lie down.

The girl declares that she remained awake until two in the morning, and that, during that time, she heard neither a movement nor a complaint. But she says that she was awakened at five o'clock by the talk of her mistress, who was speaking in a loud and high voice; and that, having enquired if she needed anything, and obtaining no reply, she took the light and went to the bed of Madame de Tourvel, who did not recognize her, but suddenly interrupting her incoherent remarks, cried out excitedly, "Leave me alone, leave me in the darkness; it is the darkness that becomes me." I remarked yesterday myself that she often repeats this phrase.

At length, Julie profited by this kind of order to go out and seek other assistance: but Madame de Tourvel refused it, with the fury and delirium which she has displayed so often since.

The confusion into which this threw the whole convent induced the Prioress to send for me at seven o'clock yesterday morning. . . . It was not yet daylight. I hastened there at once. When my name was announced to Madame de Tourvel, she appeared to recover her consciousness, and replied, "Ah, yes, let her come in." But, when I reached her bed, she looked fixedly at me, took my hand excitedly, gripped it, and said in a loud but gloomy voice, "I am dying because I did not believe you." Immediately afterward, hiding her eyes, she returned to her most frequent remark: "Leave me alone," etc., and lost all consciousness.

This phrase and some others which fell from her in her delirium make me fear lest this cruel affliction may have a cause which is crueler still. But let us respect the secrets of our friend, and be content to pity her misfortune.

The whole of yesterday was equally tempestuous, and was divided between fits of alarming delirium and moments of lethargic depression, the only ones when she takes or gives any rest. I did not leave her bedside until nine o'clock in the evening, and I shall return to it this morning to pass the day there. I will certainly not abandon my unfortunate friend: but the heartrending part of it is her obstinacy in refusing all attention and succor.

I send you the bulletin of last night, which I have just received, and which, as you will see, is anything but consoling. I will be careful to forward them all to you punctually.

Adieu, my respected friend, I am going back to the patient. My daughter, who is fortunately almost recovered, sends you her respects.

Paris, 29th November, 17★★.

148. The Chevalier Danceny to the Marquise de Merteuil

O you whom I love! O thou whom I adore! O you who have commenced my happiness! O thou who hast crowned it! Compassionate friend, tender mistress, why must the recollection of thy sorrow come to trouble the charm which I undergo? Ah, Madame, be calm, 'tis friendship which implores you. O my friend, be happy, 'tis the prayer of love.

Nay, what reproaches have you to make to yourself? Believe me, you are misled by your delicacy. The regrets it causes you, the injuries of which it accuses me, are equally imaginary; and my heart feels that between us two there has been no other seducer but love. Dread no longer, then, to yield to the sentiments you inspire, to let yourself be penetrated by all the fires you yourself have kindled. What! would our hearts be less pure, if they had been later illuminated? Doubtless, no. 'Tis seduction, on the contrary, which, acting never except by plan, can regulate its progress and its methods, and, from a distance, foresee events. But true love does not thus permit itself to meditate and reflect: it distracts us from our thoughts by our sentiments; its sway is never stronger than when it is unknown; and it is in shadow and silence that it entangles us in bonds which it is alike impossible to notice or to break.

Thus, as late as yesterday, in spite of the lively emotion which the idea of your return caused me, in spite of the extreme pleasure I felt at seeing you, I nevertheless thought myself to be called and guided still by calm friendship only: or rather, abandoned wholly to the soft sentiments of my heart, I was very little concerned to unravel their origin or their cause. Like myself, my tender friend, you experienced, unconsciously, that imperious charm which handed over our souls to the sweet impressions of affection; and neither of us recognized Love, until we had issued from the intoxication in which the god had plunged us.

But that very fact justifies instead of condemning us. No, you have not been false to friendship, and I have not abused your confidence. 'Tis true, we were both ignorant of our feelings; but we only underwent this illusion, we did not seek to give birth to it. Ah, far from complaining of it, let us only think of the happiness it has procured us; and, without troubling it with unjust reproaches, let us only be concerned to enhance it by the charm of constancy and security! O my friend, how my heart dotes on this hope! Yes, freed, henceforward, from every fear, and given over wholly to love, you will participate in my desires, my transports, the delirium of my senses, the intoxication of my soul; and every moment of our fortunate days shall be marked by a new enjoyment.

Adieu, thou whom I adore! I shall see thee, this evening, but shall I find thee alone? I dare not hope it. Nay! you do not desire it as much as I do!

Paris, 1st December, 17★★.

149. Madame de Volanges to Madame de Rosemonde

I had hoped yesterday, almost all day, my revered friend, to be able to give you more favorable news this morning as to the health of our dear invalid: but this hope has been destroyed since last evening, and I am only left with the regret that I have lost it. An event, seemingly of scant importance, but cruel in the results it caused, has rendered the condition of our invalid at least as grievous as it was before, if, indeed, it has not made it worse. I should have understood no whit of this sudden change, had I not received yesterday the complete confidence of our unhappy friend. As she did not conceal from me that you were also acquainted with all her misfortunes, I can speak to you, without reserve, of her sad situation.

Yesterday morning, when I reached the convent, I was informed that the invalid had been asleep for the last three hours; and her slumber was so calm and deep that I was afraid for a moment that it was lethargic. Shortly afterward, she awoke, and herself drew back the curtains of her bed. She gazed at us all with an air of surprise; and when I rose to go to her, she recognized me, spoke my name, and begged me to draw near. She left me no time to question her, but asked me where she was, what we were doing there, if she was sick, and why she was not at home. I thought, at first, that it was a new delirium, only of a more tranquil kind than the last; but I perceived that she fully understood my answers. In fact, she had recovered her reason, but not her memory.

She questioned me very minutely as to all that had happened to her since she had been at the convent, whither she did not remember coming. I answered her correctly, only suppressing what might have given her too much alarm; and when I asked her, in my turn, how she felt, she replied that she was not in pain at that moment, but that she had suffered greatly in her sleep and felt tired. I persuaded her to be quiet and to talk little; after which, I partly closed her curtains, leaving them half open, and sat down by her bed. At the same time some broth was suggested, which she took and found good.

She remained thus for about half an hour, during which time her only words were to thank me for the attention I had given her; and she brought to these thanks that grace and charm which you know. She then maintained for some time an absolute silence, which she only broke to say, "Ah yes, I remember coming here." And a moment later, she cried pitifully, "My friend, my friend, pity me; my miseries are all coming back to me." Then as I advanced toward her, she seized my hand, and resting her head upon it: "Dear God!" she went on, "can I not die then?" Her expression, more than these words even, moved me to tears; she perceived them in my voice, and said to me, "You pity me! Ah, did you but know . . ." and then, interrupting herself: "Arrange that we can be left alone, and I will tell you all." As I believe I have informed you, I had my suspicions already as to what was to be the subject of this confidence; and, fearing that the conversation, which I foresaw would be long and sorrowful, might, perhaps, be harmful to the condition of our unhappy friend, I refused at first, under the pretext that she required rest; but she insisted, and I yielded to her instances. We were no sooner alone than she told me all that you have already heard from her, which, for that reason, I will not repeat to you. Finally, while speaking of the cruel fashion in which she had been sacrificed, she added, "I felt very certain it would be my death, and I had the courage for it; but what is impossible to me is to survive my misfortune and my shame."

I tried to vanquish this discouragement, or rather this despair, with the arms of religion, which, hitherto, had such power over her; but I soon perceived that I had not strength enough for these august functions, and I confined myself to a proposal to call in the Père Anselme, whom I know to be entirely in her confidence. She agreed to this, and even seemed to desire it greatly. He was sent for and came at once. He stayed for a long time with the patient, and said, on leaving, that, if the physicians judged as he did, he thought the ceremony of the sacraments might be deferred; that he would return on the following day.

It was about three o'clock in the afternoon, and until five our friend was fairly quiet; so much so that we had all regained hope. Unfortunately, a letter was brought up to her. When they would have given it her, she answered first that she would not receive any, and no one pressed it. But from that moment she shewed greater agitation. Shortly afterward, she asked whence this letter came. It had no postmark: who had brought it? No one knew. From whom had it been sent? The portress had not been told. She then kept silence for some time, after which she began to speak; but her wandering talk only told us that she was again delirious.

However, there was another quiet interval, until at last she requested that the letter which had been brought should be given her. As soon as she had cast her eyes on it, she cried, "From him! Good God!" and then in a strong but oppressed voice, "Take it back, take it back." She had her bed curtains shut immediately, and forbade anybody to come near her; but we were almost immediately compelled to return to her side. The frenzy had returned more violent than ever, and really terrible convulsions were joined to it. These attacks had not ceased by the evening, and this morning's bulletin informs me that the night has not been less stormy. In short, her state is such that I am astonished she has not already succumbed, and I will not hide from you that I have very little hope left.

I suppose this unfortunate letter was from M. de Valmont: but what can he still dare write to her? Forgive me, my dear friend; I refrain from all reflection: but it is cruel, indeed, to see a woman make so wretched an end, who was hitherto so deservedly happy.

Paris, 2nd December, 17**.

150. The Chevalier Danceny to the Marquise de Merteuil

While I wait for the happiness of seeing you, I abandon myself, my tender friend, to the pleasure of writing to you, and it is by occupying myself with you that I dispel my regret for your absence. To retrace my sentiments for you, to recall your own, is a real delight to my heart; and it is thus that even a time of privation offers me still a thousand benefits precious to my love. However, if I am to believe you, I shall obtain no reply from you: this very letter is to be the last, and we must refrain from a correspondence which, according to you, is dangerous, *and of which we have no need.* Assuredly, I will believe you, if you insist: for what can you wish that does not become my own wish, for that very reason? But, before being wholly resolved, will you not permit me to discuss the matter with you?

Of the question of danger, you must be the sole judge: I can calculate nothing, and I confine myself to begging you to watch over your safety; for I can have no peace while you are uneasy. For this purpose, it is not we two who are but one, but you who are both of us. It is not the same with *our wants:* here we can have but one thought; and if our opinion differs, it can only be for lack of explanation or from misunderstanding. This, then, methinks, is what I feel.

No doubt a letter seems by no means indispensable, when we can see each other freely. What could it say that a word, a glance, or even silence would not say a hundred times better still? This seems to me so true that, at the moment when you spoke of our ceasing to correspond, the idea easily crept into my soul; it troubled it perhaps, but did not wound it. It is even, as it were, when, wishing to press a kiss upon your bosom, I meet with a riband or a veil; I do but thrust it aside, and have no feeling of an obstacle.

But, since then, we are separated; and, now that you are no longer here, this thought of our correspondence has come back to torture me. Why, say I to myself, this privation the more? Nay, is it a reason, because one is far away, that one should have no more to say? I will assume that, favored by circumstance, we pass a whole day together; must we waste the time in talking which is meant for pleasure? Yes, for pleasure, my tender friend; for, by your side, even the moments of repose are full of a delicious enjoyment. But at last, however long the time may be, one ends by separation; and then one is all alone! 'Tis then that a letter is precious! If one reads it not, at least one gazes at it.... Ah! do not doubt, one may look at a letter without reading it, as, methinks, I should still find some pleasure in touching your portrait in the night. . . .

Your portrait, do I say? But a letter is the portrait of the soul. It has not, like a cold resemblance, that stagnation which is so remote from love; it lends itself to our every movement: by turns it is animated, feels enjoyment, is in repose. . . . All your sentiments are so precious to me! Will you rob me of a means of cherishing them?

Are you sure, pray, that the need to write to me will never torment you? In solitude, if your heart expands or is depressed, if a movement of joy thrills through your soul, if an involuntary sadness, for a moment, troubles it: where will you depose your gladness or your sorrow, except upon the bosom of your friend? Will you, then, have a sentiment which he does not share? Will you allow yourself to be lost in solitary dreams apart? My love ... my tender love! But it is your privilege to pronounce sentence. I did but wish to discuss, and not to beguile you; I do but give you reasons, I dare believe that my prayers had been of more avail. If you persist, therefore, I will endeavor not to grieve; I will make an effort to tell myself what you would have written to me: but, ah, you would say it better than I; and, above all, I should have more pleasure in hearing it.

Adieu, my charming friend; the hour is drawing nigh when I shall be able to see you: I take leave of you in all haste, that I may come and find you the sooner.

Paris, 3rd December, 17★★.

151. The Vicomte de Valmont to the Marquise de Merteuil

I do not suppose, Marquise, that you deem me so inexperienced as to have failed to set its due value upon the *tête-à-tête* in which I found you this evening, nor upon the *remarkable chance* which brought Danceny to your house! It is not that your practiced countenance did not know marvelously well how to assume an expression of calm and serenity, nor that you betrayed yourself by any of those phrases which the lips of confusion or repentance sometimes let fall. I admit, also, that your docile gaze served you to perfection; and, if it had but known how to make itself believed as well as understood, far from feeling or retaining the least suspicion, I should not have suspected for a moment the extreme vexation caused you by that *importunate third party*. But, if you would not lavish such great talents in vain, if you would obtain the success you promised yourself, and produce, in short, the illusion you sought, you must begin by forming your novice of a lover with greater care.

Since you are beginning to undertake educations, teach your pupils not to blush and be put out of countenance at the slightest pleasantry; not to deny so earnestly, in the case of one woman only, the things against which they defend themselves so feebly in the case of all the others. Teach them, again, how to listen to the praises of their mistress, without deeming themselves bound to do the honors of her; and, if you permit them to gaze at you in company, let them, at least, know beforehand how to disguise that look of possession, so easy to recognize, which they confound so clumsily with that of love. You will then be able to exhibit them in your public appearances, without their conduct putting their sage instructress to the blush; and I myself, only too happy to have a hand in your celebrity, promise to compose and publish the programs of this new college.

But, until then, I am, I confess, astonished that it should be I whom you have chosen to treat like a schoolboy. Oh, on any other woman how speedily I would be avenged! What a pleasure I should make of it! And how far it would surpass that of which she believed she had robbed me! Yes, it is, indeed, in your case alone that I can prefer reparation to revenge; and do not think that I am held back by the least doubt, the least uncertainty; I know all.

You have been in Paris for the last four days; and every day you have seen Danceny, and you have seen him only. Even today, your door was still closed; and your porter only failed to prevent my reaching you, for want of an assurance equal to your own. Nonetheless, I was not to doubt, you wrote to me, that I should be the first to be informed of your arrival; of that arrival of which you could not yet tell me the date, although you wrote to me on the eve of your departure. Will you deny these facts, or will you attempt to excuse them? Either course is alike impossible; and yet I still contain myself! There you behold the force of your dominion: but believe me, rest satisfied with having tried it, abuse it no more. We both know one another, Marquise: that word ought to suffice.

Tomorrow, you told me, you will be out all day? Well and good, if you are really going out; and you may imagine that I shall know. But at any rate you will return in the evening; and, for our difficult reconciliation, the time betwixt then and the next morning will not be too long. Let me know then, if it is to be at your house, or in *the other place,* that our numerous and reciprocal expiations are to be made. Above all, no more of Danceny. Your naughty head was full of his idea, and I cannot be jealous of that frenzy of your imagination: but reflect that, from this moment, what was but a fantasy would become a marked preference. I do not think that I was made for such humiliations, and I do not expect to receive them from you.

I even hope that this sacrifice will not seem one to you. But, even if it should cost you anything, it seems to me that I have set you a fine enough example, and that a woman of sensibility and beauty, who lived for me alone, who, perhaps, at this very moment, is dying of love and regret, is worth at least as much as a young schoolboy, who lacks, if you will, neither good looks nor intelligence, but who, as yet, has neither constancy nor knowledge of the world!

Adieu, Marquise; I say nothing of my sentiments toward you. All that I can do, at this moment, is not to search my heart. I wait for your reply. Reflect, when you make it, reflect carefully that the easier it is for you to make me forget the offense you have given me, the more indelibly would a refusal on your part, a simple postponement even, engrave it upon my heart.

Paris, 3rd December, 17★★, in the evening.

152. The Marquise de Merteuil to the Vicomte de Valmont

Pray, have a care, Vicomte, and show more respect to my extreme timidity! How do you suppose that I can endure the overwhelming thought of incurring your wrath, and, above all, how can I fail to succumb to the fear of your vengeance? The more so in that, as you know, if you were to blacken me, it would be impossible for me to retaliate. I might speak, indeed, but your existence would be nonetheless brilliant and calm. In fact, what would you have to fear? To be sure, you would be obliged to leave, if the time were left you for it. But can one not live abroad as well as here? And all considered, provided that the Court of France left you in peace at whatever one you had chosen for your abode, it would merely be a case of shifting the scene of your triumphs. Having attempted to restore your coolness by these moral considerations, let us return to business.

Do you know, Vicomte, why I have never married again? It is not, assuredly, for lack of advantageous offers; it is solely in order that nobody should have the right to dictate my actions. It is not even that I was afraid of no longer being able to carry out my wishes, for I should always have ended by doing that; but that it would have been a burden to me, that anyone should have had the right merely to complain of them; it is, in short, because I wished only to deceive for my pleasure, and not from necessity. And here you are, writing me the most marital letter that it is possible to receive! You speak to me of nothing but the injuries on my side, the favors on yours! But how, pray, can one be lacking to one to whom one owes no whit? I am unable to conceive it.

Let us consider: what is all this ado about? You found Danceny with me, and it displeased you? Well and good: but what conclusion can you have drawn from it? Either it was the result of chance, as I told you, or of my will, as I did not tell you. In the first case, your letter is unjust; in the second, it is ridiculous: it was indeed worth the trouble of writing! But you are jealous, and jealousy does not reason. Very well, let me reason for you.

Either you have a rival or you have not. If you have one, you must please, in order to be preferred to him; if you have not, you must still please, in order to avoid having one. In both cases the same conduct is to be observed: why, therefore, torment yourself? Above all, why torment me? Do you no longer know how to be the most amiable? And are you no longer sure of your successes? Come now, Vicomte, you do yourself an injustice. But it is not that; it is that, in your eyes, I am not worth your putting yourself to so much trouble. You are less desirous of my favors than you are of abusing your empire. There, you are an ingrate. That is enough sentiment, methinks, and if I were to continue a very little longer, this letter might well turn to tenderness: but that you do not deserve!

You deserve just as little that I should justify myself. To punish you for your suspicions, you shall retain them: of the time of my return, therefore, just as of the visits of Danceny, I shall tell you nothing. You have taken mighty pains to inform yourself, have you not? Very well! Are you any more advanced? I hope it has given you a great deal of pleasure; I can tell you, it has not interfered with mine. All I can say, then, in reply to your threatening letter, is that it has had neither the fortune to please me, nor the power to intimidate me; and that, for the moment, I could not be less disposed than I am to grant your request.

In truth, to accept you such as you show yourself today would be to commit a real infidelity to you. It would not be a renewal with my old lover; it would be to take a fresh one, and one by no means worth the old. I have not so far forgotten the first that I should so deceive myself. The Valmont whom I loved was charming. I will even admit that I have never encountered a man more amiable. Ah, let me beg you, Vicomte, if you find him again, to bring him to see me; he will be always well received!

Warn him, however, that in no case will it be for today or tomorrow. His Menæchmus has somewhat injured him; and, if I were in too much haste, I should be afraid of making a mistake; or, perhaps, if you like, I have pledged my word to Danceny for those two days! And your letter has taught me that it is no joking matter with you, when one breaks one's word. You see, then, that you must wait. But what does it matter to you? You can always avenge yourself on your rival. He will do no worse to your mistress than you will do to his; and, after all, is not one woman as good as another? Such are your principles. She even who should be *tender and sensitive, who should live for you alone, who, in short, should die from love and regret,* would be, nonetheless, sacrificed to the first fantasy, to the dread of a moment's ridicule; and you would have one put oneself about? Ah, that is not fair!

Adieu, Vicomte; pray, become amiable once more. You see, I ask nothing better than to find you charming; and as soon as I am sure of it, I undertake to give you the proof. Truly, I am too kind.

Paris, 4th December, 17★★.

153. The Vicomte de Valmont to the Marquise de Merteuil

I answer your letter at once, and I will try to be clear; a thing which is not easy with you, when once you have made up your mind not to understand.

Long phrases were not required to establish the fact that, when each of us possesses all that is necessary to ruin the other, we have a like interest in mutual consideration: there is no question, therefore, of that. But, between the violent course of destroying one another, and that, doubtless the better, of remaining united as we have been, of becoming even more so by resuming our old *liaison;* between these two courses, I say, there are a thousand others to adopt. It was not ridiculous, therefore, to tell you, nor is it to repeat, that from this day forward I will be either your lover or your enemy.

I am admirably conscious that this choice will embarrass you; that it would suit you better to beat about the bush; and I am quite aware that you have never loved to be placed thus betwixt a plain yes or no: but you must also feel that I cannot let you out of this narrow circle without running the risk of being tricked; and you may have foreseen that I would not endure that. It is for you now to decide: I am able to leave you the choice, but not to remain in uncertainty.

I warn you only that you will not impose on me by your arguments, be they good or bad; that neither will you seduce me by any more of those cajoleries with which you seek to adorn your refusals; and that, at least, the time for frankness has arrived. I ask nothing better than to be able to set you the example; and I declare to you with pleasure, that I prefer peace and union: but, if both are to be broken, I believe the right and the means are mine.

I will add, then, that the least obstacle presented by you will be taken by me as a veritable declaration of war: you will see that the answer I exact from you requires neither long nor fine phrases. Two words will suffice.

Paris, 4th December, 17★★.

Reply of the Marquise de Merteuil
(WRITTEN AT THE FOOT OF THE ABOVE LETTER)

Very well! War!

154. Madame de Volanges to Madame de Rosemonde

The bulletins will inform you better than I can do, my dear friend, of the grievous state of our patient. Utterly absorbed, as I am, in my care of her, I only snatch from it the time to write to you, when there are any incidents to relate, other than those of the malady. Here is one, for which I was certainly unprepared. It is a letter which I have received from M. de Valmont, who has been pleased to choose me as his confidant, or rather as his mediator with Madame de Tourvel, for whom he has also enclosed a letter in mine. I have sent back the one, and replied to the other. The

latter I forward to you, and I think you will judge, like myself, that I
could not and ought not to have complied with his request. Even had I
been willing, our unfortunate friend would not have been in a condition
to understand me. Her delirium is continuous. But what do you think of
this despair of M. de Valmont? First, is one to believe in it, or does he
but wish to deceive everybody, to the very end?[1] If, for once, he is sincere, he may well say that he has been himself the cause of his own misfortune. I expect he will be hardly pleased with my answer; but I confess
that all I see of this unhappy adventure excites me more and more against
its author.

Adieu, my dear friend; I am going to resume my sad task, which becomes even more so from the scant hope I feel of seeing it succeed. You
know my sentiments toward you.

Paris, 5th December, 17★★.

155. The Vicomte de Valmont to the Chevalier Danceny

I have called upon you twice, my dear Chevalier: but, since you have
abandoned the *rôle* of lover to take up that of the man of gallant conquests, you have naturally become invisible. Your *valet-de-chambre,* however, assured me that you would return this evening; that he had orders
to await you: but I, who am acquainted with your plans, understood
quite well that you would only enter for a moment, to put on the suitable costume, and would promptly recommence your victorious
progress. 'Tis very well, and I cannot but applaud you for it; but, perhaps,
for this evening, you will be tempted to change your direction. As yet
you do but know one half of your occupations; I must make you acquainted with the other, and then you shall decide. Take the time, then,
to read my letter. It will not tend to distract you from your pleasures,
since, on the contrary, it has no other object than to offer you a choice
of them.

If I had possessed your whole confidence, if I had heard from yourself
that part of your secrets which you have left me to divine, I should have
been informed in time, and my zeal would have been less inopportune
and would not impede your movements today. But let us start from
where we are. Whatever course you were to take, your rejected would
always make another happy.

You have a *rendezvous* tonight, have you not? With a charming
woman, whom you adore? For, at your age, who is the woman one does
not adore, at least for the first week! The setting of the scene must en-

---

[1] It is because we have discovered nothing in the subsequent correspondence which can
solve this doubt that we have decided to suppress M. de Valmont's letter.

hance your pleasures. A delicious *petite-maison, which has been taken only for you,* is to adorn voluptuousness with the charms of liberty and of mystery. All is arranged; you are expected, and you burn to betake yourself there! We both know that, although you have said no word of it to me. Now, here is what you do not know, and what I have to tell you.

Since my return to Paris, I have been busy over the means of bringing you and Mademoiselle de Volanges together; I promised you this; and on the very last occasion when I spoke of it to you, I had reason to judge from your replies, I might say from your transports, that in this I was promoting your happiness. I could not succeed in this difficult enterprise by myself alone: but, after preparing the means, I left the rest to the zeal of your young mistress. Her love has discovered resources which my experience lacked: in short, it is your misfortune that she has succeeded. Two days since, as she told me this evening, every obstacle was surmounted, and your happiness only depends on yourself.

For two days, also, she flattered herself that she would be able to give you this news herself, and, in spite of her Mamma's absence, you would have been received: but you have not even presented yourself! And, to tell you the truth, whether it be reason or caprice, the little person seemed to me somewhat vexed at this lack of eagerness on your part. At last, she found a means of summoning me to her, and made me promise to forward the enclosed letter to you as soon as possible. From the emphasis she laid upon it, I would wager it is a question of a *rendezvous* for tonight. Be that as it may, I promised upon my honor and my friendship that you should have the tender missive in the course of today, and I cannot and will not break my word.

Now, young man, what is your conduct to be? Placed between coquetry and love, between pleasure and happiness, which will be your choice? If I were speaking to the Danceny of three months ago, nay, even of a week ago, I should be as certain of his behavior as I was of his heart: but the Danceny of today, led away by the women, running after adventures, and grown, as the usage is, somewhat of a rake, will he prefer a very shy young girl, who only offers him her beauty, her innocence and her love, to the attractions of a woman who is certainly very *well worn?*

For my part, my dear friend, it seems to me that, even with your new principles, which, I quite admit, are shared also in some degree by myself, I should decide, under the circumstances, for the younger flame. To begin with, it is one the more, and then the novelty, and again the fear of losing the fruit of your labor by neglecting to cull it; for, on that side, in short, it would be really an opportunity missed, and it does not always return, especially in the case of a first frailty: when such are in question, often it needs but one moment of ill humor, one jealous suspicion, less even, to prevent the most handsome triumph. Drowning virtue sometimes clings to a straw; and, once escaped, it keeps upon its guard and is no longer easily surprised.

On the other side, on the contrary, what do you risk? Not even a rupture; a quarrel at the most, whereby you purchase, at the cost of a few attentions, the pleasure of a reconciliation. What other course remains for a woman who has already given herself, save that of indulgence? What would she gain by severity? The loss of her pleasures, with no profit to her glory.

If, as I assume, you choose the path of love, which seems to me also that of reason, I should consider it prudent to send no excuses to the abandoned *rendezvous;* let yourself be expected quite simply: if you risk giving a reason, there will perhaps be a temptation to verify it. Women are curious and obstinate; all might be discovered; as you know, I am myself just now an example of this. But, if you leave a hope, as it will be sustained by vanity, it will not be lost until long after the proper hour for seeking information: then, tomorrow, you will be able to select the insurmountable obstacle which will have detained you; you will have been ill, dead if necessary, or anything else which will have caused you equal despair; and all will be right again.

For the rest, whichever course you adopt, I only ask you to inform me of it; and, as I have no interest in the matter, I shall in any case think that you have done well. Adieu, my dear friend.

I add one thing more, that I regret Madame de Tourvel; that I am in despair at being separated from her; that I would pay with half my life for the privilege of consecrating the other half to her. Ah, believe me, love is one's only happiness!

Paris, 5th December, 17**.

156. Cécile Volanges to the Chevalier Danceny
(ENCLOSED IN THE PRECEDING)

How is it, my dear friend, that I see you no longer, when I never cease to desire it? Do you no longer care so much about it as I do? Ah, nowadays I am very sad indeed! Sadder ever than when we were entirely separated. The pain I once had through others comes now from you, and that hurts far more.

You know quite well that it is some days since Mamma has been away from home, and I hoped you would try and profit by this time of freedom: but you do not even think of me; I am very unhappy! You told me so often that my love was less than yours! I knew the contrary, and here is the proof. If you had come to see me, you would have seen me indeed: for I am not like you; I only think of what will reunite us. If you had your deserts, I would not say anything of all I have done for that, and of the trouble it has given me: but I love you too well, and I wish so much to see you that I cannot refrain from telling you. And then, I shall soon see afterward if you really love me!

I have managed so well, that the porter is in our interests, and has promised me that, whenever you came, he would let you in, as though he did not see you; and we can depend upon him, for he is a very obliging man. It is only a question, then, of keeping out of sight in the house; and that is very easy, if you come at night, when there is nothing at all to fear. For instance, since Mamma has been going out every day, she goes to bed every night at eleven o'clock; so that we should have plenty of time.

The porter told me that, if you should come like that, instead of knocking on the gate, you would only have to knock at his window, and he would open at once to you; and then, you will easily find the back staircase; and, as you will not be able to have a light, I will leave the door of my room ajar, which will always give you a little light. You must take great care not to make any noise, especially in passing Mamma's back door. As for my maid's, that is no matter, as she has promised me not to awake; she is a very good girl, too! And to leave, it will be just the same. Now we shall see if you will come.

Ah God, why does my heart beat so fast while I write to you? Is some misfortune going to come to me, or is it the hope of seeing you which troubles me like this? What I feel most is that I have never loved you so much, and have never longed so much to tell you so. Come then, my friend, my dear friend, that I may be able to repeat to you a hundred times that I love you, that I adore you, that I shall never love anyone but you.

I have found the means of informing M. de Valmont that I had something to say to him; and, as he is a very good friend, he is sure to come tomorrow, and I will beg him to give you this letter immediately. So that I shall expect you tomorrow night, and you will come without fail, if you would not make your Cécile very unhappy.

Adieu, my dear friend; I embrace you with all my heart.

Paris, 4th December, 17**, in the evening.

157. The Chevalier Danceny to the Vicomte de Valmont

Do not doubt, my dear Vicomte, either of my heart or of my proceedings! How could I resist a desire of my dear Cécile's? Ah, it is indeed she, she alone whom I love, whom I shall always love! Her ingenuousness, her tenderness have a charm for me from which I may have been weak enough to allow myself to be distracted, but which nothing will ever efface. Embarked upon another adventure without, so to speak, having perceived it, often has the memory of Cécile come to trouble me, in the midst of my sweetest pleasures; and, perhaps, my heart has never rendered her truer homage than at the very moment I was unfaithful to her. However, my friend, let us spare her delicacy and hide my wrongdoings from her; not to surprise her, but so as not to give her pain. Cécile's happiness is the most ardent vow that I frame; I would never forgive myself a fault which had cost her a tear.

I feel I have deserved your jesting remarks upon what you call my new principles: but you can believe me when I say that it is not by them I am guided at this moment; and from tomorrow I am determined to prove it. I will go and accuse myself to the very woman who has been the cause of my error, who has participated in it; I will say to her, "Read my heart; it has the most tender friendship for you; friendship united to desire so greatly resembles love! . . . Both of us have been deceived; but, though susceptible to error, I am not capable of a breach of faith." I know my friend; she is as noble as she is indulgent; she will do more than pardon me, she will approve. She herself often reproached herself with betraying friendship; often her delicacy took alarm at her love. Wiser than I, she will strengthen in my soul those useful fears which I rashly sought to stifle in hers. I shall owe it to her that I am better, as to you that I am happier. O my friends, divide my gratitude. The idea that I owe my happiness to you enhances its value.

Adieu, my dear Vicomte. The excess of my joy does not prevent me from thinking of your sorrows, and from sharing them. Why can I not be of use to you! Does Madame de Tourvel remain inexorable then? I am told also that she is very ill. God, how I pity you! May she regain at the same time her health and her indulgence, and forever make your happiness! These are the prayers of friendship; I dare hope that they will be heard by Love.

I should like to talk longer with you; but the hour approaches, and perhaps Cécile already awaits me.

Paris, 5th December, 17**.

158. The Vicomte de Valmont to the Marquise de Merteuil
(Upon Awaking)

Well, well, Marquise, how are you after the pleasures of last night? Are you not somewhat fatigued by them? Admit now, that Danceny is charming! He performs prodigies, this youth! You did not expect it of him, am I not right? Indeed, I will do myself justice; I richly deserved to be sacrificed to such a rival. Seriously, he is full of good qualities! But, above all, what love, what constancy, what delicacy! Ah, if you were ever to be loved by him as his Cécile is, you would have no rivals to fear: he proved that to you last night. Perhaps, by dint of coquetry, another woman may rob you of him for a moment; a young man can hardly refuse enticing provocations; but a single word from the beloved object suffices, as you see, to dispel this illusion; thus you have only to be that object in order to become perfectly happy.

You will surely make no mistake there; you have too sure a tact that you need ever fear that. However, the friendship which unites us, as sincere on my part as it is recognized on yours, made me desire for you the experience of last night. It is the work of my zeal; is has succeeded: but I pray you, no thanks; it is not worth the pains: nothing could have been easier.

In fact, what did it cost me? A slight sacrifice, and a little skill. I consented to share the favors of his mistress with the young man: but, after all, he has as much right to them as I; and I took such scant account of them! The letter which the young person wrote to him was, of course, dictated by me; but it was only to gain time, because we had a better use for it. The one I added to it, oh, that was nothing, next to nothing; a few friendly reflections to guide the new lover's choice: but, upon my honor, they were not required; the truth must be told, he did not hesitate for an instant.

Moreover, in his candor, he is to go to you today, to tell you everything; and assuredly the story will please you mightily! He will say to you: "*Read my heart*"; this he has told me: and you quite see that that repairs everything. I hope that, while reading what he would have, you will also perhaps read that such young lovers have their dangers; and again, that it is better to have me for a friend than an enemy.

Adieu, Marquise; until the next occasion.

Paris, 6th December, 17★★.

159. The Marquise de Merteuil to the Vicomte de Valmont

I do not like people to follow up sorry conduct with sorry jests; it is neither in my manner nor to my taste. When I have ground of complaint against people, I do not quiz them; I do better, I avenge myself. However satisfied with yourself you may be at the present moment, do not forget that it would not be the first time if you were to find that you were premature, and quite alone, in applauding yourself in the hope of a triumph which had escaped you at the very moment when you were congratulating yourself upon it. Adieu.

Paris, 6th December, 17★★.

160. Madame de Volanges to Madame de Rosemonde

I write to you from the chamber of your unhappy friend, whose state has remained almost always the same. There is to be a consultation of four physicians this afternoon. That is, unhappily, as you know, more often a proof of danger than a means of relief.

It seems, however, that her mind was somewhat restored last night. The waiting maid informed me this morning that just before midnight her mistress called her; that she wished to be alone with her; and that she dictated to her a fairly long letter. Julie added that, while she was busy in making the envelope for it, Madame de Tourvel's delirium returned: so that the girl did not know to whom she was to address it. I was astonished, at first, that the letter itself had not been sufficient to inform her; upon which she answered me that she feared to make a mistake; that her mistress, however, had greatly charged her to have it dispatched immediately. I took upon myself to open the packet.

I found there the communication which I send you, which, in fact, is addressed to everybody and to nobody. I think, however, that it was to M. de Valmont that our unhappy friend meant at first to write; but that she gave way, without perceiving it, to the disorder of her ideas. Be that as it may, I judged that the letter should not be given to anybody. I send it you, because you will learn from it, better than you can from me, what are the thoughts which fill our patient's head. As long as she remains so keenly affected, I shall have no hope. The body recovers with difficulty, when the mind is so ill at ease.

Adieu, my dear and revered friend. I congratulate you upon being at a distance from the sad spectacle which is continually before my eyes.

Paris, 6th December, 17★★.

161. The Présidente de Tourvel to ——
(DICTATED BY HER AND WRITTEN BY HER WAITING MAID)

Cruel and wicked being, will you never cease to persecute me? Does it not suffice you to have tortured, degraded, vilified me? Would you ravish from me even the peace of the grave? What! In this abode of shadow, where ignominy has forced me to bury myself, are my sorrows to be without cessation, is hope to be unknown? I do not implore for mercy, which I do not deserve: to suffer without complaining, I shall be content if my sufferings do not exceed my strength. But do not render my torments unbearable. In leaving me my sorrow, take away from me the cruel memory of the good I have lost. When you have ravished it from me, trace no more before my eyes its desolating image. I was innocent and at peace: because I saw you, I lost my repose; by listening to you I became criminal. Author of my faults, what right have you to punish them?

Where are the friends who cherished me, where are they? My misfortune has terrified them. None dares come near me. I am borne down, and they leave me without succor! I am dying, and no one weeps over me. All consolation is refused me. Pity stops short on the brink of the abyss into which the guilty one has plunged. She is torn by remorse and her cries are not heeded!

And you, whom I have outraged; you, whose esteem adds to my punishment; you, who alone would have the right to avenge yourself on me, what are you doing far away from me? Come and punish an unfaithful wife. Let me suffer, at last, the torments I have deserved. I should have already submitted to your vengeance: but the courage failed me to tell you of your shame. It was not dissimulation, it was respect. Let this letter, at least, tell you of my repentance. Heaven has taken your part; it avenges you for a wrong you do not know. 'Tis Heaven which has tied my tongue and retained my words; it feared lest you should remit a fault which it wished to punish. It has withdrawn me from your indulgence, which would have infringed its justice.

Pitiless in its vengeance, it has abandoned me to the very one who ruined me. It is at once for him and through him that I suffer. I seek to flee him in vain; he follows me; he is there; he assails me unceasingly. But how different he is from himself! His eyes express naught but hatred and contempt. His lips proffer only insults and reproach. His arms are only thrown round me to destroy me. Who will save me from his barbarous fury?

But what! It is he. . . . I am not mistaken; it is he whom I see once more. O my beloved, take me in your arms; hide me in your bosom: yes, it is you, it is indeed you! What dread illusion made me misunderstand you? How I have suffered in your absence! Let us part no more, let us never part again. Let me breathe. Feel my heart, how it throbs! Ah, it is with fear no longer, it is the soft emotion of love! Why do you turn away from my tender caresses? Cast your sweet glance upon me! What are those bonds you are trying to break? Why are you getting ready those preparations for death? What can change your features thus? What are you doing? Leave me: I shudder! God! It is that monster again! My friends, do not desert me. You, who urged me to fly from him, help me to struggle against him; and you, more indulgent, who promised me a diminution of my pains, come to my side. Where have you both gone? If I am not allowed to see you again, at least, answer this letter: let me know that you still love me.

Leave me then, cruel one! What fresh fury seizes you? Do you fear lest any gentle sentiment should penetrate my soul? You redouble my torments; you force me to hate you. Oh, what a grievous thing is hatred!

How it corrodes the heart which distills it! Why do you persecute me? What more can you have to say to me? Have you not made it as impossible for me to listen to you as to answer you? Expect nothing more of me. Monsieur, farewell.

Paris, 5th December, 17★★.

162. The Chevalier Danceny to the Vicomte de Valmont

I am acquainted, Monsieur, with your behavior to me. I know also that, not content with having unworthily tricked me, you have not feared to vaunt and applaud yourself for it. I have seen the proof of your treachery written in your own hand. I confess that my heart was sick, and that I felt a certain shame at having assisted somewhat myself at the odious abuse you have made of my blind confidence: I do not, however, envy you this shameful advantage; I am only curious to learn whether you will preserve them all alike over me. I shall know this if, as I hope, you will be ready to meet me tomorrow, between eight and nine o'clock in the morning, at the entrance to the Bois de Vincennes by the village of Saint-Mandé. I will be careful to have there all that is necessary for the explanations which I still have to obtain from you.

The Chevalier Danceny.
Paris, 6th December, 17★★, in the evening.

163. M. Bertrand to Madame de Rosemonde

Madame,

It is with great regret that I undertake the sad task of announcing to you news which will cause you such cruel sorrow. Allow me, first, to recommend to you that pious resignation which we have all so much admired in you, and which alone enables us to support the ills with which our wretched life is strewn.

Your nephew . . . Gracious Heaven! Must I afflict so greatly so venerable a lady! Your nephew has had the misfortune to fall in a duel which he had this morning with M. le Chevalier Danceny. I am entirely ignorant of the motive of this quarrel; but it appears, from the missive which I found still in the pocket of M. le Vicomte, and which I have the honor to forward you; it appears, I say, that he was not the aggressor. Yet it needs must be he whom Heaven allowed to fall!

I had been to wait upon M. le Vicomte, precisely at the hour when he was brought back to the *hôtel*. Imagine my terror, when I saw your nephew carried by two of his servants, and bathed in his blood. He had two sword thrusts through his body, and was already very weak. M. Danceny was there also, and he even wept. Ah, certainly, he has reason to weep: but it is a fine time to shed tears, when one has caused an irreparable misfortune!

As for me, I could not contain myself; and, in spite of my humble condition, I nonetheless told him my fashion of thinking. But it was then that M. le Vicomte showed himself truly great. He ordered me to be silent; and, taking the hand of the very man who was his murderer, he called him his friend, embraced him before us all and said to us, "I command you to treat Monsieur with all the consideration that is due to a brave and gallant man." He further caused him to be presented, in my presence, with a voluminous mass of papers, the contents of which I am not acquainted with, but to which I am well aware he attached vast importance. He then desired that we should leave them alone together for a moment. Meanwhile, I had sent in search of every kind of succor, both spiritual and temporal: but, alas, the ill was incurable! Less than half an hour later, M. le Vicomte lost consciousness. He was only able to receive extreme unction; and the ceremony was hardly over, when he rendered his last breath.

Great God! When I received in my arms, at his birth, this precious prop of so illustrious a house, how little did I foresee that it was to be in my arms that he would expire, and that I should have to weep for his death! A death so premature and so unfortunate! My tears flow in spite of myself. I ask your pardon, Madame, for thus daring to mingle my grief with your own: but, in every condition, we have hearts and sensibility; and I should be ungrateful, indeed, if I did not weep all my life for a lord who showed me so much kindness, and honored me with so great confidence.

Tomorrow, after the removal of the body, I will have the seals placed on everything, and you can depend entirely on my care. You will be aware, Madame, that this unhappy event cuts off the entail, and leaves the disposition of your property entirely free. If I can be of any use to you, I beg you to be good enough to convey to me your orders: I will employ all my zeal in their punctual fulfillment.

I remain, with the most profound respect, Madame, your most humble, etc.

Bertrand.

Paris, 7th December, 17★★.

164. Madame de Rosemonde to M. Bertrand

I have this moment received your letter, my dear Bertrand, and learn from it the fearful event of which my nephew has been the unhappy victim. Yes, I shall doubtless have orders to give you, and it is only on account of them that I can occupy myself with anything else than my mortal affliction.

The letter of M. Danceny, which you have sent me, is a very convincing proof that it was he who provoked the duel, and it is my intention that you should immediately lodge a complaint, and in my name. My nephew may have satisfied his natural generosity in pardoning his enemy and murderer; but it is my duty to avenge, at the same time, his death, humanity and religion. One cannot be too eager to invoke the severity of the law against this remnant of barbarism, which still stains our manners; and I do not believe that this is a case in which we are required to pardon injuries. I expect you, then, to pursue this matter with all the zeal and activity of which I know you to be capable, and which you owe to my nephew's memory.

You will be sure, before all, to see M. le Président de ★★★ on my behalf, and confer with him on the subject. I have not written to him, eager as I am to be left quite alone with my sorrow. You will convey him my excuses, and communicate this letter to him.

Adieu, my dear Bertrand; I praise and thank you for your kind sentiments, and am, for life, entirely yours.

At the Château de . . . , 8th December, 17★★.

165. Madame de Volanges to Madame de Rosemonde

I know you are already acquainted, my dear and revered friend, with the loss you have just sustained; I knew your affection for M. de Valmont, and I participate most sincerely in the affliction which you must feel. I am truly grieved to have to add a fresh regret to those which are trying you already: but, alas! you have only your tears now to bestow upon our unhappy friend. We lost her yesterday, at eleven o'clock at night. By a fatality which attended her lot, and which seemed to make a mock of all human prudence, the short interval by which she survived M. de Valmont sufficed to inform her of his death; and, as she herself said, to enable her not to succumb beneath the weight of her misfortunes until the measure of them was full.

You are aware, of course, that for more than two days she was absolutely without consciousness; and even yesterday morning, when her physician arrived, and we approached her bedside, she recognized neither of us, and we could not extract the least word or sign from her. Well, hardly had we returned to the chimney, and the physician was relating to me the sad episode of M. de Valmont's death, when the unfortunate woman recovered her reason, whether that nature alone had produced this revolution, or that it was caused by the repetition of the words, *M. de Valmont* and *death,* which may have brought back to the patient the only ideas which have occupied her for a long time.

However that may be, she hurriedly threw back the curtains of her bed, crying out, "What? What are you saying? M. de Valmont is dead!"

I hoped to make her believe that she was mistaken, and at first assured her that she had heard wrong: but far from letting herself be persuaded, she required the physician to repeat the cruel story, and, upon my endeavoring again to dissuade her, she called me and whispered, "Why wish to deceive me? Was he not already dead to me?" It was necessary, therefore, to yield.

Our unhappy friend listened, at first, with a fairly tranquil air: but soon afterward, she interrupted the story, saying, "Enough, I know enough." She asked at once for her curtains to be closed; and, when the physician subsequently tried to busy himself with the care of her condition, she never would have him near her.

As soon as he had left, she similarly dismissed her nurse and waiting maid; and when we were left alone, she begged me to help her to kneel down upon her bed, and support her so. There she stayed for some time in silence, and with no other expression than that which was given by her tears, which flowed copiously. At last, clasping her hands, and raising them to Heaven: "Almighty God," said she, in a weak but fervent voice, "I submit myself to Thy justice; but forgive Valmont. Let not my misfortunes, which I admit are deserved, be a cause of reproach to him, and I will bless Thy mercy!" I have permitted myself, my dear and respected friend, to enter into these details on a subject which I am well aware must renew and aggravate your grief, because I have no doubt that that prayer of Madame de Tourvel's will, nevertheless, be a great consolation to your soul. After our friend had uttered these brief words, she fell back in my arms; and she was hardly replaced in her bed, when she was overcome by weakness, which lasted long, but which gave way to the ordinary remedies. As soon as she had regained consciousness, she asked me to send for the Père Anselme, and added, "He is now the only physician whom I need; I feel that my ills will soon be ended." She complained much of oppression, and spoke with difficulty.

A short time afterward, she handed me, through her waiting maid, a casket which I am sending to you, which she tells me contains papers of hers, and which she charged me to convey to you immediately after her death.[1] She next spoke to me of you, and of your friendship for her, so far as her situation permitted, and with much emotion.

The Père Anselme arrived about four o'clock, and remained alone with her for nearly an hour. When we returned, the face of the sick woman was calm and serene; but it was easy to see that the Père Anselme had shed many tears. He remained to assist at the last ceremonies of the Church. This spectacle, always so imposing and so sorrowful, was rendered even more so by the contrast which the tranquil resignation of the

---

[1]This casket contained all the letters relating to her adventure with M. de Valmont.

sufferer formed with the profound grief of her venerable confessor, who burst into tears at her side. The emotion became general; and she, for whom everybody wept, was the only one not to weep.

The remainder of the day was spent in the customary prayers, which were only interrupted by the sufferer's frequent fits of weakness. At last, at about eleven o'clock at night, she appeared to be more oppressed and to suffer more. I put out my hand to seek her arm; she had still strength enough to take it, and she placed it upon her heart. I could no longer discern any movement; and, indeed, at that very moment, our unfortunate friend expired.

You will remember, my dear friend, that, on your last visit here, not a year ago, when we talked together of certain persons whose happiness seemed to us more or less assured, we dwelt complacently upon the lot of this very woman, whose misfortunes and whose death we lament today. So many virtues, laudable qualities and attractions; a character so sweet and easy; a husband whom she loved, and by whom she was adored; a society which pleased her, and of which she was the delight; a face, youth, fortune; so many combined advantages lost through a single imprudence! O Providence, doubtless we must worship Thy decrees; but how incomprehensible they are! I stop myself; I fear to add to your sorrow by indulging my own.

I leave you, to return to my daughter, who is a little indisposed. When she heard from me this morning of so sudden a death of two persons of her acquaintance, she was taken ill, and I had her sent to bed. I hope, however, that this slight indisposition will have no ill results. At her age, one is not yet habituated to sorrow, and its impression is keener and more potent. Such sensibility is, doubtless, a praiseworthy quality; but how greatly does all that we daily see teach us to dread it!

Adieu, my dear and venerable friend.

Paris, 9th December, 17**.

166. M. Bertrand to Madame de Rosemonde

Madame,

In consequence of the orders which you have done me the honor of sending me, I have had that of seeing M. le Président de ★★★, and have communicated your letter to him, informing him that, in pursuance of your wishes, I should do nothing without his advice. The honorable magistrate desires me to point out to you that the complaint which you intend to lodge against M. le Chevalier Danceny would be equally compromising to the memory of your nephew, and that his honor would also inevitably be tarnished by the decree of the court, which would, of course, be a great misfortune. His opinion, therefore, is that you should carefully abstain from taking any proceedings; and that what you had better do, on the contrary, would be to endeavor to prevent the Government from taking cognizance of this unfortunate adventure, which has already made too much noise.

These observations seemed to me full of wisdom, and I resolved to wait for further orders from you. Allow me to beg you, Madame, to be so good, when you dispatch them, as to add a word as to the state of your health, the sad effect upon which of so many troubles I greatly dread. I hope that you will pardon this liberty in consideration of my attachment and my zeal.

I am, with respect, Madame, yours, etc.

Paris, 10th December, 17★★.

167. Anonymous to M. le Chevalier Danceny

Monsieur,

I have the honor to inform you that this morning, in the corridors of the Court, there was talk among the King's officers of the affair which you had a few days ago with M. le Vicomte de Valmont, and that it is to be feared that the Government will take proceedings against you. I thought that this warning might be of use to you, either to enable you to seek out what protection you have, to ward off these vexatious results; or, in the event of your being unable to succeed in this, to put you in a position to take measures for your personal safety.

If you will even permit me to give you a piece of advice, I think you would do well to show yourself less often than you have done during the last few days. Although, ordinarily, affairs of this sort are treated with indulgence, this respect nevertheless continues due to the law.

This precaution becomes all the more necessary in that it has come to my ears that a certain Madame de Rosemonde, who, I am told, is an aunt of M. de Valmont, wished to lodge a complaint against you, in which event the public officers could not refuse her requisition. It would not be amiss, perhaps, if you were able to communicate with this lady.

Private reasons prevent me from signing this letter. But I am acting on the consideration that you will not render less justice to the sentiment which has dictated it, because you know not from whom it comes.

I have the honor to be, etc.

Paris, 10th December, 17★★.

168. Madame de Volanges to Madame de Rosemonde

Most surprising and distressing rumors, my dear and revered friend, are being disseminated here in relation to Madame de Merteuil. I am, assuredly, very far from believing them, and I would wager well that it is nothing but a hideous calumny: but I am too well aware of the ease with which even the most improbable slanders acquire credit, and of the difficulty with which the impression they leave is effaced, not to be greatly alarmed at these, easy as I believe it to be to refute them. I should wish, above all, that they could be stopped in good time, before they have spread farther. But I only knew yesterday, at a late hour, of these horrors which they were just beginning to retail; and when I sent this morning to Madame de Merteuil, she had just left for the country, where she was to spend two days. They were not able to tell me to whom she had gone. Her second woman, whom I sent for to speak with me, told me that her mistress had left no orders save that she was to be expected on Thursday next; and none of the servants whom she has left here know any more. For myself, I have no notion where she may be; I cannot recollect any person of her acquaintance who stays so late in the country.

However that may be, you will be able, I hope, between now and her return, to furnish me with information which will be of use to her: for these odious stories are based on the circumstances of M. de Valmont's death; you are likely to have been informed of them, if they are true; or, at any rate, it will be easy for you to obtain information, which I beg you to do. This is what is being published, or rather, whispered, at present; but it will certainly not be long before it spreads farther:

It is said that the quarrel between M. de Valmont and the Chevalier Danceny was the work of Madame de Merteuil, who deceived them both alike; that, as happens almost always, the two rivals began by fighting and only arrived at explanations afterward; that these explanations brought about a sincere reconciliation; and that, in order to expose Madame de Merteuil to the Chevalier Danceny, and also to justify himself entirely, M. de Valmont supported his revelations by a heap of letters, forming a regular correspondence which he had maintained with her, and in which she relates the most scandalous anecdotes about herself, and in the freest of styles.

People further say that Danceny, in the first heat of his indignation, showed these letters to all who wished to see them, and that they are now making the round of Paris. Two of them, in particular, are quoted:[1] one in which she relates the whole history of her life and principles, and which is said to attain the height of horror; the other which entirely justifies M. de Prévan, whose story you will remember, by the proof it contains that all he did was to yield to the most marked advances on the part of Madame de Merteuil, and that the *rendezvous* was arranged with her.

I have, happily, the strongest reasons to believe that these imputations

---

[1]Letters the eighty-first and eighty-fifth of this collection.

are as false as they are odious. First, we are both aware that M. de Valmont was assuredly not occupied with Madame de Merteuil, and I have every cause to believe that Danceny was equally without interest in her: thus it seems to me clearly proved that she can have been neither the motive nor the author of the quarrel. I equally fail to understand what interest Madame de Merteuil can have had, assuming her to have been in concert with M. de Prévan, in making a scene which could only be disagreeable by its publicity, and which might become most dangerous to her, since she made, thereby, an irreconcilable enemy of a man who was master in part of her secret, and who, at that time, had numerous partisans. However, it is remarkable that since that adventure not a single voice has been raised in Prévan's favor, and that even from his own side there has been no protest made.

These reflections would lead me to suspect the author of the rumors which are abroad today, and to look upon these slanders as the work of the hatred and vengeance of a man who, knowing himself to be ruined, hopes, by such a means, at least to establish a doubt, and perhaps cause a useful diversion. But, from whatever source these malicious reports arise, the most urgent thing is to destroy them. They would cease of themselves, if it were to be shown, as is probable, that MM. de Valmont and Danceny had no communication after their unfortunate affair, and that no papers passed between them.

In my impatience to verify these facts, I sent this morning to M. Danceny; he is not in Paris either. His people told my *valet-de-chambre* that he had left in the night, owing to a warning he had received yesterday, and that the place of his sojourn was a secret. Apparently he is afraid of the results of his duel. 'Tis through you alone, then, my dear and revered friend, that I can be informed of the details which interest me, and which may become so necessary to Madame de Merteuil. I renew my prayer to you to acquaint me with them as soon as possible.

P.S. My daughter's indisposition has had no consequences; she presents her respects to you.

Paris, 11th December, 17**.

169. The Chevalier Danceny to Madame de Rosemonde

Madame,

Perhaps you will think the step I am taking today very unusual: but I entreat you to hear before you judge me, and to see neither boldness nor temerity, where only respect and confidence is meant. I do not deny the injury I have done you; and I should not pardon myself for it, all my life, if I could think for a moment that it had been possible for me to avoid it. Be even persuaded, Madame, that, if I am exempt from reproach, I am not equally so from regrets; and I may add, with equal sincerity, that those which I have caused you count for much in those which I feel. In order to believe in these sentiments of which I venture to assure you, it will suffice for you to render justice to yourself, and to reflect that, without having the honor of being known to you, I have, however, that of knowing you.

Meanwhile, while I groan over the fatality which has been the cause at once of your grief and my misfortunes, I have been led to fear that, absorbed in your vengeance, you would seek out means of gratifying it, even through the severity of the laws. Allow me, first, to point out to you, on this subject, that here you are led astray by your sorrow, since my interest in this matter is essentially at one with that of M. de Valmont, and that he would himself be involved in the condemnation which you would have provoked against me. I believe then, Madame, that I can count on assistance, rather than on obstacles, on your part, in any efforts I may be obliged to make, so that this unhappy event may remain buried in silence.

But this resource of complicity, which befits the innocent and the guilty alike, is not sufficient for my delicacy: while desiring to remove you as a party to the suit, I demand you as my judge. The esteem of persons whom we respect is too precious that I should let yours be taken from me without defending it, and I believe I possess the means.

In fact, if you will admit that vengeance is allowed, or say rather, that it is one's bounden duty, when one has been betrayed in one's love, in one's friendship, and, above all, in one's confidence; if you admit this, my wrongs against you will vanish from your eyes. Do not take my word for this; but read, if you have the courage, the correspondence which I place in your hands.[1] The quantity of original letters which it contains seems to lend authenticity to those of which only copies exist. For the rest, I received these letters, just as I have the honor to forward them to you, from M. de Valmont himself. I have added nothing to them, and I have only extracted two letters which I have permitted myself to publish.

One of these was necessary to the common vengeance of M. de Valmont and of myself; to this we had both a right, and I had been expressly charged with it by him. I thought, moreover, that I was rendering a service to society, in unmasking a woman so really dangerous as is Madame de Merteuil, who, as you will see, was the sole and veritable cause of all that passed between M. de Valmont and myself.

A feeling of justice also induced me to publish the second, for the jus-

---

[1] It is from this correspondence, from that handed over in the same way on the death of Madame de Tourvel, and from the letters alike confided to Madame de Rosemonde by Madame de Volanges, that the present collection has been formed, the originals of which remain in the hands of Madame de Rosemonde's heirs.

tification of M. de Prévan, whom I hardly know, but who had in no way merited the rigorous treatment which he has experienced, nor the still more redoubtable judgment of the public, beneath which he has been groaning, ever since, without any means of defense.

You will only find copies, then, of these two letters, the originals of which I owe it to myself to keep. For all the rest, I do not believe I can remit in surer hands a deposit the destruction of which is not, perhaps, to my interest, but which I should blush to abuse. I believe, Madame, that, in confiding these papers to you, I am serving the persons interested in them, as well as if I remitted them to themselves; and I spare them the embarrassment of receiving them from me, and of knowing me to be informed of adventures of which they doubtless desire all the world to remain ignorant.

I think I ought to warn you, on this subject, that the adjoined correspondence only forms part of a far more voluminous collection, from which M. de Valmont extracted it in my presence, and which you will find, on the removal of the seals, under the title, which I saw, of *"Account opened between the Marquise de Merteuil and the Vicomte de Valmont."* You will adopt, in this matter, whatever course your prudence may suggest.

I am with respect, Madame, etc.

P.S. Certain information which I have received, and the advice of my friends, have decided my absence from Paris for some time: but the place of my retreat, which is kept a secret for everybody, will not be one for you. If you honor me with a reply, I beg you to address it to the Commanderie de . . . by P . . . , under cover to M. le Commandeur de ★★★. It is from his house that I have the honor to write to you.

Paris, 12th December, 17★★.

170. Madame de Volanges to Madame de Rosemonde

I move, my dear friend, from surprise to surprise and from sorrow to sorrow. One must be a mother to form an idea of what I suffered yesterday all the morning: and, if my most cruel anxiety has been calmed since, there still remains to me a keen affliction, the end of which I cannot foresee.

Yesterday, about ten o'clock in the morning, astonished that I had not yet seen my daughter, I sent my waiting maid to know what could have occasioned her delay. She returned a moment later, highly alarmed, and alarmed me even more by informing me that my daughter was not in her apartment, and that, since the morning, her maid had not seen her there. Judge of my situation! I summoned all my people, and the porter in especial: all swore to me they knew nothing, and could give me no information upon this event. I went at once to my daughter's room. The disorder which obtained there assured me that she had apparently only gone that morning: but I found no further clue. I searched her presses, her writing desk; I found everything in its place and all her wardrobe, with the exception of the dress in which she had left. She had not even taken the small stock of money which she possessed.

As she had only heard yesterday of all that is said of Madame de Merteuil; as she is greatly attached to her, to such a degree, indeed, that she did naught but weep all the evening; as I remembered, also, that she did not know Madame de Merteuil was in the country, my first idea was that she had wished to see her friend, and had been so imprudent as to go alone. But the time which elapsed without her returning brought back all my uneasiness. Each moment augmented my trouble, and, burning as I was for information, I dared take no steps to obtain it, for fear of giving publicity to a proceeding which, afterward, I might wish, perhaps, to be able to hide from everybody. Never in my life have I so suffered.

Finally, it was not until past two o'clock, I received at the same time a letter from my daughter and one from the Superior of the Convent of . . . My daughter's letter only said that she had feared lest I should oppose the vocation, which she felt, to become a nun, and that she had not dared speak to me of it: the rest only consisted of excuses for the course she had adopted without my permission, which I would assuredly not disapprove of, she added, if I knew her motives, into which she begged me, however, not to enquire.

The Superior wrote to me that, seeing a young person arrive alone, she had at first refused to receive her; but that, having questioned her and learned who she was, she had thought to do me a service by giving my daughter shelter, in order not to expose her to further journeys, upon which she seemed resolved. The Superior, while offering, as a matter of course, to restore my daughter to me, if I were to demand her, urges me, obeying her condition, not to oppose a vocation which she declares to be firm; she told me also that she could not inform me earlier of this event, owing to the difficulty she had in making my daughter write to me, as her plan was to leave everyone in ignorance of the place of her retreat. It is a cruel thing when our children argue so ill!

I went immediately to the convent; and, after seeing the Superior, asked to see my daughter; she only came reluctantly, and in a very tremulous state. I spoke to her before the nuns, and I spoke to her alone: all that I could extract from her, amid many tears, was that she could only be happy in the convent; I decided to let her remain there, but without as yet entering the rank of postulants, as she desired. I fear that the deaths of Madame de Tourvel and M. de Valmont have unduly affected her young head. Whatever my respect for a religious vocation, I could not see my daughter embrace that career without sorrow, and even without alarm. Methinks we have already duties enough to perform, without creating fresh ones; and, again, it is hardly at her age that we best know what befits us.

What enhances my embarrassment is the nearness of M. de Gercourt's return; must this most advantageous marriage be broken off? How, then, are we to make our children's happiness, if it is not sufficient to desire it and devote all our cares to it? You will greatly oblige me by telling me what you would do in my place; I cannot fix upon any course: I find nothing more terrible than to have to decide another's lot, and I am equally afraid of bringing to this occasion the severity of a judge or the weakness of a mother.

I reproach myself unceasingly for augmenting your sorrows by speaking to you of my own; but I know your heart: the consolation which you could give to others would become to you the greatest you could yourself receive.

Adieu, my dear and revered friend; I await your two replies with much impatience.

Paris, 13th December, 17★★.

171. Madame de Rosemonde to the Chevalier Danceny

After what you have brought to my knowledge, Monsieur, nothing is left for me but to be silent and to weep. One regrets that one still lives, after learning such horrors; and blushes to be a woman, when one finds one capable of such excesses.

I will willingly concur with you, Monsieur, so far as I am concerned, in leaving in silence and oblivion all that may relate to these sad events. I even hope that they may never cause you any other grief than that inseparable from the unhappy advantage which you obtained over my nephew. In spite of his errors, which I cannot but recognize, I feel that I shall never console myself for his loss: but my eternal affliction will be the sole vengeance I shall permit myself to obtain from you; I leave it to your heart to appreciate its extent.

If you will permit to my age a reflection which is rarely made at yours, it is that, were one enlightened as to one's true happiness, one would never seek it outside the bounds prescribed by religion and the laws.

You may rest assured that I will keep faithfully and willingly the deposit you have confided to me, but I ask you to authorize me to give it up to no one, not even to you, Monsieur, unless it should become necessary for your justification. I venture to believe that you will not refuse me this request, and that you have already realized how often one laments for having indulged in even the most just revenge.

I do not pause here in my requests: convinced as I am of your generosity and delicacy, it would be very worthy of both of these if you were also to place in my hands the letters of Mademoiselle de Volanges, which, apparently, you have retained, and which, doubtless, are of no further interest to you. I know that that young person has wronged you greatly; but I do not think that you have thought of punishing her; and, were it only out of respect for yourself, you will not degrade the object you have so greatly loved. I have no need to add, then, that the consideration which the daughter does not deserve is due at any rate to the mother, to that meritorious woman, in regard to whom you are not without having much to repair: for, after all, whatever illusion one may seek to impose on oneself by a pretended delicacy of sentiment, he who first attempts to seduce a heart still virtuous and simple makes himself, from that fact alone, the first abettor of its corruption, and must be, forever, responsible for the excesses and errors which ensue.

Do not be surprised, Monsieur, at so much severity on my part: it is the greatest proof I can give you of my complete esteem. You will acquire fresh rights to it still, by lending yourself, as I desire, to the security of a secret the publication of which would do yourself a wrong and deal death to a mother's heart which you have already wounded. In a word, Monsieur, I desire to do this service to my friend; and, if I could be afraid that you would refuse me this consolation, I would ask you to reflect beforehand that it is the only one you have left me.

I have the honor to be, etc.

At the Château de . . . , 15th December, 17★★.

172. Madame de Rosemonde to Madame de Volanges

Had I been obliged, my dear friend, to await and receive from Paris the enlightenment which you ask me for concerning Madame de Merteuil, it would have been impossible for me to give it you as yet; and doubtless that which I received would have been vague and uncertain: but there has reached me information which I neither expected nor had reason to expect; and this is only too certain. O my friend, how that woman has deceived you!

I shrink from entering into any details of this mass of horrors; but, whatever may be reported, rest assured that it still falls short of the truth. I hope, my dear friend, that you know me well enough to believe my word for it, and that you will require no proofs from me. Let the knowledge suffice you that there exists a mass of them, and that, at this very moment, they are in my hands.

It is not without extreme pain that I beseech you also not to compel me to give a reason for the advice you ask of me, respecting Mademoiselle de Volanges. I recommend you not to oppose the vocation she displays. Assuredly, no reason can justify one in forcing such a condition of life upon one who is not called to it: but sometimes it is a great happiness that it should be so; and you see that your daughter tells you herself that you would not disapprove, if you knew her motives. He who inspires our sentiments knows better than our vain wisdom what is right for each one of us, and, often, what seems an act of His severity is, on the contrary, one of His clemency.

In short, my advice, which I am quite sensible will afflict you, and which, from that fact alone, you must believe I would not give you unless I had greatly reflected upon it, is that you should leave Mademoiselle de Volanges at the convent, since this step is of her own choice; that you should encourage, instead of thwarting, the project she seems to have formed; and that, in awaiting its execution, you should not hesitate to break off the marriage you had arranged.

After fulfilling these painful duties of friendship, and in the impotence in which I am to add any consolation, the one favor it remains for me to beg of you, my dear friend, is to ask me no further questions bearing in any way upon these sad events: let us leave them in the oblivion which befits them; and, without seeking to throw useless and painful lights upon them, submit ourselves to the decrees of Providence, and believe in the wisdom of its views, even where we are not permitted to understand them. Adieu, my dear friend.

At the Château de . . . , 15th December, 17★★.

173. Madame de Volanges to Madame de Rosemonde

O my friend, in what a fearful veil do you envelop my daughter's lot! And you seemed to dread lest I seek to raise it! What, pray, can it conceal which can affect a mother's heart more than the dire suspicions to which you abandon me? The more I think of your friendship, of your indulgence, the more are my torments redoubled: twenty times, since yesterday, have I tried to escape from this cruel uncertainty, and to beg you to let me know all, without considering my feelings and without reserve; and each time I shuddered with dread, when I remembered the prayer you made me not to question you. Finally, I decide upon a course which still leaves me some hope; and I depend upon your friendship not to refuse me what I ask; it is to answer me whether I have, to a certain extent, understood what you might have to tell me; not to be afraid to let me know all that maternal indulgence can forgive, and which it may not be impossible to repair. If my misfortunes exceed this measure, then, indeed, I consent to leave you to explain yourself by silence alone; here then is what I know already, and the point to which my fears extend.

My daughter has shown that she had a certain inclination for the

Chevalier Danceny, and I have been informed that she has gone so far as to receive letters from him, and even to reply to them; but I believed I had succeeded in preventing this error of a child from having any dangerous consequences: today, when I dread everything, I can conceive that it may have been possible for my surveillance to have been deceived; and I fear that my misguided daughter may have set a seal upon her wrongdoing.

I recall to mind, again, several circumstances which lend weight to this fear. I told you that my daughter was taken ill at the news of M. de Valmont's misfortune; perhaps this sensitiveness was merely due to her thought of the risks M. Danceny had run in this combat. Afterward, when she shed so many tears on learning all that was said of Madame de Merteuil, perhaps what I thought to be the grief of friendship was but the effect of jealousy, or of regret at finding her lover to be unfaithful. Her latest course may again, it seems to me, be explained by the same motive. It often happens that one believes oneself called to God, only because one has revolted against men. Finally, supposing these facts to be true, and that you have been informed of them, you may have found them sufficient to justify the rigorous counsel you gave me.

However, if this be so, while blaming my daughter, I should still believe it my duty to try every means to save her from the torments and dangers of an illusory and transient vocation. If M. Danceny is not lost to every sentiment of honor, he will not refuse to repair a wrong of which he is the sole author, and I am entitled to believe that a marriage with my daughter is sufficiently advantageous to gratify him, as well as his family.

This, my dear and revered friend, is the one hope remaining to me; hasten to confirm it, if you can. You may judge how desirous I am that you should reply to me, and what a terrible blow your silence would inflict.[1]

I was about to close my letter, when a gentleman of my acquaintance came to see me, and related the cruel scene which Madame de Merteuil underwent the day before yesterday. As I have seen nobody for the last few days, I knew nothing of this adventure; here is the relation of it, as I have it from an eyewitness:

Madame de Merteuil, on her return from the country on Thursday, alighted at the Italian Comedy, where she had her box; she was alone in it, and, what must have seemed most extraordinary to her, no gentleman of her acquaintance presented himself during the performance. At the close, she entered the withdrawing room, as was her custom; it was already crowded; a hum was raised immediately, but apparently she was not

---

[1] This letter was left unanswered.

aware that she was the object of it. She saw a vacant place on one of the benches, and went and sat there; but at once all the women who were there before her rose, as if in concert, and left her absolutely alone. This marked sign of general indignation was applauded by all the men, and the murmurs, which even amounted, it is said, to hooting, were re-doubled.

That nothing might be lacking to her humiliation, her ill luck had it that M. de Prévan, who had shown himself nowhere since his adventure, should enter the withdrawing room that same moment. As soon as he was recognized, everybody, men and women, surrounded and applauded him; and he was carried, so to speak, in face of Madame de Merteuil by the crowd, which made a circle round them. I was assured that Madame de Merteuil preserved an appearance of seeing and hearing nothing, and that she did not change her expression! But I think this fact exaggerated. Be that as it may, this truly ignominious situation lasted until her carriage was announced; and, at her departure, the scandalous hooting was re-doubled. It is fearful to be related to such a woman. M. de Prévan met with a great reception the same evening from all the officers of his reg-iment who were present, and there is no doubt but that he will shortly regain his rank and employment.

The same person who gave me these details told me that Madame de Merteuil was seized the following night with a violent fever, which was at first thought to be the effect of the terrible situation in which she had been placed; but it became known yesterday that confluent smallpox had declared itself, of a very dangerous kind. Truly, it would be a piece of good fortune for her if she were to die of it. They say, further, that all this adventure will damage her case, which is on the point of being tried, and in which they assert that she had need of much favor.

Adieu, my dear and revered friend. I see the wicked punished in all this; but I find no consolation in it for their unfortunate victims.

Paris, 18th December, 17★★.

174. The Chevalier Danceny to Madame de Rosemonde

You are right, Madame, and certainly I will refuse you nothing within my power to which you attach any value. The packet which I have the honor to forward you contains all Mademoiselle de Volanges' letters. If you read them, you will see, not without astonishment perhaps, what a wealth of perfidy and ingenuousness can be united. That is, at least, what struck me most, on my last perusal of them.

Above all, can one refrain from the liveliest indignation against Madame de Merteuil, when one reflects with what a hideous pleasure she brought all her pains to bear on the corruption of so much innocence and candor?

No, my love is dead. I retain nothing of a sentiment so basely betrayed; and it is not that which makes me seek to justify Mademoiselle de Volanges. Nevertheless, would not that simple heart, that gentle and pliable character, have been influenced for good more easily even than they were seduced to evil? What young person, issuing similarly from a convent, without experience and almost without ideas, and bringing into the world, as almost always happens then, an equal ignorance of good and evil; what young person, I say, would have been able to offer more resistance to such culpable artifices? Ah, to be indulgent it suffices to reflect upon how many circumstances beyond our own control the terrible alternative between the delicacy and the depravation of our sentiments depends. You rendered justice to me, then, Madame, in deeming that the wrongs of Mademoiselle de Volanges, which I felt most keenly, did not, however, inspire me with any ideas of vengeance. 'Tis quite enough to be obliged to renounce my love of her! It would cost me too much to hate her.

I needed no reflection to desire that all which concerns and could harm her should remain for ever unknown to the world. If I have seemed to delay the fulfillment of your desires in this matter, I think I need not conceal my motive from you; I wished to be sure, beforehand, that I was not to be troubled with the consequences of my unfortunate duel. At a time when I was craving your indulgence, when I even dared believe I had some right to it, I should have feared to have too much the appearance of buying it by this condescension on my part; and, convinced of the purity of my motives, I was proud enough, I will confess, to wish you to be left in no doubt of them. I hope you will pardon this delicacy, perhaps too susceptible, in view of the veneration which you inspire in me, and the value which I attach to your esteem.

It is the same sentiment which bids me ask of you, as a last favor, to be so good as to let me know if, in your judgment, I have fulfilled all the duties which have been imposed upon me by the unhappy circumstances in which I was placed. Once at ease in this respect, my intention is fixed; I leave for Malta; I will go there to make gladly, and keep religiously, the vows which will separate me from a world of which, while still so young, I have had such good reason to complain; I shall go, in short, to seek to lose, beneath an alien sky, the thought of so many accumulated horrors, whose memory could only sadden and wither my soul.

I am with respect, Madame, your most humble, etc.

Paris, 26th December, 17★★.

175. Madame de Volanges to Madame de Rosemonde

The fate of Madame de Merteuil, my dear and revered friend, seems to be at length complete; and it is such that her greatest enemies are divided between the indignation she merits and the pity she inspires. I was right, indeed, in saying that it would be a happiness for her to die of her smallpox. She has recovered, it is true, but she has been fearfully disfigured; and, in particular, she has lost an eye. You will imagine that I have not seen her; but I am told that she is really hideous.

The Marquis de ★★★, who never misses an occasion for saying something malicious, said yesterday, in speaking of her, that the disease had transformed her, and that now her soul was to be seen in her face. Unhappily, everyone found the expression just.

A further event has just come to add to her disgrace and to her prejudice. Her case was tried the day before yesterday, and the verdict was given against her unanimously. Costs, damages, restitution of the funds received, all was adjudged to the minors: so that the small remnant of her fortune which was not compromised in this case is absorbed, and more than absorbed, by the costs.

Immediately she received this intelligence, although still sick, she made her arrangements, and started off at night, alone and posting. Her servants say today that none of them would follow her. It is believed she has taken the road to Holland.

This departure makes more noise than all the rest, from the fact that she has carried off her diamonds, a possession of great value, which should have returned to her husband's estate; her plate, jewels; in short, everything that she could; and that she leaves behind her nearly fifty thousand livres of debts. It is a real bankruptcy.

The family is to assemble tomorrow to make arrangements with the creditors. Although only a distant relation, I have offered to contribute, but I shall not be present at this assembly, having to assist at an even sadder ceremony. Tomorrow, my daughter takes the habit of a postulant. I hope that you will not forget, my dear friend, that, in making this great sacrifice, I have no other motive for feeling compelled to it than the silence which you have maintained toward me.

M. Danceny left Paris nearly a fortnight ago. It is said that he is on his way to Malta where it is his intention to remain. There would be still time, perhaps, to recall him! . . . My friend! . . . My daughter is guilty indeed, then? . . . You will forgive a mother, no doubt, for only yielding to this awful certainty with difficulty.

What a fatality has fallen upon me of late, and stricken me in the objects dearest to me! My daughter and my friend!

Who is there who would not shudder, if he were to reflect upon the misfortunes that may be caused by even one dangerous acquaintance! And what troubles would one not avert by reflecting on this more often! What woman would not fly before the first proposal of a seducer! What mother could see another person than herself speak to her daughter, and tremble not! But these tardy reflections never come until after the event; and one of the most important of truths, as it is, perhaps, one of the most generally recognized, lies stifled and void of use in the whirlpool of our inconsequent manners.

Adieu, my dear and revered friend; I feel at this moment that our reason, which is already so insufficient to avert our misfortunes, is even more inadequate to console us for them.[1]

Paris, 14th January, 17★★.

---

[1]Private reasons and considerations, which we shall ever make it a duty to respect, force us to halt here.

We cannot, at this moment, give our reader the continuation of Mademoiselle de Volanges' adventures, nor acquaint him with the sinister events which culminated the misfortunes, or completed the punishment, of Madame de Merteuil.

Perhaps someday it will be in our power to complete this work; but we can give no undertaking in this matter: and, even were we able to do so, we should still deem it our duty first to consult the taste of the public, which has not our reasons for taking an interest in this narration.

Appendix

The two letters which follow appear in the MS. of the book, but were not included in the printed editions published in the author's lifetime. The first was replaced by the note to Letter 154 (see p. 261), the second appears at the end of the MS. as one which was mislaid and recovered.

I. The Vicomte de Valmont to Madame de Volanges

I am aware, Madame, that you do not love me; I am not ignorant that you have always been against me in your communications with Madame de Tourvel, and I have no doubt that your feelings are still the same; I agree even that you may suppose them to have some foundation. Nevertheless, it is to you that I address myself, and I do not fear, not merely to request you to place in the hands of Madame de Tourvel the letter for her which I enclose, but also to beg you to make sure that she reads it; to dispose her to do so by assuring her of my regrets, my repentance, and especially of my love. I am sensible that this request may seem to you a strange one. It astonishes even myself; but despair lays hold of any means, and does not calculate too nicely. Moreover, an interest so great and so dear as that which, at the moment, we have in common must thrust aside every other consideration. Madame de Tourvel is dying, Madame de Tourvel is unhappy; life, health, and happiness must be restored to her. That is the object to be secured; all means are good which may assure or hasten its success. If you reject those I offer, you will be responsible for the result: her death, your own remorse, my eternal despair—all will be your work.

I know that I have unworthily outraged a woman who deserves all my adoration; I know that the terrible wrongs I have done her are the sole cause of the misfortunes she is experiencing; but, Madame, fear lest you become an accomplice in them by preventing me from repairing them. I thrust the dagger into your friend's heart, but none save I can withdraw the steel from the wound. I, I alone, know how it may be healed. What matters it that the guilt was mine, if I can be of use to her? Save your friend! save her! she needs your aid, not your vengeance.

Paris, 5th December, 17★★.

II. The Présidente de Tourvel to the Vicomte de Valmont

O my friend, what is this distress of which I am conscious since the moment of your parting from me! When calm is so necessary to me, how comes it that I am given up to an agitation so great that it becomes even pain, and causes me real terror? Would you believe it? I feel that even in order to write to you I need to collect my strength and to call reason to my aid. Yet I tell myself, I repeat to myself, that you are happy; but this idea, so precious to my heart, which you so rightly called the sweet calmative of love, has on the other hand become its ferment, and makes me succumb under a felicity too strong for me, while if I try to snatch myself away form this delicious meditation, I immediately fall once more into cruel anguishes, which I have so earnestly promised you to avoid, and from which, indeed, I ought to protect myself so carefully, since they lessen our happiness.

My friend, you have easily taught me to live only for you; teach me now to live when I am not with you. . . . No, that is not what I wish to say, but rather that, far from you, I would not live, or at least would forget my existence. Abandoned to myself, I can endure neither my happiness nor my suffering; I feel the need of repose, and all repose is impossible to me; in vain have I called on sleep, sleep has fled far from me; I can neither occupy myself nor remain idle, turn by turn a burning fire devours me and a mortal shudder annihilates me; every movement wearies me, yet I cannot keep still. Well, what shall I say? I should suffer less in the throes of the most violent of fevers, and, without my being able to explain or even conceive it, I yet feel assuredly that this state of suffering arises only from my powerlessness to contain or to direct a crowd of feelings, to whose charm I should nonetheless be happy to be able wholly to deliver up my soul.

At the actual moment when you went out, I was less tormented; some agitation indeed was mingled with my regrets, but I attributed it to the impatience caused me by the presence of my women, who came in at that moment, and whose service, always too dilatory for my taste, seemed to me to be prolonged a thousand times more than usual. Above all, I wished to be alone; I doubted not, when surrounded with such sweet remembrances, that I must find in solitude the only happiness of which your presence left me susceptible. How could I have foreseen that, strong as I was when with you to sustain the shock of so many varied feelings, so rapidly experienced, I could not support the memory of them alone? I was soon most cruelly undeceived. . . . Here, my tender friend, I hesitate to tell you all. . . . However, am I not yours, wholly yours, and must I hide from you a single one of my thoughts? Ah! that would be indeed impossible; only I claim your indulgence for involuntary thoughts which my heart does not share; I had, as my custom is, sent away my woman before retiring to bed. . . .